PRAISE FOR SOMEDAY I'LL FIND YOU

"An enthralling page-turner set in World War 2—it's a novel you will not be able to put down. This book is not simply a war love story; it is so much more." Valerie Green, *BC Review of Books*

"An absolutely wonderful novel...driven by fast-paced adventures and intrigue that held me spellbound the entire way through. Oh! And it is so romantic!" Genevieve Graham, *Letters across the Sea*.

"Humphreys's newest novel is a beautiful, morally complex, and achingly honest portrayal of people caught up in the violence and uncertainty of war." Natalie Jenner, *Bloomsbury Girls*

"A fantastic double-whammy! An edge of the seat war story and a nuanced, intriguing romance."—Diana Gabaldon, *Outlander*

"A beautifully written, riveting, deeply moving novel about a man and a woman at war." John Pigeau, *The Humm*

SOMEDAY I'LL FIND YOU

C. C. HUMPHREYS

TWO HATS CREATIVE INC.

International Edition Trade Paperback ISBN: 978-1-989988-16-9 (Ebook) 978-1-989988-17-6

Penguin Random House Canadian eBook ISBN:9780385690522

Names: Humphreys, C. C. (Chris C.), author.

This book is a work of fiction. Names, characters, places and incidents are products of the author's imagination or are used fictitiously. Any resemblance to actual events or locales or persons, living or dead, is entirely coincidental.

Cover design: Juan Padron www.jcovers.com

With love and deep appreciation to:
Flight Lieutenant Peter Humphreys, RAFVR, and Ingegerd Holter,
Spy, Royal Norwegian Navy. And to Cat Cooper because . . . well, you
know.

...Necessity and chance
Approach not me and what I will is Fate.

John Milton
Paradise Lost, Book VII

PART 1
PRELUDE

ONE
LONDON'S BURNING

London. December 29, 1940

WHEN HE SLAMMED the front door of his boarding house and stepped onto Carter Lane, Billy Coke had no idea he was stepping to his fate. He didn't hear its beating wings, just the shriek the slam drew from his landlady, Mrs. Slade. The pleasure that noise gave only lasted him as far as the postbox. There he stopped, looked down, and shook his head.

There'd been a time when his enemies had held guns, not dish-cloths. When he'd fought for freedom, not a denied extra spoonful of reconstituted egg. "What a hero you are, Billy," he muttered. "What a bloody hero!"

He looked up, tasted the air. The sky was that streaked and sooty grey only London, in his experience, seemed to offer: a low ceiling of thick cloud, smothering the earth. Studying that, Billy concluded that it was foul weather for flying, and no Huns would be coming this night. They had come for fifty-seven in a row, from the 7th of September to the 2nd of November. Sporadically since. There'd been one small raid on December 22 and an even lighter one on the 27th—that one hadn't even made the front pages of most newspapers.

4:45 p.m., the light almost gone and people scurrying everywhere, seeking sanctuary. Ten minutes or so till the blackout, when it would be harder to get about. Less so for him; his eyesight was good and not much compromised by night. Besides, every third lamppost was painted with broad white stripes, beacons in the dark; and his feet knew this path by themselves. They had beaten it often enough in the last few weeks, since he had discovered the Globe Tavern by Moorgate station.

It was a pub that shouldn't be open on a Sunday but was, filled with those who shouldn't be above ground when the Huns came, but chose to be. Who knew, as Billy did, that even if the odds were lower of dying in Anderson shelters, brick cellars and Tube stations, lots of the unlucky were still buried in them. Which was why many, like him, decided to take their chances behind a pub's thick velvet blackout curtains—for if they were to die, at least they'd do so with a pint in their hands and a song on their lips.

It was his ability with the latter that led to Billy's right hand being kept occupied with the former. Once the Globe's landlord, McGovern, knew that Billy had trodden the boards and had the repertoire of songs and the pleasing baritone to prove it, he welcomed him back every night he chose to come, keeping his glass filled with mild-and-bitter and slipping him the odd pork pie, chicken leg or plate of eels that required no ration book—for McGovern ran a profitable sideline on the black market.

When Billy reached the corner of Cheapside and Bread Street, he looked up at St. Paul's. It would only be moments before they turned out the lights on it. For now, it stood brightly, its dome a pearl against that grey ceiling of cloud. He dipped his head at it, then walked slowly on in the gathering dark as the last city lights winked off around him. It was just past 5 p.m. when he turned onto London Wall. The Globe was about twenty painted lampposts away.

It was then he heard it, just before the sirens started and he could hear little else. His ear was more attuned to the sound of a plane engine than most Londoners', being as it was a sound he loved, that he craved, a tune he thought better than any of the songs he sang, especially if he could listen to it within the cockpit of a plane he was piloting.

But this engine's sound did not bring him joy. It was out of synchronization, deliberately so, to throw off anti-aircraft tracking equipment.

I was right and I was wrong, he thought, speeding up, risking a tumble on the darkened street. The Huns aren't coming. The Huns have come.

AS IT HAPPENS, Ilse Magnusson was also thinking of fate just before the bombs started to fall. She'd been led there by a complex trail of thoughts—almost as complex as the music she was playing in the church of St. Giles' without Cripplegate. The building itself had started her down the trail, when the man who'd brought her to it, Petr, had excitedly shown her around.

"And this is the tomb of the English poet, John Milton," he'd said. "Do you know him?"

"I do."

She did. Her father, Wilhelm Magnusson, was obsessed by poetry, and Milton was a favourite, only one rank below the incomparable Goethe. So, when she looked at the tomb, a quote came easily to her, in her father's voice.

. . . *Necessity and chance*
Approach not me, and what I will is fate.

She spoke the words only in her head. She really did not know so much about this Petr, only that he was thirty-five years old, that he had fled Czechoslovakia a week before the Germans invaded, and that he played the viola. They'd shared a table at the Lyons Corner House by Charing Cross, and when he discovered that she was a flautist, he'd invited her to play in this church with him, another exile on violin and the church's rector on cello. She recognized that he desired her and since she thought it a possibility she might sleep with him, part of her restraint in not quoting Milton aloud was that she'd found a lot of men were frightened by her intellect. If she did decide to take him as a lover, the last thing she'd want him to be was frightened.

The main part of her restraint, though, was the memory Milton had brought of her father, whom she had not seen in three years but whom she might be fated to see soon enough in their hometown of Oslo if, as in *Paradise Lost*, necessity and chance did not approach, and she kept exerting her will. She would always love her father but he had become her enemy, though he did not know that yet and, with fortune, would not for many years. As soon as she saw him, she would lie to him. It would pain her to do so, even though it was vital that she did.

It was a relief to escape such thoughts in music. It had been a long while since she'd played with others; yet if she'd been a little nervous, so had they. The priest, complete with collar and robe, was named Sandy and proved solid if uninspired on the cello. Petr was a good viola player, while his friend, a Slovak called Janos who had no English, was an excellent violinist. So good in fact that Ilse was sure he was, like her, a professional, and that he probably resented having to play second violin—for, of course, the flute replaced the first violin in a flute quartet. It put extra pressure on her. Which pleased her, as she brought metal to lips for the first time.

The best quartets took years to coalesce but the four of them did well enough. They eased into it with some Haydn. Yet, in a London where death came for some each night from the skies, she'd discovered that people chose to move quite swiftly to their greatest pleasures— one reason she was even considering Petr as a lover. It was Janos who suggested the next piece, grunting it in German at Petr. She spoke the language fluently, even better than she did English. But her handlers, those who were so carefully considering her fate, had urged her to cultivate the habit of revealing almost nothing of herself, in any circumstance. She practised that now, looking both surprised, which she wasn't, and pleased, which she was, when Petr translated.

"Janos has suggested Mozart. Flute Quartet No. 1, D Major. Shall we?"

Petr had known where this would lead. He'd brought the music for the four parts in a battered leather portmanteau. He produced them now and they arranged the sheets on their music stands. As Janos counted them in, he lifted his eyebrows, looking straight at her. It was a challenge. She took it up, joyfully.

She was fair on the Allegro. But on the Adagio she soared, along with her notes which rose in the glorious acoustics created by the ribbed vaulting of the church's ceiling. Though each movement high-lighted her instrument—it was a flute quartet after all—the Adagio had only the violin underneath it, which was not even bowed, but plucked.

There was another reason she loved the piece—it was based on an old troubadour song. The pinnacle of medieval romance, perfect for this setting. Yet now, even as she took the music and let it take her, she recalled that troubadours sang of an ultimate love that was, at its heart, unattainable, unfulfilled . . . unrequited. And so, when she glanced again into the yearning eyes of Petr, she knew suddenly that his love would remain all of those. It was neither her fate nor his, she decided, for them to be lovers. Or maybe, she thought with an inward smile, it was Mozart who had decided for both of them.

So caught up was she, in her thoughts, in the music, that she was the last to hear the sirens—she became aware only when Janos stopped plucking, and Sandy stood up. "Air raid," he said unnecessar-ily. "You must all go to the crypt." They'd been playing right in the centre of the nave, and he walked quickly to the entrance of the church under the tower, re-emerging with a metal helmet and an ARP armband. "Swiftly all. I must get to my post and watch for incendiaries."

"The crypt? Is it . . . good?" Petr asked, his Adam's apple bobbing.

"This church, sir, survived the Great Fire of London in 1666," Sandy said, firmly ushering them towards the altar and the steps down behind it. "I doubt that Herr Hitler will have any more success now than the devil did then."

They collected their instruments, moved down the nave. It was when Ilse was at the head of the stairs that she remembered something. It froze her and she stopped. "I must go," she said, turning back.

"No." Petr took her arm. "Do you not hear that?"

'That' was the *ack-ack-ack* of the anti-aircraft batteries starting up. It was one of the worst sounds in the world, remorseless, relentless, a drill bit driven into the brain.

"I hear it," replied Ilse, laying her hand on top of his, "yet I must go."

"Where, for God's sake?"

"To my hostel." She raised her voice, above siren and gun noise, to still his protests. "It is close. It will take me no time. Listen, the bombs are not falling yet."

He swallowed. "I come with you."

"No," she said, sharper than she meant, lifting his hand away, then continued, softer. "It is my mistake. No need for both of us to risk it. Besides"—she smiled, squeezed his hand, released it—"it is the Young Women's Christian Association hostel. They will not allow a man into their shelter. Not even Herr Hitler could make them."

She moved away fast, down the nave to the church door. "Mistake?" she heard him call, but she lost his other words to the racket, which, as she stepped outside, went up so many decibels she ducked, stopped, suddenly hesitant.

Her instructors at the Special Operations Executive had given her a Morse code textbook to study in case they accepted her for training. They'd told her that it must never be out of her sight. "Hold it closer than any lover in the night," they'd advised. "Bite the hand off anyone who tries to touch it."

She'd put the book beside her flute to bring with her to the church. But she'd picked up the one and not the other.

Everything SOE did was a test. If the hostel took a hit or was partly burned out and the book lost—so was her career as a spy. She'd never be able to return to Norway to fight the Nazis.

Clutching her flute case tight to her chest, she set out, bending into the raid-roar as if into a strong wind. A dozen paces and she heard them—incendiary bombs falling. Hitting the roofs of buildings, puncturing some and glancing off the sloping tiles of others to skitter down to the pavement. One exploded three paces in front of her. The bomb itself was small, one foot long, two circled hands wide. But it threw out an impressive fountaining of sparks in a ten-foot radius. Some landed on her foot, and she paused to rub the glow off with the sole of her other shoe. It would be a minute or so before the bomb would burn at its most intense—2,200 degrees Celsius, she'd been told. But since this one had landed on stone, it should burn itself out quite fast.

Milton, she thought, as she started running again, was both right and wrong. Sometimes necessity and chance approach whether you want them to or not. And my fate is no longer entirely in my own hands.

AS HE PILOTED his Heinkel 111 towards London, Oberleutnant Klaus von Ronnenberg was also considering death—unsurprising, since he was about to help deliver so much of it to the English capital this late December night. He was also thinking about a woman. Not one specifically, and certainly not the woman who would soon be skirting one of the first bombs he dropped, and whom he was fated to meet, to both their joy and their sorrow.

Death and the Maiden, he mused. Was it the hardest thing Schubert ever wrote? Will I never get it right?

Whenever the Kampfgruppe, his bomb wing, was making its final approach to the target, he liked to focus on his bowing technique. Often this piece. The fiendishness of the composer's triplets, especially in the Presto, that mad last movement of the String Quartet No. 14, kept him calm, distracted not at all from his flying. Though, unlike in most missions he had flown, tonight there was little actual flying to be done. The new equipment, the X-Apparatus, saw to that. He didn't fully understand how it worked; he was a pilot, after all, not an engineer. He just knew it did.

"To the left, Oberleutnant." The voice of his navigator, Kreutz, crackled in his ear.

Klaus shifted the rudder a hair, applied left aileron. "Yes," the voice came. "Yes. So."

Klaus was now back along a radio beam laid down from Station Anton on the Cherbourg peninsula. Kreutz listened to the signal that would tell him if they'd strayed from course so his commander could adjust—like he just had. So, until the next call came, Klaus could return to the music, its complexity. His left hand was on the stick, and he fingered it as if it were the strings of his violin.

The crackle. Kreutz again. "First beam, sir. First beam."

"Good. Received."

They had flown through the first electronic cross-beam. Kreutz would have started the timer immediately, which in turn engaged the automatic mechanism. Now Klaus had to keep an eye on his speed, maintaining it for precisely ten minutes. They had tested the X-Apparatus on the English city of Coventry six weeks before. It had worked perfectly—if perfection could be found in the hundreds who had died that night.

Klaus glanced into the night sky around him, seeking lights. He was a sitting duck if there were English night fighters about, because he could not evade them—he could not throw himself "off beam," or off course, if he wished to do his duty. He shivered, tried to re-engage with the music, failed. His fingers went quiet on the stick. But the tune of it was still in his head, under the throb of the Heinkel's twin engines. *Death and the Maiden,* he thought. How many English maidens will we kill tonight? Some of his fellow pilots in the elite squadron complained that the Apparatus was unsporting, removing the skill of the pilot and bomb aimer to deliver the goods—skills they'd honed in Blitzkriegs across Poland, Belgium and France. Klaus never complained because he had never considered war a sport, only a necessary evil. He fought because it was his duty, and he believed in the cause of his nation. Yet he preferred to fight soldiers. Targeting civilians would never sit well with him.

It seemed far less than the required time when Kreutz spoke again. "Five minutes, Oberleutnant. Five minutes."

The pilot glanced back to make sure he was not hearing things. Kreutz was looking at him and raised his thumb. Facing forward again, Klaus checked his gauges. There was so little he could do, but he did that little, flew on with his deft touch on throttle, on rudder, on stick.

"Main beam!" Kreutz cried, so soon. "Main beam."

It was the moment. They were over the target. The bomb bay was linked electrically to the signal. There was nothing else they need do. All felt the shudder pass through the plane as the bay doors opened. "Bombs gone! Bombs gone!" called Kreutz. They were 288 incendiaries lighter, and the Heinkel turned from carthorse to colt; like Klaus, she yearned to gallop. He pulled back on the stick, began the climb to twelve thousand feet.

Kreutz gave him his headings. With a deep sigh, Klaus set his attention for the base at Vannes, Brittany. The pathfinder wing had only dropped incendiaries, as required—to make a giant blazing beacon for the hundreds of planes that followed them, wave after wave of heavy bombers, who would drop thousands more incendiaries, hundreds of 550-pound bombs, on and on into the night until, with the devil's luck, London burned to the ground.

Once the euphoria of survival had passed, Klaus started thinking again about *Death and the Maiden* and the difficulties of playing it, looking forward to his next opportunity to do so—which he was soon to learn would never come. For the rain that had been threatening all night finally arrived, becoming heavy by the time he was circling over Vannes. The mechanic on the ground didn't notice Klaus's lights, didn't hear the Heinkel's engines since the rain was pounding so hard on his roof. Besides, he had not been told to expect the pathfinders back quite so soon, which was why he was driving his repair truck across the runway when Klaus brought his bird in to land.

For a long time after they took his left arm, Klaus could still feel his fingers. Caressing the stick of his airplane. Pressing down on the violin's strings.

MAJOR ERICH STRIEGLER, flying the leading aircraft of 1 Gruppe Kampfgeschwader 54, did know someone in the city. Indeed, the major had been thinking of him as he flew over the English Channel. Nearly always thought about him sometime during a bombing raid. For they'd met after one, three years before, in Spain—though at that time it had been the other man who was doing the killing.

It had taken a year for the memory of that day to be reborn from terror into hate. Which Striegler could use and did, always happy to kill any enemies of the Reich: Poles, Greeks, Norwegians, Belgians. Yet his greatest delight came from killing those who had brought his country so low after the Great War—the French and, especially, the English. He had dropped bombs on the Tommies' helpless formations as the Panzers drove them to Dunkirk, blown up their ships in the water and circled back to watch them burn and drown, hoping that each waving arm might belong to that Englishman he'd encountered not far from a town called Guernica one day in 1937.

But would he get a chance to kill any enemies this night? Peering through the cockpit glass, he saw only the same nothing. A cloud ceiling to six thousand feet, bleak and unremitting. His navigator, Barheim, was intoning what he calculated from his charts—that they'd passed over the coast of England at a place with the absurd name of Bognor Regis twenty minutes before. That London should lie directly ahead. There was flak ahead certainly, great arcs of red tracer punching up through the grey, but flak did not really concern him. Even on a clear night, the enemy would be lucky to hit him—firing blind through cloud posed little danger. And even if by a miracle RAF night fighters found him, his plane, a Junkers 88A, was a new breed, a wonder bomber. With a maximum speed of 416 kilometres per hour, he was confident that he could outrun and outmanoeuvre any Brit fighter.

Returning to base then was not the problem. Completing his mission was. He'd thought it was absurd, setting out in this weather. He was convinced of it now.

"Guildford. Guildford below," his navigator droned.

Another suburban town, filled with bourgeois shopkeepers—and Jews, no doubt. English society was riddled with Jews. It was one of the reasons they were going to be beaten. Perhaps he should just unload there and kill a few?

No. His orders were London. He would obey them as well as he was able. He knew that the glory boys of Kampfgruppe 100 were meant to light the path. He'd heard they even had some fancy new apparatus that guaranteed they'd reach their target. They'd probably still fucked it up. Thought they were an elite, superior to the pilots of any other Geschwader...

The major blinked, rubbed his eyes, looked again. He'd thought exploding flak might have dazzled him. But it was not so. There, a little to his right, was a wide circle of cloud, dusky pink. Lit from below.

It appeared that the glory boys had not fucked it up after all.

With a touch of rudder and aileron he altered his course, levelled; flew straight for the glow. "Barheim," he called to his navigator. "Into position."

His man was a better bomb aimer than he was a navigator. Now Barheim moved to lie belly down in the Junker's Plexiglas nose, and his voice was no longer a drone. "Left a few degrees. That's it. Steady. Steady."

Striegler leaned out of his seat to peer down. They were approaching the centre of the light. The bomb bays were already open. In a moment he felt the shudder, and the words in his headset that accompanied it. "Bombs gone! Bombs gone!"

Striegler opened the throttle, pulled back on the stick. He would climb fast and high before beginning his circle back. The rest of his wing would be following him in. Others were on their way from France. They each had their altitudes, to avoid any chance of a collision.

In those first few seconds of the climb, he thought of the bombs he'd let fall, the mix of incendiaries and high explosives, going the opposite way, to earth. He imagined Englishmen looking up, hearing the whistle of their approaching doom. And then, as ever, he imagined one face. That of the man who'd put a gun to the back of Gootsie's head and blown his brains out. Who would have done the same to Striegler if a Spanish priest had not stopped him by calling out the murderer's name. The name Striegler would never forget.

The major closed his eyes. Saw his friend's head on the ground, haloed in blood. "Die," Erich Striegler said, while his bombs still fell. "Die, Billy Coke."

JUST AS BILLY reached the pub, the Globe's front door opened and the landlord stepped out, followed by half a dozen of his customers. Each had a bucket filled with sand and all were looking to the skies. " 'Ello, lad," said McGovern, the rumble produced from his huge chest carrying over the wail of sirens, air raid and fire engine, the jabber of flak. "Not sure you'll get any singing in tonight."

"Big one, you think?" Billy stopped, caught his breath. "Shouldn't you be in the cellar, Mac?"

"Not yet. No bombs, only fucking incendiaries right now. One was in me yard, one come down through me roof. Both out. No fucking Hun's going to burn down my boozer. Not this night or any other. Mind yourself!" he added in a roar, pushing Billy back into the pub door. An incendiary crashed to the ground a dozen feet away in a cascade of sparks. One of his punters ran forward and smothered the glow in sand. "Grab yourself a bucket, boy. There's more inside."

Billy took a step but then McGovern's voice halted him. " 'Ello? 'Oo's this?"

Billy turned. A woman was running down the street towards them. She was well dressed, in a black winter coat with a fur collar. She clutched an oblong case to her chest. She was fifty yards away when an incendiary fell between them. It exploded, and the woman lurched sideways, stumbling into a wall.

Snatching a bucket from one of the men, Billy ran forward, tipped sand over the bomb. The woman was just pulling herself up when he put an arm under her elbow to help her. "Come on, love," he said gently, "there's a shelter here. Let's get you into it, eh?"

She stood straight. Retrieved her arm. "I cannot. I have to go."

He was about to tell her not to be silly, take her elbow again and lead her—when he saw her face. It wasn't the beauty of it that caused him to pause, though he noticed that in an instant. It was the absolute calmness in her pale-blue eyes, that calmness in her voice too, which came again now, with an accent he realized was European, light. "There is something I must get. From my hostel. It is close. Thank you."

She took a step and he halted her, not with touch, with words. "Your case."

She stopped, looked at what he now held. "Oh, my flute. Thank you," she said again, reaching. But when she took one end of the case he didn't release it to her, and they were joined by it for a moment.

"Where's this hostel?"

"By Broad Street station."

It wasn't far, a few streets away. But with bombs falling on all of them? "I'm coming with you," he said, letting the case go.

"No. You do not have to—"

"I'm coming."

Ilse looked at him for a moment longer. Remembered Petr, the look in his eyes, his offer. She held out her hand. "Ilse Magnusson," she said.

He took her hand. "Billy Coke," he replied.

His hand felt warm in hers, despite the chill of the night. Steady, despite the falling bombs. After a few seconds, she shook, firmly, once, then began to walk fast away.

He watched her for a dozen paces. So that's it, he thought, shaking his head. That's what they've been singing about.

He followed, where fate willed him to go, the shouting of his friends at the pub doorway not slowing him at all.

TWO

BOMBS GONE

London. December 29, 1940

THERE WAS NO POINT trying to talk. The clamour of the raid made anything short of a shout inaudible. Besides, thought Billy, what would I say? Her name, her hand in his, the way she'd looked at him. It had taken his words away. For now, he was just happy to follow her, one pace behind.

It may be a cacophony, Ilse thought, but there are layers to it. Like Schoenberg, perhaps, a composer of "degenerate music," according to the ultimate commander of these bomber pilots, Adolf Hitler. Or like an opera, Wagner maybe, both the Führer's and her father's favourite. The throbbing of fire pumps and the drone of aircraft engines were the bassline held together by the staccato beat of the ack-ack. The chorus was the rise and fall and rise of the warning klaxons, with sopranos joining as the fire engines rushed closer, deftly dropping a fifth and changing key as they passed. The timpani was the crack-clatter-crack of incendiaries bouncing off roofs, onto paving stones, and the sucking noise a roof made when a stick bomb fell just so, punching through the tiles to be swallowed within, there to burn.

At the entrance to Finsbury Circus they had to halt, step into the railings because a fire engine roared towards and past them, skidding around the corner. A taxi followed. Though its hail light was lit, the driver was not seeking trade but only to get the fire pump he was pulling to the flames. The skyline was aglow, fires climbing heavenwards at a score of points. Where Billy and Ilse headed was dark, except where it was split by searchlights moving on the clouds, crossing and re-crossing, coalescing for a moment before breaking apart, as if the operators were playing some madcap game.

The ack-ack gun in the Circus had stopped firing to reload. For a moment the loudest noise was the hum of engines above. "They won't find them," Billy said, pointing at the beams. "Why would any flyer drop below those clouds?"

"But how do they see through them?" Ilse stared up. "How are they landing so many bombs?"

Without waiting for an explanation he would have struggled to give anyway, she set off at her previous pace. The anti-aircraft battery started firing again as they passed the middle of the Circus and they both covered their ears with their hands.

The YWCA was a tall Victorian brick building near the end of a terrace behind Broad Street station—the only feature distinguishing it from its neighbours was the brass plaque on the right door column which read "Young Women's Christian Association." Below that someone had handwritten in black capitals: 'Men admitted to public areas only. No men admitted after 5pm.' Someone had had a go of scrubbing out the l in "public"—Billy smiled, wondering if it had been some denied lover.

Ilse stood with her hand on the doorknob. "Come inside," she said.

He pointed to the sign. "Forbidden."

"Come to the hall. No one will be around. They will all be in the cellar."

He followed her in. The hall was less plain than the exterior, painted a bright primrose that would have glowed in sunlight, the walls hung with several pastoral scenes and one frowning matriarch. There were chairs, some tables, with cribbage boards and magazines dotting them.

"You will wait?" she asked.

"Sure. Can I smoke?"

"I'm afraid not. You wish to wait outside?"

"No, that's fine."

She moved rapidly to and up a staircase. The Victorian lady glared down at him. "OK." He shrugged. "You got me."

Upstairs, Ilse's door was unlocked as always. It was also ajar. She hoped that was only because Margriet, the Dutch girl who shared the room, had forgotten to close it in her rush to the shelter. But she also knew that SOE did not simply caution their prospects as to security. They tested them. Taking a breath, she pushed the door wide, looking straight to the small table where she'd left the Morse code book.

It was not there.

She hurried in, looked all around—floor, bedside table, bookshelf. Not there. SOE had sent an operative. They had taken the book. She had failed; they would fail her. She would not return to Norway to fight. She would take a secretary's job and type out the war, ninety words per minute.

The pit in her stomach filled with equal measures of relief and disappointment.

And then she looked at the mantel, above the fireplace that was never lit. There she saw the book in its innocuous teal cover. She crossed to it, picked it up to make certain. *Sonata at Midnight* was embossed in faded gold on the spine. She'd thought it an odd title— some kind of test too, as if they knew she played music. The first fifty pages was a rather florid romance. Only at page fifty were the three dense pages of Morse abbreviations written. "QRV: I am ready." "QRU: I have nothing for you."

Holding the book, her heartbeat gradually returned to normal.

She looked around, noticed again how tidy the room was. Margriet's home in Leiden had been destroyed in the German assault, reduced to splintered wood and ash, both her parents killed. She tidied the little they had three times a day.

Ilse took a step back towards the door, then paused. The noise of the raid, which had receded in her panic, returned now, the full orchestra. The closest sounds, the loudest still, were the fire engines, the sirens, the ack-ack. But under them she could hear the drone of engines. The Germans were still coming, in numbers greater than she had yet heard during the whole of the Blitz. The bombs might be falling elsewhere in the city for now but she had no doubt that they would come close to her again this night—that this room, this building, might be reduced, like Margriet's home, to splinters and ash.

She'd been about to go downstairs to tell the man she'd met whose name she'd forgotten, whose touch she had not, that she was safe, that he could go. Instead, she grabbed a canvas satchel, threw the book into it, and piled a few essentials on top—lipstick, nylons, toothbrush; finally, the Norwegian flag that she'd bought in Brooklyn three months before, just prior to boarding her ship.

She heard the voices as she descended the stairs—the man's, low and gentling, the woman's shrill, commanding. "What is it?" Ilse asked, stepping into the hall.

The man was standing, hands raised as if surrendering to the woman before him. She was the house supervisor, Beatrice Marber, and she looked most unhappy. "Miss Magnusson," she said, "this man says he is here for you. I told him he cannot be here, even during a raid. That he must leave forthwith."

Forthwith. It was the kind of word Ilse collected for her father. They laughed about the English, their ways and words. But Miss Marber, spinster, did not look as if she would appreciate laughter now.

"I was trying to tell her," said the man. "I was only waiting to make sure you were OK, that you'd found what you needed."

"I did. All is well, Miss Marber."

"All is not well, Miss Magnusson. There is a big raid on, and you must join us immediately in the cellar. While this fellow must leave."

"He will. I will see him off." Miss Marber looked like she would object. But as the house shook with a blast then, and they all swayed, the older woman huffed to the cellar stairs, disappearing swiftly down them.

"So, this is goodbye?"

"No. I do not like this shelter." She jerked her thumb over her shoulder. "They sing hymns. Badly. Do you know somewhere better? Not far away, I think."

He tipped his head to the side. He'd been planning on spending the night in the Globe, singing for beer. But it was in the area already bombed and burning. And he wouldn't want her there anyway, subjected to McGovern and his crew's rough humour. "I know somewhere. It's close," he said, "and they make a nice cup of tea."

"Ah, the English answer to everything. Hitler will never triumph as long as there is tea." She smiled. "Then let us go."

As he led her back the way they'd come, the scale of the raid became very clear. London burned, so many fires everywhere now that, in the little time they'd been inside, it had become one inferno. They could feel the heat of it on their faces, taste it in the acrid air.

Though much of the action appeared to be ahead and to the south of them, some incendiaries were falling nearer. In Finsbury Circus again, air raid wardens and volunteer firefighters scurried about, dumping buckets of sand on every sparking cylinder. Those they took longer to reach glowed bright, turning the world phosphorescent—running men became stick figures, etched in white fire. The orchestral cacophony continued, and once again Ilse and Billy covered their ears with their hands as they ran past the ack-ack battery at the centre of the Circus. Yet as they passed it, all the guns of the battery suddenly and as one ceased firing. Gunners either fell to the ground or stepped away from the hot metal to bend over and rest their hands on their knees.

It was nowhere near silent. Sirens still wailed, fire engine alarms clanged, men ran and shouted. But the contrast of before and after was marked . . . and strangely ominous.

Ilse and Billy both dropped their hands from their ears, halted. "Why do they stop?" asked Ilse. "Is the raid over?"

"No. Listen." He pointed skywards. The drone of engines, the note under everything, was as constant as ever.

"Why are they not shooting at them?"

"I think . . . I think we must be sending up the night fighters. Give them a chance to shoot the bastards down. Don't want to hit our boys." His eyes narrowed as he gazed again at the sky. "The engines are different now, as well. Do you hear?"

"No. How different?"

"The planes before, the first ones? They were Heinkels. But these are heavier bombers. Junkers 88s probably." He looked at her. "Haven't you felt it? They've only been dropping incendiaries up to now. Those up there?" He swallowed. "They'll be carrying the bigger bombs as well. The high explosives."

"How do you know so much?"

"I'm a pilot."

She took a deeper breath. The air was so hot now she seemed to need more. "We should get to your shelter."

"Yes."

They'd only gone twenty yards when the first 550-pound bomb hit. One moment they were hurrying along, the next the pavement tilted, their feet lifted, and they were hurled sideways into railings. They slipped down them, lay dazed in a tangle of limbs. The sound appeared to reach them afterwards; or perhaps it was that the roar was so long, loud, continuous.

"You OK?"

He wasn't sure if she heard him, but she understood, as he did her mouthed, soundless reply. "Yes. I think so. Yes."

He looked ahead. The bomb had fallen somewhere beyond the Circus's last houses, beyond sight but not feeling. A dozen paces away, an ARP warden was on his back. Billy rose, staggered over to him. The man's eyes were open. He looked surprised by death. There was not a mark on him.

Sound returned in accelerating noises. Shouts, screams, sirens. Billy closed the man's eyes then went back to where Ilse was rising. "You sure you're OK?" he asked.

She nodded, bent to pick up her bag. Straightened. "Is he . . ." she asked, nodding over Billy's shoulder.

"Nothing to be done," he said, and took her arm.

They felt more bombs drop, electric jolts running up through their bodies and battering at their hearts. But they did not stumble again and, within two minutes, stood before their destination on Moorgate. "Thexton and Wright's," Billy said, ushering her through the entrance. "They don't let you smoke down here, which is a bit of a bugger. Other than that, it's great. Though I should warn you—they serve the driest scones in London."

He'd discovered the cellar of the old building on one of his nightly rambles. It slept a hundred, and one Mrs. Bishop ran it, shelter and canteen both. He'd been lucky, because he'd been probably the ninety-ninth client and she would admit no more. But so long as he returned a couple of times a week, he was guaranteed his place.

Mrs. Bishop's eyes lit up when he approached her counter, narrowed when she saw he had someone with him. He held up both hands. "I know, Mrs. B, I know. But I couldn't leave her out on the street, now could I?"

Mrs. Bishop was a dragon when she needed to be—and a dove when she chose. She appraised Ilse for a long moment, then nodded. "Some of me regulars haven't made it tonight, so there's room. Just this once, mind. Don't make a habit of it."

"I won't."

"I suppose you'll both want tea?" On their nods she began pouring from a vast urn. "And scones? I baked 'em tonight."

"Please."

"That's two bob, love." She took Billy's florin, then waved it at him. "But it'll cost you more than this. Two songs tonight, not one."

"It's a deal."

"Songs?" Ilse asked, as he led her across to a table against the far wall, weaving through crowded tables, families already spread out on blankets on the floor.

"I sing. A bit. To lighten the mood."

"A singer *and* a pilot?"

"Not very good at either but . . ." He sat, nodding at a couple of men and women he recognized at the other end of the table, the same ones he saw there each time, because most people always went to the same spot in a shelter if they could, as he did. "So, you know everything about me. I know nothing about you."

"That's not true." She smiled. "You know I play the flute."

"And you live in the YWCA. That's the sum of my knowledge." He smiled. "So, where are you from?"

Once it would have been the easiest of answers. But her handlers at SOE, in her initial interviews, had emphasized that all information was potentially dangerous. That all strangers should now be considered guilty until proven innocent—and then doubted again. They could have sent this . . . Billy Coke, she remembered his name now. One more test. She hated that she had to weigh her words. She hated the consequences of not weighing them more. Still, this was an easy answer, as was the story, part true, part false, that would follow.

"I am Norwegian. And you are English."

"Yes—and no. I wasn't born here but I grew up mostly here."

"Where were you born?"

"Canada."

"Montreal?"

"No, the west. British Columbia, the province is called. On a small island."

"Why there?"

"My father had a farm."

"He was Canadian?"

"English. He'd gone out there, uh, during the first war."

"Why did you leave?"

"He died."

"Oh. I am sorry. How old were you?"

"Seven."

"Your mother?"

"Gone before."

"Dead?"

"Just gone. My dad's family were here, so I came and—" He raised a hand. "Hey, I thought I was asking the questions."

"Why would you think that?" They both laughed and she continued. "Besides, there is not much to tell of me."

"Well, that's obviously not true." He picked up his scone, tapped it on the plate. "Mrs. Bishop's scones have been known to suck all available moisture from the body. One bite, I won't be able to speak for a minute, minimum. So off you go. How are you here?"

He took a bite. She studied him. He is handsome, she thought, not quite movie-star handsome but good-looking. Dark-brown hair, thick, Brylcreemed down. A Roman nose, his mouth strong also; his eyes were heavily lashed, which she envied, the eyes themselves a bluey-green, like a stream in sunlight. There were laugh lines beside them, laughter in the eyes, for now. But something else behind that, something wary. It reminded her to be wary too.

Her perusal had been silent. He waved her on, using the scone like a baton.

"I was a passenger on a cargo vessel. On my way back from South America when the Germans invaded Norway. The captain and crew voted to go to England when they heard things were not going so well back home. So, I am here."

Billy swallowed, took a sip of tea, spoke. "Did you get a vote?"

"No. But I wanted to go home."

"Someone waiting for you?"

"Father. Brother. Friends." She smiled. "No one else, if that is what you are asking."

"Never crossed my mind." He raised the scone. "Would you still rather be home? I mean, considering how safe and friendly London is right now?" He jerked his head towards the outside world. The building's cellar was deep, and the raid's noise only came now in the faintest of siren wails, the shudder of bombs.

She shook her head. "No. Perhaps here I can help my country better than there."

His mouth was full. He asked with a raised eyebrow.

"Oh, nothing much. I am not very daring. But I can type. The Norwegian government in exile needs typists."

It's odd, Billy thought. Everything she said sounded true—until that. He didn't doubt that she could type. He just guessed that wasn't the limit of her ambitions. He'd noted the way she'd dealt with the woman at her lodgings, had seen her on the streets as the bombs fell. She was, if not unafraid, at least undaunted. She'd chosen to go back out with him, despite the danger, which thrilled him, and perturbed him, adding to the feeling he'd had from the first moment he saw her. It wasn't simply her beauty—the perfect oval of a face, silken skin, ice-blue eyes, white-blonde hair. It was the immediate and intense certainty that the face was simply a stunning mask—and his realization that he would trade his life right there and then to see behind it.

Around them, some people began to sing. It was a music hall favourite, "Roll Out the Barrel."

Neither of them joined in as he studied her. The lies and half-truths didn't bother him so much; tell him all her secrets at once, he might have to start telling his. This was the game people played. Before the war, it was one that could drag on for months, years even— especially in England, where people kept so much veiled. Bombs had changed all that. Almost everyone had their dead, and wondered what their dead would have done with what remained of life had they known what was coming. So the game was played faster now.

He finished chewing, was about to probe a little more. But one of those 550-pound bombs dropped nearer—all felt the crump, the shock of it, coming up through the soles of their feet and the seats of their chairs. The room shuddered, dust fell from the ceiling, everyone stopped singing. Then, into the silence, Mrs. Bishop called, "Go on, Billy Boy. It's time. Sing us one."

He looked at Ilse. She raised her hands, gesturing him up. He stood. "Requests, Mrs. B?"

A few voices came, titles called. Her voice topped them all. "Anything you like, love. You choose."

Billy stepped away from the table, looked at Ilse again. Thought about what she hadn't said, what she had. Of all he'd like to say. Then he began to sing.

If you were the only girl in the world
And I were the only boy
Nothing else would matter in the world today
We could go on loving in the same old way
A garden of Eden just made for two
With nothing to mar our joy
I would say such wonderful things to you
There would be such wonderful things to do
If you were the only girl in the world
And I were the only boy.

Ilse was surprised. She'd played with classically trained singers, had always been in awe of their power. This Billy Coke didn't sing like them. But his voice, a light baritone, was true, clear, without any vibrato. It filled the room, yet he didn't seem to be making any effort to do so. Sang as if he were continuing a conversation. He didn't look at her, at anyone, only across the room, beyond it. Because of that, she thought, he is every boy in this room, singing to every girl.

While he sang, she looked around. Most people, old and young, were gazing at him, smiling. Some of the couples were looking at each other, mouthing the words. Mrs. Bishop behind her trestle had a cup in her hand, a dishcloth pushed into it, but was not using it, frozen. A vibration shuddered through the room again, rattling teacups in their saucers. This time, no one noticed.

He returned to the beginning of the song. His eyes focused, he looked around the whole room, raised both hands. People took the cue, and their voices rose. Hers too.

If you were the only girl in the world
And I were the only boy
Nothing else would matter in the world today
We could go on loving in the same old way
A garden of Eden just made for two
With nothing to mar our joy
I would say such wonderful things to you
There would be such wonderful things to do . . .

He didn't gesture, yet everyone stopped singing all at once. Ilse realized that this was something he'd done before. And that they all wanted only his voice at the end, singing for all of them.

She looked back—and he was looking at her for the first time. Singing the climax slowly, straight at her.

If you were the only girl in the world . . .
And I . . . were the only . . . boy.

The last pure note hovered in the air. He extended it out to the room again, and closed his eyes.

Everyone clapped, some whistled. Billy bowed. Other song titles were suggested. "Give us a moment to wet my whistle," Billy called, and sat.

Conversations began again. Mrs. Bishop returned to cleaning. "Well," Ilse said, as he grinned shyly at her, "you have a lovely voice."

"Thank you."

She couldn't help herself. "I bet it gets you many girls, doesn't it?"

His eyes went wide. "Girls? Hmm," he replied, running his hand through his thick hair. "That's interesting. I never thought of using it on girls."

He held the look for a moment—then they both burst into laughter. "Truly," she said, "you sing so well. You must be a professional."

"Was. For a time. More an actor than a singer truly. In the provinces, mainly."

She raised an eyebrow. "Provinces? Like in Canada?"

"No, no. Sorry. English acting term for regional theatre. Most towns of any size have a repertory theatre. You put on a new play every week. Mostly silly comedies, mysteries, some light musicals."

"So an actor—and a pilot? How does that work?"

"Ah," he said. "Now *that* is a long story."

She smiled. "I'm not going anywhere."

Billy stared into the ice of those eyes. There was something in them, an invitation maybe, her own secrets certainly, that made him want to tell her everything: Spain, that war; this one; why he was on the streets. Everything. Stuff he'd never told anyone. He couldn't, though. No, not yet. She had her mask and he had his and he wasn't ready to lift it. But what little half-truths could he speak that might keep her interested? Because he wanted this, more than he'd wanted anything in a long time: to keep those eyes on him.

As he debated, the door to the cellar clattered open. All looked up. Mrs. Bishop stepped forward to reject any interloper—other people had followed Billy and Ilse in, and the room was at capacity. Though it was not a refugee that stood there but a middle-aged fireman in his full black garb, his face rimed with soot, his eyes vividly white. "Sorry to disturb, Mrs. Bishop. We're taking a helluva pounding up there. 'Ole bloomin' city's burning. Bombs demolished the building at number 84. We think there's people inside, but my lads are trying to fight the fire. Any blokes 'ere can lend a hand with some diggin'?"

Billy, along with a number of the men, stood up immediately, stepped forward. Ilse rose too, followed. But when she reached the bottom of the stairs, the fireman spoke. "Sorry, miss. Chief says only men."

"I can help—"

"I'm sure you can. But you'd also get in the way. 'Ow about 'elpin' Mrs. Bishop make some tea for the lads. They'll be needin' it soon. Fires make you thirsty." Ilse started to protest, but he turned away. " 'Elmets at the top of the stairs, lads. Axes and ropes too. Quickly now."

Billy turned back. Ilse shook her head. "I would like to help with more than tea."

"I know. But they'd just send you back down."

"Come on, young fella," called the fireman. "Kiss 'er and 'ave done. Adolf's waiting."

"One moment." Billy turned back again. "May I—?"

"Kiss me and have done?"

He smiled at the challenge in her eyes. "Rain check on that. But may I see you again? Perhaps tomorrow?"

She didn't hesitate. "Yes. But I have an appointment. I don't know exactly where I'll be."

"Nor me. Or if where we want to be will still be standing." He crossed to the trestle. "Got a pen, piece of paper, Mrs. B?"

She handed him both. He scribbled and passed the paper to Ilse. She read and her eyebrow rose again. "The Honourable Gervase Coke? Who is he?"

"My cousin."

"Your cousin is 'Honourable'? Does that make you a knight?"

"Not exactly. It's, uh, another long story." The fireman bellowed again, and Billy stepped away. "I'll come back here later if I can, or to your hostel tomorrow. But if . . . if we miss each other, he'll know where I am." He shrugged. "We're not close, but he's the only family I have here, so I'll leave a message with him." He held out his hand. "I enjoyed meeting you, Ilse. I hope to see you again."

She took his hand. "And I you, Billy."

He held her hand for a moment, then squeezed it, turned, exited. He was the last volunteer, and the fireman pulled the door shut behind him.

Mrs. Bishop came up beside her as Ilse stared at the closed door. "'E's a lovely boy, our Billy," she said.

"Yes."

"You going steady?"

"Oh no." Ilse turned. "We only met tonight."

"Wouldn't have thought it by the way he sang to you." The older woman leaned in. "My advice, love? Don't wait too long." She raised her eyes to the ceiling. Dust was falling from it again, as it shook from another explosion. "Hitler's not." She smiled. "Help me make some sarnies for our boys up there?"

"Gladly," Ilse replied, and followed Mrs. Bishop behind the trestle.

THREE
RENDEZVOUS

London. December 30, 1940

AS HE TRUDGED TOWARDS his digs the next morning, Billy Coke didn't think he'd ever been so tired.

It was light, though few would actually call it that. Rain clouds hung thick and low over the city; squalls spat out chilled drops, lashed into his face by the still-ferocious wind that had so driven the flames of the night before. But beneath the God-made clouds hung others that man and the devil had fashioned, as foul and black as any mystic's vision of hell.

London had burned. Still burned in places, even if the worst of it was past. The rain had helped, dampening some of what the over-stretched firemen could not yet reach. It had also halted the attack. Billy was certain that, were it not for this terrible weather, the Germans would have been back in relentless waves. The first incendiaries had been to light the place up for the hundreds that would follow. He had seen the Nazis do that in Spain, seen the results. But not even Hitler would order his pilots back if they would not be able to land at their airfields on their return. He would need them again, in better weather, to kill even more efficiently. Billy had no doubt that they would come back to finish the job as soon as the clouds cleared.

They had come close enough. He had spent the whole night around Moorgate, going from building to ravaged building, hacking away at debris, pulling away bricks, stones and wooden rafters. His hands were raw, scraped and scratched, with splinters under most of his nails, and covered, as all of him was covered, in an unshiftable layer of soot. That was streaked in red—his blood, and blood from the bodies he'd reached, the dead and the dying and those few who survived.

The buildings that still stood were mainly shells, walls around gutted interiors. It was Destruction's Lottery though, some buildings untouched beside ruins. It seemed to Billy that a disproportionate number of pubs had survived, as if even the devil, after his work was done, would need a pint. He'd passed the Globe, seen McGovern slumped at the door, clutching an empty sand bucket. The man had stared at him but did not acknowledge him, probably did not recognize him, just another soot-faced spectre. Billy couldn't speak, his throat a desert; hadn't stopped. Stop and he'd lie down and not get up again. And the place he knew he had to do that was in his own bed, on Carter Lane.

That lottery of fire and bomb had spared many streets towards the river. He walked down Moorgate, passed the undamaged Bank of England, cut down Queen Victoria Street, its buildings still standing. Beyond it though, as he walked along Watling Street, he could see columns of smoke rising high over the area around St. Paul's. The dome was wreathed in it, like fog tendrils clinging to a mountainside. The cathedral stood, somehow. He felt a sob come when he saw that, stifled it. If St. Paul's had gone, perhaps London would have too.

It got harder to walk then, scenes from his night repeated here. Buildings collapsed, bricks and beams crashed across glistening pools of black water, fire hoses snaking through the carnage. Many were manned, exhausted men clutching them, barely containing the writhing. Fire within buildings and without, plumes of it jetting from burst gas mains. The stench was awful, shattered sewers disgorging their filth. The main sound was the clink of broken glass being swept into bins.

The closer he got to Carter Lane, the greater the devastation. The dome of St. Paul's might have survived but very few buildings around it had been as lucky. So complete the destruction, so numb his mind, that he got lost, streets he knew well blended into chaos. Until he stopped and realized that his feet had brought him where his mind could not, and he was looking at what had once been his digs. He only recognized the place because wedged into a tumble of bricks was the house's door knocker, a bronze lion. The house, together with the Anderson shelter in the tiny walled garden where Mrs. Slade and her son would have taken refuge, was gone.

He felt another sob rising. He may not have liked his landlady. But he didn't wish her dead.

"Gone. All gone."

The voice came from right beside him. He had heard so many calling from the rubble that, by the end of the night, he was hearing voices where there'd been none. So he didn't turn—until the voice came again. "They've taken it all. I've nothing left."

He turned. She was standing beside him, staring at what had been her home, her hair in curlers under a scarf, though several strands had come loose. She was wearing what she always wore in the Anderson — a patched dressing gown over a winceyette nightdress and slippers. "Mrs. Slade, are you . . . are you alright?"

She didn't look at him. "Nothing left," she said again, and rubbed at her chin, adding more soot to it. "All gone."

He stared at her helplessly, so tired he didn't know what he should do. So he put his arm around her. Slowly, she lowered her head onto his chest.

He heard slipping on the tumbled stones behind him and turned to see her son—"my Rodney," as she called him—coming towards them. "Come on, Mum," he said gently. "Let's get you away." He held out his arm, and Mrs. Slade passed from one man to the other.

"It's all gone," she told him. "They've taken it all."

"I know, Mum." Rodney turned, then started when he realized that the man who stood there was Billy. "Mr. Coke," he said. "We thought you must be . . ." He looked back at what remained of his home. "We was lucky. Didn't think so at first, when an incendiary got the house and it was too hot in the Anderson. We'd just gotten to the corner when the bomb fell." He wiped his nose, carving a line of wet through the soot. "Sorry about your stuff, Mr. Coke."

Billy tried to find words, failed. The son led his mother away, while Billy stood and watched them, uncertain what to do now. Then he remembered the one other place in London where he could go. He was not welcome—except, he'd been told, in an emergency. Well, he thought, looking down at himself, then up at the smouldering city, this will have to do until the real emergency comes along.

He threaded his way through bricks, puddles and hoses until he reached Farringdon Road on its approach to Blackfriars Bridge; crossed the street, walked along Victoria Embankment. After fifty yards, he heard an engine. Turned, and saw a taxi approaching. It had its sign lit and it wasn't pulling a fire pump. He raised his arm and it pulled over.

"15 Cheyne Walk," he said, falling onto the back seat. The driver grunted something about filth but drove off anyway.

He had to wake Billy at his destination. "Wait here," he told the driver, and lurched up the steps, rang the bell, then leaned against the portico column, the plaster cool on his head. Footsteps approached and the door opened. A man in a black frock coat stood there, staring at him in angry suspicion—until he recognized him. "Master William," he said. "Whatever has happened to you?"

"The Blitz, Jeffers," Billy replied, then jerked his head over his shoulder to the taxi. "Would you mind . . . ?"

"What? Oh, of course, sir."

When the butler returned from paying for the cab, he found Billy slumped on one of the Chippendales in the hall. "Master William," he said, "your cousin is with the regiment. I am expecting him later today but—"

"That's OK, Jeffers. He's not the first thing I need. The first thing I need is a bed."

The butler looked him slowly up and down. "If you will forgive me, Master William, the first thing *you* need is a bath."

ILSE SAT in the first-floor office of the Special Operations Executive in Chiltern Court, Baker Street, studying the annihilation of her country. She had sat there twice before, staring at the map of Norway on the wall behind the desk. It had been extensively used during the short campaign earlier that year, the British operatives in the new Scandinavian section of SOE charting, in various coloured inks, her country's two-month fall to the invading Germans.

The initial shocking Blitzkrieg on April 9 that had seized Oslo, every other main town and almost every important strategic site in the country in one day was marked in blunt, black spear points. The brave, brief struggle of the massively outgunned Norwegian army was charted in red arrows, with red stars indicating the few minor triumphs—in Valdres and Midtskogen, at the Hegra Fortress, and at Oscarsborg, where the German heavy cruiser the *Blücher* had been sunk. Mostly, though, every red arrow led to a cross where surrenders had taken place. Only in the far north was there a constellation of success, near Narvik. The port had been retaken by the Norwegians and a supporting British invasion force and held for a while. But it was a short respite only. A date was inked in the waters next to the city: June 7, 1940. The day the British suddenly withdrew, evacuating King Haakon VII of Norway—marked there as 'H7,' the new symbol of his country's resistance—as they did so.

Someone had drawn over the centre of the country a large swastika. Ilse had cried the first time she'd seen the map, tears for her beloved country, for all her countrymen who had died in the lost cause. Boys she'd been at school with among them, no doubt—her fellow students who had tied one knot in the tassels of their graduation mortarboards for every dawn they'd witnessed. Gone now.

She didn't cry this time. She wasn't here for that. She was here for a job, and tears would not help her get it.

The door behind her opened. She turned to see one man she knew, and one she didn't, enter the room. "So sorry to keep you waiting, Miss Magnusson," said Major Cholmondeley-Warren, walking round to lob a thick, string-bound folder of papers onto the desk before dropping into the chair. "Jerry's raid last night caused delay everywhere, I'm afraid. Were you caught up in it at all?"

"I was. But I was fine, I found—"

"Good, good," the major interrupted. His first name was St. John, which she'd discovered was actually pronounced *Sinjin*, and his surname was not *Cholmondeley* but *Chumley*. More British eccentricity, added to by his fellow officers addressing him as "the Saint." He did not, however, have the proverbial patience of one, she'd swiftly learned. Hence his interruption. He was short and near-hairless, save for thin eyebrows and a pencil moustache.

Happily, the man who he introduced now had thick red hair at beard and head, and just the one name. "Lieutenant McBride. Irish, but he can't help that. Navy, which he could have, if he'd thought it through. With our customary lack of imagination, we call him Danny Boy." He waved at Ilse. "Miss Magnusson."

The younger officer—perhaps he was twenty-five—held out his hand. "Delighted to meet you, Miss Magnusson. How are you today?"

He'd spoken in clear, if accented, Norwegian. She replied in the same. "I am well, thank you. You speak our language."

"Not as well as I used to, I'm afraid. I was at school there for several years, while my father was based in Ålesund. He was—is—an importer of fish. From Belfast, though my mother was from Dublin and I grew up between the two." He glanced down at the major, who was looking at them both with impatience. "The Saint here speaks not a word. Which can be useful, actually." He smiled. "We had better revert to English," he added, reverting, "so our colleague can keep up, eh?"

"Keep up? I suspect I shall be far ahead of you as usual, Danny Boy." Cholmondeley-Warren turned to Ilse. "We have quite a lot to get through. May we begin? Do you need tea?" He asked it in such a way that indicated acceptance would be seen as a form of weakness. So when she shook her head, he continued, briskly. "McBride here is going to give us a brief summary of where SOE stands right now vis-à-vis Norway, since he has only recently returned from there. We shall then discuss a couple of different options for how you may be able to help. Is that acceptable?" Without waiting for a reply, he waved his hand and barked, "Proceed."

"I will, in a moment. But first I have an important question I need to ask."

"Oh, for God's sake. You Irishmen. Ask her out for a drink on your own time."

"It's not that." McBride smiled. "Though I may later—just to practise my Norwegian, you understand. No, my question is simply this." He leaned back to perch on the desk's edge. "Miss Magnusson, do you believe we are going to win this war?"

It was not at all what she was expecting. She frowned. "Do you mean make a peace? Or defeat Germany?"

"The latter."

"I—"

"You see many, perhaps most, here and abroad, don't believe it. And you can understand why." He pointed to the map behind the desk. "Your country. Occupied. The rest of Europe?" He gestured to the map of the continent she knew was on the wall behind her. "The swastika flies over near all of it. France, Belgium, Holland, Denmark,

Poland. Where it doesn't, Hitler has his chums—Mussolini in Italy, Franco in Spain. Or neutrals frightened of him—the Swedes, the Swiss. The other Irish." He smiled briefly. "He has his non-aggression pact, of course, with Joe Stalin, and they've carved up Poland between them. All that's left is tiny old Britain. Whose army left most of their equipment in Dunkirk. Whose capital city the Luftwaffe nearly burned to the ground last night and will try to do so again, no doubt. Preparatory to an invasion which we should be hard-pressed to prevent succeeding."

"There's America?"

"Also neutral. With most of the country dead-set against involvement across the water. 'America First' is the cry there. Even Roosevelt, who likes us, can't support us openly, given the mood of many of his fellow citizens. So I ask again"—he scratched at his thick red beard— "do you think we can win this war?"

For a short time she had considered defeat. Who hadn't? When her own country fell so fast, when the Great Powers crumbled before the onslaught, when Nazism spread, unstoppable, across the map of Europe like some black plague? But she hadn't considered it for long. "I do not wish you to think my reply is bravado, or ignorance. It may be naïveté. But I have long recognized that Hitler and his lot are evil. I . . . experienced a little of it first-hand, before the war." She swallowed. "And I am convinced that evil never triumphs. In the short run, as now, perhaps. But never in the long." She uncrossed and recrossed her legs, leaned forward. "The simple answer then is yes. Yes, I believe utterly and completely that we will win this war."

There was a moment's silence—then McBride smiled. "Good show," he said. "I happen to agree with you. As do we all, here at SOE, and on up through the High Command. As the prime minister said in the house only the other night—"

"Enough," growled the major. "Get started on what Winston says and we'll never be done here. To business, Lieutenant."

"Sir." McBride reached back to the manila folder on the desk and undid the strings. Constrained papers sagged and he delved, withdrew a sheet. "How aware are you of what is happening in Norway right now?"

"Not very. You asked me to avoid my countrymen at Norway House." She'd arrived by boat from America in June, and later found out from the major that her surname had been immediately flagged in her initial immigration interview, then forwarded to SOE. It was why they'd made that first contact. She cleared her throat. "But you never really told me why."

Cholmondeley-Warren scratched at his bald scalp and a few flakes fell. "For this reason. And it's not that they are not splendid chaps in the main at Norway House. But as always there is a bit of a, uh, bun fight about which direction we should be taking." He glanced at McBride. "There's a difference of opinion about how, ah, vigorous our operations should be."

"You mean whether to indulge in sabotage and risk reprisal executions?"

"Very good. Precisely," said the major. "Though I believe, as do many others, that you can't make an omelette, breaking eggs and all that." He waved his hand. "But keeping you apart now may keep you safer later. It does mean, though, that you will be working for us here at SOE. Not for Milorg or another of the resistance groups." He narrowed his eyes at her. "Will you be alright with that?"

Ilse thought for a long moment. "All of us will be fighting for the same result. The liberation of Norway. The defeat of Hitler."

"Indeed."

She nodded. "Then I am alright with that."

"Good." He gestured at McBride. "And so, to the lieutenant's question?"

"My knowledge of what has happened in Norway? I have kept up a little. One of the secretaries at Norway House, Kirsten Larsen, I was at school with. When I ran into her on the street, I couldn't avoid her. We meet up, but always away from the Circus. I also asked her to not tell anyone that I was here."

"That's good. We know about her, and we're fine with it. So, can you summarize what you have learned from Miss Larsen?"

"Well," she sighed, "it's mainly not good. The country was so shocked by the suddenness of occupation. People died, many industries shut down, hundreds of thousands were out of work. Most people just wanted to feed their families. The Germans offered them work and food. Most took it."

"Some took it more eagerly though, didn't they? Welcomed it, in fact."

"You are referring to the Nasjonal Samling, Lieutenant?"

"The NS, yes. Vidkun Quisling and his crew. Norway's Nazis."

Ilse shivered. "There has always been that element there. They used to be laughed at, with their parades and salutes and black uniforms."

"Not laughed at so much now though, are they?" The major leaned forward. "Now that they are running the government under the Reichskommissar imposed from Berlin."

"No, I suppose not."

"Yet there is resistance," said McBride, taking another sheet. "A growing resentment. Acts of sabotage, larger and small, some carried out by the Norwegian military resistance, Milorg. Other groups have formed in all areas of the country, and SOE are in contact with them. We have landed Norwegian soldiers by boat, dropped them by parachute. The problem being that most of them, and most of the ad hoc groups, are exposed quite quickly. Betrayal by the NS and, I'm afraid, simple stupidity." He sniffed. "People talk too much in Norway, Miss Magnusson."

"You have to give us time, sir," she replied. "One hundred and twenty-five years with no war. We were innocents."

"There is no time." Cholmondeley-Warren sat back and stared down his nose at her. "Innocence is dead. Ruthlessness must prevail. If we are to win as you wish."

"I agree."

"You say you do. But do you have what it takes to be ruthless?"

Ilse shrugged. "You will only know that if you test me. As you have been doing already."

"Only in very minor ways. The testing will get tougher if you are to proceed."

"To what?"

McBride took over. "There are two options. The first is far easier and will allow us to perhaps practise Norwegian a lot together." His quick smile came and went. "You work for us here at Chiltern Court. You translate, collate, analyze. Prepare reports, brief us."

"I become a secretary. Like Kirsten."

"Do not dismiss her work with a label," snapped the major. "Accurate information, acted upon, is what will win us this war, far quicker than bravado."

"I apologize. I did not mean to—" She took a deep breath. "What is the second option?"

"That after suitable training, we send you back to Norway—as a spy."

Ilse nodded. It was what she had hoped for—and dreaded, almost equally. But she didn't let anything show on her face. Just said, "I prefer this option."

"You are at liberty to change your mind—after what we tell you next." He jerked his head at the papers. "Now's the time, McBride."

"Sir." The lieutenant reached into the pile again and pulled out a sheet which he unfolded and handed to her. It was a photo of the front page of the main Norwegian newspaper, *Aftenposten*. It was dated six days before, Christmas Eve—the day her country celebrated the holidays. "There," he said, tapping an article halfway down the page. He removed his finger and she saw the byline: "Wilhelm Magnusson."

Her father.

"Please read it."

It was an opinion piece rather than a report, and continued on a second page. She read, instantly connecting again with her father's voice: the humour in it, the wry depiction of some of his countrymen's foibles, especially at this time of year. The main subject was lutefisk, that strange Yuletide delicacy that few other nations under-stood—since, essentially, it was rotted fish. Her father wrote of a stan-dard Norwegian figure, the simple farmer, and the lengths he went to in order to have a normal festivity under wartime restrictions; aided, in this case, by a bemused young German soldier.

She finished, looked up, to both men's stares. "Read it again," McBride said. "Then tell us what you think it's about."

She re-read. But this time, the voice, the story, didn't amuse. There was a thread in it that she teased out, and when she got it, she nodded. "Well?" asked the major.

"It's to do with acceptance. How life can get better if you just go along with it. Whatever the difficulties, simple pleasures can still be had by simple folk."

"Admirably summed up. And what, from our perspective, do you think we'd find wrong with that?"

"The article speaks to the status quo. Accepting what is. Enjoying it even—especially, perhaps—when people of different countries can find common ground."

"In rotting fish. Don't understand it myself." The major shud-dered. "But I am sure many of your countrymen do, am I right?"

"They would, yes."

"He's a good writer, your father, isn't he? Won awards."

"He has. In Norway, Sweden, Germany."

"Germany?"

"He is half German. My grandmother—"

"We know. But this is not typical of his output, this piece. The German award was for a play, no?"

"One of the awards. For a historical piece. About hardy fishermen."

"Hardy Norse fishermen?"

"Yes. But the Germans liked it because it spoke of 'Volk.' The people. A sense of Northern European identity."

"A sense of racial purity, perhaps?"

"In a way. Though he wasn't . . . he had Jewish friends . . . he—"

Cholmondeley-Warren interrupted her stumbling. "Did you know that your father has joined the NS?"

Ilse shook her head.

"Does it surprise you?"

"I imagine that to get ahead in Norway now it would help to be part of the establishment."

"You're defending him." The major raised his hand against her interruption. "No, no, it's good that you still love your father. It will help in what we are going to ask you to do."

Love her father? Of course she did—this man who, as a widower, had raised her and her brother, who'd taken her everywhere with him, introduced her to literature, to history, to music. Allowed her to go abroad at seventeen to study when many fathers wouldn't have. She'd always known there was a shadow to his politics, which had started with a hatred of Bolshevism, of the horror stories coming from Stalin's Russia, and expanded through his love of all things German into a support for Hitler's solutions, his European New Order. When she'd left to study in America, she'd been too ignorant, too timid, to confront him. And she had never wanted to do it in letters. He was the writer, not her.

She realized she'd gone inward, and looked up again at the men staring intently at her. What had he said, the Saint? Her love would help in the work they were considering her for? She was about to ask when McBride spoke.

"When did you last see him?"

"Three years ago. 1937."

"Where?"

"In Berlin, actually. My father was there to receive another award. For journalism this time."

The major glanced at some notes before him. "Ah, yes. An exposé of some of the horrors Stalin perpetrated in the Ukraine. Admirable. I remember reading and enjoying it at the time." He looked up. "You accompanied him."

"Yes. I went also to see my grandmother before I travelled to America." She cleared her throat. "I left to study music in New York."

"No visits home? Awfully long time to be away."

"I was studying. I worked to help pay for classes."

"Hmm. Did he know, or has he become aware since, that you might not share his, uh, political views?"

"No. We have not discussed it. Maybe we would have if I'd gotten back in time before the invasion."

"Fortunate again for us that you did not. That no one in Norway appears to know where you are." The lieutenant looked at his superior, received a nod. "So, Miss Magnusson . . . Ilse, if I may? You say you prefer this second option. That you wish to become a spy. But I must warn you, it is not as glamorous as the word suggests. Most of it is dull, tedious work. Which is simultaneously very, very dangerous— as several hundred of your countrymen have discovered. You may still reconsider."

"I do not wish to." She shifted, recrossed her legs. "What will I do?" she asked.

McBride nodded. "Well, first there will be some training. A month's worth at our facility, Fawley Court, in Henley-on-Thames. Not as comprehensive as we might wish, but it will cover the essentials. You will learn the basics of coding, how to set up and run a secure cell, how to operate a transmitter. You will improve your Morse. A little minor sabotage, without explosives. If there is time, we may teach you how to kill someone."

"I see. And would I need to learn parachuting as well? I am not very good with heights but—"

"In this case, we would seek to introduce you into Norway over the Swedish border. We are concocting a suitable story as to how you made your way there. Sometime in February we think. You would then proceed to Oslo."

"And do what?"

"Nothing." It was the major who took over now. "We wish you to do nothing at all, for several months at least, maybe half a year. You will make no contacts in the resistance. Cells are going down with alarming frequency right now. You will lie doggo, take notes but only in your head, observe." He leaned forward. "Especially, you will help your father. Argue a little, as daughters do. Slowly become a convert to the cause. Become his helpmeet, his confidante. Have him take you deep into the pro-Nazi establishment. Befriend all the main Nazis in Norway, German and Norwegian."

She looked from one man to the other, gauging again what the major had just said, before replying. "So, that is it. You are asking me to betray my father."

"That, as you say, is it." The major glanced at McBride, before fixing her again with his eyes. "Will you do it?"

It was not that she hadn't thought about him. She and her father had always been close, almost too similar in many respects. His letters before the war had been filled with its coming, and a growing admiration for the way his mother's countrymen were shaping Europe's destiny. She had written one letter arguing strongly against his beliefs but had never sent it—why, she hadn't been certain. Now she thought she knew.

Could she betray him? This man she loved and respected? Every day she was with him?

She could. She would have to. Because, in the end, it was simple. As simple as her belief that this war would be won. "Yes," she said, "I will."

"Good lass," McBride exhaled loudly. "We were hoping you'd say that." He looked at his watch. "I am afraid, Ilse, that we must now go to another meeting. We are briefing Winnie himself as to our progress. We will add your decision—but not your name of course—to our list of successes." He grinned. "May help persuade the PM to funnel some extra cash our way."

The major had stood, was packing up the folder. "The next wireless course at Fawley Court begins a week today—Monday, January 6

—so you'll move down Sunday. Any questions?" he asked, eyes on his task.

"One, yes."

"Go on."

"How do you know that the daughter of such a man is not a Nazi double agent?"

That stopped the major's packing. He looked sharply at her—while McBride whistled. "You know, we were hoping you might ask us that," he said. "And I can tell you this much . . ." He glanced at the major, looked back to her. "Our first two interviews with you. We are trained to watch for subterfuge, as you can imagine. Also, you have been thoroughly vetted. We have friends in America and they know, uh, friends of yours." He smiled. "Of course, we could still be mistaken. But if you are a German spy I would say your career choice was all wrong. You should never have taken up the flute. You should have become a bloody actress!"

"Language, Danny Boy!" Cholmondeley-Warren reprimanded, but without any true colour. He studied Ilse for a long moment, then said, "Do you have any pin money?" Without waiting for an answer, he bent to write something on a scrap of paper, then continued. "Take this to accounts on the floor below. It's an order for, uh, ten pounds. How you spend it is up to you, as long as you are in Henley on Sunday night." He handed her the paper, then picked up the folder and peered at her. "My suggestion, young lady, is that you get away for a few days. Take a little holiday. It may be the last one you have until . . ." He smiled—the first time he had since the interview began. "Well, until the war is won." He put out a hand; she stood and shook it. "Come, Danny Boy. Let's go see Winston and sing for our supper."

He strode out. McBride shook her hand as well, held it a moment in both of his. "Thank you," he said. "It's a bit ramshackle, the Good Ship SOE, as you will discover. But we think it has the capability of sinking a few Jerry destroyers, and considerably shortening the war.

Welcome aboard." He squeezed her hand, then added, in Norwegian, "Happy New Year. May 1941 be the year that the tide turns."

He left, and she turned to pick up her handbag from beside the chair. As she rose, she looked again at the map behind the desk, the chart of her country's fall. But instead of focusing on the large swastika in the centre of the map, she looked to the top of it, to a far smaller symbol— King Haakon's 'H7.' That new symbol of resistance.

"My All for Norway," she said softly. "Happy New Year."

FOUR

THE GETAWAY

London. December 30, 1940

BILLY COKE WOKE to a voice and a gentle shaking.

"The master has returned, sir. He awaits you in the dining room. There's tea here."

"Jeffers?" Billy yawned, sat up, more than a little confused. He'd been deep in a dream about mountains. "What time is it?"

"Four p.m., sir."

"Four?" He stretched his arms, yawned widely again. Most of it came back. The air raid, getting to Coke House. Nothing after. He looked down. "How did I get into these pyjamas? And who put these plasters on my hands?"

"I helped you, sir. After the bath."

"The bath?" Billy scratched his head, looked around. "Where are my clothes?"

"Your clothes were ruined, sir. Too much dirt, too many gashes. I have hung one of the master's old suits in the closet, along with socks, underwear and a shirt. Summer-weight, I am afraid. I also regret that

his shoes will not fit you, so I have cleaned yours as best I could."
Jeffers pointed. "There's a basin of hot water on the chest of drawers,
and a face cloth."

He went to the door. "Is my cousin pleased?" Billy called. "About
lending me all his stuff?"

Jeffers turned. He paused before speaking. "In confidence, sir, I
would say that the master is not pleased about anything to do with
your presence."

"Thanks for the heads-up. And for all your kindness." He smiled.
"I suppose I still can't persuade you to call me Billy?"

"Heavens, no, Master William." The old butler bowed his head.
"The dining room, sir. As soon as you are ready."

Billy picked up the teacup, the aroma rising before he laid his lips
on the fine china. He sighed. "Lapsang souchong," he murmured.
Almost impossible to find since the war began. But Coke House
would have enough to last the war, no doubt. Infinitely better than
the last cup of tea he'd drunk. Where had that been? Oh, yes, Mrs.
Bishop's.

Then he remembered. "Ilse," he said, sipped, and smiled.

JEFFERS WAS RIGHT. The Honourable Gervase Coke did
indeed look anything but pleased.

"This *is* an emergency, is it?" he snapped by way of greeting. "We
had an agreement that I would be in touch with you, should I have
news."

"And good afternoon to you too, cousin." Billy sat at a place
setting on the opposite side of the table, lifted the metal warming lid.
"What's this? Welsh rarebit? Yum!"

He tucked in. He'd rarely been this hungry. Gervase threw down
his own knife and fork on his part-eaten food and regarded him
glumly. His large round face and bulbous nose gave him the aspect of
a particularly angry frog. Indeed, all of him was big, which explained

why even his ancient cast-offs hung so loose on Billy. Neck folds bulged over his uniform's collar. He had the epaulettes and pips of a captain, and the shoulder flash of the Devonshires—the Coke family's regiment.

Billy looked at the flash. "Shouldn't you be in India?"

Gervase sighed. "The first battalion is in India, the second in Malta, as you well know. I am captaining a company in the newly raised 50th, the Holding Battalion."

"Holding what?" said Billy, through a full mouth.

"England, you bloody idiot."

Billy smiled and kept eating, pausing only to slurp the coffee that Jeffers had arrived to pour. He had a long history of riling his cousin, couldn't think of any other way of acting with him. Gervase, two years his senior, had disapproved of him from the moment he arrived as an orphan from Canada, aged seven, and had made that clear from the off. Billy had seen no reason to court his approval since.

"Well, is it?" Gervase asked testily. "An emergency?"

"Did Jeffers not tell you? Look, are you done with that? Thanks." He reached over and snagged his cousin's half-finished rarebit, to grunted protests. "My digs were destroyed. I spent the night fighting the fire. I had nowhere else to go."

If Gervase hated one thing more than Billy, it was Germans. "Bastard Huns," he spat. "I hear they nearly burned down the city."

"Much of it, yes. It was"—Billy closed his eyes briefly—"terrible."

"I am sure." Gervase regarded his cousin with a moment of rare sympathy before the scowl returned. "I just don't know what to do with you. Perhaps that's the service you should join. Become a fireman. I understand they are so short of men they will take anyone— even a godless communist like you."

Billy chewed his last bite of melted cheese and bread, then carefully aligned his knife and fork on the plate, which Jeffers immediately swept up. This was old ground, a familiar battlefield. "I am sure I have told you before, Gervase," he said slowly, "that though I am certainly godless I was never a commie." He beamed. "I am an anarchist."

His cousin's nostrils flared—a sure sign of impending battle. "They say it happens in the best of families. But it never had in ours before your father. He was certainly a rebel, taking himself off to Canada before the first war was even over—"

"Having taken a sniper's bullet at Ypres. I'd leave my father out of it, if I were you," Billy warned. "Besides, from what he told me, the founder of the Coke fortunes was a rebel too. And a thief."

Gervase's eyes bulged. "Are you referring to—"

"Sir William." Billy gestured to the portrait that dominated the dining room behind Gervase's chair. *Sir William Coke, Baronet,* looked down from the wall, wearing an ermine robe, a long curled wig and an ambiguous smile. He had a pistol in his right hand. "Dad told me that, before he was knighted, he was a highwayman. That's why he's holding the pistol."

Gervase snorted. "Nonsense. Our ancestor fought for the first Charles, Charles the Martyr, God rest his soul, in the Civil War, and was knighted by the second Charles and given our estate, Torsham Abbey, for services rendered. He also helped found the Devonshires—"

"Quite. And in between the wars and the knighting and the founding he made a living holding up stagecoaches."

"Romantic rubbish!" exploded Gervase. At which point, Jeffers stepped forward and in a gentle tone enquired if the master might wish to take some fino. His cousin took a deep breath, nodded and, while Jeffers poured the pale sherry into two crystal glasses, stared balefully at Billy. He took a gulp, then said, "I don't understand you at all. This ceaseless ingratitude. My father took you in when your father died—"

"And whipped me off to boarding school straight away. That . . .hideous place. I'd come from a farm, for God's sake."

"Yes, and your manners needed mending. You were almost feral."

"Hardly. I just didn't like uniforms and stupid rules."

"Which you proved again and again. How many schools was it, in the end?"

"Two or three."

"More like five. And then, when you joined me at Repton you got yourself expelled, fully and finally. At sixteen." Gervase shook his head. "For punching your housemaster!"

"True. He'd had his hand down my rugger shorts. When I removed it he called me insolent, and decided he'd cane me. I decided he wouldn't."

"Indeed. That expulsion was hardly the first disgrace you brought on the family. But you eclipsed it later, by God, didn't you?"

"Really? How else?" Billy knew his sins well enough, but he was always delighted to watch his cousin tally them, mainly for the colours he turned.

Fingers like pork bangers came out, to count off. "You became a bohemian. An actor, prancing and singing for money. Then you went off to Spain to fight for communism."

"To fight against fascism." Billy took a gulp of sherry, put the glass down. "If more in Europe had joined us then, and halted fascism in its early incarnation, we might not be watching the Nazis trying to burn London down now. The continent might still be free—"

"Oh, yes. You were such visionaries, you . . . anarchists," Gervase sneered. "What a brave workers' paradise you were going to make."

"A better world than rests now under Hitler's boot!"

"You—"

"More sherry, sir?"

Jeffers's hand slid the cut-glass decanter in between the two heated faces that had gotten closer together. Both cousins leaned back, took deep breaths and picked up their crystal to drink.

And resume, Billy thought. Over the years they'd had arguments that could go on for hours. Twice, when they were still at school, they'd ended in blows. Now though, his cousin gave a vast sigh, sipped, put his glass down and, oddly, spoke in a calmer voice.

"I said before that I didn't know what to do with you. That was not in fact true. Something has come up."

"A commission in the regiment?" Billy had even considered joining the Devonshires, just to take up the fight again. His every attempt to join the Royal Air Force, to use the skills he'd acquired, had been rebuffed by buffers like his cousin—all because he'd flown and fought for the Left in Spain.

"Great Christ, no! I couldn't take the responsibility. You'd probably punch a drill sergeant before basic training was done." Gervase ran his tongue around the inside of his lips. "No. Against my better judgement I may have found someone willing to let you fly again."

Billy's breath caught. He felt suddenly cold. "The RAF will have me?"

"Again, no. But I met a fellow at White's last week, guest of another member. A Canadian flyer. RCAF—squadron leader, I think. Decent chap, for a colonial. He talked about the deep losses all squadrons sustained in the recent Battle of Britain." Gervase lifted his glass, took another sip of fino. "They are rebuilding, training young men as fast as they arrive off the boat. I mentioned you, without going into any of your, uh, criminal history, aside from that you were born in Canada. He asked to meet you on Friday at Cranwell, the air force college." He raised an eyebrow. "Think you can stay out of trouble till then?"

Billy, finding he needed a gulp of sherry, took it. "Do you know what his squadron flies?"

"Vintage biplanes? Does it matter? You'll be in the air again." Gervase's brow furrowed. "No, wait, he did tell me. We'd taken a few snifters on board so . . ." His brow cleared. "Hurricanes. They fly Hurricanes."

Fighters! His cousin was right, he'd have flown anything to get aloft again. But a fighter was the dream. He'd flown a Polikarpov, the Russian fighter, in Spain, towards the end. "You know, cousin," he said, "I could bloody kiss you."

"You better bloody not." He eyed the suit Billy was wearing. "I suppose you lost everything in the Blitz?"

"What little I had is lost, yes."

"Well, you can keep that. Hated the check anyway. Maybe Jeffers can roust you out some other cast-off togs. You can go to the family tailor, Dege and Skinner, on Savile Row, to have them altered. I'll let them know to put it onto the Coke account."

"Thank you."

"It's not for you. I do this for the family name. Can't have you showing up at your regiment looking like a tramp." He sighed. "I suppose you need money too?"

"Well . . ."

"Jeffers will loan you a tenner from housekeeping. Note the word *loan*. I shall expect it back."

"Of course." Billy smiled. "Honestly, Gervase, I am grateful. And a little surprised."

"Don't be. I do this only to get you off my back. I still don't like you and never will. You are a disgrace to our name, sir." He wagged a finger. "But perhaps up there"—he pointed the finger to the ceiling, beyond it—"you can redeem yourself, what?"

———

BEFORE HIS FITTING at the family tailors, Billy used their phone to call the YWCA. Ilse was out at a meeting, he was told, was expected back for dinner at seven. He left a message: would she have dinner with him instead? The lady he spoke to was that same spinster who'd disapproved of him the night before and continued to do so now. She agreed, however, to pass on the message.

He formed a plan for beyond dinner while he waited for the 38 bus. There was a place he had to go to see if he could make it work. A man he had to see.

"Billy!" McGovern cried as the young man pushed through the doors of the Globe. "You're alive!"

"You too." Billy allowed the big man to take his hand and near crack his knuckles in a vigorous shake. "How did this place survive? It's about the only building still standing on London Wall."

"God. Me, that is!" McGovern replied, tapping his chest. "The lads and I put out every fire. And all the big bombs missed us, just. Molly!" he called, and his wife appeared from behind the bar, her blonde hair dishevelled, streaks of soot across her face, carrying a tray. "Look what the cat dragged in."

" 'Ello, Billy, love," she said, leaning in to kiss him, a smacker on the lips. "Want some chicken?"

He looked at what she held—carcasses in various states of dismemberment, mostly blackened. " 'E didn't get every fire," she said, "whatever this 'ero tells you."

"Fuckin' Adolf killed all my chickens. They was great layers too. What are we going to do for eggs now?"

"Eat powdered egg like everyone else?"

"Fuck that. Tastes like shit. Besides, eggs is my currency, trade 'em on the Black for all sorts."

The idea that Billy had been forming now took a turn. He'd thought of simply asking the husband and wife, who'd become like family to him this last half-year, for a favour. Now he could do them one in return. "You get your chickens from the country, don't you?"

"Yeah, from my brother Don, who runs the family farm out near Lowestoft, Suffolk."

"Why don't I do a run out there and collect a flock for you?"

"That'd be nice, Mac," said Molly. "The kid could really 'elp us out."

"Wait a minute." McGovern looked at Billy suspiciously. "You never wanted to be involved in the Black before. Offended your *h*anarchist principles, you said." His expression changed. "This 'asn't got anything to do with that piece of skirt you went 'aring off after last night, deserting your post 'ere?"

Billy grinned. "Might have."

"Let me see if I got this straight." Mac put a hand to his forehead, as if he were a medium receiving messages from the beyond. "You want me to pay for you to gallivant off with her? Have a nice little day trip?"

"Actually, I was thinking three days."

"You cheeky little—"

Molly grabbed her husband's arm, halting his flow. "I think it's a lovely idea, Billy." She looked up. "Why not, Mac? He can collect that other stuff too." She poked him in the ribs. "Go on! We was young once, remember?"

"Yeah, before the Boer War." His voice was still gruff, but there was a smile in his eyes. "Alright, you little sod. There's enough petrol to go and come back—with my chickens, and a few other things. I'll make a list, phone Don, let 'im know you're comin'. Tomorrow. I need the van tonight." He tapped Billy's chest. "Three days tops, mind. Back Thursday night, latest. And you'll owe me a night of singing when you're back."

"I'll sing you one now, if you like." Billy grabbed Molly, swung her around, pulled her close, swayed. " 'When we're out together, dancing cheek to cheek.' "

"Bloody 'ell." McGovern shook his head as Molly giggled. "Daft bugger's in love."

IN HER ROOM at the YWCA, as the last day of 1940 began, Ilse looked at her few possessions, neatly packed into the small case on her bed. Done, she thought, closing the lid. As she did, a van's horn sounded outside. Three short notes, one long. *Duh-duh-duh . . . duhh.* Beethoven's Fifth. The rhythm Billy had told her he would use—on the phone the night before, when she'd turned down his dinner invitation. She'd told him she couldn't join him because she so badly needed a good sleep. It was only partly true. She mostly needed to consider again what she was doing here. Taking this trip with this handsome . . . actor. Excitement had warred with fear.

Yet now, as she heard the notes, she smiled. She'd always enjoyed that symphony; now she knew something else about its first bar from her studies in Morse—three short, one long was also code for the letter *V*. And *V* stood for *Victory*. The BBC evening news opened their daily European broadcasts with those notes from the Fifth to bring hope to the defeated, the occupied. Then, after the news, they would include other coded messages for those who resisted—usually bits of nonsense or lines from a poem which only made sense to the ones receiving them: information about weapon drops, agent landings, requests for sabotage. Now she hoped that if all went well at Fawley Court in the next month, she would be back in Norway soon, be among the people listening for those special messages, hoping that one was for her.

For now, though, as the last long note from Billy's horn faded, what she really heard was possibility. This singer, this pilot, this stranger she was about to accompany into the English countryside for three days. If nothing else, it would be a holiday, perhaps her last for years - until the day "V for Victory" announced a truth, rather than a hope.

"Here we go," she said, and snapped shut the clasps of her case.

PART 2
ADAGIO

FIVE
A DRIVE IN THE COUNTRY

London. December 31, 1940

THE FURTHER THEY GOT from London, the more they left the war behind them.

Not at first. They'd had to drive out through the East End and, as usual, the poorest area of the city had suffered the worst of the bombing. Closest to the docks, one of the main targets of the Luftwaffe during the fifty-seven-day Blitz, it had been struck hard again in what was already being called, as Billy had read that morning in the *Daily Worker*, the communist newspaper, "the Second Great Fire of London." He found himself wondering if his ancestor, the highwayman whose name he shared, had endured the first, just as Billy had the second.

Whitechapel was near impassable, with fires breaking out again and again, no matter the fire engines pumping endless water into shattered cellars, their hoses blocking the roadways that the tumbled walls had not. He'd been forced northwards into Bethnal Green, which was not much better but through which he'd managed to snake a route, gradually creeping east. There, he was stopped by the authorities. The pass that McGovern had given him, detailing why he was taking a truck out, using rationed petrol—for the purposes of restocking Shoreditch's devastated food market—passing muster with a harried, smut-streaked constable.

As they passed through more rubble, bouncing over tumbled brick, Ilse murmured, "Jews."

He glanced, saw what she was seeing. Jews indeed, five of them, Orthodox, hair coiling down beside their faces from under homburg hats. They were staring at a collapsed building, and in his glance, Billy saw shattered benches, a curving wall still standing, a large, leaning Star of David. "Looks like their synagogue," he said, accelerating as they left the last of the rubble behind and the vehicles ahead sped up. "Poor bastards. Still, they're better off here than in Germany, aren't they?"

"They are," Ilse whispered.

He glanced across, caught a look that fleeted in her eyes and was gone. Pain there, some nerve touched. What's that about, he wondered. They hadn't talked much since he'd picked her up—or hadn't talked *about* much. Chit-chat. Mainly him doing the chitting and the chatting. Come to think of it, he thought, it was me doing most of the talking at Mrs. Bishop's two nights before. They were meant to have gone for dinner last night, but she'd said she needed a good sleep, and that there were also things she needed to do, people to say goodbye to, as she would be leaving the YWCA when they got back from their trip. To go where, she hadn't said. Secrets on secrets, he thought.

She was preoccupied, staring out at the devastation, keeping all her answers brief. As ever, he didn't like silences, always strove to fill them. To entertain.

He thought back to what they'd seen in the East End, what he'd read in the *Daily Worker* earlier. Began to sing.

It's the same the whole world over
It's the poor wot get the blame

It's the rich wot make the profit
Ain't it all a . . . crying shame.

He'd sung it in his best music hall style, plenty of vibrato. She turned to him. "I thought it was 'fucking shame,' " she said.

"Ah." He was slightly startled. "I always try not to swear in front of a lady. At least before noon."

"Who told you I was a lady?"

He looked at her again. For the first time that morning, she was properly smiling. Her eyes—those ice-blue eyes, the first thing he'd noticed about her outside the Globe as the bombs began to fall—were filled with light now. Mission accomplished, he thought, and stared a moment longer than he should have, seeing as he was driving. He turned forward, eased back from the bumper of the car ahead. Blimey, he thought, just as he'd thought in that first glance two nights before. His stomach shifted, and he couldn't work out if it was from excitement or terror. Both of which he'd felt the moment she'd said yes to his proposition on the phone. He'd also been a little surprised. This might be 1940—still, just—and many of the rules that had bound people before the war had already begun to slip away. Still, she was, what, early twenties? And yet she hadn't hesitated when he'd suggested the trip. Who was she?

Yup, he realized, terror and excitement both, as the road opened before them.

From the corner of his eye, he saw her pick up the newspaper between them. "*Daily Worker*," she announced. "This is the communists' newspaper, is it not?"

"It is."

"Are you a communist?"

"No. Used to be." A car pulled out ahead of him and he declutched down.

"Seen the error of your ways?"

He shook his head. "Nah. They were too tame for me."

"So now you are . . . ?"

"Anarchist. We don't have a newspaper." He grinned. "That would be too . . . organized."

"I see." She laughed. "I don't think I have ever met an anarchist before."

"You may have. There isn't a look."

"Hmm. I don't think we have them in Norway."

"You'd be surprised."

"You want to tell me why you are this?"

He could, he thought. He had some pretty good set speeches down, passionate, funny. He could give her Bakunin chapter and verse; regale her on the needed breakdown of society into smaller self-governing groups, and on the vital importance of teaching people to read, to think for themselves. He could trot out some of his favourite quotes, capping it all with "A new world will only be gained when the last king is strangled in the guts of the last priest." However, he'd discovered that such talk was not the most conducive to romance. Except perhaps with some of the tougher Andalusian girls he'd met, though it truly wasn't the talk but the action they'd wanted.

Which was another thing. If he talked of it, he would have to talk of Spain, where he'd learned it all. And he did not want to think about Spain. Not now. Not on this day when the clouds had pulled back and bright sunlight filled the land. Not when tumbled brick was giving way to green fields, and shrouded bodies to flocks of sheep. Not when he had three days' holiday before he had to go back to war. Three days with the most beautiful woman he'd ever met, who had agreed to come with him for . . . for what was yet to be decided.

"A Marxist, an anarchist and a nihilist walk into a bar," he said. "And the bartender says, 'Sorry, we don't serve anyone under twenty-one.'"

She smiled. "Are you saying you only believed in it when you were young?"

"No, still believe, it's just—" He broke off. To be honest, he knew it was a joke that worked better in a trench in Navarre than a truck in Essex. And he really didn't want to get into it all.

She continued, her voice low. "I think I would like you to tell me sometime. There is much of the world I . . . I have never tried to understand. Felt no need. I had music and . . ." She looked out the window. "Now I feel the need."

Billy couldn't see her eyes. But he could hear it in her voice. That darkness, back. Yet he fought back his first impulse—to make it go away, entertain it away. The darkness was a part of her. It might even be the core of her. And he wanted to know all of her. Or at least as much as he could uncover in the three days they had.

"I'll tell you anything you want to know," he said. "In time. But you have to tell me stuff too. I need some *quid pro quo*."

"You know Latin too?" she asked, without turning.

"I kinda speak it. At one of my schools, we did a Latin play every year. I first got into acting by playing Seneca."

She turned. "Your school. Tell me of that."

"Uh-uh. First, *audi alteram partem*."

"Which means?"

"I will 'listen to the other side of the case.'" He smiled. "In other words—you talk first. Tell me about you."

"Me?"

WHAT CAN I TELL HIM? she wondered. How much is allowed?

This was one of the reasons she had almost cancelled the trip. This moment she'd known she would have to face. The reason why she had chosen not to go to dinner with him the night before, while she tried to figure it out. Really, it had only been when she'd heard possibility in the sound of his horn and when she'd seen again the face she only half remembered because it had been glimpsed by incendiary light and in the dimness of an underground tea room. When she'd heard the voice again, that pleasing baritone that had so delighted her, with its English accent and a little of something else in it too, and had viewed again the smile, finally, indeed, the smile—

"boyish" is what the English would say, "gutteaktig," she'd call it in Norwegian—that she knew she couldn't disappoint him. He was going to war, to be a pilot, and she knew that so many of those young men would die. She was going to war too, where the life expectancy of an agent, she suspected, was not much longer than a pilot's. But for a few days, they could leave the war behind.

Actually leave it, in devastated London. She'd seen when he looked at her, in that first moment, what her beauty had done to him. It had happened with men before, several times. What her French lover, Armand, had called *un coup de foudre*: the lightning bolt of an immediate, dazzling love. She had only been the recipient of it, had never been struck blind herself. It annoyed her, truly, that men fell so easily for what they could only see. But the truth was also that she liked men. She liked the feel of them, the weight of them, the smartness and, yes, even the stupidity of them.

None of which she could say to him now. But what could she say, to end the silence that had lengthened since he'd quoted his Latin and asked about her? Some things perhaps. This first, she thought, even though this too is a risk.

"Billy. Listen."

"I am."

"You told me on the phone that you are finally going to war?"

"I hope so, yes." He frowned, accelerated around a tractor, settled again to his normal fast speed. "If the RCAF will have me."

"So I . . . I am going to war too."

"How?"

"I cannot tell you."

"I see. At least I think I do." He geared down, slowing as they entered the outskirts of a village. "And where will you fight the war? Norway?"

She shrugged. "It is something else I cannot tell you. But will you"—she grabbed his hand—"will you remember that when I don't answer your questions it is not because I do not want you to know about me, but because I *cannot* answer? Also, this . . ." She squeezed his fingers. "That when there is a silence between us, it does not require you to fill it?"

"Hmm. I'm not very good with silences."

"I noticed. Will you try?"

He ran his tongue around his lips. "That I will."

"And can we just have . . . a good time? For three days? For this, our three-day holiday?"

"That we can. And it begins now." He jerked his head back. "Behind my seat. The paper bag."

She reached, pulled the bag out, opened it, extracted a waxed-paper package. "What's this?"

"Corned beef and mustard. And in that flask back there, tea. Molly McGovern made us them." He grinned. "A holiday begins with a good breakfast, don't you think?"

She peeled the paper away, held out the sandwich to him. He didn't take it, just leaned close and took a large bite. Then, even as he chewed, he began to sing—the same song he'd sung to her two nights before. It sounded different through margarine and beef.

If you were the only girl in the world
And I was the only boy . . .

———

"THERE MAY BE no signs of war out here," Billy said, an hour and a half later, pulling the truck over to the verge, "but there are also no signs."

Turning off the engine, Billy stepped out. He'd stopped at a cross-roads, of sorts. Straight ahead, he knew that the road they'd driven on all the way from Hackney Wick—the A12—led to Lowestoft. How far away that was, he had no clue. To either side, narrow lanes ran off between tall, winter-bare hedgerows.

He looked in a ditch beside the roadway. The signpost pole was there. The sign itself was not. "They took 'em all down when they thought the Nazis were about to invade," he said. "Think they still might." He took off his trilby, scratched his head. "Don't know what that might do to Jerry but it's confused the hell out of me."

She got out of the truck, came to stand beside him. "Is that your map?"

"For what it's worth." He scanned McGovern's drawing, scratched on the back of an envelope.

"That was, ah, Blythburgh we passed through?"

"Yup—no sign of course. But the postmaster hadn't scratched the name off his post office very well."

Ilse turned the map back and forth. "The sea is that way, I can smell it. But this . . ." She tapped the map crossroads. "This could be any one of half a dozen we have passed through."

"Oh, I know. Hold up. Here comes a local."

The man—a farm labourer by his attire of muck-splattered boots and baggy wool trousers—was leading a cow up the seaward lane towards them. He had his eyes to the ground and was both chewing slowly and whistling off-key. When he reached the crossroads, he looked up, and started when he saw them. He was probably in his sixties, corpulent and grey with the years. His coat was split at both shoulders. "Eh now," he cried, jerking to a halt. The cow pulled over to the hedge and began tugging at some red berries.

"Good morning," Billy said, stepping towards him. "I wonder if you could help us. We're a little lost."

The man leaned away and spat some tobacco juice beside the cropping cow. "Well, that depends, see," he replied, wiping his mouth, his voice a low rumble, his eyes flicking between the two of them.

"On what?"

The labourer shifted the tobacco wad over to his other cheek, his eyes narrowing. "On whether you be Nazi spies, see."

"Ah. And why might you think we were?"

"Why? Everyone knows theys being dropped all over. Saboteurs, prior to the invasion." He said it like a quote from some newspaper or off the BBC. "You talk proper too. Like a Nazi might." His gaze shifted to Ilse, standing just behind Billy. "Her looks like a German too."

"I'm Norwegian."

"So you says."

"Look, I can show you our papers," Billy said, turning back to the truck.

"Papers can be faked, see. Everyone knows that." The man turned and spat again, hitting the cow on her muzzle this time, which did not deter her from her munching. "You tell me where you is trying to find, and I'll tell you if I can tell you where it be."

"Sotterley."

"Oh, aye?" He said it like the village was the secret centre of the national defence.

"Well, just outside. I'm trying to get to Don McGovern's. Lowcroft Farm?"

This raised an eyebrow. "You know Don?"

"I know his brother." Billy didn't know the publican's first name; everyone just called him by his surname. His wife called him Mac.

"Does ya?" For the first time, the man smiled. "Charlie? He was a right young rogue. Poacher 'ere. Ran off to London to escape the squire's gamekeepers when he was barely out of his . . ." He took off his cloth cap, scratched at the grey stubble on his head. "What's he up to now?"

"Runs a pub in the city."

"Sounds about right." The man put the cap back on, glanced at the truck. "And you be 'ere to fetch him some livestock, like? On the Black?"

Billy shrugged. "I think that's between me and his brother, don't you?"

"Fair 'nuff." He tipped his ear towards his right shoulder, looked past Billy. "Don's farm is down that lane. A little ways on the right." He took up the slack on the rope, jerked the cow away from the hedge. "Tell him Frank Whittaker says 'ello, and I might be down to see 'im tomorrow. With the, uh, milk?" He gave an exaggerated wink, then tugged at the brim of his cap. "Miss," he said, then growled at the cow, who was trying to nibble again, jerked the rope, and turned along the main road south.

Billy and Ilse watched him go for a few moments. "Well," Ilse said. "I think Britain is safe from invasion with men like him confusing the Germans."

"I think you're right." Billy turned back to the truck. "Shall we?"

The directions were good. There was a sign for Lowcroft Farm at the corner of a lane on the right. Billy took it, both sides of the truck scraping the hedgerows, the wheels slipping on slick, churned mud. A hundred yards and they pulled into the farmyard, buildings on three sides—a barn before which a dozen chickens pecked and rooted, a pen filled with sheep, and a thatch-roofed, whitewashed farmhouse.

The door of the latter opened as Billy cut the engine. The land-lord of the Globe was a big man but his brother—there was no mistaking the family look, black hair, wide face—was huge. He was wiping his hand on a tea cloth, staring suspiciously. "Who be you?" he said, as Billy and Ilse got out of the cab.

"I'm Billy Coke, Mr. McGovern." The wide face didn't change expression. "Uh, your brother sent me? From London?"

"I don't know nothing 'bout that."

"He said he'd phone you."

"Phone lines been down out of Lowestoft since that last German raid." He stared at them. "Did 'e send a note with you?"

"No."

"What you 'ere for?"

"To collect chickens. A few other things. For the pub?"

"Oh, aye." The farmer laid the towel over his shoulder, put his hands on his hips, eyes narrowed. Then they widened a fraction. "'Ere, you ain't that singer he told me about? Entertains in the pub? Canadian fella?"

"I am."

"Can you prove that?"

Billy glanced at Ilse, who was smiling at him. He thought of what he'd been singing that morning. Except now she *was* the only girl in the world, and that song belonged to her. So he squared his shoulders and began to sing something else he'd loved. It was an old one from the music halls, written for a "girl" to sing to a "boy." But in the revue they'd done at the theatre in Bath, there hadn't been an actress in the company who'd had the range for it, so the musical director had changed the lyrics and given it to Billy. It was the last song he'd sung there, in fact, before going to Spain.

The girl I love is up in the gallery
The girl I love is looking now at me.
There she is, can't you see, waving her handkerchief.
As merry as a robin that sings on a tree.

As he sang, a woman came out and stood behind the farmer in the doorway. When he finished, she started a round of applause.

"Lovely," she said.

"That's better than a phone call, I 'ave to say." Don McGovern was all smiles now. "Come in, the pair of you, and let's 'ave a cuppa. This 'ere's my wife, Noreen."

"Mornin'," the woman said.

They followed the McGoverns through the front door, entering straight into a small, warm kitchen. Over at a wood-fired range, an old lady in a smock, her grey hair up in a bun, was bent over, pulling a tray of something from one of the ovens. "Mother," McGovern said, very loudly, but the woman did not turn. "Deaf as a post," he sighed, before crossing and tapping her on the shoulder.

She started. "Eh?" she said, looking up.

"Guests, Mum," he said, very loudly. "We got visitors. Friends of Charlie's. Up from London."

"Oh, yes." She put the tray down on the stovetop, turned, her wrinkled face cracking into a smile that revealed very few teeth. "Friends of my boy, eh? I'll put the kettle on."

They sat around a messy table. Drank tea and ate some of the delicious scones—which put Mrs. Bishop's to shame—hot from the oven, complete with jam and cream; no rationing on a farm, it appeared. After the farmer caught up with his brother's news—he shouted the basics at his mother, who did not sit but beamed at the visitors and bustled about—both he and his wife shook their heads over what Billy could tell them of the terrible raid on London, which the BBC had not fully detailed. After they politely turned down a third scone, McGovern took them outside and got down to business.

"You'll 'ave to wait a few days for them chickens," he said, leading them across to the barn, "because you see—"

Before Billy could reply that they planned on staying till Thursday anyway, he saw McGovern's reasons—the chickens were still in chick form. Under a single red bulb's light, two dozen moved around in a mesh pen. "Most was only born in the last coupla days. Shouldn't travel for a coupla more if 'n you want them to arrive alive." He bent, picked one little yellow ball up, placed it in Ilse's hand. "Can you spare the time?"

"Actually, we were planning on it." Billy looked at Ilse, who was nose to beak with the little bird, her eyes wide in pleasure. "Would day after tomorrow work?"

The man nodded. "Should be alright. Give us time to get them other things Charlie wants." He glanced at Ilse before heading back to the yard, Billy following. She stayed behind, still captivated by the chick. "You and your, er, wife got somewhere to stay?"

Billy thought for a moment. But something about the big farmer made him think that he needn't lie. "We're, uh, not actually married."

"Hmm. Might be tricky. 'Otels round 'ere can be a bit . . . prudish."

"We'll manage."

"Well, if you don't, you come back here. We got a spare room over the barn. Wife and I aren't prudish at all." He winked. "Naturists, we is."

The sudden image of the very large farmer naked threw Billy a bit. Ilse joined them at the truck and the two men shook hands; then, before Billy could climb in, old Mrs. McGovern came slowly out of the farmhouse with a basket. "Just a few things," she said, very loudly, handing the basket to Ilse. Billy glimpsed some more scones, pots of cream and jam, their tea flask—no doubt refilled—a bottle of what could be cider, a paper wrap of crumbly cheese.

"Thank you very much," Ilse said, taking it. "You are very kind."

The old lady squinted up at her. "And you are very beautiful," she replied, squeezing her hand, before looking at Billy. "I hope you know you are a very lucky man."

"Believe me, I do." He nodded at the farmer beside him. "Thank you, again. See you Thursday."

Billy took a step towards the cab. As he did, Don bent and snatched up a chicken that had been rooting around at their feet. Lifting the canvas back flap, he dropped it into the truck. "Never know," he said. "It's amazing how the idea of a nice roast chicken can overcome some people's prudery."

To waves, they drove off back down the muddy lane. "Very kind people," Ilse said, peering into the basket.

"English farmers. The salt of the earth."

She looked at him. "Do you think the farmers in Germany would be any less kind?"

He glanced at her. For a little time, laughing in a farmhouse, the war had gone. Now it was back in those eyes.

He didn't answer her. "Which way?" he asked instead, stopping the truck at the junction with the A12. "Right is back towards London. There's that small fishing port we came through that you said looked charming—Blythburgh, on the estuary." He nodded left. "Bigger town up there, Lowestoft. Lots to see."

Ilse was looking straight ahead. "That way is the sea." She turned. "I want to go to the sea."

She turned back, leaning forward, determined. "As my lady commands," he said, and put the truck in gear.

The lane leading to the sea dipped and rolled, and at the crests of the little rises, glimpses of water came, sparkling in the winter sun. Ilse was staring ahead, scarcely blinking. "You like the sea, then?" Billy asked.

Without looking at him, she nodded. "I am Norwegian," she said.

It obviously needed no further explanation, and he didn't ask for one. Besides, he was focusing on the truck, which had started to sputter. When he pulled into what was perhaps a car park for summer visitors, the engine cut out without him turning the key.

They stepped down from the cab on either side, met at the front. "Shall we?" she said, nodding up the slight slope topped by swaying marsh grass. Beyond it, they could hear the whoosh of waves.

He studied her. She had retreated again, behind those cool blue eyes. He wondered if perhaps a little time alone would bring her back. Besides . . .

"You go ahead." He gestured to the truck. "Want to take a look at the intake valves. Bloody petrol they're giving out now is full of little bits. Clogs things up. Don't want to get stuck here."

"You are a mechanic as well?"

He shrugged. "Know my way around an engine."

"You don't want to see the sea?"

He grinned. "Not going anywhere, is it?"

She didn't look too disappointed. "OK. You catch up."

She climbed the little slope, crested it, raised a hand to wave, vanished.

He watched the place where she'd been for a moment, then shook his head and went to the back of the truck. The chicken was sitting on McGovern's tool bag. Billy scooted it away, to protests. He saw why— it had an egg under it. He put that on some hessian sacks that lay in another corner, where the hen swiftly reassumed its perch. Then he picked up the tool bag and went to deal with the engine.

ILSE HALTED on the other side, just below the crest. Out of sight, but perhaps not out of Billy Coke's mind. She didn't know why she'd gone so cold so suddenly.

Then all her thoughts were taken by the sight before her.

It was true, what she'd said. Norwegians loved the sea. They were a sea people, from the wanderers called Vikings—traders and raiders — to the present day. And though the sight before her was so very different from the sea she'd spent so much of her life beside—holidaying every summer at the family hytte at Vessøya, on the southwestern shores of Oslofjord—she closed her eyes now and filled her other senses with the similarities.

The sound of waves sucking at the land, like a long breath drawn in and slowly breathed out. The scent of it, rich in salt and vegetation, seaweed rolling in surf, ground upon the rocks. The touch of the wind as it flushed her skin, lifted her hair, seeped beneath her chilled eyelids, drawing instant tears. Not sad ones though; joyous, as she opened her eyes again. The land beneath her hytte was rock, dark granite thrusts and jagged spills, coves carved by relentless waves, where at low tide stretches of sand and rock pools were left behind, filled with life—clams to be dug up, beds of mussels to be peeled from small cliff faces, crabs to be chased, all for the family pot, the feast that night. This English beach was long, shallow, disappearing on both sides in sand and shingle as far as she could see. The sand was coarse, pitted with small stones and with rocks, many wrapped in seaweed.

One thing was the same. There was a horizon. A blue-black line surmounted by a bank of white cloud. As she stared at it, her eyes narrowed against the sharp sun, she realized that it was perhaps the horizon she had missed most of all. Seeing . . . distance. Nothing ending, everything limitless, everything possible. If she reached those clouds, there would be another bank in the far distance, and then another, then another.

She walked to the water's edge. Picked up a pebble and threw it into the foam of a wave, then backed away so her shoes did not get wet. Maybe she'd take them off, roll up her skirt so she could wade in. It was the one sense she had not felt yet—sand under her toes, water at her ankles.

She squinted up at the sun. It was high and she knew it was

nearly noon. Years with the Norwegian Guides had taught her much about finding directions. She knew how England faced, how she was looking off the country's eastern edge. She turned to her left, stared northeast; across those waters, beyond all those horizons, lay her homeland. Saw it, even if she couldn't see it.

She turned southeast. That way lay Germany—and suddenly she knew why she'd gone cold, why she'd withdrawn, back in the truck.

It was the grandmother. Handing her the basket filled with treats she'd made. It had taken her back to another land she loved. To a man she loved and now was trying not to, in the place where she'd last seen him.

There, she thought. That way. Looking, she remembered.

SIX

CONCERT FOR A KING

Seelow, Germany. May 17, 1937

HER GRANDMOTHER HAD SHOWN her the way of it once—twelve years before, when she was five. Ilse had been distracted then, wanting to be off chasing her cousins through the woods. She had forgotten how to make one almost immediately. Now she focused, repeating each stage in words, asking questions, as Oma created magic from a forearm's length of freshly cut willow branch.

Finally, after all the paring and tapping, the cutting and the adjusting was done, Oma raised the bark flute and blew. A sweet, clear sound came. She played a rise of notes, then handed it across. "Your turn."

Ilse took it, placed her lips on it, blew. It took a while to get the first note, then longer to make a run of three. They were not as clear as her grandmother's. She handed it back. "I'm used to keys," she said, apologizing.

"This doesn't have any. You need to use your breath, child, your lips." Oma raised the flute, played again. A simple tune Ilse recognized, from the region where the house was, where her grandmother had grown up: Seelow, about seventy kilometres east of Berlin. A tune for the season. For the sap that had risen in the willow, the leaves on the trees, the wisteria just coming into bloom around her front door. As her grandmother played, Ilse looked above her, at the small, white-walled house that she loved, that she'd visited so often over the years to be with the woman she loved who lived there.

Oma. Who stopped playing now, quite suddenly, reaching for breath. Her grandmother, who'd always been able to play an afternoon through, and now could barely get through a song. Who'd been a big woman once, and now was shrunken.

"Take," she gasped. "Play."

Ilse took, didn't play. "Shall we go in, Oma? Aren't you getting cold?"

"Not yet. The sun is nice, isn't it?" She lifted her wrinkled face into a sunbeam, closed her eyes, smiled, then shivered. "Perhaps my shawl?"

Ilse rose, went into the house. On a chair in the small hallway was a red wrap. Middle Eastern designs on squares of ruby, ochre and gold. Patterns of poppies; lozenges of gold and silver thread filled with half-moons and five-pointed stars. Brought back from some exotic souk by the man who stared down from the wall above the chair, in his high-buttoned naval uniform, his lips pursed within his large but well-trimmed beard. Her grandfather, Rolf, the Norwegian sea captain. Drowned these thirty years.

She took the wrap outside, placed it around her Oma's shoulders. It was warm against the whitewashed wall, but the old lady shivered still. "Shall we go in? I'd like to see those albums."

"In a while, gulljente." 'Golden girl' in Norwegian. She'd lived in Norway for years, even after the captain didn't come back, raising her children there as Norwegians. Only when the last of them—Ilse's aunt Leni—was married and gone did she declare her desire to return to the home she'd come from, her father's house near Seelow. Her own mother had still been alive then; she had two sisters, widows from the war. Lost three brothers in that too. Now she was the last.

Not for long, Ilse thought, and looked away so Oma would not see the tears.

Perhaps she heard them. Ilse felt a hand on her arm. "When is the car coming for you?" her grandmother asked.

"Father said he'd send it around ten." She wiped her cheek, turned back around. "I'd rather stay here with you."

"You've been here three days." The old lady put a hand on Ilse's folded ones. "It has been lovely. But you must be bored here. In the city, all that excitement." Her eyes gleamed. "Berlin is a marvellous place again, full of wonders. Or so I have been told." She sighed. "Oh, there was a time in Berlin, long before the war, when I—"

She broke off, staring above her into the wisteria, through that into memory. Ilse turned her hands up, took Oma's in them, startled by how small they had become. Her father had often complained of his mother's large hands, how they could fetch him such a clout when he was naughty. "Come now, Oma. With me."

"Oh, if I only could!"

"You can. You must. Father has gotten me a room at the Adlon."

"The Adlon!"

"We can share a bed. Like we did when I was young."

Her grandmother stared at her for a moment, then shook her head. "No, child. I will not leave here again."

"But . . ."

"No. I must die in my father's house. My house." Oma shook the hands that held hers gently. "Besides, you will be too busy at the reception. Flirting with all those handsome young officers in their smart black uniforms." She smiled. "There was a ball I went to once at the Adlon, I remember. I was no older than you. All the officers were back from that first war with France. 1872, perhaps? There was a young officer in the Uhlans. Kasper? No—Kasper-Georg, that was his name. We danced every dance. No other officer was allowed to squire me. He told me he'd challenge any who tried to a duel. That I would have their blood or his on my hands if I was so cruel." Her misted eyes came back. "Killed, of course. Killed in '15, or '16, like so many of them." She looked at Ilse. "Ha! Listen to this old fool. Last few moments with her beloved gulljente and she spends it in history. Tell me," she said, her eyes bright, "if your father has arranged it, what do you think you will play tonight?"

"I hope he hasn't." Ilse shivered, but not from the cold. "Because he is not musical, he thinks it an easy thing. That a quartet or quintet or whatever grouping we will be can just let me in and we will all be wonderful."

"But you are wonderful, Liebchen. You played so beautifully for me here in my house last night. And you are going off to study at that prestigious American school—what was its name again?"

"Juilliard. Another reason I'd rather stay here. Spend my last night with you before I fly from Tempelhof in the morning. Not at some event with strangers."

"Not just strangers, Liebchen. My son told me that the greatest men of our age will be there. Of any age." Oma's eyes were bright again, and clear. "Did your father not tell you too? The Führer himself might be there!"

"It is possible. Generalfeldmarschall Göring will be there for sure."

"Another great hero! Ah, now, you do make me want to come with you."

Ilse looked at her grandmother. The age, the illness, had slipped away. She had the same look she'd had when she'd talked about dancing with the cavalry officer, sixty-five years before.

Ilse didn't understand politics. She didn't want to. "Is he so very special? Herr Hitler?"

"Special?" A different look came into the filmy grey-blue eyes now. Serious. Passionate. She stared straight into Ilse's. "You must understand, Ilse, what Germany was like for so long. We lost the war —and then we lost the peace. Those French, those Britishers, they set impossible terms, took our best lands, created enemy states on all our borders, made us pay and pay even when we had nothing left to pay with." She sighed. "So when the Depression came we had nothing in reserve. You exchanged a wheelbarrow of Reichsmarks for one loaf of bread. So many of my friends lost their homes, had to give them away, for nothing. For . . . more wheelbarrows! I only just kept . . . this!" She reached to her side, taking a frond of wisteria in one hand, running her thumb through the lavender petals as if stroking a cat. "There was fighting in every city. Even out here in Seelow, communists burned barns, attacked officials."

She broke off, staring ahead of her, lost again to memories, unpleasant ones this time. "And then?" Ilse asked.

The eyes cleared. "Then *he* came. The Führer. A man with a vision. Who was elected fairly, took power, dealt with his enemies. Ruthless, yes—perhaps—but he needed to be. Once again, Germany had purpose, control. We took back our industrial lands, built up again our army. Got our Reichsmarks again in envelopes, not . . . wheelbarrows. And he restored the connection that had been broken, between the German and his land. Between blood and soil." She took Ilse's hands again, squeezed. "Do you remember, Liebchen, last year, how the world came to Berlin, to the greatest Olympic Games ever staged?"

Ilse did. She'd seen films of races, flags raised, anthems played. Mostly "Deutschland, Deutschland über alles"—the home nation had won so much. Something about it had disturbed her, but her Oma had a smile now, and she didn't want to take it away. "I do," she replied, squeezing back. "It was wonderful."

"It was." Her grandmother nodded. "We had our pride again. Our destiny. Because our man of destiny had come."

"I see." Ilse's father had talked about the rise of National Socialism in the same terms. Glowingly. "It makes my German-half proud," he'd told her once. "It is my motherland, my mother's land, after all."

There was one thing that Ilse still didn't understand. Her father had shrugged when she'd raised it and changed the subject. But Ilse knew her Oma wouldn't. "What about the Jews?" she asked. "Is it fair what is being done to them?"

"Fair?" Ice shifted the fire in her grandmother's eyes. "Those friends who had to sell their houses for nothing, they were bought out by Jews. They ran so much of the business in the country, sticking to their tribe, shutting out the true German who had come back from defending his country to find it taken over, no way back in." She shook her head firmly. "The policies are right. Fair and just."

"But . . . but I know several Jews, Oma. I am sure you do as well. I have played music with them often. They are . . ." She hesitated. "They are like us."

"As individuals, perhaps," her grandmother conceded. "But as a tribe, no. They must leave. Go to their own lands, in Palestine. Go to other countries where so many of their tribe already live, like America. Leave here. And leave behind what they have looted from us."

"I see." She did. She understood. If her Oma—the flute maker, the baker, the kindest, sweetest person she'd ever known—believed this, how could she not?

Gravel crunched on the driveway. Ilse turned to see a giant black Mercedes sweep into the yard. She stood as the engine cut out and the driver lowered his window. "Fräulein Magnusson?" he asked.

"Yes?"

"Ach, good." He stepped from the car, a young man in a smart black uniform. He put on his cap and saluted, arm straight and angled up. "Heil Hitler! I have been sent to collect you and take you to Berlin."

"We have been expecting you, my good young man." Ilse's grandmother pushed herself slowly off the chair. "May I offer you some coffee?"

The driver hesitated, then shook his head. "Much kindness, good lady. But it took me a while to find your house and I must have the Fräulein back in Berlin by noon. For her rehearsal. I am afraid we must leave promptly."

Her grandmother clapped. "So you will play! Wonderful!"

Ilse still wasn't so sure if it was. "My bags are in the hall just here. I'll get them."

"Please, allow me."

The young man preceded her through the door. He picked up her small valise, her flute case and her vanity case, took them back out. Ilse collected her coat and cloche hat from the stand, put both on, adjusting the hat in the wall-hung mirror. Her grandmother had disappeared, but now she came back, carrying a basket, a linen towel over the contents. Ilse could smell spices rising from it—cardamom and clove, cinnamon and nutmeg.

Oma pulled the towel back, revealing neat rows of two kinds of cookies. "Make sure you eat your fill of these, or hide them for your trip, before your father smells them." She tapped the darker ones. "Chocolate Lebkuchen. When he was nine, he found a tray of them hot from the oven in our kitchen in Bergen. He ate ten and was sick for two days. Didn't stop him doing the same thing the next Christmas. Save him one, perhaps." She pointed to the lighter cookies. "Linzer. They have my own raspberry jam. Wilhelm is less fond of them but I'd still keep them out of his way. Here."

She held the basket out. Ilse didn't take it. She looked at her Oma. Down at her, when she'd spent so much of her life at her hip, looking up. Her softness was gone, taken by the cancer. But her eyes were still the same.

Ilse burst into tears, stepped in, wrapping her arms around the old woman, who held the basket to the side in one hand, patting with her other, murmuring endearments, German and Norwegian: "Gulljente, Liebchen." They held each other for a long while until the engine started up outside and Oma pulled away. "Go," she said. "Go and play beautifully."

Ilse took the basket, then seized a hand. "I will be back," she said, shaking it. "I will see you again."

"Of course you will," her grandmother replied, both of them nodding and smiling through the lie. "Now go, so you can come back quicker. Oh, wait!" She went back into the kitchen, came back with a flask, handed it over. "Coffee, for the fine young man. Lots of sugar—young men like that." She lowered her voice. "Did you see the badges at his collar? The runes of victory? He is Waffen-SS. The elite. Perhaps even from the Führer's own guard."

They went out again to the porch. The willow-bark flute lay on a chair. Ilse carefully picked it up. "I'll play this. Perhaps I'll even play it tonight."

"No, Liebchen. Tonight, you play with your wonderful metal flute. And this?" She tapped it. "The sap will dry, and because it is really only bark, it will fall apart. Maybe you play it for three days if you are lucky."

"That's sad."

"Dear one, no! Not sad. This is called the Instrument of Spring. We make it now, we play it only now, with joy, for the beginning of the season." Oma shook her head. "It is right, for right now, so it is the opposite of sad. It is . . . pure happiness. Also, since you now know how, you can make a new one each spring, and think of me when you play it, yes?"

"Yes. Yes, I will."

Ilse thought there must be something else she needed to say. But she couldn't find the words. Then the driver stepped from the car, coughed, and said, "Excuse me, Fräulein, kind lady, but—"

"I am ready."

The officer went around to the back passenger door, opened it. Ilse slipped in, carefully laying the bark flute on the seat beside her before handing him the flask. "Coffee," she said.

He muttered his thanks, then closed the door on her, went round to the driver's side. Paused there. "Heil Hitler," he called, saluting her grandmother.

"Heil Hitler," Oma called back, saluting too.

The car pulled away, and Ilse looked out of the rear window, watching the house recede, her grandmother recede. Oma held the salute till the car was nearly at the stone pillars of the driveway, then lowered her hand, changing the gesture into a wave before turning back to the house. Grey merged with lavender and white, dissolving into wisteria.

―――――

THE LAST NOTES HELD, ceasing suddenly at the violinist's sharp nod.

"Not too bad," Günther said, taking the violin from his neck, his lips pursed. "Though we all need to crescendo into that last phrase." He looked at the cellist, Walther. "In the first eight bars, you can be more legato. And you"—he focused on Ilse—"more fortissimo. Other than that . . ." He shrugged. "Yes, not too bad."

It hadn't been. Ilse was surprised. But then she always was when musicians who had only met at lunchtime were reasonably proficient by dinner. The cellist was a little weak. She'd played with better, even here in Germany at the music camp she'd attended in the Black Forest when she was twelve. But the repertoire was not the trickiest. Some Mozart, of course, considering where they were. More Boccherini, since he had written eighteen quintets for flute and strings.

"Have a break, eat a little, drink some water, or tea," Günther added, then waved a finger. "No champagne!"

He directed this warning straight at her. Was it because she was the stranger in the group, the Norwegian among the Germans? She had acquitted herself well, she knew that. No, she realized, he was suspicious because of the question she'd asked, after the first Boccherini piece they'd played. She'd already noticed that weakness in the cellist. He wasn't bad, simply . . . uninspired. So, as she flicked through the scores for the next piece they'd rehearse, she'd asked after another cellist, one she'd played with at that music camp near Munich five years before.

"Has anyone heard from Felix Rachmann?"

Everyone froze, then looked elsewhere. Except for Walther, who stared hard at her, past the neck of his cello. "Rachmann? A Jew.

They are not allowed to play in public anymore. They wouldn't make the standard anyway."

It was palpable nonsense. Felix, at eleven years old, had been the most naturally gifted musician she'd ever met. But she didn't say anything. Partly because she'd noticed, for the first time, the pin in Walther's suit lapel. Within a small white circle centred in a red one, the whole rimmed in gold, was a black swastika. Her driver from Seelow had worn one on his uniform too.

Walther was a member of the NSDAP—the Nazi Party.

They'd played on, and she'd asked no more questions. Now, as they all moved away from her in a group, she sat a moment longer and worried again about the evening ahead. She was most nervous about her duet with the harpist, Greta. It would be played last but had been practised first, since the harpist had classes to attend that afternoon at the Berlin Musikakademie. It was the shortest work they were playing, barely a minute and a half. One of Edvard Grieg's *Lyric Pieces*. A tribute to the great Norwegian composer, to her nation, to her.

The ballroom of the Adlon was festooned with flags—two flags. The Norwegian red with its blue cross on white, alongside the flag of Germany, the red surrounding, as with the badge, the black swastika in a white circle. The party was being held to honour several different things. First, her father was being presented with one of Germany's most prestigious awards for journalism, Die Schweibart Politischerpreis. The day chosen was Norwegian Constitution Day—Syttende Mai, May 17—celebrating the day that Norway got its own constitution, freeing itself from Denmark. Finally, as the alternating flags testified, the event was a tribute to the lasting amity between these two northern nations that shared so much—ancient gods and common folklore being but two.

She looked down at her costume, traditional for Syttende Mai. Her bunad. The dark blue skirt, with its decorative panels all around the hem, rose to her bodice—blue also, cross-laced in the middle, with the curling leaves and flowers of the bergfrue, the national flower that she'd embroidered on it, lining it up to her neck. There, her white blouse was fastened by a button on its simple collar.

She picked up Oma's basket and crossed the hall, passing waiters laying the last glittering cutlery and polishing the crystal on the many round tables—and the one long table, raised on a platform, upon which the most eminent guests would sit. She paused in the gap between the dining hall and the smaller reception room, halted by the heat, the buzz of chatter, laughter. It was packed—black and field-grey uniforms dotted among the sober suits, and the brighter colours of evening gowns.

She scanned the room, looking for her father. It wasn't that hard to find him. In a room of tall men, at six foot six he was still one of the tallest, and his hair, thick as a lion's mane, was a silver beacon drawing the eye. A shorter man stood next to him, but what he lacked in height he made up for in girth. He was also a contrast in colour. Her father had brought his own bunad from Oslo for the occasion—a beautifully tailored black frock coat with silver trim and buttons, a red waistcoat beneath. The other man was in a uniform of sorts, though even to her inexpert eye she was not sure that it belonged to any service. To begin with, it was powder blue, with scarlet collars and cuffs—which she saw flash as he waved his arms about. A massed rank of medals bounced, gleaming on his vast chest, metal reflecting the light from the cut-glass chandeliers above.

She made her way across the room, weaving through the crowd, ducking under the arms of waiters bearing trays of champagne flutes. Eventually, she reached the two men. They were standing at the room's end in front of a long table, linen-swathed and covered in plates of meats and cheeses and bowls of black caviar. She suddenly realized that she was hungry, had barely eaten since leaving her grandmother's.

Her father was in mid-flow, extolling something. But he stopped when he saw her and smiled. "Ah, Ilse," he declared loudly, as if she were across the room. "Hermann, may I present to you my daughter, who will be playing for us later tonight? Ilse, my darling, please greet Generalfeldmarschall Hermann Göring."

The large man—even more the peacock close up, with his purple neckerchief and its single pearl pin, his knee-length boots tipped with spurs—immediately handed his champagne glass to a uniformed aide beside him, then bent and seized Ilse's right hand. "Gnädige Fräulein," he murmured, attaching large, moist and rubbery lips to her hand, lingering in the kiss. When he finally rose, he fixed his eyes on her—eyes, she noticed, that were not only wet and somewhat glazed but subtly lined in pencil—then spoke. "My good friend Wilhelm, your father, informed me that you were an attractive young lady. He completely failed to do you justice. You are quite beautiful."

Ilse blushed. "Thank you, sir."

Göring forged on. "Beautiful in the most Aryan way. Nordic. Teutonic. I hope, my dear," he squeezed the hand now which he had not relinquished, "that you are planning to have many beautiful children to the glory of your nation—and ours." He smiled widely. "Perhaps I can introduce you to some fine young officer here tonight. Perhaps then you will remain here with us, gracing our new Germany."

"I . . . I thank you, sir. But I leave for America in the morning. For . . . for my st-studies."

"America?" The eyes narrowed.

"My daughter has won a scholarship to their finest music school, the Juilliard, Herr Generalfeldmarschall," her father said.

"Well." Göring shrugged. "If we must lose her, we must." He pulled her forward by the hand he still held, leaned into her ear. "Just don't study with too many Jews, eh?" he whispered. "Lots of Jews in America." Those lips touched her ear like they'd touched her hand, and then he moved back, releasing her. She must have looked startled, because her father took her arm.

"What is in the basket, my darling?"

Ilse looked down, startled again. She'd forgotten she was holding it. "Lebkuchen, Father," she replied. "For you."

His eyes gleamed. "My mother's Lebkuchen?" he exclaimed. He seized the basket, peered into it, looked a little disappointed that there were only six—Ilse had heeded her Oma's warning, and the rest, along with the Linzer, were in her hotel room—then offered the basket to Göring. "I can promise you that my mother, a proud German, makes the greatest Lebkuchen you will ever have had."

"Quite the boast," Göring replied, reaching into the basket. But when he took a bite, his eyes rolled up in his head in delight. "By heaven, you are right!" He swallowed the one he had in two bites, delved for another. "But, Wilhelm, can we eat the rest out on the terrace?" he said, waving it. "I need that smoke." He turned again to Ilse. "Your father and I were about to go outside for a cigarette. We cannot smoke in here."

Ilse looked around. She hadn't noticed what was suddenly obvious: the crowd was not standing under the usual blue-grey cloud. She must have looked puzzled, because the Generalfeldmarschall explained.

"The Führer cannot stand smoke. So we cannot do so in any room he might come into. Even though he may not come tonight." Göring sniffed. "He doesn't much enjoy events like this. He does not drink alcohol, so all the toasts bother him. He is vegetarian, and even the smell of meat upsets his stomach." He turned his eyes back on her, and they narrowed. "Still, I hope he does come. Because one thing he *does* enjoy is a beautiful young woman. So I know he would like to meet you."

He stared a moment longer before swallowing the Lebkuchen he held, then snapped his fingers. Immediately his aide placed a cigarette, in a long, black holder, in his hand. "To the terrace," he cried. He clicked his heels to Ilse, the spurs jangled, and he moved away, followed by his entourage.

Her father lingered. "You must forgive him. He is somewhat brash. Also, he drinks perhaps a little too much. And there are . . . other things. Wounded badly in the war so—" He broke off, studied her. "You must eat, my darling. You look pale. Don't want to faint when you play."

"I will, Father."

"Good girl." He gave her shoulder a swift squeeze. "*Gratulerer med dagen*," he said.

"*Hurra for Syttende Mai*," she replied.

"I will see you afterwards," he said, and went out to the terrace.

Ilse turned to the food. She was no longer hungry. Reaching up to her ear, she wiped it with the cuff of her blouse, then rubbed the back of her hand across her skirt.

BEFORE DESSERT, the speeches began.

Generalfeldmarschall Göring made a long one, slightly slurred yet filled with high praise for her father and the work for which he was being honoured this day—a savage denunciation of Stalin and all his works, his terrible crimes against his own people, his starving of millions in the Ukraine famine, his slaughter of millions more in his purges. It was impeccably researched but not academic, Göring extolled, because Wilhelm Magnusson was not an academic—the Generalfeldmarschall in his tone implying that academics were suspect—but rather a journalist of the highest order.

Toasts followed, in imported aquavit—it was Norway's day after all, so their national liquor must be drunk. The award—a silver dove of freedom taking off from an oak branch—was presented. Her father's acceptance speech was shorter, less bombastic, equally passionate.

"Though the Generalfeldmarschall is accurate in his summation of my book and the horrors I witnessed, there is one key point he left out."

Wilhelm paused, took time to gaze around the whole room. When he started again his voice was quieter, even more intense. "What the Bolsheviks have done, in what they term 'collectivization' is to remove the people from their own land—sever the sacred bond between the peasant and the earth where his ancestors have lived and died for millennia. The New Germany has done the opposite. Has strengthened that sacred bond. Between the German and his land. Between blood and soil."

There it is again, Ilse thought, as Wilhelm sat to a standing ovation. What her Oma had said earlier in the day. *Blut und Boden.*

The speeches ended—and the music began. The audience was more than a little inebriated, clapping loudly between each piece, men thumping the tables. This despite Ilse feeling the quartet was not quite as good as when they'd rehearsed. Walther, the Nazi cellist, was especially error-prone. But the crowd loved it.

It came to the last item of the evening—her duet with the harpist, Greta, who returned now to play her only part: the Grieg. It was from his Opus 47, No. 6, arranged for flute and harp.

Ilse raised her flute to her lips. She looked across at Greta and nodded. The harpist played the two-bar introduction, and Ilse joined.

It was a piece based on a folk song Grieg might have heard in the countryside of Norway. "Spring Dance" it was called, fitting for the season and this day, her country's special day. The flute led it, the harp underneath providing rhythm and counterpoint, echoing and matching the trills of the woodwind, Ilse's notes like birds calling or snowmelt running down the rills and mountains, both summoned by the returning sun.

They built the piece to its climax, the flute carrying the last phrases alone, ending on a single, pure, sustained note.

There was silence as she and Greta nodded at each other. Broken by a single pair of hands clapping—those of a man standing at the division between the two rooms. Some, who did not see him, immediately joined in the applause. But the clapping and table-thumping was swiftly lost to other sounds: chairs scraping, pushed back hard; crystal falling as people grabbed the linen at table edges to help them rise; above all, the swelling chorus of voices as everyone did see him, greeted him.

"Heil Hitler! Heil Hitler! Heil Hitler!"

He continued to stand in the doorway, acknowledging the cries, the straight-armed salutes, with his own right hand simply raised palm-out at the level of his shoulder. He seemed small to Ilse, but perhaps that was because of the two huge men who stood immediately behind him in the same midnight-black uniforms that her driver had worn.

Adolf Hitler, Ilse thought, rising, flushing in sudden awe, her flute still clutched in her left hand, her right rising without her seeming to do anything, to parallel the other salutes in the room, like the one her grandmother had given from beneath her wisteria earlier that day.

As the cries changed to "Sieg Heil!" Hitler moved, crossing towards the band—towards her, she realized, her heart starting to pound far faster than when she had been playing. He reached her, still trailed by his giant bodyguards. Closer to, he was neither small nor tall. His eyes, when he halted before her, were level with hers. He regarded her unblinkingly, and she felt her knees wobble, could not hold his gaze. Looked up to his forehead, which seemed waxy to her beneath its eaves of thick black hair, then down to his small, bushy, square moustache.

He continued to study her, while the noise diminished, then finally and suddenly died all around them, like a stop at the end of a musical piece. The only movement in the room was the lowering arms, and her father as he crossed to her, Göring a step behind.

"Mein Führer," Wilhelm said, "if I may present my daughter, Ilse Magnusson?"

Hitler didn't lift his hands, did not speak, just kept staring at her. Ilse decided she could not curtsy—she wasn't sure she wouldn't keep going down if she bent her knees. She managed a head bob, but still couldn't raise her eyes again to his.

Then there was a hand at her chin. A slight pressure, forcing her head up. She had to look at him. When she did, Hitler spoke.

"Beautiful lady," he said, his voice soft, a little crack in it as if strained, nothing like the voice she'd heard in newsreels, shouting from podiums. "My dear Hermann sent me a message that I ought to come and hear you play. Though I am not well today, I am so happy that I did."

She tried to answer, but her throat was not working. A small sound emerged.

"Are you very proud of your father today, Liebchen?"

She coughed, managed, "I am, sir."

"Good, good. A daughter should be proud. As I am sure your father is proud of you, no?"

His eyes still did not leave hers, though he turned his head slightly to his right.

"Very, mein Führer."

"Good, good," Hitler said again. Then his fingers, which had not left her chin, grasped her left cheek. Twisting it hard he said, "Beautiful, beautiful!" She held back a cry of pain as he turned and walked away. Not just from her—out of the room, the cries of "Sieg Heil!" resounding again as he did.

She flopped onto her chair. There were voices around her, saying things she didn't really comprehend. Congratulations, enthusiasm. She felt her father's hand on her shoulder, squeezing. He said something which again she did not take in. Her cheek hurt, and she raised her fingers to it, rubbed. Suddenly the fact that she had not truly eaten anything except cookies came back to her, and she wondered if she was going to throw up.

The crowd moved away and onto the desserts which had been laid out on the tables in the reception room. The musicians left too, to eat. When Ilse looked up, only the harpist, Greta, was still there. She pulled up a chair next to Ilse and sat. "You were very honoured," she said, her voice soft.

"Yes, yes."

"The Führer honoured me too, not long ago."

Ilse swallowed. "Yes? How so?"

"I have two grandparents who are Jewish," Greta continued, her voice even lower. "So I could be called a Jew as well. Instead, I am a Mischling."

"What is that?"

"Mixed race. But I was given the Deutschblütigkeitserklärung — the German blood certificate. Each one must be approved by Hitler himself. If he grants it, it is . . . an act of grace."

Gnadenakt. That's what she said. Except she did not look like she was "graced" at all. Only furious.

"So you are . . . German?"

"Oh, yes. Still German, by the grace of our Führer. Not so my Opa and Oma. They have already left, for Holland." She turned and looked at Ilse now. "I am sorry. Perhaps I should not be speaking to you like this. Your father—"

"Is not me." Ilse finally dropped her fingers, rubbing the tips.

"And you asked before about Felix Rachmann. You sounded like a friend of his so I thought . . ."

"I am—was—his friend. Do you know how he is?"

"Not how. I have not seen him for a while. But I do know *where* he is." She stood, leaned down, kissed Ilse on the cheek, kept her head close, whispered, "It is in your flute case. Take money if you can." She stood. Walther, the cellist, was coming towards them, two plates of cake in his hands. "I must go. This Nazi desires me. It is all I can do not to slap him."

Walther arrived. "Cake for you, Greta." He looked at Ilse. "I am sorry, I have hands only for two."

"She may have it. I must go," Greta said. Over his voiced disappointment, she turned back and held out her hand to Ilse, and they shook. "We play well together, yes?"

"Very well."

"Good luck in America," she said, and walked away.

Walther followed her, protesting. Ilse looked around. No one was near or watching her. She opened her flute case, laid her flute in it— but not before she saw the scrap of paper, a Berlin address she didn't know scrawled on it.

"My child," her father called. She shut the case, stood to meet him. "Hermann has suggested we go on to what he terms a 'delightful little nightclub.' Hard to find, he said." Wilhelm shook his head. "I asked if you could come, and he suggested . . . not."

He smiled and she shrugged. "That is alright, Father. I am tired anyway. I will get an early night."

"Good. And we will have breakfast tomorrow? Before the limousine takes you to Tempelhof?"

"Yes."

He looked at her for a moment. "So, you met the man of destiny, hmm? What did you think?"

"Interesting."

"Isn't he? I have a problem with a few of his policies, of course. But what he has done for his country? Marvellous."

"Yes."

Göring's aide crossed to them. "Sir, the Generalfeldmarschall is keen to be away."

"Indeed. I come." He turned back to Ilse. "Sleep well, my darling."

"I will."

IN HER ROOM, Ilse changed quickly from her bunad into a simple dress and flat shoes, put on her coat, hat. She checked her purse. She'd discovered in the limousine that Oma had shoved an envelope of Reichsmarks into it, with a note that read "to buy some pretty thing." It was still there. At the concierge's desk, she asked about the address she'd memorized.

He frowned at her. "Dear lady, this address is in Scheunenviertel. It is a bad area, dangerous at night. A slum." He leaned closer and lowered his voice. "It is filled with Jews."

"I am going to see a friend there. A girlfriend." She swallowed. "Not a Jew," she added; she didn't know why.

"Then I'll get you a taxi. Boy!"

He raised his hand to a bellboy. "No," she said sharply. Suddenly the idea of someone knowing where she was going worried her. "May I go by tram?"

He looked at her a long moment, then sighed, waving the bellboy away. "You may. There is a stop around the corner from the hotel. One tram, you needn't change." He pulled out a large city map in a wooden frame. "The tram drops you here." He tapped on a square. "You must then walk here." He tapped again. "But again, I must warn you: these are not good streets. Few lights. Abandoned houses. Let me call you a taxi."

"No, thank you. Have you a map?"

"No," he snapped. A concierge was used to having his advice taken. Then he relented, sighed again and said, "I will draw you one."

THE TRAM steadily emptied as they proceeded north. Lost to her thoughts and her concerns, she finally looked up to realize that the lively, well-lit parts of Berlin were behind them. There the street lamps had all sported long flags with the swastika. The street lamps were fewer now, and all were undraped. Few shops were open, and those that were had a different symbol painted on their windows—the Star of David.

The tram stopped; most people got off. She checked the concierge's map again. It was her stop too. She descended; the tram pulled away. There was one streetlamp at the stop, its beam shuddering. She crossed the street and entered an alley.

If it had been poorly lit before, it was worse here, and even more so in the maze of alleys beyond. But it was one month before Midsummer's Day, and at nine thirty at night a faint light in the sky still came down from the five-storey rooftops of warehouses. She was just able to make out street signs, turned into one called Dead Chicken Alley, walked twenty paces, and stopped.

According to Greta's note, Felix lived at number 47. But that seemed to be all of the five buildings in front of her, which ran for close to a hundred paces each way. Every window had broken panes. No light came through any of them.

Somewhere nearby she heard a skittering. Turned, and saw a small brown shape dart behind a pile of broken planks. She felt the last of her courage ebb away. Turning back the way she'd come, she took a step— and heard it. Mahler. Mahler, but only just recognizable, as it was being played so very badly.

One of the doors into the warehouse was ajar. She followed the music, which grew louder as she crossed the cavernous empty space. Eventually there was light as well, so she followed that.

She stopped in the doorway to a smaller room, what might once have been an office. Saw immediately why the music had been poor.

Three boys were there, the eldest no more than ten. Two sat at stools before music stands, one with a violin, one a viola; the last at a small, much-battered upright piano. There was only one man in the room, though truly he wasn't so very much taller than the tallest boy.

Felix Rachmann held a cello. "Stop!" he yelled as Ilse appeared at the door, but not because he'd seen her. "Franzel, my darling lad," he said to the piano player. "You are meant to be the calm at the centre of Mahler's storm. The life raft we all cling to. Instead you are floating away"—he waved his bow—"disappearing over the waves, leaving us far behind you. The beat is so . . ." He raised his bow, moved it like a conductor, down, to the side, up. "And one, two, three, four. You see? Legato. Sempre legato." He laid the bow on his strings. "Watch me. And one, two, three, four."

He nodded, played a note—the only one to do so. "Herr Professor," said Franz at the piano, nodding at the doorway.

Felix looked, stood. "Yes?" he said, his voice high-pitched, sharp. "What do you wish?"

Ilse realized she was in the shadows, so she stepped into the light. "Hello, Felix," she said. "Do you remember me?"

He peered, puzzled. Then his brow unfurrowed. "Yes," he said at last, "I remember you." He said it flatly, no colour to it. "How did you find me?"

"Greta. I . . . I don't know her last name. Harpist. She gave me your address."

An eyebrow went up. "Did she?" He said this as if he wasn't pleased. "Why?"

"I asked about you. She thought I might—" She broke off, looked at the three boys, each staring at her, their eyes wide. "May we talk? I can sit, wait for your practice to be done."

"It is done." He tapped his bow against the top of his cello. "Finish for today. Same time Saturday. Till then, you know what you must do?"

"Practise, Herr Professor. Practise."

They said it like a teacher would, and he gave a faint smile. From their leather satchels, the violin and viola players carried forward two glass jars, filled with something pale, cloth caps tied around them with string. The pianist was last, and hesitant, putting out a wrap of folded newspaper, something inside. "Mamme says this is all we have today, but there will be more next time . . ."

"It is alright, Franzel." Felix tousled his hair. "Next time is fine."

The boys stared at Ilse as they crossed the room slowly. Then they were out the door, and she heard running feet, giggles. "You made them happy," Felix said. "End of practice was really in another half-hour."

"I am sorry, I—"

"It does not matter." The cold tone was back. He laid his bow beside his cello on its stand, then faced her. "So now why don't you tell me why you are here . . . Ilse Magnusson."

He rolled the name out as if it was something grand. She studied him, saw the boy still, but only a little—in the dark hair that had lost its boyish curl, the height, scarce above five foot four, the green eyes. Mischief had ruled those at the music camp; he'd got more thwacks with the teachers' batons than all the other children combined, for his chatter, his mad practical jokes. The man before her now did not look like he joked much.

Suddenly she felt as if fingers were on her cheek, twisting. She flushed, raised her hand to it, and for no reason that she could understand said, "I met Adolf Hitler tonight."

It was obviously nothing like what he'd expected her to say. "You *met* him?" he gasped.

She dropped her hand. "Played for him, with Greta, others. Walther Schwimmer."

His eyes narrowed again. "Walther Schwimmer," he breathed. "How is the dear fellow?"

"He's . . ." She saw the lapel badge again. "He's a Nazi."

"Of course he's a Nazi. You become a Nazi if you want to get on, whether you believe or not. If you want to play for the Berliner Philharmoniker, the Sächsische, the . . . I would have been delighted to join the party, to play. But, of course, they would not have me." He sniffed. "Maybe my playing wasn't good enough."

"You are the best cellist—no, the most gifted musician—I have ever met," Ilse said.

"Maybe once." He stared at her, shrugged, looked away. Then he began to laugh. "You met Hitler. The star! The legend! It is like saying you met . . . Greta Garbo. It is like saying you met Clark Gable!"

"Do you still love the movies?"

"Yes, I love them. But I do not go to them. You need money for tickets, not"—he bent, peered at the contents of one of the jars— "schmaltz herring."

"I have money," she said softly.

He looked up at her fast then, emotions pursuing each other across his face. Hope, suspicion, anger, hope again. "How much?" he said, but before she could reply, he continued. "I am sorry, that was rude of me. I have forgotten how to be polite. You were a friend."

"Are."

"Are. Yes, perhaps." He picked up the jars, and the wrap of news-paper. "Come, let us go to my place and talk."

"Is it far?"

"Not very." A smile came, with a hint of that mischievous boy in it. "Come."

They left the room. But instead of walking to the warehouse's front door and out, Felix led her to some stairs, up them. Four flights, then he went down a corridor, opened a door. "Not far." He grinned, gesturing that she should go in. As she passed him, she became aware of his smell. She suspected he couldn't bathe very much. She turned her face away so he would not see anything on it.

The door opened onto a tall-ceilinged loft running a good forty metres along the building. Large windows faced the street. None of these panes were broken. The space was cavernous yet did not seem so— because almost every part of it held furniture. Standing cupboards, oak dressers, piles of chairs, three dining tables, dozens of paintings stacked five deep, wing-backed armchairs and sofas; a jumble, filling the space.

He saw her surprise, smiled. "If my people manage to get out of the country, some of them refuse to sell for the tiny prices they are offered. They stack it here and hope for better days when they can return. But if I need to sell some, I am allowed."

"Do many get out?"

"Some. It is harder now." He made his way between a dining table and a huge armoire. "Look, it is not all random. We have made rooms. Here is the kitchen. Sit, please." She did, on a stool, as he bent down. "Ha, yes!" he said. When he straightened, he was holding a bottle. "Schnapps?" he offered.

She did not really drink. But it seemed right to, now, so she nodded. He found two glasses, blew dust from them, set them on the nearest dining table and poured two shots. "What shall we toast?"

"Getting out?"

His eyes narrowed again. Then he shrugged. "Sure," he said, and shot his glass. Ilse sipped, still coughed, and he laughed, poured himself another, sat.

"Can you get out?" she asked.

"It was never easy. But it is much harder now." He stared at the liquid in his glass. "Most countries will not take Jews. The Americans, their trade unions? They say we come to steal their jobs. Others say we must have enough money to live when we arrive. Yet to leave we must pay ninety percent of all we have to the German State, as a tax. A penalty for, uh, *exploiting* the country in which we are aliens." He swallowed, as if he had something bitter in his mouth. "In the war, I lost three uncles and five cousins in the trenches. My father won the Iron Cross, First Class, at Verdun. He never walked straight again. I am glad he never lived to know that the country he loved would call him an alien."

He shot off the schnapps, put it down. "Can you not go to Palestine?" Ilse asked.

"Our people's home?" He laughed, the sound without humour. "The first Rachmann came to Berlin in 1780." He ran his fingers through his lank hair. "I am a German. I was raised on German music, German literature. I have lived all my life in the greatest city in the world. And you want me to go and live in a desert? What have I to do with all those . . . Jews?"

His voice cracked. He reached for the bottle again yet did not pour. "No, Felix. I just want you to live." She laid a hand on his arm. "Can you not sneak across a border?"

"I can. Maybe. But my mother? My sister?" He lifted the bottle, tilted it at her. She shook her head and he poured himself another. "No. I must try to raise enough money for the bribes."

"Then maybe this will help."

She reached into her purse, brought out the envelope Oma had given her. He put down his glass, regarded the envelope. "How much is in there?"

"Ha! Do you know, I have not looked."

Felix took the envelope, slid his finger along the seal, pulled out the money, counted. "One thousand marks," he said. "This is about two hundred and fifty American dollars."

"Is that enough?"

"No. But it helps. It helps a lot." He looked at her. "Are you sure? Do you not need this?"

"No. I go to America tomorrow."

"America? Why?"

"I have a scholarship. To the Juilliard."

"The Juilliard?" He looked above her, his eyes misting.

A noise came from the stairs. Footsteps. She started, and he smiled. "Don't worry. It is only Horst."

A voice came from beyond the door. "Fixx, Fixxie, I found some —" A tall man entered, broke off when he saw them sitting there. He had a package under his arm.

"It is alright, Horst," Felix said, standing up. "This is . . . an old friend, from music days. Ilse Magnusson."

She rose too, held out a hand. "I am pleased to meet you."

Horst came in, put the package down on the table. Shook her hand and gave a sharp head-bow, also clicking his heels. "Charmed," he said. She studied him, wondered who he reminded her of. Then she remembered. At the tram stop in Königsplatz near the Adlon there had been a poster, urging people to join the NSDAP—the Nazi Party. On it, set against the Eagle of Germany, a perfect Aryan family had been gathered—a mother in a headscarf holding a baby, a blond boy, and a girl with curly fair hair to her waist. All held within the embrace of the handsome, tall, blond father and husband who gazed fondly down.

Horst could have been the model for the man on the poster.

Perhaps Felix picked up on her appraisal. He punched Horst on the shoulder. "Always with the heel clicking!" he laughed. "I try to get him to be less of a fucking Nazi. But when you are christened Horst von Brensen, it is hard, no?"

The tall man laughed too, undid his tie. He was wearing a formal office suit. "How was work, Liebchen?" Felix asked.

Horst frowned at that, his eyes moving to Ilse. Felix smiled. "It is alright. When I say she is a friend, I mean it. She does not despise me for being a Jew. And she will not despise me for . . . loving you." He put a hand on the big man's shoulder. "Though of course the laws against such love are now as harsh as those against Jews. So I am twice persecuted." He turned back to Ilse. "Horst works for the Ministry of Culture. We met at a concert before . . . before my papers were inspected properly and my, ah, *tainted* bloodline established." He smiled. "It is his duty to have many fine sons for the Fatherland." He reached up and pinched Horst's cheek. "Do you think it is too late for my Horst to find a nice German Mädchen to settle down with?"

"Much too late," Horst murmured softly, squeezing Felix's hand and kissing it briefly, before releasing it and reaching for the package on the table. "Fixxie, that shop that was closed is open again. The one that makes the best Spätzle? I bought all he had left—some Currywurst. Some wine too."

"So, we have a feast! You stay, Ilse, yes?"

"I can't." Over their protests, she continued. "I have an early flight. I must pack, sleep."

"Oh, yes. Horst, she leaves for America tomorrow. Also, she has given me a gift." Felix raised the envelope of money. "Perhaps this helps us to come and see you there."

"That would be wonderful." Ilse picked up her purse, closed it. "Goodbye, Felix."

"Wait. Can I not give you something?" He gestured around the loft. "There are trays of jewels, nice paintings—"

"I don't need anything," she replied. "Except maybe . . ."

"Yes?"

"Will you play something for me before I go?"

He stared at her for a long moment, and then he smiled. "Of course I will. Come, we go down."

They descended the stairs, went again to the office that was now a music room. Felix sat behind his cello, tuned it. When he was satisfied, he asked, "What would you like to hear?"

She knew. Had known from the moment she first walked into the warehouse. "Mahler," she replied. "Not what you played with the boys. The Second Symphony."

"The *Resurrection*?" He took his lower lip between his teeth. "Isn't that what we played at the music camp in Bavaria?"

"I think we tried."

"It will not sound so . . . full with only the cello but"—he shrugged—"of course I'll play it." He lifted his bow, paused. "You know, it is forbidden to play so much these days. Any Jewish music. Mendelssohn, for whom I was named. Mahler. So I play them as often as I can. I teach them."

She went to him, bent, hugged him. "Play as I leave, will you? I'd like the music to come with me, back to the tram."

"As will Horst. The streets of Scheunenviertel are not safe. Goodbye."

"Goodbye, Felix," she said. "Good luck."

"Good luck to you," he said. "In America . . . and in the fight that is coming. Everyone must pick a side now." He waved his bow at himself and Horst. "We have."

"I have too. Now."

He laid his bow on the strings, closed his eyes, then began to play the cello theme from the second movement, as she knew he would. She listened for a while, her eyes closed too, then walked away, Horst beside her. The notes accompanied them across the empty warehouse, out into the street, a little away along it. Music for life. For death.

For resurrection.

SHE DIDN'T SLEEP MUCH, was awake at six, and was bathed, packed and in a taxi for Tempelhof Aerodrome within an hour. Her father would be calling for her for a last breakfast at eight, but she'd decided she couldn't face him, couldn't make small talk or listen to him again extolling the virtues of this New Germany. She left him a note, saying that Lufthansa had called, bad weather was predicted, the flight must leave early. It was a lie and not even a very good one, with the clear blue skies over Berlin. But she didn't care. At the airport, she checked her valise for the Paris flight. She'd collect it, go to Gare Montparnasse for her night train to Cherbourg and the ocean liner to New York the next morning.

When they called her flight, she walked out onto the tarmac holding only her purse—and Oma's wooden flute. She was following a young man who suddenly cried out and turned sharply back into her. "Excuse me," he said, rounding her, running back towards the terminal.

She looked at what she now held—the flute, crushed and in two pieces. Felt a moment of sadness when she thought of Oma making it, playing it. Then remembered what her grandmother had spoken of afterwards. Of Germany's man of destiny, who had left his mark on Ilse's cheek. Of Blut und Boden.

Dropping the remains of the flute to the tarmac, she ground it into German soil and boarded the plane.

SEVEN
OPIUM DREAMS

Rennes, Northwest France. December 31, 1940

KLAUS VON RONNENBERG LOVED MORPHINE.

For someone who had only ever consumed stimulants such as cigarettes, beer and schnapps, and all those in moderation, it surprised him how much he loved it. He'd thought it was something only those of weak character could become addicted to. But he'd been wrong to think that, so wrong. Morphine was something that everyone should have, all the time. It should be included with field rations, instead of those amphetamines that the soldiers who'd blitzkrieged through Europe were given.

It wasn't only the relief from pain; though when the drug was losing its potency, and the day nurse, the otherwise delightful Almuth, was delayed on some other business, some other patient, he certainly felt its absence, crying if the minutes extended. No, it was more the dreams that came. Sleeping ones, waking ones, slipping seamlessly between the two.

Most were pleasurable. Friends would visit, from his childhood, his university days, the various musical groups he'd played in. Quartets became quintets became orchestras, and he played with them all, better than he'd ever done, his missing left arm restored, lost fingers moving so easily over the violin's frets.

Sometimes though, the dreams were not so pleasant. The night nurse, Lena, was more distracted than Almuth, came less often. On the second night, when his weeping finally drew her, she gave him a larger dose than prescribed, to quiet him so that she could return to her lover, a sergeant of Panzergrenadiers whose distant grunts Klaus heard in bass counterpoint to her shrill soprano during their midnight duet.

He celebrated the end of the year differently. He welcomed visitors that night. Often they were dead but that did not stop them talking to him, laughing with him. Some, though, reproached him. Not so much for what he'd done, he'd not harmed them in life. More for what he hadn't done. Mainly for the fact that he was alive, and they weren't.

His father came, who'd died when Klaus was fourteen, still as disappointed as ever that his son was a musician, a scholar, and not the woodsman, hunter, Olympic cross-country skier that he himself had been. Pieter Raumann came, the boy from his fraternity at Heidelberg, who'd pushed a weak heart too far trying to pass his initiation, goaded and bullied by older students, which Klaus had observed though he had not intervened.

Yet neither of them disturbed him as much as the third who came. Unlike Pieter, he'd at least tried to save her. Failed. Which no doubt was why she was here now.

Gretchen.

"Is that . . . is that you, Gretchen?"

"Yes, Klaus. Yes, my love." She clasped his left hand, which was strange because he knew they'd taken that. "I am here." She smiled, her green eyes crinkling the way they always did. "I always come to Gehrden for Christmas."

"I am at Gehrden?"

Yes, he had to be, yes, yes, and it had to be Christmas Eve because he could see the candles on the pine tree had all been lit. Delicious scents were rising from the cauldron above the fire, the spiced Glüh- wein within it. His belly was stuffed with roast goose, red cabbage and Kartoffelkloesse, though he knew he'd still find room for several slices of Elsa the housekeeper's Stollen.

Except his stomach was fluttering every time he glanced at his cousin Gretchen, who had grown up with him and had never looked at him the way she did now, her gaze moving up and down his blue- grey Luftwaffe uniform, the pilot's wings newly and proudly displayed on his right breast, the single seagull pips at his collars for his recent commission as Leutnant. He hadn't wanted to wear his uniform, had thought to wear civilian clothes at what could be his last family gathering in a long while. But his mother had insisted. The look in Gretchen's eyes made him happy that she had.

"Gretchen," he murmured, squeezing her hand. "We are so naughty. We shouldn't."

"We must." She kept his hand, drew him from the corridor he'd crept down, into her room.

Every night, for six nights, the same. The family in their beds, he in hers, each of them learning about this different way of love.

Gretchen who, despite an appreciation for his uniform, hated Hitler and was a leader of students at the University of Hanover distributing anti-Nazi pamphlets.

Gretchen, who'd been arrested and sent to Sachsenhausen concentration camp for "re-education." His mother had been assured that her niece would be freed after a few months having learned her lesson. But typhoid killed Gretchen before she did.

Klaus looked at her. Now her rosy skin was pale, her face thin, her long auburn hair suddenly cropped close to her head. She took her hand away. Walked backwards to the door, her eyes never leaving his.

"Gretchen," he cried. "Don't go! Don't go! Don't die!" The door opened and closed. She was gone.

"No!" he cried.

A touch on his arm. He held his breath. Perhaps it was day, perhaps Almuth had come, bringing her pricking, sweet relief.

A voice. A man's. Not hers. Klaus couldn't hear what he said. "What?" he mumbled.

"I said that I have sent an orderly for the nurse. She will be here very soon."

Klaus opened his eyes. He regarded the man sitting by the bed. He wore an army greatcoat. The epaulettes on his shoulder showed him to be a Generalmajor. He looked familiar. Klaus could not remember his name. Yet he was almost certain that he was alive.

The other man must have seen the question in his eyes. "Hans Messer," he said, dipping his head slightly. "We met before. I was a guest at Gehrden. Christmas 1938."

Gehrden. The von Ronnenberg family hunting lodge. That Christmas when he'd just earned his wings. That Christmas when he and Gretchen became lovers. It made Klaus wonder again if the man before him was real, not imagined. It seemed too . . . coincidental, his being there, just after Gretchen.

Messer went on. "I am an old friend of your mother's, which is why I was there. Also why I am here. I have been reorganizing our office in Paris. She reached me there. Told me about your—" He broke off, took Klaus's hand where it lay on the coverlet. "Are you understanding me, my young man?"

Klaus tried to speak, found he couldn't, coughed. Immediately, Messer went to the side table, poured water into a glass, helped Klaus rise slightly, drink. When he'd had enough, the other man lowered him slowly back to the pillow.

Despite the pain that was building, in his severed bicep, on his burned face—or perhaps because of it—Klaus was able to focus on the man before him. Messer was handsome, his mother's age, early fifties, with neatly cut, short blond hair. A smile warred with concern in his bright-blue eyes. "I remember meeting you, Herr General," Klaus croaked. "It was a . . . a happy time."

Messer nodded, "It was." He took Klaus's hand again. "Your mother asked that I visit you, see if you needed anything, send her a report. The doctors tell me that you will recover well."

"Recover? Recover! How?" Klaus looked down to where his other arm should be, to the bandaged stump there. His eyes flooded. "I will never fly again. I will never play the violin again. I will never—"

The tears poured out. "Shhh," Messer whispered softly, shaking the hand he held. "No, you may not do some things again. But you will still do much in the world. Because you are intelligent, gifted in many areas. And because I will help you." He sat back, took out a gold cigarette case, placed two cigarettes between his lips, lit both and put one in Klaus's mouth. "You speak several languages, yes?"

Klaus inhaled deep. It wasn't morphine but it helped clear his head a little. "I speak English, French, some Russian, some Norwegian—"

"Norwegian? Why?"

"Since I was twelve, my mother took us to Norway every summer for holidays. There . . . there was a girl I wished to talk to."

"Ah, *cherchez la femme*, as they say in this country." Messer gave a smile—which went fast. He leaned closer, lowered his voice. "I remember another girl, from that Christmas. Gretchen. Your cousin, wasn't she?" Klaus swallowed, turned away, as Messer continued softly. "Your mother also asked me to help her. I tried, but I was . . . too late." He squeezed the hand he'd taken up again. "But I promise you this: I will not be too late with you."

Nurse Lena burst in. Her uniform was creased, and she'd failed to tuck all her hair under her cap. "What is this I hear, Leutnant? You've been complaining that I've been neglecting you?" She took Klaus's cigarette from his mouth, stubbed it out. "And you?" She turned to Messer, her voice continuing her scold. "Who are you to disturb my patient when he should be sleeping, huh? Shoo!"

She waved Messer away and put a small metal tray down on the bedside table. Klaus looked at it longingly, and was gratified to see, cradled in the white linen towel, a syringe.

Messer was buttoning his greatcoat. "I go, my young man. I will call your mother. Reassure her. Heal swiftly. We have work to do."

Nurse Lena was folding back the half-sleeve above the bandage. Done, she reached for the syringe, raised it into the light, squirted a little, tapped. Klaus was almost too distracted, too anxious. But there was something Messer had said that he needed to understand. "What work?" he called.

The Generalmajor had one hand on the door, was about to step through. "Eh?" he said, turning back.

"What work do you have for me, sir?"

"Oh." Messer put on his cap. It had his rank in gold upon its brim. "Perhaps you didn't know. I am the deputy chief of the Abwehr. So when you are fully healed, as I am certain you will be soon, under this attractive young lady's attentions"—he smiled at Lena, standing poised beside the bed, needle raised, and she blushed—"you will report to me in Berlin. I have a job for you, one that you will enjoy. Where you will find, ah, purpose again, yes?" With a snap of his heels, a salute—an army, not a Nazi one—he was gone.

Lena bent to the arm. "Such an impressive man," she said, wiping Klaus's skin with a wad of impregnated cloth, and giggled, all her fierceness gone. "And so handsome too." She sighed, placed the needle, pushed it in, depressed the plunger. "What did he say he was deputy chief of? I can never remember all those military departments."

He felt it immediately, the easing of pain, the pleasure. He was in love again. He looked forward to the dreams that love would bring. But his friend had asked him a question.

"Abwehr," he murmured. "Wehrmacht intelligence." She said something which he didn't catch, and he wasn't sure if he spoke again or just thought he did. "I am going to be a spy."

EIGHT
RUINS

BILLY COKE STEPPED OUT from under the truck's hood, dropped it back into place, then wiped his hands on an already dirty cloth. It hadn't been an intake valve, but rather a misfiring spark plug. Fortunately, McGovern had spares in the truck's toolbox, but it was a more laborious job than Billy had hoped, the day was unseasonably warm, and he'd taken some time.

He looked to the line of marsh grass, the sea sounding beyond it. Ilse had been gone a while. Putting the toolbox in the back of the truck—he was startled by the chicken, whom he'd again forgotten, flapping up — he walked up the slight, sandy path, and onto the beach.

She wasn't far away. She was sitting between the grass and the tideline, knees drawn up, arms wrapped around them, staring at the sea. He studied her profile. Exquisite, he thought. Movie-star beautiful. She looked like that Austrian actress he'd seen in a film the previous year. With Charles Boyer—*Algiers*. What was her name? "Hedy Lamarr," he murmured. When she'd appeared on the screen in the cinema on Shaftesbury Avenue, many in the audience had actually gasped. He thought he might have been one of them.

He'd gasped again on London Wall when he'd met Ilse Magnusson.

Was she out of his league? He wasn't sure what his league was. He'd slept with exactly five women. He'd even been engaged once, briefly—to Rosie, a fellow player at the Bath Rep. When he'd decided to go and fight in Spain, she'd decided not to wait for him. He smiled. Rosie. He'd heard she'd married the company's leading man, Earl Herriot.

Ilse did not move, just stared. At what, he wondered, aside from water. Into memory? He felt a vague unease. Her moods changed fast. They'd left the farm both glowing, he'd said something about the generosity of the English, and she'd replied with something about how German farmers would be just as kind—and the temperature had dropped about twenty degrees. What had that been about?

Well, I'm not going to find out staring like a fool, he thought. He walked closer. "Hey," he called.

She started, looked up. Something was in her eyes, something sad, but it went when she saw him, and she smiled.

"Penny for your thoughts," he said.

"Not sure if they are worth so much," she said, stretching her legs out, her arms parallel and high, like a diver's. "Though I think I would like to swim."

"Are you kidding me? In that?"

"Why not? I jump in the Oslofjord in May."

"I'm sure you do. But that's the North Sea. In January."

"You think it will be much colder?" She stood up, brushing sand from her dress. "Do you English not jump in that pond in the park tomorrow, on New Year's Day?"

"The Serpentine? Some nuts do, sure. This will be much colder."

She looked up into the clear sky. "But it is warm today, yes?"

"Not really. Only . . . less cold."

"I thought you said you were born in Canada. It is cold there, no?" she said as she pulled off her sweater, dropped it.

"Which is why we don't jump in the ocean at New Year's."

"Then," she said, crossing her hands at her hips and taking the material in her fingers, "you can watch and hold my dress." And with that she pulled it up and over her head. Her eyes disappeared into cloth, reappeared a moment later. The challenge was still in them.

His dropped down to the slip she wore underneath, which strained against her breasts. He forced his eyes up again. "Well, OK," he growled, "since you're making it about national pride, I guess I have no choice."

She laughed then, her face transformed by glee, and in the instant he saw the little girl she had been not so very long ago. He dropped to the sand, grabbed at the laces of his boots. As he struggled out of them, the slip dropped over his head. When he pulled it off and looked up, Ilse was running naked into the sea.

It didn't take him long to strip. With a yell, he ran down to the water's edge, hurdled the first few waves, and plunged in.

Christ, it is fucking fr-freezing, he thought, immediately striking out in a fast front crawl. He made for Ilse, who was on her back floating, if you please, uttering little cries of delight. He reached her, grabbed her, pulled her towards him. "You're insane!" he cried, as their bodies collided.

"Completely," she shouted, pushing him off, swimming away. He pursued her, but she was a better swimmer than he was. She laughed, teased him with closeness, took off again. Now she was making for the beach, and he let her go, watched her stand, stagger, stumble onto land. A wave lifted him, he looked back, saw bigger waves coming, swam fast ahead of one, caught it, rode it, arms stretched out, adapting to the surge and the curve of it, until he felt the shingle on his thighs and belly. He remembered when he'd last caught a wave, in a different season and a much warmer sea. But he still didn't want to think about Spain. Not now. Not now, when he was finally happy.

He pushed himself up with his hands to his feet. Ran to where Ilse had gathered her clothes. "*Now* I am cold!" she shrieked, and he saw her lips were purpling, and the skin that wasn't hidden by cloth was pimpled with goosebumps.

"The truck," he yelled, snatching his own clothes up.

They half stumbled, half ran, both giggling like schoolchildren. At the truck, he opened the cab door, flung his clothes in. "Give me yours," he said.

She was looking down. He looked too. "Hey," he said, "I've been in a December sea. Give a guy a break!"

"Of course," she replied, warmth in her voice, warming him.

He grinned. "Get in," he said, opening the door wider. "I'll get the engine going—and I have a towel in my suitcase."

"I have one in mine too. Bring it," she said, and got in.

He ran to the back, threw up the canvas flap, climbed over the door. The chicken was perched on the raised shelf, its head angled to the side, peering at him as if about to ask a question. "I have no idea," he said, and laughed.

Back in the cab, she was shaking, teeth chattering wildly, "ugh, ugh, ugh" coming through them. He threw her one towel, took the truck out of gear, cranked the engine. It fired, smoothly running, no more stutters. It would take a while for the heater to make a difference, so he towelled himself vigorously, as she did herself beside him. Clothes were tumbled back on then, but he'd also brought other things from her suitcase and from his.

"That's a lovely shirt," she said, one eyebrow raised. Red striped flannel, he'd bought it in Bilbao for the winter nights. Since he'd been wearing it the night of the air raid, it was one of the few items of clothing that was his own, not scrounged from his cousin. He sighed, threw it at her, slipped back into the cotton shirt he'd been wearing. Pulled a green army jersey over it, then shimmied into his trousers. He'd brought some blue woollen slacks and a sweater from her suitcase. The sweater was the last thing she put on, and he saw that what he'd mistaken for a jumble of patterns was symmetrical—snowflakes and spheres in white bands set against red. Hand-knitted, for sure.

She started towelling her hair, which fell in thick, sodden curls below her shoulders. "May I?" he said. At her nod, he took the towel, caught strands of her hair in the fabric folds, rubbed them.

"You can go harder," she murmured, turning her back slightly to him, tipping her head.

He obeyed, moving from tips to the scalp, using more pressure there. Her chattering ceased. Her eyes closed. He thought she might be purring.

After a while, he leaned back, opened the heater vents a little more.

She swivelled to face him. "Better?" he asked.

"Warmer, sure," she replied. "But is this heat better than that cold?" She poked his chest. "Admit. It was good, wasn't it?"

"Not bad."

She laughed. "You English! 'Not bad' is the ultimate for you, no? This fantastic feast? Not bad. This stunning view? Not bad."

He smiled. "So are you warm enough now?"

"Outside, yes. But I am—what is that expression? 'Chilled to the bone.'" She shivered. "Back home, after a cold plunge, we used to go to a fire. Really warm ourselves."

"We could find a pub. They might have a fire going." He reached into his shirt pocket and drew out his wristwatch, placed there for safekeeping. "Nah, just past two. They'll be shut. Maybe a hotel up in Lowestoft? Down the road in Southwold?"

She rubbed the window clear of the steam that had formed. "It's still so lovely outside. And the dark will come soon enough. Can we find somewhere, make a fire?"

"A fire?" He grinned. "Sure, why not? Let's go look."

He turned the truck, swung it out of the car park and headed back down the lane to the main road. Turned left there, the direction they'd come from London. There was something he'd glimpsed before as he'd looked for the side turning that would take them to the McGovern farm. Seen, it had stirred some memory; dismissed. He half remembered it now. Spotted it again about a quarter of a mile along, on the right. "Let's try here," he said, swinging the truck onto a track, part gravelled, mostly mud, and all but hidden by the winter-bare branches of two willows.

"What is this?" Ilse was peering through the windscreen at the narrow lane ahead.

"Not sure." He jerked his thumb over his shoulder. "Did you see those stone pillars? The sign on one?"

"No."

"It said 'Hatton House.'" Probably a manor of some kind. Maybe abandoned."

"Why would you think that?"

"Well, it didn't actually say Hatton House but 'atton ous.' Rust had taken the rest. No English gentleman would allow that, so . . . ah, lookee here."

The lane had widened a little and then opened onto a semicircular forecourt. Looming over that was a three-storey Victorian house in an advanced state of dilapidation. The slate roof had tumbled in at various spots, there was no front door, nearly all the windows were broken.

He came to a stop, turned off the engine, stared. He remembered the memory that had come when he'd first seen the sign, the driveway. When he'd been at his boarding prep school—Forest Dene, where his uncle had sent the little orphan almost as soon as he was off the boat from Canada—he'd swiftly formed a gang of toughs who would slip away on Sundays to range over the local woods. They'd found an abandoned manor house, set up a base in the ruins, used it to fuel fantasies of war and adventure. It had been worth the thrashing he got when they were eventually followed by the masters and caught, for the escape it had provided. For those few hours every Sunday he'd been free, like when he'd lived with his father on Salt Spring Island in British Columbia.

He turned to Ilse. "Shall we explore?"

They went to the entrance. It opened into a wide hall, staircases curving up on either side. The door was lying flat within, one part of a jumble of debris—fallen slates, peeling wallpaper. He smelled mould, and perhaps something worse. It didn't make him want to go in; plus, when he looked up and saw sky, he thought it might even be dangerous. "Not very pleasant," he said. "Let's check around the back."

They followed a gravel trail that girdled the house. Huge, winter-bare rhododendrons sprawled close, pushing into the broken windows, and they moved through their branches, emerging at the back to a terrace of cracked paving stones above a muddy lawn, three rusting croquet hoops thrusting out. At the bottom of the lawn was an overgrown hedge. Beyond that he could see sunlight glinting on water.

"What is that?"

He followed Ilse's pointing hand. To the left, close to that water, stood another structure. "Perhaps a summer house? Let's go see."

As they made for a gap in the hedge, he felt that rush of joy he'd had as a schoolboy. That sense of freedom. Pleasure that only increased when Ilse took his hand.

Unlike the main house, the structure standing by what turned out to be a large, willow-lined pond was relatively intact. It was mainly glass, with only a few broken panes. Inside, there was the strange sense that people had been there recently. There were canvas-backed lawn chairs, some stacked, two unfolded beside a table on which stood cups, saucers and a small china teapot. Croquet mallets, three balls and the striped centre pole were in one corner next to an old archery butt. There was an arrow in that: bull's eye. On the floor beside it were two badminton racquets, a feathered shuttlecock. Ilse came close, took his arm at the bicep. "Ghosts," she murmured.

"I know. I love ghost stories, don't you?" He grinned, nodded outside to the water. "You're not going to want another swim, are you?"

"Oh no." She shivered. "My bones are still chilled."

He laughed. "Then I'd better see about making my lady that fire."

He left her in the summer house, went back outside. To the left, down towards the water, he found what he'd suspected might be there—a small circle of earth two arms' lengths across, edged by stones. He squatted, looked carefully around. There, under an oak, was a low-roofed structure. Within it, neatly stacked, was a triple row of small logs.

"That makes life easier," he said. The wood was grey, dried out, several seasons old. There was no kindling, but he could manage that.

He went back to the summer house. Ilse was sitting in one of the lawn chairs. "Just going back to the truck to fetch some things to make a fire," he said.

"Do you need help?"

"I'm fine."

"Hurry back. Now I am cold." She stretched out a hand to him and he took it. "See?"

She was. He bent, turned her hand, blew on the palm. "I'll hurry."

He whistled a show tune as he returned to the truck. When he threw up the canvas, he didn't see the chicken—until movement drew his eye. It was crouched behind some potato sacks but rose, giving a little squawk as he reached near it to a pile of old newspapers. He pulled three off the top and was about to leave when he saw the spare petrol can. Shaking it, he felt a little slosh inside. He eyed the chicken. "Bit of a cheat, eh?" he said. The bird looked away as if embarrassed.

He'd spotted an old palette inside the house, and spent some time stomping that into kindling. Took his booty back to the fire-pit and began arranging it—balled newspaper first, kindling on top, smaller logs in a loose circle, larger ones around that.

He heard her approach, then stop behind him. "S-soon?" she asked, her teeth chattering.

"Sooner with this," he replied, spilling some petrol around. He took out his matches, struck one. "Stand back," he said, and when she took a step away, he threw the match into the pyre.

Whoosh! Instant flame, heat, the stench of gasoline. He stepped back. "Cheating," he said, putting an arm around her. "My uncle used to tell me: 'To be a proper man you must be able to start a fire from scratch, kill and butcher an animal, and sire a son.'" He'd used a gruff, upper-class voice and grinned. "I was going to impress you with my fire-making skills but decided it was more important to warm you up quickly."

"Which you have done." Ilse nodded at the fire, which had caught fast, paper gone, kindling blazing, logs beginning to glow. She extended her hands, palms out. "And the other two things?"

"What?"

"Can you kill and butcher an animal?"

"I know the mechanics."

"Even a chicken?"

He shrugged. "I made my first fire at four and killed my first chicken at five."

"On the farm in Canada where you grew up?"

"Yes." He turned back to the fire, stared into flame. He didn't want to think about the farm, his father. "You hungry?"

"Starving."

"Then, my lady, roast chicken it is."

He took his arm from around her, turned to go. She caught a trailing hand. "And the third thing?"

He was ahead of her this time. "The siring?"

"Yes. Have you?"

"Not as far as I know."

"Not as far as you know," she repeated softly. "But you know . . ." she looked above him for a moment, into rising smoke, ". . . the mechanics?"

He looked at her. Her thick golden hair still damp, tamed with a band, tied back. What was she anyway? Twenty, twenty-one? The sea had scrubbed her beautiful face clear of makeup, making her look even younger. Holy Jesus, he wondered, is she a virgin? With her poise, her foreign mystery, her swift acceptance of his invitation, surely she had to be . . . experienced? Now, looking like she was about fourteen, he wasn't so sure. He looked into those eyes, which returned to him only a steady stare. What had she asked, he wondered?

"Dinner," he said, swallowing, and headed for the truck again.

When he reached it, the chicken was in plain sight this time—sat on the raised bench, staring at him, almost defiantly. It didn't have a lot of room to escape, so he caught it fast, stretched its neck long, jerked it sharply upwards, heard the crack. On a nearby stump he beheaded it with a hatchet from the tool kit, grabbed the large cooking pot Don had stuck in there, and returned to the fire.

Ilse had brought the two lawn chairs to the heat, was sitting in one. "Want to help?" he said, holding the chicken by its neck.

"Of course." She rose. "What can I do?"

"Fill this from the pond."

He gave her the pot. While she went to fetch water, he put down the chicken and collected the metal croquet hoops from the hut and the lawn. The flames had died a bit, but the logs were burning well, so he quickly shoved the hoops into the centre of the fire, making a rack. She came back, he set the pot on them, put the lid on it. When the water looked about right, he tested it, heated it a little longer, then dunked the chicken into it, holding it by its legs, scalding it for about forty seconds. Then he pulled it out, set it on the edge of the blanket and began pulling the feathers off. She knelt beside him, and they made short work of it.

When they were done, he took out his knife. "If you want to skip the messy bit, there's some potatoes and carrots back in the truck. Also, a cloth bag with some salt, pepper, plates, cutlery."

"My father is a hunter," she said. "I always quite enjoyed the messy bit. I'd help him clean all his kill." But she stood anyway, walked away, and he set to gutting and dressing the bird.

By the time she returned, the carcass was ready. Billy had found a metal chair, its seat patterned with decorative holes. While he worked its legs into the fire above the hoops, Ilse rubbed the chicken with salt and pepper. "Look what I found," she said, and held up a spray of rosemary. "Big bush behind the house." Breaking off a piece, she shoved it into the cavity.

He took the bird from her, laid it on the chair, fed some logs onto the fire. She placed the potatoes and carrots in the ashes at the fire's edge.

They waited, turning the food occasionally. Fat soon began dripping, flames spurting in sudden flashes, a delicious savour filling the air. The sky had darkened, a few tendrils of cloud holding the fleeing sun in shades of purple. He went back to the truck, grabbed cups, the bottle of cider, a torch, a gasoline lantern. When he returned, she wasn't there, so he brought out the small table from the summer house, arranged the cutlery.

It was fully dark when they ate, their backs warmed by a blanket apiece, their fronts by flame, their insides by food that not only their hunger told them was delicious. The chicken was perfect—tender, smoky; the potatoes were filled with cream in lieu of butter and all the richer for it. Rations had been short in London for a long time, feasts rare, so they ate more than they might have done before the war. The cider was local, dry and sharp, like some of the fino sherries he'd tried in Spain. Strong too, blurring the edges of the night, darkness and light.

Billy continued eating after Ilse, gnawing the flesh off one last leg. Sated, he hurled the bones into the fire. They stared as the flames took them, and finally he said, "I suppose we should look for a hotel."

"We should," she breathed, "but not yet."

He looked at her. Her eyes were half closed, her lips parted in a slight smile. He leaned, awkwardly, from his chair to hers, and kissed her.

There was shock, a literal one, like they'd both walked across thick pile carpets. There was a flash of being in that sea together earlier—salt, motion, thrilling, chilling, churning. He'd kissed, been kissed, before. Never like this. Not even close. How long did it last? A second, an hour. Not a clue. All he knew was that he rose from it, desperately needing air. And with the certainty, sudden as it was absolute, that this was what he'd sought for as long as he'd been seeking.

Both pulled away, both gasped. "Holy mackerel!" he said.

Her eyes, wide as his, widened further. Suddenly she was laughing, and he was laughing, and then they both stopped at the same time. "Where?" he murmured. "Truck?"

"Here," she said, reaching for his shirt front, pulling him towards her. His chair tipped. He shot a hand to the ground, stopped his tumble.

"I don't think it's possible in a deck chair," he said, in a voice like a BBC announcer's, suddenly matter-of-fact.

She laughed again. "We need more blankets," she said, "then we can stay here by the fire."

"Truck," he said again, thickly this time, rose, staggered off, yes, staggered. "Fuck me," he said, and tried to get his wobbly legs to move quicker.

When he came back, the detritus of supper was gone along with the chairs. She was gone too, and he dropped the blankets atop the other two, looking around wildly. He felt that if he did not kiss her again now, right now, it might all turn back into the dream that everything was starting to seem like. And he didn't want a dream. He wanted to prove that kiss was real, that she was real, that they could be real together. He'd never wanted anything, anyone, so badly.

And then she reappeared, emerging from the summer house. Firelight moved over her face, he could see her smile, hear a tease in her voice as she lifted something and spoke. "Look what I have found," she said, and raised it to her lips.

He saw what it was. He shivered, worse than he had when he'd emerged from that frigid sea.

"No, please," he said, stepping towards her. "Don't."

"Just a little song," she murmured. "A song from my land."

He took another step and froze, as Ilse played the first notes on the recorder. He turned away, and now it wasn't her playing. It was Andoni, and the flames Billy gazed at weren't in a fire-pit in the east of England but surging through a town in northern Spain, on a day of death.

On a day of murder.

NINE

MURDER

The Basque Country. April 26, 1937

"BEELEH! BEELEH! " The voice accompanied the slap of rope-soled shoes on cobbles. Billy Coke glanced sideways from where he lay under the truck's engine and saw the shoes approaching. They stopped as he turned back to his task. "Ah, you are there! I practise song. I know it now." The little foot tapped Billy's big, booted one. "Come up, Beeleh. I play, you sing."

"Momentito."

Billy wound the wire tight around the plastic tube's end, sealing it onto the engine's gas intake valve. It wasn't a perfect join, but there hadn't been any new parts of machinery since the war began. Everything was improvisation. And ever since the people of Guernica had discovered his skill with engines, he had become the small town's chief improviser.

He shuffled his way out on his back, stood and brushed himself down. "Pump the pedal five times. Then try," he called in Spanish to the farmer whose truck had refused to start after he'd taken down his stall, all his produce sold, and loaded it onto the flatbed. It was perfectly blocking the main but narrow entry into the square in front of the railway station. Down the road, a line of farmers waited to bring their own trucks to collect their stalls and any unsold produce from the Monday market. He could see the anxiety on those nearest. Everyone was anxious, with the war drawing ever closer. Everyone wanted to be back in their own home.

The engine turned, coughing like a tubercular old man. The small gas ration the farmers could get now was heavily adulterated, of poor quality. It was no wonder that every second vehicle in the waiting line was pulled by a mule.

The engine heaved, gave an enormous bang that made everyone around them jump, then started. The farmer gave Billy a clenched-fist salute, and the truck lurched away. There was a cheer from down the line; farmers rushed for their cabs, started their own engines.

"Beeleh! Beeleh! Now! Now! I play, you sing."

"OK, kid. But let's get out of the way here."

He put his hand at the back of Andoni's neck, roughhousing the nine-year-old into the portico of a shop. As Andoni started to blow at his recorder, excitement blurring his notes, Billy watched the activity in the square.

It was a fine day. Late April, a real warmth again on the land after the month's early, heavy rains, reflected in the first bounty that the region's farmers had brought to market. He felt his stomach bubble and heard its growl. Rations had been short for some months now— more so since the fascist offensive had begun three weeks before, all along the front. Increasing numbers of refugees had to be fed— Basque traditions of hospitality meant there was no other choice. And Bilbao, the capital city, was being blockaded by the Nationalist navy, its population slowly starving. An officer passing through the town on his way to the front had brought the scale of suffering home when he casually mentioned "the soaring price of cat." It had shaken Billy. He had always loved cats. Tonight though, he thought, we will feast. In his three months in Guernica, market day had always ended in celebration. This one— which might, depending on the fortunes of war, be the last for a while—would be especially celebratory, he felt. I'll get drunk again, he mused, scratching at his stubbled chin. The last time, though. Tomorrow . . . or the next day at the latest, I have to leave. Have to. Even without the papers.

He hadn't planned on staying in Guernica for three days, let alone three months. He'd only come because he'd been so bored in Bilbao, with no money to relieve the boredom or stop the growling of his stomach. Refugees from other parts of Spain had swarmed the town, and casual work was scarce and fiercely fought over. While it had been made clear that the only job he really wanted to do—flying planes— was closed off to him. Ever since the Soviet squadron had arrived, cockpits were reserved for Russians and the very few Spanish flyers who could prove their fervent adherence to communism. Billy had already been marked as an anarchist by the pilots he'd flown with in the Republican Air Force, their archaic Hispano-Nieuport 52s and Letov 231s shot out of the sky by the massively superior German and Italian machines—the Heinkels and Fiats. It hadn't mattered to them; they'd accepted his politics because he could fix their engines, and in return they'd taught him to fly. But it mattered to the political commissars who accompanied the Soviets, who had come to Spain in support of the international brotherhood.

As Andoni struggled to play single notes—he hadn't got the simple tune yet, despite his boasts—Billy looked into the clear sky he longed to be soaring through and shook his head. Fucking communists and fucking Nazis, he thought. Sent to fight a secret proxy war for their Red and Black allies in Spain. It was not something he'd thought about back in England, nor heard about as he'd attended the recruitment meetings for the International Brigades that were forming to defend Republican Spain. He hadn't thought about it that Saturday night when he'd hung up his black tie and tails in his dressing room at the Theatre Royal in Bath, having finished the last play he would do there, and walked out the stage door and into the truck that would drive to Southampton, without even saying goodbye to his now ex-fiancée, Rosie, or to any of the other actors, hoping the letters he'd left would explain all. There had been fierce but friendly debates in the hold of the steamer making for Bilbao—communists, syndicalists, trade union socialists and old fashioned English liberals arguing for their causes, all subsumed in the greater cause of freedom. He hadn't even thought about it after he'd walked across the Pyrenees into the Basque Country, when the ship had been diverted to Biarritz in France and he'd chosen not to wait. It was only after the Soviet commissar had escorted him off the flying base at pistol point that he'd been forced to think about it. Liberty's cause was a lot more complicated on the ground than in the air, and he'd discovered that mouthing off his beliefs like the hothead he was would get him nowhere. So he'd figured out a plan . . . one that the man now weaving towards him between the dismantling of stalls had promised to help him with.

"Hola, Comrade Flyer."

"Hola, Comrade Priest."

The tall, thin man ran his hand over the grey stubble of his shaven head and looked nervously around them. "Shh, hombre," he hissed. "Do you wish to see me put up against a wall?"

The fear was largely false. Though rumours of priest slaughter had come from the south—from Madrid and especially from Andalusia— the Basques still loved their church and their church-men. Besides, Billy had learned that very little frightened the former Jesuit Father Xabier. "Do you have news for me, comrade?" he asked.

"News—and something more." The priest tapped the breast pocket of his ragged black suit jacket. "Shall we find a copa to discuss it over?"

"A copa—or three. If you have what I hope you have in your pocket, I'll be paying."

A salt-and-pepper eyebrow rose. "You have come into some money, comrade?"

Billy frowned. "Ah. No. But perhaps Mamá Rosarita will let me sing for my supper, as she often does."

Xabier sighed. "Or she will let me pay. As she always does." He put his arm around Billy's shoulders. "Come."

Billy looked down at Andoni. The boy had stopped playing, was frowning at the recorder. "Something wrong with it," he muttered. "I was good before."

"You keep practising, and we will sing later," Billy said, running his hand through the lad's thick corn-blond hair. "I need to speak to the pri... to my comrade here. Come to Mamá Rosarita's in half an hour."

"I will!" Andoni's dark eyes, which were a little crossed anyway, crossed further. "How do I tell the half-hour again, Billeh?"

"When the big hand goes round to six."

"Ah yes. Of course I remember." He lifted his arm. Hanging loosely at his wrist was Billy's wristwatch. Andoni squinted at the watch face. "Which is six again, Billeh?" When Billy tapped it, the boy grunted. "Of course. I know this." He shook his head. "But I think I wait right outside Mamá Rosarita's now, in case."

The three of them crossed the square, threading through the crowds of black-swathed women still at several stalls. Many only came out at the end of the day, figuring that farmers would take lower prices then. There was a lot of guttural haggling going on.

They left Andoni with an orange soda and his back to the bar's outside wall, playing notes. Though the place was already filling up with some farmers wanting a drink before heading back to their farms, a group rose to leave just as the two men passed their table. Billy swooped, Xabier went to the trestle from behind which Mamá herself—nearly as broad as she was tall—tapped one of the large stone barrels into a pitcher. Xabier returned with it, two cups and a plate of olives in oil.

"The war seems far away, doesn't it?" commented Xabier, looking at the laughing clientele.

"It does," Billy replied, even though for him it never was.

"Topa!" the former Jesuit said, raising his cup. "Or as you say in English, *good health.*"

Billy raised his, and replied in the same language. "Fuck the pope," he said, made eye contact, took a hefty swig. It was the local cider—the main drink of the region and as dry as sand. When he'd first tried it, Billy had been tempted to use it to remove rust from propellers. But like a lot else that had been strange in Spain, he'd grown to like it.

Xabier shook his head. "Billy, I may be a lapsed Jesuit," he said, "but it is still hard for me to think of sex with El Papa."

"Just trying to help with your escape from Catholic dogma, comrade," Billy replied, grinning. "Just as you are trying to teach me Basque."

"Well, I am not sure Basque will be much help where you are going." The priest reached into his suit pocket, took out a tattered envelope and laid it on the table.

Billy eyed it, did not reach. He'd been disappointed too many times before. "Is that it?" he asked.

"It is . . . everything." Xabier took another sip, sat back. "It is one reason I was in Bilbao for a week. With the war getting closer," he sighed, "I thought it was best to come back with everything."

Despite his sudden flush of excitement, still Billy did not reach. If all he needed was truly in the envelope, then he would be gone fast. Perhaps even tonight. Once a course was chosen, he hated delays. Hated goodbyes more—the tears, the promises for a reunion all knew would never happen. He'd avoided it in Bath with his fellow actors, and with Rosie most of all. He also knew that these goodbyes would be worse. In the three months he'd been here, he'd come to love the town, its people. The kindness with which they'd taken in this stranger; the generosity with which they'd made him feel at home, which he had almost never felt. Not at the schools his family had forced the Canadian orphan into, certainly not at their homes. Briefly perhaps in a few theatre companies. But he'd felt it everywhere among the Basques. They were passionate, romantic, funny as all heck. And their belief in the necessity of this war, the chance it offered of a truer freedom, brought the cause of revolution home to him far more clearly than any lecture or studied text. What sealed his love was that they were singers too, almost every one of them—one of the reasons they'd adopted him, when they'd realized he had that gift, that passion, too.

There are two I will miss most though, he thought—the boy by the door still trying to play single notes, and this man sitting across from me.

Xabier was sixty-six, with the swift and piercing mind of the Jesuit he'd formally been; gifted in analysis, in argument, deeply read in literature and politics. Billy had fury and conviction, but Xabier could shatter every one of his arguments with devastating acuity if he chose to, which he rarely did. The former priest preferred simple reason, gentle persuasion. Over long nights of cider and a chessboard, they had discussed the world and everything in it. He spoke excellent English—had lived in Boston for many years. Yet what had made Billy love him most was how he had explained his own loss of the thing that had held him all his life—his faith. "It was like a much-worn shirt I'd been wearing, heedlessly," he said one night, after perhaps one too many copas—or perhaps just enough. "Held together by the threads that were rules I'd accepted since childhood yet never thought about." He'd stared into the fireplace, for it was a cold winter's night at Mamá Rosarita's, and flames had moved in his grey eyes. "But when I came back to Spain, when I saw how my coun- trymen lived, most of them so poorly. How the priests lived, most of them so . . . high, I began to unpick each stitch. Seeking what it held for me, its true meaning behind its so-called truth. And one day, when I'd finished, the whole shirt just"—he shrugged—"slipped from my body, taking with it the scales from my eyes."

Xabier was as dedicated to the cause of revolution as he'd ever been to that of religion. He worked for that cause, for the betterment of all men—in the debating chambers, and the halls of power. He would never handle a gun. He could never kill, he'd told Billy. But he could work, and did work, ceaselessly, for that better world.

"What?" Xabier said now, as Billy continued to stare at him.

"Nothing," said Billy. It was another part of the goodbyes he hated: saying how much he'd miss someone. So instead of saying it, he opened the envelope and slid its contents out onto the table.

The money was easy to identify—about two hundred pesetas in various notes. That made about twenty dollars, give or take. Less than five pounds back in Britain. Not much—but a lot more than Billy had seen in many a month. "It is little, I know," said Xavier. "But I think perhaps with these other things, you will not need to buy much food."

Billy unfolded the first of the two papers. It was tatty, its creases lined in black, some of the ink blurred with use and age—including the name, which was odd since it was his and so had to have been added recently, along with one of the two passport photographs he'd given the former priest. Billy held it up. "So, I have been a member of the SRI since 1934? About two years before I actually got to Spain?"

"You have. We made you join a little earlier. Lots became members of the Socorro Rojo Internacional in 1934 after the miners' strike in Asturias." He smiled. "You are an actor, so you can make up stories about how you were there, and the barricades you stood behind."

"Sure can." Billy looked down. "And I am a communist too?"

"Most are in the SRI. You said you needed to be a communist, yes? Not a *fucking anarchist*."

Billy smiled. Xabier almost never swore. But he could not say the word *anarchist* without doing so. Billy's allegiance had caused some of their fiercest arguments. "If I want to fly again, then yes," he replied. "The Soviets are in charge of the Republican Air Force now. If you want to fly for them—get one of their fancy new Moscas or Chatos—you first need to be able to quote Lenin."

"Which you can do?"

"Sure. I learned those lines and can say them convincingly, like with any role. And 'The Internationale' is a catchy tune." He looked up. "How the hell did you get this?"

Xabier grinned. "It is interesting how so many former Jesuits are now communists."

"Like you, Comrade Priest?"

The Basque didn't answer, just gestured with his chin to the second piece of paper. Billy unfolded it, and gasped. "This is an American pilot's licence! How the hell"—he squinted—"did you get it *and* get my name and photo put onto it?"

"Ah, there I think I was most cleverish!" Xabier took a gulp of his drink and smacked his lips. "Is this a word? Perhaps." He leaned in. "An American journalist arrived in Bilbao to report on the war. Very big, very loud man. Got very drunk. Said he needed to hire a plane to fly himself over the lines. When he was told this was impossible, he got very angry and waved his licence around. Then somehow," he shrugged, "he found himself in bed with a young . . . OK, with a not-so-young lady. Actually, she is the former abbess of the nunnery of Amorebieta and an old friend." He grinned. "So, we, uh, take it."

Billy turned the paper more into the light, whistled. "You've got some good forgers in the cause."

"The best. Still, I would not let anyone study either paper *too* long." Xabier smiled. "But I think, with these two, you will get up there again." He raised his eyebrows towards the ceiling.

Billy looked up too, lost for a moment in the sky he couldn't see above the town. "God willing," he murmured.

"Oh, so *now* you appeal to him?" Grey eyes twinkled at Billy. "When you spent so much energy trying to convince me that he can't exist?" Xabier poked the pesetas on the table. "As I say, it is not much. But there is a truck leaving for Barcelona, avoiding the fascists, and from there, with the SRI paper, you should be able to get rides all the way to Madrid. That is still where you think the new esquadras will be forming?"

"I am sure of it." Billy reached across, laid a hand on one of the other man's. "Thank you, my friend. *Esskerik asko.*"

"*Ez horregatik*, comrade. All for the cause."

"All for the cause." Billy kept hold of the other man's hand, shook it gently. "When does this truck leave?"

"Midnight."

"This midnight?"

"Yes."

"Good."

It was as if they both became aware again, simultaneously, of the notes being played on a recorder just outside the door. Perhaps it was because they were being played well now, each one clear. Perhaps because both men knew that, now the leaving was decided, there was one person for whom it would be the hardest of all.

Two people. Billy would miss Andoni more than anyone he'd ever left before. The nine-year-old had found his fellow orphan on Billy's first day in Guernica. Billy had fixed a resident's broken car in Bilbao, and that man—Mikel, who ran a small garage in the town—had invited him back to work for room and board. Since both had become precarious after the communists booted Billy out of the esquadra, he'd accepted. Andoni was a limpiabotas and could not be dissuaded from shining Billy's scuffed boots as soon as he stepped out of the car. Since he had not a single duro to pay for it, later that day he split his first wages, for the repair of a sewing machine—a bowl of bean soup and a rock-hard bocadillo—then taught the kid how to thumb-wrestle. Andoni had barely left his side in the months since. Especially after Billy swapped a wheel replacement for the recorder.

"You will not tell him?"

Billy chewed the flesh from a small, green olive, spat the pit onto the floor, then shook his head. "I can't."

"Maybe just him? Try to explain—"

"What? That, like everyone else, I'm abandoning him too?" Billy snapped, then held up his hand in apology. "I am sorry."

"Por nada. I understand. I will take care of him."

"You will? I'll write a note, saying I have to go fight the war in—"

"Do not say where. He would try to follow."

"I won't. Will you . . . will you take him with you? To Bilbao?"

"Yes. I am too busy and never at home. But my friend, the one who used to run a nunnery and now runs a different establishment, she has already said that Andoni can live there, with her."

Billy, who was rarely shocked, was now. "You are going to put Andoni into a whorehouse?"

"I cannot think of a better place. He will have so many mothers," Xabier grinned, "and get such a varied education."

Billy slapped the table and laughed. "You truly have fallen far, priest!"

"You think so?" The grey eyes sparkled, and he raised his copa. "Then here's to falls—and risings. Long live the Revolution."

"The Revolution!"

Their toast was loud, and drew a response all round, the cry spreading to each corner of Mamá Rosarita's. It also drew a small figure into the doorway. "Billeh?" Andoni called, waving the recorder. "I have it now. Come, sing!"

"I'm coming." Billy collected all the papers in the envelope, tucked that into his flying jacket's inner pocket and the money into his trousers. It would not take him long to pack, since much of what he possessed was on his person. Two spare pairs of undershorts, two vests, his much-darned last two pairs of socks, one sweater, one red flannel shirt. His Ruby pistol for which he'd never had a holster. A hat for his head, a stick for his hand? He grinned. He was excited to leave. Until he heard the boy calling again from the doorway.

His smile left and he stooped till his head was near Xabier's. "I'll take him now," he said softly, "sing with him, play with him, tire him out, sing him to sleep. He's always exhausted by nine or so. I'll leave him in my bed. You'll be there when he wakes?"

"I will."

"Good."

He stood straight, and Xabier surprised him again by standing up himself, leaning in and pulling him into a hug, which he'd never done before. "I know we don't believe in him anymore," he whispered in Billy's ear, "but vaya con Dios, mi hermano."

"Vaya con dios, Comrade Priest. Thanks for all this," he tapped his breast pocket, "and for your friendship." He went to arm's length.

"And we will meet again. When the fascists are beaten. In a free Euskal Herria."

"I will show you now, Billeh!" Andoni was hopping from foot to foot. "I have it perfectly. Hear!"

He put the wooden tube to his mouth, his eyes crossing down its length. Billy moved to the door, looked into the square. The market hadn't cleared much, still many people lingering, talking, haggling, or simply leaning, eyes shut, faces turned to the spring sun. There was a busker in one patch of it, a fiddler playing a lively folk tune. His hat, upturned before him, had some coins in it, though more produce— carrots, leeks, an onion. "I don't think he will appreciate the competition, Ando. Let's find a better place."

Billy put a guiding hand on the boy's shoulder, steering him to the square's exit and through it. Guernica was not a big place, and they soon came to an open area before an abandoned gas station with half a roof and only three leaning walls. Several farmers had pulled their trucks over, waiting their turn to collect their stalls. Men smoked, talked, passed wineskins. No one seemed in much of a hurry. "What time is it now?" Billy asked.

Andoni squinted at his watch. "The small fat hand is on four, the big thin hand is on six, so . . ." He frowned. "So, it is exactly four minutes after six."

"Ando, how many times must I explain—"

The solemn face dissolved into a huge grin. "It is four thirty! Four thirty! I fool you good, Billeh!"

"You little monkey!" Billy grabbed the boy by the arm, twisting it. Letting Andoni twist his in his turn, till his own arm was up his back.

"Do you surrender?" Andoni cried. "Do you cry *uncles?*"

"*Uncles! Uncles!* Have mercy!"

He was released. With a flick of the head, Andoni stood tall, raised the recorder as if he were in a concert hall, nodded once, and began to play.

He had indeed got it. Very few notes were blurred, and the rhythm was steady. The song was simple, an old Basque lullaby,

"Haurtxo Polita." Once, Andoni had told him that this was the song he wished to learn, Billy had agreed to learn the words in Basque, even though he still didn't know much of the language. Andoni was fluent in both Basque and Spanish. His parents had been immigrants from Andalusia and had taught the boy Spanish before they died of influenza when he was five— and so he and Billy were able to converse, with the odd English word thrown in. Indeed, Andoni had got Billy to teach him English and he'd picked a lot up, fast. He was a natural linguist.

Both orphans also appreciated a lullaby sung to a child by loving parents.

Billy let him play it through twice and the boy got more confident each time. On the third he joined in and, as often happened when he sang, people stopped what they were doing, the conversations they were having, to listen; then, on the chorus, they joined in.

Applause came, as the baby was urged to sleep. Andoni beamed and bowed. "Again, Billeh!" he called. "Again!"

He lifted the recorder to his lips—but Billy laid his hand on it. "Wait," he said, looking up.

He'd heard it first under the song. Had an ear for that different music, almost as beautiful to him—a plane's engine. Lately, though, with the fascist dominance of the skies, it was less lovely. It usually meant death to someone, somewhere nearby.

Like him, others in the crowd had their necks bent back, hands roofed to foreheads, peering up. The sky was mainly blue, though studded with a few clouds. Out of one of these a shape emerged— flying at about five hundred feet, Billy guessed, by how easily he could see its details. The black saltire cross, the insignia of the German Condor Legion, was on its tail fin. Its unique cockpit was a bulbous glasshouse, shot through with sunlight.

"What is it, Billeh?"

"A Heinkel 111."

"Fighter?"

"No." He reached out and pulled the boy close. "Bomber."

"So it does not come for us!" Andoni looked around. "Nothing to bomb."

"No," Billy murmured. "Nothing."

The plane flew directly over the small town. Because of all that glass, he could see the pilot in his cockpit, peering down. Billy looked at the bomb bays in the Heinkel's belly as it passed over. They did not open. Why would they, he thought? It was on its way to Bilbao, to drop bombs on the docks, as planes did most nights recently.

Most . . . *nights*. And never a single plane, but squadrons.

He found he was holding his breath. Yet the plane passed over swiftly enough, the sound of its engine fading from roar to growl to whine to . . . silence. He exhaled, loudly, with many others.

"Now we play again, Billeh!"

"Sure, kid, sure." Billy ran a hand over his forehead, felt the wetness. "I'll count us in. One, two . . ."

A single note sounded, clung in the air, faded. "Billeh," said the boy.

"I know."

He put his arm around Andoni again, as the reverse sounds came — whine, growl, roar. This time the Heinkel's belly was open. Now he could see the squat shapes of the bombs.

"With me!" he cried, but he didn't bother to wait for assent, just bent, snatched the boy up, ran into an open field, away from the leaning walls of the old gas station.

He threw the two of them to the ground, lay on top of Andoni— who squirmed. "I want to see, Billeh! Let me see!"

His head popped up. Billy let it, shifted his weight off the boy, because the bombs were already falling, but not on them. On the town centre, about two hundred yards away. Falling in a tight group, an arm's length between each of them, easy to count. Six fat bombs, shrieking as they fell.

The ground on which they lay seemed to rise and press itself against their bellies. The sound came next, six fast explosions melding into one long roar. That faded slowly, as other noises began to grow, like an organ in a church, playing separate notes—structures tumbling, glass shattering. People screaming.

Billy looked around. Others had followed his example, fled the ruined gas station, pressed themselves into dry earth and grass stubble. He pulled Andoni close as the plane passed over them. "Stay here. Do not move. Do not get up."

He made to rise, but the boy clung to him. "Do not leave, Billeh!" Andoni's face was a grimace of terror. "Where do you go?"

Billy forced his voice to calm. He ran a hand over the boy's sweaty head. "I go to help them," he said.

"I come help too!"

He tried to rise. Billy gripped his arms. "No, little one. Buildings will not be safe. There will be"—he swallowed—"hurt people. I cannot help them if I am worried about you, yes? Yes?"

The boy nodded, though Billy could see his reluctance, and he still clung on hard. "What if the bomber comes again?"

Billy freed himself from his grip, stood, brushed off some earth. "He won't. I think the pilot decided not to fly to Bilbao alone and decided to get rid of his bombs on something before landing." He spat. "Coward."

Andoni gave a little smile. "*Fucking* coward, yes, Billeh?"

He said it in English. He'd insisted Billy start teaching him the bad words he already knew in Spanish and Basque. Billy nodded, tousled his hair, and ran.

The noise got worse the closer he got. Screams dominated. Agony, anguish, fury. When he reached the square, he had to climb over the wreckage of a truck to get in. In the cab he saw his first body, or what remained of it. There was blood and limbs, half a face. A single, shocked eye stared at him.

His stomach heaved and he turned to puke between the twisted metal and the tumbled brick of the wall, the little he'd consumed earlier passing bitter through his mouth. Kept moving, burned his hand on the hot engine whose casing had been ripped away. Dropped to the cobbles, slick with leaking gas, leaking blood.

He had nothing left to puke, spat bile away. He'd seen bodies, helped pull them from the ruins of houses on the docks of Bilbao. One or two. There were dozens here, between the dead and the dying. He couldn't move, couldn't lift himself from the ground. A weight pressed on him, made up of sight and sound and stench.

When he'd left the market fifteen minutes earlier, no one had been in a hurry to leave. Farmers and their wives still trying to sell the last of their produce to black-clad housewives seeking bargains, their voices raised in argument, in gentle insult. Now they were gone, most of them; the six bombs that had landed precisely in the square had vaporized some as if they'd never been there, halved others, flung still more up or over. Men and women were melded with splintered carts; lay across or under animals. A one-winged capon flapped about. A rabbit sat oblivious beside its smashed crate, chewing at a pile of beets. A horse lay on its side, still in its traces, its guts spilled beside it, trying to roll up onto its two remaining legs. Of all the shrieks that filled what had been Guernica's main square, that animal's were perhaps the worst.

Still Billy could not move. The world swam, nothing made sense to his eyes. So he looked up, sought steadiness in the familiar, found it in the sign of Mamá Rosarita's cantina. It was still perched on the lintel above the entrance, which was the only part of the building standing. Behind it he could see what looked like kindling laid out for a fire, made up of smashed tables and chairs. One of the great stone jars still stood. The other was sheared off halfway down, tipped onto its side. Amidst all the smells, rough cider filled his nostrils, stung his eyes.

He looked straight ahead to the train station that was still standing, though its facade looked like someone had smashed it with ball hammers. His bed was in its eaves—a dormitory for a few of the homeless.

Above the cries he now heard some calmer voices calling urgently. Glanced left and saw Xabier—Xabier lived!—bending to a fallen woman who screamed when he put his arms around her and dragged her from beneath her stall.

"Move," Billy ordered himself, obeyed, rose, staggered over, crouched down. "Xabier!" he said, then yelled it when he got no response, shook his arm. "Xabier!"

The man looked up sharply. His glazed eyes cleared when he saw who called. "Billy," he shouted, then made a circling motion around his left ear. "I cannot hear so well." Then he looked about him, shook his head. "Help?"

"Yes," Billy shouted back. "How?"

Xabier looked around again, so Billy did too. Others were coming from outside the square, from untouched buildings, moving to the wounded, lifting them, carrying them into the railway station's hall. "First," said the priest, swallowing, "help that animal."

It was still the worst of the screams, high-pitched, agonized, somehow terrifying, even piercing deafness. Some men and women stood, bloodied or not, unmoving, eyes clenched shut, their hands over their ears, trying to block it out. "Yes," Billy said, and lurched up, wove between the bodies, the rescuers, the wounded, made it to the train station, climbed the stairs to his room in the attic. There was no one in any of the five beds. He stooped, snatched up his bag, flung the strap over his head, took out the gun, a Spanish Ruby, checked it—the pistol was Great War vintage and the safety often slipped—then went back the way he'd come, down the stairs, out again into the square. Walking straight up to the horse, which was still shrieking, still trying to rise, he flicked the safety off, pulled the slide back to chamber the first round, placed the barrel in the rough white star in the centre of its forehead and squeezed the trigger. The gun was old and cheap, and misfired every fifth or sixth time. This time it didn't. The loud shot, the sudden cessation of the loudest scream, brought almost a silence to the square, from the humans in it at least, as if everyone had taken a breath at the same time. The noise returned the next instant, doubled, in pleas and groans. Dropping the gun into his bag, Billy moved back to Xabier, picked up the legs of the woman—who screamed when he did—and helped carry her into the station, laying her out in what had become the first row of wounded.

Some order returned. Xabier, the town's mayor, the police—organizing water, stretchers, bandages. Two doctors appeared; they'd been on their way to help the Basque forces fight the war twenty-five kilometres to the east. Instead, the war had come to them.

Billy got a stretcher with Xabier, brought more injured into the hall. The Jesuit kept shaking his head as if to clear it. When they went out for their fourth trip, he stopped, turned, called loudly, "Billy, say something."

"Can you hear me?"

"Eh?"

"CAN YOU HEAR ME?"

"Ay, not so loud! Yes, I hear you better."

"What happened to you?"

"I'd gone out back to relieve myself. I was halfway through when the bomb . . ." He swallowed. "The back wall came out, covered me. When I dug myself out, I couldn't hear—and Mamá Rosarita's was gone." He was still talking loudly. Now he swivelled to face the remains of the bar, and his voice dropped. "Gone," he whispered. He swung back. "Why did they do it, Billy?" he asked, his voice harsh. "I know this is war, but these here"—he gestured with his head around the square—"these are not soldiers. They are Spaniards, like the ones who drop the bomb."

"They weren't Spaniards. They were Condor Legion. Fucking German mercenaries." He flicked his head. "Come on. More wounded to bring in."

He gripped the stretcher handles tightly, tried to shove forward, but Xabier did not move. "You don't think . . ." He licked his lips, "You don't think they'll come again?"

"Why would they? It's not a military target. Even the Germans—"

He broke off. Because *his* hearing wasn't compromised. "Planes," he murmured.

Xabier put a hand behind his ear. "What?"

"They've come again."

Billy dropped the stretcher, wove through the wreckage of the square, the smashed stalls and folded bodies, shimmied over the truck still wedged into the entrance, and ran twenty yards to the open street beyond, looking into the eastern sky.

He'd said planes. He'd heard more than one this time. Now he saw them—five of them. Three Heinkel 111s and one Dornier Do 17, also a bomber. Two others were a ways behind, but then caught up fast, shot past, peeled away, one left one right, accelerating into the sky. He'd never seen them before, but he knew what they were. Before he was thrown out of the esquadra his comrade pilots had talked about them in frightened whispers.

Messerschmitt 109s.

For a moment he was lost in awe. He could see the bird's unique design even in a glimpse—the enclosed cockpit, the shorter wings, the double machine gun mounted on the cowling. Most miraculous of all were the wheels, which were folded up into the wings. When his awe passed, two feelings came: fear for the pilots he'd left behind, that they had to face such a foe. And relief. Fighters meant that this squadron *was* on its way to Bilbao, because there was no point having a fighter escort over a town that had no air cover, not a single ack-ack gun, no defences of any kind. He'd been right, the single Heinkel before had been a cowardly rogue.

Then, just as he was turning back to return to the square, almost out of the corner of his eye he saw the shapes above change as their bomb bays opened.

He ran, screaming a warning, as the first bombs fell.

He made the square. People were frozen everywhere in it, statues staring up. "Take cover," he yelled, running towards Xabier, who'd rolled a young man onto the stretcher and was staring up like all the others. Billy grabbed his end. "Go! Go! Go!" he screamed.

They reached the three stairs that led up to the station as the first bombs struck. But this time there was no explosion, nothing blasted them off their feet. Instead, Billy heard the smack of metal on tile, heard things roll down the sloping roofs, saw something drop, bounce and skitter at his feet, then suddenly burst into incandescent light.

"Incendiaries!" Billy cried, in English because he had no Spanish, no Basque word for them. He heard them everywhere, clattering and skittering off cobbles and tiles, looked up to see some strike then vanish through roofs as if sucked into quicksand. Behind already-shattered windows, interiors began to glow, suddenly, and explode into flame.

The Condor Legion had come to burn Guernica down.

"We can't take him inside," Billy called, then reversed his grip so he was leading the way out to the side of the station, onto the tracks. When they'd laid down the young man—who reached bloodied arms out to both of them, beseeching them not to leave him—Billy took Xabier by the shoulder and propelled him back towards the station. Smoke was already seeping from its windows. "We've got to get them all out. Otherwise they'll be burned alive."

The hall was smoky and glowing. People were smothering some of the incendiary bombs with blankets. Not enough.

While Xabier shouted orders and people moved to obey, Billy ran upstairs again. He had his new papers in his jacket pocket still, but he'd need his others too, not least his British passport. There were also his few clothes, one spare ammo clip for his pistol, and his anno-tated Bakunin, the father of anarchists. He flung it all into his satchel, then ran back down the stairs.

The railway hall was streaked with flames and filling with smoke. Flinging a sleeve before his face, coughing, he made his way to Xabier, who was organizing a chain of people to get the patients and themselves out onto the platform then down onto the tracks. Billy hoisted one end of a stretcher, moved.

Half-choked, he and the others returned again and again to the furnace the hall had become, extracting the wounded until the last of them was out.

Billy lay for a moment between metal rails, trying to find air.

Bombs continued to fall, some with whistles, screaming as they fell, making the earth groan and shift beneath him when they hit. Beneath all that, and always, the sound of engines in the sky. The Germans were sending in wave after wave.

It was then that he heard another sound. Lighter than the crump and thud of the bombs. Followed by a different kind of screaming.

He stood, swayed. Xabier grabbed his arm, shouted something he didn't hear—Billy shrugged him off, found his way as much by touch as by sight across the smoke-filled square, squeezed his way past the truck and the first body he'd seen. Beyond, the cobbles were broken apart, shattered, with bodies splayed over them.

The staccato punches of bullets called him. He looked down the street. He could not see the football field where he'd left Andoni, but he could see the Messerschmitt swooping over it, hear its blazing guns.

Billy ran.

LEUTNANT ERICH STRIEGLER banked his Heinkel 111, swinging wide over the estuary then back on a straight bearing for Guernica. It was going to be his last run. Even he could no longer ignore the climbing temperature of his heat gauge, the wisps rising from his port engine. He had a leak in his coolant system. His ground crew had wanted him not to go back up when he'd landed to reload at the Vitoria air base of the Condor Legion. But he'd been the first pilot to drop his bombs on the town. If he could not be the last—they'd been ordered to make three runs—at least he would see the effect his first had had, muddled though it would be by all the others of the Geschwader who'd followed him in. He knew his bomb aimer, Wolfgang, had been accurate. He could hardly miss, the way Erich had flown.

Most of the crew had not been happy about going up again. But of course they obeyed his orders, and ceased grumbling on his snapped command. Only Gustav grinned at him, giving him the thumbs-up from his position in the belly of the plane, where he was the gunner. He'd known 'Gootsie' since school. They'd both grown up in Karlsruhe, were avid supporters of the local team, Karlsruhe SC. They'd joined the Party on the same day, were the only ones in the crew who wore the Nazi badge on their uniforms—frowned upon by some military sticklers. Still, no one complained too much these days.

The goldfish-bowl cockpit of the Heinkel gave him an excellent view. And what a view! Erich, looking down the length of the river to the town ahead, saw that the first two 'tactics' they'd been briefed to use— heavy bombs and incendiaries—had been most successful. Guernica was a mess of collapsed buildings. Smoke spiralled up in tight black coils from scores of fires. And even as he approached the town's northern perimeter, he witnessed the third tactic in action as two Messerschmitts shot past him, swooped low and fired short bursts, strafing the main road, their machine gun rounds exploding cobbles among the fleeing figures, many of whom were caught, reeled, fell.

"Glory boys," Erich muttered. He'd applied to transfer to fighters; been rejected. They'd told him he was too old, at twenty-three. "They want them eighteen and fearless," his commandant had said. Well, I am fearless too, he thought. And my bird can do as well as theirs.

He peered ahead. There was a football field just beyond the town centre. Small black figures dotted it. "Gootsie," he called through his headset. "Want to shoot some rabbits in a field?"

The laughter came crackly into his ears. "Love to, Herr Leutnant."

Erich next heard the voice of Wolfgang, his navigator and bomb aimer, in his headset, even as he saw the man wave from his position in the nose just below him. "Leutnant, the engines . . ."

Erich glanced at the pinched, anxious face. "Just one last run before we go home," he called, and using the ailerons and rudder, he banked around to the right, swung out over the estuary again, swung back. Once more he was coming straight towards the town centre. The Messerschmitts had cleared the streets of people. But that football field lay ahead. Pushing the stick forward, he descended, till he was only about eight hundred feet from the ground, flying in and out of the smoke columns. "Now you see me, now you don't," he muttered. People were indeed crouched like frightened rabbits all across the field. "Karlsruhe scores to win the title," he laughed, and took them still lower. He'd be safe, drop to five hundred to give his comrade a sporting chance.

He felt it, an extra shudder through the fuselage as Gootsie let fly. Saw those stitched earth lines, as neat as any fighter could make. Saw someone leap, fall. He pulled back sharply on the stick to start the fast climb away.

Then he felt it—a hard shake, accompanied by an immediate drop in power. The wing dipped, he glanced left, even as he corrected, and saw his left engine feather to stillness. The plane yawed violently left. He kicked the rudder hard, tried to bank, reducing power to try to level . . . and the right engine cut out too.

The sudden machine silence was shocking, the wind now so loud despite his flying helmet. Instinct and ceaseless drills took hold of him. He had never crash-landed. He knew what to do.

"Brace!" he screamed, fumbling for his own safety harness which he hated to wear. "Brace for crash landing!"

He peered ahead. Beyond orchards, farmhouses, barns, walled enclosures, he saw . . . fields! Spring wheat, green ears, waving. They are far, at my limit, he thought, but he needed to reach them, so needed to stretch the glide. He'd pulled the stick back to counter the loss of power, the sharp yaw. Now he eased it forward, lowered the nose. Too much! A little back . . . there. The angle was everything. Too steep and they'd lose altitude too fast, be destroyed in the force of the crash. He didn't put his wheels down, it would drag the bird, he wouldn't make that field. The plane was almost certainly a goner, but if the field was flat, he could glide in on its belly and save his crew.

They were as drilled as him. He sensed rather than saw what

they did. Windows were cracked, doors opened to a latch. A crash would crunch the fuselage, jamming everything. They would need to get out fast or be burned in their seats.

He was maybe one hundred feet off the ground. Saw a farmer looking up in a cow pen, his beasts around him. The field was still too far. He pulled the stick back and the nose lifted, heavy, reluctant, only a little. Enough, maybe enough.

Something screamed along the belly of his bird, gouging along the metal, echoing up through his empty bomb bay. Gootsie screamed too, crouched beside his machine gun.

The field was so close below him! It was not wide, a stone fence and trees beyond. Erich pushed his stick down, held the wings level, moved the rudder left and right, fishtailing. The tail swung side to side, he slowed, dropped, Gootsie gave another scream, lost in the louder shriek of belly-metal grinding along the ground. The plane bounced, slid, slewed, spun. Three circles and it ploughed side-on into the stone wall before finally, fully halting.

ONE MINUTE EARLIER...

He'd been decent at the hundred yards at school. This was at least double that. The second Messerschmitt overtook him, just before the finish. With lungs afire, he rounded the corner of the last building, saw the field.

People were stumbling across it, dodging the earth exploding around them, little mounds of it thrown up to the sounds of the Messerschmitt's machine guns, as if someone was stitching the earth with metal thread. He saw a woman snatched up and knocked forward, her child flung out before her. In a moment, bullets ripped the length of the field, all the way to the goalposts.

Where he'd left Andoni.

Somehow, he found the air he needed. Tripped on one body, vaulted others, hands reaching out to delay him, he made the posts.

The boy was lying where he'd left him. He wasn't moving, and searing pain shot from Billy's lungs into his heart.

Then a little fair head popped up. "Billeh!" Andoni called. "I stayed, like I promised you."

Billy dropped down beside him, gasping. Found enough air to say, "Now we go." Because even as he heard the Messerschmitt's engine fade, he heard another's grow—and recognized the twin-engine voice of the Heinkel 111. Knew, because he'd studied a downed one once, that it had machine gunners in its nose, rear and belly.

He picked the child up. Andoni cried something out and tried to wriggle from his arms, but Billy held him tightly and began staggering back to where they'd come from—the leaning walls of the abandoned gas station, about one hundred yards away, now the safer place to be. Especially as the engine was growing louder, the screams around him louder. Then, in the uncut grass just beyond the faded white line of the field's boundary, Billy tripped over a body he saw too late.

He sprawled, Andoni spilled forward. But the boy was up again in a moment, turning and running back the way they'd come, as the engines grew still louder.

"My recorder, Billeh!" he cried.

Billy grabbed for his legs, missed him. By the time Billy was on his feet and running himself, Andoni was fifty paces ahead, fresh legs powering him away. "Andoni! Get down! Down!"

The boy probably didn't hear him above the engines' roar, the plane so low. Perhaps he did hear and ignored him, too intent on his prize.

No, Billy mouthed, no sound coming, as he ran again, as the central gunner in the Heinkel opened up, laying down another metal line from one set of goalposts to the next, just as Andoni reached them. He was picked up, flung against one post, the force cracking it, though it didn't break.

Billy reached him. "No," he said, aloud this time. He could see the boy was dead because no one could survive what the machine gun had done to him. There was a hole the size of a fist in his back, the edges of the torn flesh scorched. Billy didn't need to turn him over to know that the exit wound would be twice as big.

Andoni's arm was thrust out ahead. Clutched in his hand was his recorder.

Billy looked up. Now he made sense of what he'd been hearing as he ran. The Heinkel hadn't gone as far away as it should have, and he could see why—neither propeller was turning. The plane was dropping fast. Yet with his own pilot's eye, Billy could see what the German was doing—stretching the glide. He was trying to get over the barns and the orchards. He was trying to crash-land in Gueterria's wheat field.

Billy started to run again. Surprisingly, he found that now he wasn't tired at all. Perhaps because others were also running beside him, and it was easier to run in a pack.

LEUTNANT STRIEGLER HELD his left arm in his right hand. He wasn't sure if the left was broken, or the shoulder dislocated. He only knew that he was in a lot of pain. He'd been unable to aid the unharmed Gootsie help the others from the wreckage.

Ernst Frohmann, the rear gunner, was writhing on the ground, clutching his ribs, red froth at his lips. Willie Martz, the dorsal gunner, was sitting, his knees drawn up, his nose broken, a large cut on his forehead leaking blood into his eyes. Only Wolfgang hadn't made it. He'd been in his position in the front of the glasshouse canopy, which was what had smashed into the farmer's wall. He dangled from his straps now, head lolling, eyes open. Erich had to look away from them, from what had been his cockpit. It was a miracle he'd survived with nothing more than whatever his arm injury was.

His plane had not exploded either—another miracle, but one that might not hold. He could smell leaking gas, leaking glycol. It was that coolant that had cut his engines, downed his plane. He should have listened to the mechanics at the base. Next time he would. Next time …

He looked up, "Gootsie," he called. "We must move further away from the plane."

But his Karlsruhe comrade was not listening to him. He was staring back across the wheat field, along the avenue of flattened sheaves and gouged earth that marked their plane's glide. So Erich looked there too—and saw the running men and women.

He swallowed. He had a pistol, but he couldn't use it, there were too many coming—besides, his best hope now, for himself, for his men, would be to get some medical aid. He would be a prisoner for a while, perhaps. He'd heard of another German airman who'd been captured on the Madrid front. He'd been roughed up a little when taken, but then had been held in a jail. Three months later he'd been swapped for one hundred Republicans. That's what would happen to him and his crew.

Almost weeping at the effort, he pulled himself first to his knees and then onto his feet. Awkwardly, he pulled his gun holster over his head and held it out to the first man who reached him. "Kamerad," he said, raising one arm high, in half the gesture of surrender. "I am Leutnant Erich Striegler. I demand—"

The man—taller than the others, not as dark—screamed something and slapped the holster from his hand. Then he thrust his other hand into Erich's throat and threw him backwards.

He hit the ground hard, agony shooting through his wounded arm. He let out a high-pitched scream, echoed by his crewmen, who other men and women had jerked up, struck, then forced onto their knees. The one who'd knocked him over reached down, grabbed him by the back of his flying jacket, dragged him into the rough line that had formed, threw him down next to Gootsie. Erich yelped, then shouted in German, "We surrender! We are your prisoners." Heard the reply.

"No, Leutnant Striegler. You are fucking murderers."

It was strange for Erich because he understood what the man had said, and he didn't speak any Spanish and certainly no Basque. Then he realized—the tall man had spoken in English, which he did speak, a little.

"You are Englander," he said, in that tongue. "Please help we. We surrender."

"No, you don't," the man replied. Then he stepped behind Gootsie. He was the only one able to put both his hands up on the back of his neck, the other gesture of surrender. Erich's comrade craned his neck around to look up at the man standing behind him. Gootsie spoke no English, so he said, in German, "Prisoner of war."

"That wasn't war," growled the man, taking out his pistol. Pulling the slide back, he put the muzzle to Gootsie's head and shot him.

Screaming began, from the crewmen, from the crowd. Some of them grabbed the Englander, were trying to tug him away. Others were shouting, urging him on. He threw off those who tried to hold him, stepped behind Erich.

"Nein! Nein!" Then he remembered one other phrase in English. "I beg you!"

The man did not respond. He just thrust the muzzle of the gun into Erich's head and pulled the trigger.

Erich felt his bowels go, his thighs instantly hot and wet. But he didn't feel anything else. He heard—an English curse, the pistol's slide being worked; then the muzzle was shoved again against his head. Heard another click, then a roar as the man threw the gun away, bent and picked up Erich's Luger, pulled it out of the holster, slid off its safety. By the time he did this, more people were shouting at him. Still, he ignored them, stepped forward again.

"Stop! Stop this!" It was a different voice that spoke. English still, accented, urgent.

The Luger's muzzle was pushed into Erich's scalp. "Why should I? Did you see what they did to the town?" A sob escaped; the voice rose. "They killed Andoni."

"Yes," came the new voice again, still calm. "And killing these men will not bring him back."

Erich turned slightly to look up at the newcomer. He had grey stubble on his head, grey eyes. Now the man slowly reached towards the pistol, and spoke again, just as calmly. "This is not the Basque way, my friend. And this is also not you, Billy Coke."

The muzzle did not move. Erich looked down at his childhood friend, his head the centre of a spreading red halo. It reminded him of a stained-glass window in the church his mother would take him to at home. Some saint. Erich closed his eyes.

IT WAS ONLY when Xabier said his name that Billy returned to himself. He hadn't been himself for a while, had no memory of who he was. All that had been in his mind as he'd done what he'd done were the holes that German bullets had made in Andoni's body. But now, in his friend's voice, he remembered himself.

But memory gave him no motion. He couldn't move. Xabier touched his hand, gently wrapped his fingers around it, and lifted it from the kneeling man's head till the Luger's muzzle was pointed at the sky, before easing the gun away.

When it left his hand, Billy finally looked elsewhere. To his friend, staring at him, tears in his eyes. To the blond hair on the back of the head he'd nearly exploded. To the head on the ground that he had. Swivelling, he walked back the way he'd come, along the avenue the plane had scythed through the spring wheat.

Xabier called, "Billy? Billy Coke? Wait for me in the town. We must talk. Billy?"

He heard the call. Felt the eyes that followed him, all the eyes. Even felt the qualities of their seeing. Compassion. Wonder. Hatred. Yet he did not turn around. He would never see the priest again. He was leaving Guernica. But before he did, he had a boy to bury. Then he had a war to fight.

TEN
THE COPPICE

Southwold, Suffolk. January 1, 1941

WRAPPED IN A BLANKET against the morning chill, forehead pressed to the window, Ilse watched the action in the truck's side mirror. The wide glass was almost like a movie screen and there were players moving across it: the two men from Adnams Brewery, where they'd come to collect McGovern's ales. And Billy Coke. He was the focus of the action, had most of the dialogue. He was the professional, after all. She could not hear what he said, could only see its effect: taciturn local men, dragged out of bed on what should be a holiday, going about hard work on a frosty January morning, thawed by a performer's charms. She saw them smile, then laugh. When Billy tap-danced on the yard's cobbles, the younger of them applauded and Billy bowed, then rose to help lift one of the wooden barrels into the back of the truck, vanishing from her sight. When he stepped down again, they were still laughing, because he was still talking, more words in half a minute than he had spoken over their whole breakfast in the Swan Hotel's musty, cold dining room.

This is his . . . front, she thought. Was that the word in English, the same as in Norwegian? Or perhaps *fasade* was better, almost the same in both tongues. The face he showed the world—the carefree man, a song always ready in his mouth, a sparkle in his eyes.

"Never trust an actor," her father, who had written plays, once told her. "They make their living from deceit. Even . . . no, especially, when they believe their own lies."

She shivered. *He* could talk. She didn't want to think about her father. If all went well with SOE, she would be thinking of Wilhelm Magnusson too much, and soon enough.

Besides . . . she knew she had not been deceived by Billy Coke. Yes, there was the actor, the entertainer, telling his stories, trying to amuse her. But everyone had a front, especially strangers who would be lovers. She had hers—the mysterious Nordic beauty, revealing little of her past, nothing of her future. Yet she knew she'd glimpsed behind his *fasade*. When they'd come out of that frigid sea, when they'd laughed and shivered, discovered the abandoned house, explored it like children on an adventure, built the fire, ate by it, looked at each other across the flames. And when they'd touched, when they'd kissed? The promise of those kisses! She'd known desire before, with Tomas, her first lover, in New York. But this was different. Tomas had chosen her—his student—wooed her at the music school, gradually broken down her resistance. But here, now, she'd chosen Billy as much as he'd chosen her. They had been about to make love, there by the fire, and again later in some hotel, and again and again for all the time they had. She'd known it. She could see he knew it too, wanted it as much.

Then something had happened. She had thought to play him a silly tune on the recorder she'd found, entertain him for a moment with her skills as he had entertained her with his. But it had changed everything; he had cried out "No!" then vanished inside himself. She had taken his hand, but the electricity of their touches had gone, their fire quenched, now as cold as the sea they'd swum in, as cold as the bucket of pond water he'd thrown on the flames as he withdrew from her, telling her they should go find a hotel. And when they did, he didn't even bother to protest when the landlady, all English morality, refused them a room together because they couldn't produce a marriage licence. When they'd parted in that carpeted, dank corridor outside their rooms, Ilse knew he would not steal into hers in the night. And over a breakfast of cold, overcooked eggs, greasy bacon and foul coffee, he'd scarcely met her eyes, and the few words he'd said were to do with the day's practicalities: collecting beer, collecting the chicks from the McGoverns' farm, getting back to London, a day before they were due, something muttered about a meeting he'd forgotten, a line so poorly delivered she'd never have believed it upon a stage, let alone in a frigid dining room in Suffolk.

Is that it, she wondered, as she watched Billy shaking hands with the two men, the younger one pulling his hand back and staring at it in surprise, at the coin that had appeared magically in it—do we drive back to London in silence, on the first day of a new year, to the war that neither of us might survive? The memories of fingers, and lips, and the light in eyes fading as a mistake behind both our *fasadene*?

Not if I can help it, she thought.

He climbed back into the cab. "Cold?" he asked, as he turned the key and the engine kicked into life.

Yes, she thought. "No," she replied.

"Right, the farm," he said, and steered through the brewery's gates. She looked at his profile as he negotiated the scant early-morning traffic on the streets of Southwold. His eyelids were low, as if they were veils— though that could just have been the sun piercing the morning mists, bright now in the windscreen.

They cleared the town, turned left onto the main road, headed south again. She'd been this way enough to know that they were not far from the farm. More loading, more . . . *acting*. Then London.

"What is a coppice?" she said.

"What?"

"A *coppice*? I do not know this word."

"It's, uh . . ." They'd been forced to a halt behind a tractor that had suddenly pulled out then stopped. "A coppice is a type of wood-land. In medieval times, they'd cut young trees to grow wood in a certain way. To turn into charcoal, or to make fences, furniture, beams for houses."

"You sound like a professor."

"I was a bit of a history buff at school." He glanced across. "Why do you ask?"

She replied by pointing. He peered. Half-hidden by a dangling branch, a wooden arrow pointed along an overgrown path into a forest. "'Wenfold's Coppice,'" he read. "Hmm. Local authorities must have not seen that one or they'd have taken it down."

"Do you think, um, Wenfold's Coppice will be a major German military objective?"

At least that brought a grin. "Probably not."

"I've always wanted to see a coppice."

"Even though you've only just heard of one?"

"Even though."

She watched his eyes narrow, saw the calculation in them, then the decision. "Happy to fulfill a lifelong desire," he said, and when the tractor finally started again with a bang and a puff of blue smoke, he followed for a dozen yards, then pulled the truck over on a wider part of the verge. When he jumped down on the driver's side, she climbed down on hers. Before she shut the door, she reached back and picked up the blanket.

The path had not been attended to or used for a while, and they had to push through low branches, step over deadfall. The faintest of trails marked the path's continuation up a small hill, leading towards a line of trees on its crest. As they climbed, sheep regarded them incuriously until they got too close, sprinting off then with panicked bleats.

Billy led and, when they reached the hilltop, stopped and turned about. "My," he said. Ilse turned too, gasped. It may not have been much of a rise—he had told her that Suffolk was a very flat county—but the little there was allowed them a view over the trees along the road and beyond. Straight ahead, the sea was about a mile away, steel blue in the growing light, white horses foaming in, the horizon a shimmering line impossible to focus on. To their left and right the land fell gently away, more fields punctured by bursts of trees.

"The sky," she murmured. It made her dizzy, and she stumbled slightly, grabbing at his arm. He steadied her as she looked up. It was so . . . *vast*, quite different from any she'd seen before, in all her travels. The city skies of London or New York always seemed low to her, pressing down. In Norway, up in the mountains where she loved to walk, snow-lined granite peaks pushed up into the blue, linking earth and heaven. This sky felt . . . untethered, a huge hemispherical dome, cloudless and beyond blue, and she held him tighter as she tried to see it all.

"I know," he said, laying a hand over hers on his arm. "You should see the paintings that have been inspired by it."

"How could anyone paint this?" she murmured.

They stood, stared for a moment longer. "Shall we?" he said, and turned her into the trees behind them.

There were the remains of a fence, broken slats prone on the ground which they stepped over. "We call this a *copse*. Do you have that word in Norwegian?"

"No." She pointed. "Do you know that one?"

He peered at the main trunk, then up into the branches. "That's, uh, yes, that's a hazel—you know, where we get the nuts from?" He pointed to another. "That's an ash, and that one over there is a, uh, field maple, I think."

She smiled. "So you are not only a history bluff, but a botanist bluff too?"

He smiled back. "Buff," he said, then looked up into the branches. "I had a teacher at school. The only one I liked, really. He taught me lots of stuff. He was a loner, like me . . ."

"You? A loner?" She laughed. "Come on. I see you with others—in that tea house the night we met, at the farm, even just now with those men at the brewery. You"—she gazed up into the blue, seeking a word—"*attract* people. You make friends easily."

He raised an eyebrow. "*Do* I?"

"Yes."

"Yeah, well, that's . . ." He broke off, his gaze too, looked away into the trees. "That's acting."

"Is it? You made me a friend. Easily. Acting too?"

"No! No, I . . ." He swallowed. "Look, English schools like that, they're . . . terrible places. Especially for someone like me. I'd been living on a farm on an island in Canada, with only my dad. Then he . . . died."

"You said. How?" He turned away. She took his hand. "How did he die, Billy?"

He looked at her, took a deep breath. "Alright." He stared up again, into the canopy. "Our farm was in a forest. Very different to this. Huge trees—giant firs, cedars. My father was clearing the land. One day he was felling a tree. He didn't notice the widow-maker—"

"The what?"

"It's . . ." He pointed up. "Do you see there, where the tops of those two trees nearly meet? There's a small branch, see, broken off the top of one, caught in the crook of the other?"

"I see it, yes."

"Canadian trees, they're much taller. Hard to see the tops. And branches, or the tops of trees, can break off, get caught up there. Much bigger than that. So you need to be careful when you cut one down." He shrugged. "My father didn't see the widow-maker. It fell and broke his back."

She took his hand again. "Oh, Billy. Did you find him?"

"I was with him."

"With . . ."

"Yes. I was seven. Kept thinking he'd wake up." He looked down at the ground. "Sat there for two days, waiting for him to wake up."

"Where was your mother?"

"Oh, she'd . . . she'd left us a long time before."

"That is terrible. I am so sorry."

"Yeah, me too. But it made me . . . left me . . . alone."

"A loner," Ilse murmured. She looked down. She was still holding his hand. It was warm to the touch. It made her think of another hand she'd held. Cold, getting colder, as life left it. "I know this feeling," she took a deeper breath, "because . . . because I lost a parent too. My mother."

"How?"

"Cancer. I was ten. They let me in, but only . . . only at the very end." She removed her hand from his, used the back of it to catch the tear that ran down one cheek. Then she gave a choked laugh. "So perhaps cancer is the widow*er*-maker, yes? My father—" She shook her head, turned away, needing both hands for the tears now. "I was sure that if I kept holding her hand then she could not be dead. That she couldn't leave. But my father came, made me let her go." She swallowed. "Let. Her. Go."

Billy shifted closer behind her. "I felt the same, in the forest. That as long as I didn't go, he . . . he couldn't be dead." Billy stared at her back. "Ilse?" She did not move, speak. "Ilse?" He put his hands on her shoulders.

She turned at his touch. "Tell me," she said, fast and fierce.

"What?"

"Why, when I played the recorder, did everything change?"

His eyes went wide, then hooded over. "We should be getting back."

He stepped away, but she grabbed both his hands. "Tell me."

"There's nothing to tell."

"Don't lie to me!" She kicked a branch on the ground. "Don't . . . *act* for me anymore! You just told me about your father."

"Yes, but that's different. That . . . that *happened* to him. I wasn't . . . I didn't . . . *do* anything."

"So tell me what you did *do*."

He stared at her. "I can't," he said, then shouted, "I bloody can't!"

"You wish to start what . . . whatever this is between us . . . with lies? Evasions? We don't have the time!" She glared up into his eyes. "Or do it, then. Go to your war, Billy Coke, I will go to mine, we will never see each other again. Never know what *this* is." She shoved him, palms into his chest, and he stumbled back a pace. "Or could have been. That, or . . . or you can tell me now." She took a deep breath, "Why, when I started to play, did everything change?"

He stood where her shove had sent him, still swaying. When he looked at her now, she saw panic in his eyes. "It is not a . . . it is not a nice story."

"You think those are all that I want to hear? Nice stories? Funny stories, like the ones you told those men at the brewery this morning?" She waved a hand to the world beyond the wood. "Do you remember what is happening out there? In my homeland, the Nazis rule, killing my friends, torturing my countrymen." She choked, swallowed, went on. "Do you remember that man in that square three nights ago, killed by a bomb, without a mark on him? What is *nice* out there anymore?" She shook her head, took another breath, centred her voice which she knew had risen high. "So you have a choice now. Tell me your not-so-nice story. Or drive me back to the war, say goodbye forever, and never, never know."

"Alright!" he shouted, then stepped to her, gripped her arms, hard and high up on each. His eyes were fire now, but seen through water. "Alright," he said more quietly. "I'll tell you. Tell you about Spain. Tell you who I really am!"

So he did.

The anger left him as he talked. For a time, it was matter-of-fact, filling in details. Occasionally there was a hitch in the throat, usually over names, strange names she'd never heard before—Xabier, Andoni. A place called Guernica, which she had heard of, read about. Then his eyes left hers, his lids closed—perhaps to hold back his tears which, like hers, they failed to do. His voice deepened, went ragged, the smoothness of the performer entirely gone. And without Ilse realizing how they'd gotten there, they were on the blanket, his back against a trunk, her on her knees before him, saying nothing. Listening. Listening and, at one particular moment, wishing that she'd never learned to conjure music from wood.

He was right. It was not a nice story. The man whose shoulder she now pressed with one hand was a killer. More than one victim, in that war in Spain, shooting Spaniards and Italians and Germans out of the sky. But it was only the first one that had made him cry.

At last, when all his words were gone and he looked straight at her, Ilse saw so many things in his eyes. There was the man in the dock of a court, awaiting judgement, fearing it yet defying it too—knowing the worst was inevitable, wanting it done. Yet somewhere deep, deep behind that, was a boy in a forest by a body, waiting for someone to come.

She stared back. At last, he grunted. "So there," he muttered. "That's why."

" 'Why'?"

He shook his head, swallowed, looked away. "Why I've ruined everything."

She took his chin, turned his face back to her. "No, Billy," she said. "You've made everything." And saying it, she leaned into him, and kissed him.

He resisted, at first, but only for a moment. His lips were cold, deadened . . . until they weren't, until they were the opposite, and she sank into them, into him, and he came away from the tree trunk, pulled her down, lay beside her, sank into her, pressed her into the ground.

It was a blur then. Sweaters fumbled over heads, clasps unclasped, snaps unsnapped, the sound of zippers sliding the loudest noise in a copse where even the birds seemed to be holding their breath. She was ready for him—more than ready, instantly ready, as he was for her. She gasped as he entered her, suddenly and all at once, and he murmured a question, something about pain, which she answered by pulling him deeper.

For a time, they lay like that, still, joined. She was below, then somehow she was above, seeing him as if for the first time—no, *like* that very first time, in that street when the bombs were falling, that moment he'd touched her hand. Everything since had been veils, thrown up because it was what people did, how they got to know each other, only gradually pulling them aside. This, then, was the promise of that first naked look, that first truth fulfilled.

She'd had lovers before. Three. A kind one, a fast one, an angry one. Billy Coke was none of these things, though he was gentle for a time, until she didn't want him to be. And when, from on top of him, she cried out, throwing her head up to that impossible sky, when he cried out too as he pushed himself deep, she knew what she never had before. That though she'd taken pleasure and given it too, it wasn't what each did to the other that truly mattered. What mattered was what she'd never come close to finding before—the sudden certainty that love was something made by two people, not one. And in that certainty, the realization that she was no longer alone in the world.

They lay there for a while, Ilse having found a place that felt as if it had been moulded for her alone, so perfectly did her head fit between his shoulder and his chest, so completely did his arms enfold her. Birdsong returned to the copse, light through the bud-less trees. Until suddenly, simultaneously, totally—

"Y-yikes," he said. "Are you . . . ?"

"Yes. Fr-freezing."

Fumbling reversed, clothes back on. Yet they were still cold because, despite the sunlight and the lovemaking, it was January in England. "Truck?" he asked.

"Yes. And then the f-farm." She laughed. "What is it you English always say: 'I'd kill for a cup of tea?' "

She suddenly regretted her choice of words. But no shadows came into Billy Coke's eyes now. Only a smile.

"So would I."

HE WOKE, but he didn't open his eyes. Once he did, the day began. Leavings, partings, a war. Better to lie there, tethered to sleep.

Perhaps it was the wood pigeon that had woken him. It had roosted in the elm that edged the barn, calling to the rising sun. It was such an *English* sound, one of the first he'd come to love—but only grudgingly as he'd clung to Canada, to the island he'd been dragged from, to his father. Refusing to assimilate no matter how hard they tried to make him at their schools, with their Latin and their patriotic hymns, and the sticks they broke on him. Later, at Repton, he'd met Owen Wells, who the other kids called Frankenstein because he had half a leg, half a face, both torn away by a German bomb in a trench in Flanders. A recluse shattered by war and a boy shattered by circumstance—the two loners had found each other, and the teacher had not only taught Billy about engines, as he rebuilt a scrapped sports car, but also about a different England, one worthy of his love, its music from the soil not the church, with heroes who wore no crowns. The land of radicals and revolutionaries, where birds sang equally for all men.

"Do you hear it, Cokey?" he'd say, about this bird, or that one. "Wood pigeon. A series of croons. And wait! Wait for that single note! Hear how it leaves it in the air, like a question? There. There! Ah!" The teacher had given him what passed as a smile for a man with half a face. "'No bird soars too high if he soars with his own wings,'" he'd quoted. "Who's that?"

"Blake, sir?"

"Blake indeed. Read him, and Clare, and Hopkins sometimes, and you can forget your 'Half a league, half a league, half a bloody league onward,' eh?"

"Sir."

"Call me Owen, lad." That half-smile again. "Or 'comrade,' if you prefer."

For his sixteenth birthday Owen had given Billy a copy of *The Communist Manifesto*.

The pigeon ended with his single note and immediately began

another set. Billy heard other birds now. Too early in the year for the migratory ones, these were the natives: tits, great and blue. A chaffinch, loudest of all, calling his challenge again and again.

Yet under all those sounds, a finer one, rhythmic—breath taken in, blown softly out. Yes, he thought. Listen to that, the song in that. With luck, comrade, you'll hear birdsong all over the world. None will sound as lovely as this breath in, that breath out.

He could not only listen for long. He opened his eyes.

Ilse lay on her side, her face on an old pillow, its case embroidered with hedgerow flowers long ago by the grandmother who sat in her rocking chair by the range in the farmhouse kitchen. She and the McGoverns had plied the couple with blankets and sheets, more than they needed, worried about the draughty barn on a January night. They needn't have. The two had made their own warmth through a night of waking dreams. Their lovemaking wasn't in bursts; it had felt continuous, this moment blending into the next, as varied as any dream's imagery. But he must have slept. He'd just woken, after all. She slept now, lips parted, eyelids fluttering with some or other vision. Whatever it was pleased her, because she smiled, gave a happy sigh.

He held her within sight, as he had within his arms. This— remember this, he told himself. This exact fall of hair, this shape of nose, this curve of jaw, with the faintest line of a white scar, like jagged lightning, under her chin. These . . . specifics. They will keep you, in all the dark nights to come.

If fate has a death in mind for me, falling from the blue where the birds soar, he thought, let this be what I think of last. Not terror, not fury. This.

And this, he now realized, this most of all. These eyes open now, filled with light, looking back at me.

"Good morning," she whispered.

"Good morning." He opened his arms, and she fell into him again.

He held her, they lay still, only his one hand moving, running through her white-blonde hair in gentle strokes. He felt her pressed to him in various places. Her forehead rested on his cheek, one breast was on his chest, one hip pushed into his, the length of her thigh matching the length of his, for she was tall. Her foot fitted under his, her toes thrust into his sole.

They lay, their paired breathing soft, as the birds sang. He wondered if they could make love again, after a night of it, thought not; changed his mind when he ran his hand down the length of her silken back and she made that sound again in her throat, not entirely human. "Really?" she said, amused, stretching her arm, which had been pinned as she'd pressed against him, fingers unfurling, wrapping around his. "Again?"

He could still count the number of women he'd been with on one hand—plus the second thumb now. Only two longer-term. Rosie. And Maria, in Madrid, black-haired, black-eyed, fiery during the love-making, weeping in his arms afterwards for her dead husband who'd been killed by fascists in the early days of war. Neither experience, nor the few fumbles that followed, had been close to what he'd felt last night. It was as if he finally understood, had unlocked a code that had forever puzzled him.

"Oh, why not?" he breathed. She laughed and rolled on top of him. As the sun climbed and the birds called, they made love, slow at first, then faster, an urgency to it, as if both knew it was the last time. Afterwards they lay once more in the same position as before, though the skin that pressed together now was hot, slick. "Ilse," he murmured at last, turning, but she lay fingers on his lips.

"Hush now," she said. "Hush."

"Listen. I want to tell you—"

He got no further. "Hallo-oh?" came the man's voice from below, followed by a gentle knocking on the barn door. "You two awake?"

"Yes."

"Good," said Don McGovern, continuing. "Mother wants to know if you'd like your eggs scrambled or fried?"

"Fried," Billy said.

"Scrambled," Ilse said at the same time.

They both laughed, as did the farmer. "Be about ten minutes," he called, moving away.

"Ilse, listen," Billy tried again, but she was already out of the covers, snatching up flung garments.

"Didn't you hear, slowpoke? Ten minutes."

Billy watched her dress, striped by sunbeams through the gaps in the barn's planked wall. What could he say anyway? What could he promise, or expect? The world beyond had called in the farmer's voice. The first of many voices that would pull them apart.

IT WAS LATER than he'd thought, close to nine by the time they walked into the farmhouse, so breakfast was a little rushed. Don teased them, his wife hushed him, his mother said nothing, just kept heaping eggs and rashers of bacon onto their plates, urging them with gestures to eat more, ever more. She may have been old and deaf, but she knew they were heading back to a hungry city and to meagre rations.

Sated—stuffed, truly—Billy went and helped Don load the last of the supplies: a crate of tweeting chicks, just old enough to travel now; a half-dozen chickens, killed that morning; a flitch of bacon, a half-dozen huge pork pies, and three large stone jars of cider. With the beer they'd collected the day before, McGovern at the Globe Tavern would be well supplied for a while. There might be short rations in the land, but farmers, publicans and royalty would feel neither hunger nor thirst.

The first parting of the day was swift—a firm handshake from Don McGovern, a hug from his wife for the both of them. Grandma stood in the doorway and Ilse went to her, was pulled into a hug, held in it, as the old woman whispered into the younger one's ear. Then they were gone, the drive to London fast, then slowing as they approached the city and traffic built. The sky had darkened, a light rain starting to fall, as they drove the last streets, which had been cleared of most debris, the tumbled bricks, broken glass and charred beams. Billy had almost hoped they would not have cleared away everything from the raid of three nights before, that their passage would be slower, the inevitable postponed. London, though, was not like that. England was not. Fighting Hitler meant not only bullets and bombs, it also meant sweeping away the traces of his attacks. It meant, simply, carrying on.

They'd certainly carried on at the Globe, their first stop. As Billy and Ilse helped McGovern and Molly unload, he saw that all the windows broken in the raid had either been taped across the cracks or replaced by boards, while every scorch mark from the incendiaries had already been sanded down and painted over. When they'd finished the transfers, they were each given a pint of beer—"Never too early for a pint of mild," said McGovern—and a pasty fresh from Molly's oven. McGovern was a little miffed that Billy didn't hand over the truck's keys straight away. But Billy told him he had to drop the lady home.

"They love you, these people," Ilse said, as they climbed back into the cab.

"Do they?" He shrugged. "Well, they are the closest I have to family here."

"Closer than the Honourable Cokes?"

Billy chuckled. "Much." He turned the key and, with a stutter that caused him to frown, the engine growled into life. "If you ever need to find me, McGovern and Molly will know where I am."

All too soon they were parked in front of Ilse's hostel. Billy didn't turn off the engine; it had stuttered on the short ride over, and he wasn't sure it would start again. Or maybe that was his excuse. He'd always hated farewells, never made them if he could help it. He hadn't had last words when he'd held her that morning. He couldn't think of any now.

"Billy."

He'd been staring at nothing through the rain-spotted wind-screen. Now he turned.

Her eyes were bright. "Thank you," she said.

He swallowed. "It was fun."

"It was more than fun. You know this."

"I . . ." This was why he wanted to be gone. What could he say? What promises could they make? Somewhere far away, beyond the truck's spluttering noise, he heard the faint call of an airplane's engine. That's where he wanted to be now. Back in the blue. That return began tomorrow, when he reported to RAF Cranwell. "What did she say?" he blurted.

"Who?"

"The old lady. Mrs. McGovern. What did she say to you?"

"Ah." Ilse glanced out the window. "She told me you were a good boy. She said you were . . . I did not know this term." She looked back. "She said you were 'a keeper.'"

"Did she?" He shook his head, as it hit him, hard. "Did she remember there was a war on?"

"Oh, she remembered. She knew we had to part too, because I'd told her that we needed to fight the war . . . in different ways."

"I see." He looked away again. "Did she have any advice?"

She laid fingers on his cheek. " 'Just love him,' she said. And just let him love you.' "

"I do!" He swung back to her now, grabbed the hand that touched him, squeezed it hard, words coming fast. "Ilse, I have never known anything like this. And I've known enough to know that this is not just the . . . the madness of love. Or of war. This time and place." He jerked his head to the world outside the truck. "This is different. And it breaks my heart that we have to part. That the war is going to take you from me. That one or both of us might not make it through. That I might not . . . ever again know you . . . hold you—"

He broke off, his voice choked. She reached again to his cheek, thumbed the moisture into his skin. "Billy. We will. Once you showed me this, who you are, told me of Spain, of your darkness, I knew. No man has ever done more than see my beauty. No man has ever . . . trusted me like you did. No man has ever . . . touched me like you did, in all ways. Trust me, it is not something I will forget, no matter what I . . . what I must do to fight, as I must fight."

He took both her hands now, pulled her closer. "Then listen to this. I can't believe that I have been given this glimpse of what should be, only to have it taken away. It's ridiculous. If the Germans couldn't kill us the other night, they are never going to. I'll go and fight my war, and you will go and fight yours, and someday, I'll find you again."

"Yes!" she cried. "Yes, you will, my love, you will. Or I'll find you!" He kissed her then, she kissed him back; it lasted a long while, a keepsake kiss. Lasted till the engine, with a great groan, shuddered to a stop. He leaned away, to look at her. "Tell me this. How can I hear about you?"

"Billy, you know I am going to be doing . . . secret work. I don't think they allow—"

"Tell me! Even if I don't see you until the Nazis are beaten, I must know you are alive at least."

"Then . . ." Ilse looked down, her forehead furrowed. Then it smoothed and she reached into her purse, pulled out a scrap of paper and a pencil. "My friend, Kirsten Larsen. This is her office number. She will stay in London. She works in Norwegian naval intelligence. She will perhaps know . . . something. A little."

"A little will be enough. Have to be enough."

"Then I will see her, tell her of you."

"Will she believe you? That I . . . I mean enough to you to . . ."

"I will make her." She laid a finger on his cheek, traced a salty trail. "But it may be years till the Germans are beaten. So we must both . . . forgive anything that the other must do. Do you understand?"

He stared back at her. "I will never love anyone like I love you."

She laughed. "You better not," she replied. "But you can love another a little perhaps. Yes, Billy Coke? Until we meet again."

He nodded. "Until we meet again. But when we do, we will never need to part."

"A deal, my keeper," she said, then leaned in and they kissed again. It went on forever, ended too soon, and she was out of the truck, up the stairs, through the door of her hostel, which closed behind her. He stared at it for a moment, then turned the key. To his surprise, the engine fired straight away.

He drove off and, just like her, didn't look back. He hurt all over . . . but he was smiling. She was on his lips, on his cheek, throughout his body. Most of all, in his memory. He would always have her there. Until he found her again.

As he would.

PART 3

ALLEGRO

ELEVEN
THE PROPELLER

Sicily. August 2, 1943

"HERE' S LOOKING AT YOU, KID."

It was Bogart who spoke. But he didn't think it was Rick shaking his arm. That guy was in Casablanca, or the Hollywood version of it anyway. They'd all watched the movie against a canvas wall two weeks earlier, on the eve of their departure from Malta. It had arrived on a British destroyer three days before that, and there had been three showings a day to packed pavilions.

In the moment he had before he was forced to surrender sleep to the arm-shaker, he looked again at who Rick had spoken the line to. It had shocked him when the character had first appeared in the film, because the women he and Rick loved had the same name. Rick's was played by a Swedish actress. A stunner, no question. Couldn't hold a candle to his own Ilse.

"Eat your heart out, Ingrid Bergman," Billy muttered.

The shaking stopped. Because he'd chosen to sleep under his plane's wing rather than in his tent, he'd used an oily rag to cover his face in a doomed attempt to keep the mosquitoes off it. This was now whipped away.

"That's right, Cokey. Ingrid's here. Now pucker up and kiss me."

Billy heard the smooches getting closer. He put a hand out, planted it in the face that approached, and shoved hard. "Get off me!"

"Aw, really?" Billy came up on an elbow and opened his eyes to see Pilot Officer Franklin "Hot Dog" Darby on his ass, grinning at him. "Come on!" the Yank continued. "Keep your eyes shut and you wouldn't know the difference between me and your sweet Martene of Malta."

Billy squinted at his wingman. "Martene didn't have a moustache."

"Buddy, pal, she kinda did."

"OK, maybe a little one," Billy conceded. He slapped the tickle at his neck. Wiped the corpse and his own blood on his shirt. Then sat fully up. Regretted it immediately. "Ouch," he said.

"You and Ingrid sink a few last night? Oh, yeah, lookee here." Franklin reached and grabbed a wine bottle from near his feet. "You didn't drink all of this by yourself, did you, Cokey?"

"No, I shared it with the local sheep, what 'ya think?"

Franklin peered at the bottle, sniffed its lip and grimaced. "You know, at least the stuff we had back at the Mess had labels."

"Sure they did. Slapped on yesterday morning by the same guy who sold me that."

"Still, you'd have had company."

"Yeah, and the Walrus glaring down his nose at me every time I opened my mouth."

"Well, you get up his. When you're drunk you spend a lot of time quoting commies."

"Anarchists. And I *do* that to get up his nose." He stared up at the bottom of his Spitfire's wing. "My school was filled with fuckers like him."

"Well, this fucker sent me to request your company at 0900. We're getting our orders."

"What orders?" Billy felt the tingle he always felt when the call to action came.

"We finally get to use the latest, uh, refinement." Franklin reached up to the wing and tapped the bomb rack.

"Fuckers," Billy muttered, about no one in particular. The Spitfire Mk VIII was one of the finest fighters in the world. Its success came from its speed and manoeuvrability. "Bomb racks? It's like strapping coal sacks on a racehorse."

"So true. But since we shot the Eyeties and the Krauts out of the sky, the generals don't need us to duel in the blue. They need us to bomb and shoot the shit out of the Nazi trenches to support our boyos going in." Franklin slid from under the wing, stood, reached a hand back. Billy took it and, ducking under the wing, rose too. "And the generals are the bosses, right, pal?"

"For now. But come the revolution . . ." Billy leaned back down and snatched up his toolkit.

Franklin eyed it. "You been tinkering again, Cokey? You know we have mechanics for that, right?"

"Sure. But I've been asking them to take a look at my intake valve for a week. Nada."

"They don't like you fucking around with the engine."

"Yeah, well, they don't have to fly her."

They began walking and soon cleared the trees. The land dropped quite steeply away from them. The airstrip was on the ridge, but the camp was near half a mile away. It kept the personnel safe from night bombing raids and artillery attacks, which had been a consideration when they'd first arrived two weeks before and the enemy front line was less than five miles away. Less so now since the German and Italian forces had been steadily squeezed back by the multi-pronged Allied invasion and advance. And as Franklin had said, the dogfights had all happened in the first ten days, when the enemy fighters had still been contesting the airspace over the island. They'd been outnumbered, and the Italian Macchis and Fiats were not as good as the Brits' and Yanks' Spits and Mustangs. That was also true of their pilots. The captured ones were young, inexperienced. The German Fockes and 'schmitts had been scarce in the air, even if their pilots were better.

Quite the reversal, Billy thought, as they cut down towards the main track to the camp to make better time. When he'd first joined 73 Squadron in Libya in April '41, they'd been the ones outnumbered— five to one— and their old Hurricane Mk IIs were easily outflown by the German aces in their 109s. Most of the guys he'd flown with then were flying the heavens now.

"Oh, you missed something else last night, buddy." They'd reached the road, and as ever Billy was struggling to keep up with the long-legged Yank. At six foot three he was really too big to be a fighter pilot, his knees near his ears in the cockpit.

"Another sermon from the Walrus? He should wear a dog collar not a silk scarf. Hey, ease up, will you?"

Franklin slowed marginally. "Nah. We had guests in the Mess. German prisoners."

"Army?"

"Luftwaffe. Reconnaissance boys. Flak got 'em over Castellana and they crashed into Lentini Lake, which as you know is more a puddle these days. We were the nearest 'drome so they were brought to us for the night." He shrugged. "Quite decent fellas, actually. The navigator, Richter, speaks pretty good English."

"Oh." Billy stepped around a pothole. This code of honour among enemies was so British. It had irked him at school, and it did so here. Didn't bother most of the squadron except him and Kowalski, a Pole who had seen what "decent fellas" had got up to in his homeland, as Billy had in Spain.

"You'll see them at breakfast, if they haven't been taken yet."

Billy grunted. He could do without it.

Attuned to his moods—he'd been Billy's wingman for a year, after all—Franklin stopped talking and increased his pace again. This time Billy just kept up, sweat starting to run. Seven a.m. and already hot as hell. The camp was soon in sight, at the top of the next hill. It was concealed in an olive grove, with further cover provided by canvas flysheets and some "drogue" netting, left behind by the fleeing enemy, in patriotic red, white and blue. In their time there, the squadron had already scrounged all the necessary accoutrements of camp life from nearby abandoned villas: chairs, tables, glasses, a collection of Italian operettas to play on the gramophone Franklin had brought from Malta on his lap, along with five vinyl 78s they'd acquired there. They ate well too. Not the food provided by the army, which consisted of small quantities of hardtack biscuits and tins of cheese, but gathered from the fields nearby: melons, tomatoes, lettuce, onions, leeks. "Fine food for fucking rabbits," Franklin, the cattle rancher's son from Texas, had complained. But they didn't go hungry, as they knew the infantry boys did, slogging their way across the Sicilian fields. And of course there was always booze—lots of local wine, stolen or traded for, with every plane arriving from Malta with a liquor bottle tucked behind the seat.

Billy made for his own tent first, threw on his jacket and his marginally cleaner spare pair of shorts. As he walked towards the Mess tent, he knotted his blue polka-dotted silk scarf around his neck.

Halfway there, he was hailed by the two rookies in the squadron — both Canucks, identical twins from the small farming town of Three Hills, Alberta: Pilot Officers Jake and Jimmy Dent. All of nineteen, still too young and stupid to be truly scared. It was the ideal age for a fighter pilot, it was said. After that, a man started to have more sense, took fewer risks. At twenty-six, Billy often felt like an old arthritic hound lying by a fire, being nipped and pawed at by two young pups.

"Sir! Sir! Look what I got from that Jerry pilot!"

Billy squinted at what the boy held. It was a bronze cross, with swords between the cross's arms. On each blade, an eagle carried a swastika in its talons. There was another larger swastika in the medal's centre. "Don't know it, Jimmy. Did he say what it was?"

"I'm Jake, sir. He's Jimmy. And no, he didn't say. Couldn't. Didn't speak no English. But I offered him a mickey of whisky for it, on accounts of we don't drink, bein' God-fearing." He gave a toothy grin. "And he took it." Jake threw the medal into the air, caught it. "You speak German, right, sir?"

"Some."

"Because I asked him to write down what it was before they left."

"They're gone?"

"Yup, Military Police took 'em away in a jeep ten minutes ago."

Good, Billy thought. Last thing he wanted was to talk with Krauts. He took the piece of paper Jimmy held out to him. Unfolded it. Read the German words.

Deutsche Spanienkreuz.

His hand began to shake. Something must also have shown on his face because the other young Canuck before him, Jimmy, said, "You alright, sir?"

Billy inhaled deeply. "Fine." He handed the paper back to Jake. "It means 'German Spanish Cross.'"

"Spanish? Why?"

"Some—" Billy cleared his throat. "Some German pilots flew for squadrons that Hitler sent to help the fascists in Spain."

"Did they? Hot damn, never knew that." The kid was turning the medal over and over. "So this was, like, an award for bravery?"

"Sure. Brave men bombing towns with no defences. Murdering civilians."

"Sir?" Both the boys looked at him, eyebrows raised, puzzled by Billy's voice, the deadness of it. By his eyes, so cold.

Franklin stepped out of the Ops tent. "We're starting, fellas."

From around the camp, the pilots were making their way over. Still puzzled, Jake slipped the medal into his breast pocket. Both twins turned and ducked under the tent flap.

Billy didn't move. He stared after the kids, not seeing them. Seeing instead another kid, his blood soaking into Spanish soil. Then he suddenly wondered if somewhere, perhaps not even far away, another pilot was telling stories in *his* Mess about his time in the Condor Legion. Showing off *his* medal for bravery.

"Erich Striegler," he murmured. Not a name he'd ever forget. Nor a face.

Franklin was in front of him. He looked as puzzled as the twins. "You OK, Cokey?"

"Fine." He rolled his shoulders. "What's going on?"

"The briefing, buddy. Let's go." He squeezed Billy's arm and went into the tent. Taking a deep, steadying breath, Billy followed.

The easel the army captain was standing in front of had their usual two maps on it—one a general one of eastern Sicily, the other an aerial map of the local area. Pinned beside these were two new photos. The officer was studying his notes. The Walrus stepped up beside him, as the men scrambled for the assortment of stolen seats: wingbacks, dining chairs, a sofa and one pew. Franklin had beaten him to the most comfortable one, known as "the throne"—a Queen Anne in plush emerald velvet—so Billy just leaned on the back. Around him, most of the flyers looked at the photos and muttered.

"Right, chaps, quiet now, pay attention." The chat ceased and the Walrus continued. "This is Captain McLune of the Royal Irish Fusiliers, liaison officer for air support. He'll explain what he requires of us today."

The captain put his notes down on the inverted wine crate in front of him. Billy reckoned him to be mid-twenties, but he looked older, with large bags under his eyes. "Good day to you, gentlemen," he said, smiling, his Irish accent soft and southern. "'Tis a pleasure as always to be addressing our brave Canadian allies. Sure, and didn't I spend a happy year studying in Montreal. Jaysus, though, I'd never been so fucking cold in my life."

The Walrus bristled, because he was a devout Christian and tried to minimize the blasphemy and swearing in his squadron—which was a little like trying to contain a fire with a squirt gun. Billy, like the rest, laughed, looking around. 92 *was* a Canadian squadron, and each man wore the Canada shoulder patch, but like in every squadron he'd ever flown with, RAF or RCAF, the pilots were a mix of nationalities. There was Franklin the Yank, Kowalski the Pole, plus two Aussies, a

South African, a Rhodesian, a Czech, a Dane. The Walrus was a Brit, as was Flight Sergeant Carrington-Jones. Which left the Brothers Dent from the Prairies, and Billy, born in British Columbia, as the only Canucks.

McLune continued. "As you will have guessed from the bombs being fitted to your planes, this is a Rhubarb. A low-level attack. And my boys on the ground will be delighted to know such an illustrious outfit as 92 will be clearing a path for them and keeping the Kraut faces in the dirt as they advance"—he picked up a baton—"here."

He tapped the blown-up photograph. Whispers ran through the group. "Yes, I know you all know it. Hard to miss, eh?"

Centuripe, thought Billy. It was about twenty-five miles north of them, and indeed was impossible to miss. Spread out over the hills in four directions, it resembled a man lying down with arms and legs outstretched. As drawn by someone like Matisse, Billy had always thought. If ever a pilot was lost in this part of the world, which happened far too often, a glimpse of Centuripe would orient them easily.

"Yup, Centuripe—and the key to the enemy's whole defensive line." On the main map, McLune ran the tip of his baton from the northern coast down. "Break them here, and the line folds. So today, my comrades in the London Irish have been ordered to take the three hills above the right arm, which will make the taking of the town itself much easier. Your mission is to fly in following the artillery bombardment, drop your loads on the hill we call Point 704, then strafe it, return to base for more bombs—"

"Sir! Excuse the interruption." Franklin had his arm raised. "Which is the right arm, and which is the left?"

McLune squinted at him. "What do you mean?" He tapped the map. "This is the right. That's obvious, isn't it?"

"Not really. Who says the guy is lying face up?"

"Who says it's a guy?" It was an Aussie voice that chipped in, Flight Sergeant "Chips" Woods. "That's my girlfriend you're talking about, mate! Look at those spread legs!"

More harrumphing from the Walrus, more laughter, McLune joining in. "OK," he said, "let's call her Sofia. And she's lying face up. Waiting for you, mate." The laughter rose, then subsided as he continued. "So you bomb this hill, Point 704, at noon plus fifteen. Strafe, then back to base, re-arm and, if all goes well and we have 704, we'll send you a signal to bomb the second hill, Point 703, here." He tapped. "More of the same, and if that goes well, we might need you a third time, for the third hill, 611." He tapped again, put down his notes, took the baton in both hands. "Questions?"

Arms went up. He pointed at Kowalski.

"Please, sir, is there ack-ack?"

"Not much, we think. A battery at the very pinnacle of the town, beside the church. It's so high up you can probably fly beneath it—but I'm not a pilot, so . . . your call." He pointed at Chips. "Yes?"

"Will they not have fighter cover? Our Spits are kinda hamstrung in a dogfight carrying those bombs."

"Again, we doubt it." McLune reached up and scratched his head under his cap. "They gave up all their bases when we bombed the crap out of them, and they had nowhere to land. They must fly out from the mainland, so they need a lot of warning. Besides, we're launching diversionary bomber raids on Adrano and Catania to make 'em think we're going there first. If they scramble fighters, we're sure that's where they'll send them."

He nodded, definitively, while Billy shook his head. HQ was always so *sure*. But they weren't the ones being bounced by Messerschmitts or Fockes out of a sky that was meant to be clear of them. It had happened time and again in North Africa, over Malta.

The key questions had been asked. The other arms dropped. McClune nodded, picked up his notes and shoved them into his breast pocket. "I'll leave you gentlemen to discuss the details of how you do all this. Flying is a foreign country to me. I get nauseous standing on a chair." He grinned, saluted. "Good hunting, chaps."

The Irishman marched out of the tent to a waiting jeep, which revved and took off. The Walrus pulled another easel forward, with a blackboard on it. There, on the fixed grid, their flights were chalked in white. The twelve planes were in groups of four. Three sections. Billy was relieved to see two things—the Walrus wasn't leading, wasn't even flying. His plane had a damaged undercarriage from a prang in their move to Lentini which was beyond the skills of the ground crew to patch up. They were waiting for parts from Malta. He could have pulled rank, taken one of the younger pilots' planes. But he'd torn knee ligaments in that same prang, and they had not yet healed. Or so he said. Billy was a little surprised to see that he wasn't in command. Kowalski was, his designation "Top Hat." Then Billy saw why. In his section were chalked the names Darby, Dent and Dent.

He was "Bowler"—and he was to mind the children. It made sense. The Alberta boys had been in one brief dogfight and had never bombed and strafed in anger, only in practice. Franklin had, but he would be the "Arse-End Charlie," also known as "the weaver," because he would weave about three thousand feet above his comrades, keeping an eye out for "bandits." You needed an experienced pilot to do it because, of course, no one wove above the weaver.

As they left the tent and walked to the truck waiting to take them to the strip, the sound of needle on vinyl came. The Dents had been assigned the role of music officer between them. They'd chosen Glenn Miller's "American Patrol" a few weeks before in Malta, and it had become the favourite song of the squadron for takeoff. When they returned, whoever got back first played Miller's older hit, "I'm Thrilled." It was only 0930 and takeoff was noon, but pilots were happier waiting with their crates. They clambered into a truck, which bounced them up to the ridge. There they settled into the olive grove beside the strip. The Dent boys found some branches and a stone, and went off to play a game that kind of resembled hockey, but on dirt not ice. Billy lay down again under his Spit's wing. As he closed his eyes, he thought about her, as he usually did before sleep.

Ilse.

He opened them when a hand shook his arm. "Cokey," said

Franklin, handing him a cup of tea. "Quarter of noon. Waiting for the call."

Kowalski gathered them at the edge of the grove. Beyond the tree-line, on the edge of the escarpment, the ack-ack gunners were checking their 3.7-inch AAs. Behind him, ground crew were swarming over the Spits, doing last-minute checks. Billy watched Flight Sergeant Jenkins bend under the open canopy of his engine. By the way his back stiffened, he'd obviously seen what Billy had done to the carburetor intake the crew had failed to fix. He frowned at Billy, dropped the canopy, climbed down. The Pole's instructions were succinct, expressed as usual in his idiosyncratic English. Assemble at ten thousand feet. Radio silence till target. Three waves going in, on his call.

When they broke, each man went to an olive tree and pissed.

As Billy was buttoning himself up, the phone rang. Kowalski himself picked it up. Listened, said, "Right," then hung up. "Scramble," he called. This wasn't the mad sprint of Libya, Egypt or Malta. The enemy wasn't coming in force and fast. The pilots walked to their planes.

Corporal Dunald was waiting with Billy's gear. "All tickety-boo with the bird, Corporal?"

Dunald was a scrappy little tyke from London's East End. He was incapable of speaking a sentence without saying "fuck." He'd been a good amateur bantamweight boxer and Coke had once seen him fell a giant American paratrooper in a bar in Valletta with a single punch.

"Tickety-fucking-boo alright, sir. Fucking gremlins came in the night and fixed your intake. Jenkins is fucking furious. Nearly 'ad a stroke." He grinned. "Fucking love to see that!"

"You'll probably see more of it before this war is over."

"Fucking great." He handed Billy his gear—jacket, helmet, goggles, Mae West, parachute pack, gauntlets. He put them on, one by one, then pulled himself onto the left wing and over the folded-down door.

Dunald folded it up. "Good hunting, sir. Fuck those fucks, eh?"

"I'll certainly fucking try, Dunald."

The corporal jumped down. Billy lowered his seat—Jenkins had probably raised it as petty revenge. When he could squint through the gunsight, he stopped, settled back. Billy wouldn't close the canopy till takeoff, it was too hot and his jacket was fleece-lined. Hell on the ground in a Sicilian summer. Heaven at ten thousand feet in an unpressurized cabin.

Up ahead he heard the firing of the first cartridge in Kowalski's Spit, followed by those in his section. Blue smoke blew and propellers turned. He looked at his watch. Bang on noon. He'd wait till the fourth plane in Top Hat section started taxiing before firing his own. Spits would overheat if they idled on the ground too long.

It didn't take long. As the South African, de Klerk, moved off, Billy thrust his arm up, circled his hand, hit the starter button, and pulled his canopy closed.

He and his flight were airborne moments later.

They assembled at ten thousand feet, over the sea to the west, then flew back, passing over the airstrip and the Lago di Lentini as they went. Top Hat section under Kowalski took the lead, three planes flying in a line with three hundred feet between their wingtips, and their weaver, de Klerk, a thousand feet above. Billy put himself and the two Dents of his section—Bowler—one thousand feet behind Top Hat, with Franklin weaving above. By the time Trilby section, with Mikos as leader, tucked in behind, the squadron was in formation.

It took them just five minutes to reach Centuripe. And there he— or she, if Chips had his way—was. A human figure anyway, arms and legs splayed, stretched out over the hills. Billy could see the enemy's defensive lines around most of the town. Could also see to the northeast, the three hills that were their objective that day. Marked clearly because of the smoke rising from them, the twenty-five-pounders of the British artillery having done the first of the bombardments that the RCAF were to conclude.

Way over to his left, and at least five hundred feet below, Billy saw a flash, followed by a mushrooming black cloud. McLune had warned about a battery of 88s at the highest point in the town. The odds of them hitting fast-moving fighters at ten thousand feet were small but grew with every thousand feet they dropped. The Irishman had been right though—they could fly below the guns, which could not angle down. Would need to anyway, to accurately drop their loads.

At last Kowalski broke radio silence. "Top Hat to Bowler and Trilby. Receiving?"

Billy had kept his mask off. He didn't need oxygen at ten thousand and below. But now he needed the radio. As he slipped it on, he spoke. "Bowler to Top Hat. Receiving."

His earphones crackled as Mikos spoke. "Trilby to Top Hat. Receiving."

There was just static, and then the Pole spoke again. "Follow me in, boys, in sections. Tally ho. Tally ho. Out."

Immediately Kowalski, followed by his whole section, peeled hard to the left, lowered his nose and began a steep dive. He was as experienced as Billy at this type of mission—had busted tanks in Hurribombers all over North Africa.

Thrusting the stick forward with his right hand, Billy pushed the throttle with his left, gaining speed, feet working the rudder and ailerons. The Spit responded as superbly as ever. He went into the same sharp dive as Kowalski; sensed, rather than saw, his section follow. Franklin had cozied up, become the fourth finger. He was a weaver no more. For now, they were all bombers.

Some more flak burst ahead of them, a little closer, still not enough to worry. And then his altimeter told him he was low, one thousand feet up, and so he began to flatten the dive, pulling back on his stick and his throttle, levelling, slowing. He dropped it to 250 miles per hour. Any faster and he'd overshoot the hill.

Out of the corner of his eye, another Spit appeared, overtaking him. "Bowler One to Bowler Two. Slow the fuck down! On my tail. Out."

He heard a faint, crackled "Oops" and Jimmy Dent eased back. Billy again turned his attention forward.

Ahead of him, Kowalski was approaching the hill, his section now in a line behind him. There were some black puffs from flak above them— the 88s on the hill couldn't swivel down far enough, not to six hundred feet. Which was the height from which the Pole released his three bombs. "Bombs away!" he shouted as he went into a steep, fast climb. "Bombs away" came three more cries, and then his section followed him out.

Billy wasn't watching. In ten seconds he was nearly at the target. He heard a few strikes like hailstones against the base of his plane. Germans shooting at his belly with small arms. As much chance of piercing his armour as a pebble thrown at a barn wall.

Target below. He glanced down, pulled the bomb lever. "Bombs away," he called, accelerating up and away like those before him who he now saw climbing into the sun.

The calls came, again and again, in staccato static: "Bombs away." Three times. His boys had done the business. Four more calls came from Trilby, while Billy was climbing high. Again, a few puffballs exploded. Again, not even close.

Banking, Billy levelled at five thousand feet and followed Kowalski out to the north.

They made their turn. The second run would be different. Strafing always was. Required more flying. He was never sure of the effect of it. Perhaps psychological, not physical, because the Germans would be in slit trenches with one helmet on their heads and a second on their ass. No one would be stupid enough to be on open ground.

He saw it then, a flash of it anyway—a football field, bullets ripping up the ground like stitches from some giant sewing machine. A boy's body torn apart.

He shook his head, thought of two other boys, not too much older than Andoni had been. He pressed his radio button.

"Bowler One to Bowlers Two and Three. Over."

The brothers came on simultaneously, their words jumbled.

"Shut up, Bowlers Two, Three, and listen up. Remember how I trained you. Thirty-degree dive, strafe at one thousand feet, two seconds on the teat, get out. Got it, Bowler Two?"

"Got it, Bowler One. Bowler Two out."

"Bowler Three?"

"Got it, Bowler One. Bowler Three out."

He'd tried to train them at strafing when they'd first joined the squadron as replacements in Malta. But it was a skill rarely used, and there were other survival skills that had been more immediately necessary. Dogfighting ones.

Billy dropped his plane down, down, following Top Hat. Then, half a mile out, he put his crate into a steep, fast climb. At one thousand feet he spun it over, flying on his back, looped, dived faster. Steeper than he'd advised the twins, fifteen degrees, because he knew what he was doing, had done it so often. Would fly lower before he fired for the same reason.

The shriek of the air rushing past him, the G-force building, at five hundred feet and with trench lines in his sight he squeezed the teat, felt the shudder as his Hispano 20mm spat cannonballs into the earth. A two-second burst then he pulled the stick back hard at four hundred feet, slamming the throttle forward. The positive Gs hit him hard and fast as always, squished him down into his seat as his vision tunnelled, and he felt like someone had dumped a sack of coal on his shoulders. It eased as he climbed, levelling again at two thousand feet.

The scream was very loud, very short. He looked in his mirror, couldn't see anything. He waggled his wings, looked down each side, still saw nothing. "Bowler One to section. Bowler One to section. Report."

It took a moment. Then Franklin spoke. "Bowler Two is down, Cokey. Repeat, Bowler Two is down."

Before Billy could reply, another voice cut in. "Jimmy? Where are you, Jimmy? I can't see you! Jimmy?"

Billy knew what had happened—what he'd always feared might happen. The other brother had dived too steep, or gone too low, pulled out too slow. At that height off the ground, there would have been only one result. Nothing that a twin brother needed to hear right then.

"Bowler Three, this is Bowler One. I have a visual on him. Plane ditched but in a field. He'll be OK. Return to base."

The radio crackled again. "But I should go see. See he's OK."

"Negative, Bowler Three. Obey orders, into the finger. On my starboard wing. Return to base. Understood? Over."

The voice came on a small sob, a single word. "Understood."

Fuck, fuck, fuck, Billy thought, as he watched the surviving Dent line up three hundred feet away on his wingtip. He'd known he'd needed more time with them. He'd known it. But he couldn't mourn him now. He'd ground the surviving brother at Lentini—he'd flown his last mission. The Dent family of Three Hills, Alberta, would not lose their last son. Air force rules.

Once more the radio sounded. The words loud. "Bandits!" yelled Franklin. "Bandits, one o'clock."

Billy craned his neck, looked up. Sun flashed in his eye; blinded, he looked away, blinked at his panel. He'd levelled at two thousand feet. The bandits would already be doing what he'd be doing in their place: diving down on them out of the sun.

They'd been bounced.

A voice on the radio, the accent Polish. "Top Hat leader to all sections. We're coming back for you. Break! Break!"

Billy was already breaking as the words came. The bandits would be with them in seconds. He was too close to the ground to dive. And if the bandits were Messerschmitt 109s they were better divers than Spits anyway. He had to get up, up and away.

He pulled his stick sharply towards him, used hard left aileron. He banked, climbed, presenting a side-on silhouette to the enemy dropping on him from above. Not a second too soon.

He saw the tracer bullets thrum perhaps an arm's length over his port wing, before he shot past the enemy, going down as he went up. It was less than a second's glimpse, but he could have sworn the pilot was waving. The glimpse showed him one other thing—a white cross on the tail-fin. A Macchi 205. At least some of the bandits were Italian.

There was a myth—a series of jokes about the prowess and courage of Italian flyers. In countless duels, from his early days in Spain, through North Africa and over Malta, Billy had never found them lacking much of either. And here they were, defending their homeland. He knew how he'd have felt, over Kent, over British Columbia.

His climb was steep, deliberately so. But he could only hold it so long. As soon as he felt his stick start to loosen, the slide of the seat of his pants sideways, he knew he was in danger of a stall. He levelled and swivelled his head so fast he nearly gave himself whiplash; looked ahead, to each side, above, below. There! Below, planes all over the sky. At least twenty, theirs and ours, impossible to tell which, he thought. He checked his altimeter. He was now the one at five thousand feet. With one last glance above into the empty sky, Billy put his plane into a shallow dive. There were birds everywhere, firing, avoiding fire, tracer flying through the air like coils of white rope. Billy saw the white fin-cross of a Macchi ahead as it banked to chase a weaving Spit—Billy didn't know whose. The Italian was intent on his pursuit, weaving as well, firing short bursts from his machine guns, the only weapons the Macchi had. Deadly—but not as deadly as Billy's 20mm cannon.

He followed him. At four thousand feet, flying a little to port so that his comrade being chased was well out of his shot, he brought the Italian plane into the left quadrant of his gunsight. It was a mix of geometry and guesswork now. Deflection, speed, angle, and as much pure instinct as anything else. As ever for him, everything slowed. He didn't seem to be flying the plane anymore, it was flying itself, like he'd let go of the reins of a horse, the beast knowing where it had to go and how to get there. When he had no time, he seemed to have so much. Breathing out, banking ever so slightly, Billy squeezed the teat.

A three-second burst. He saw the cannonballs strike into the side of the engine. Immediate white smoke. A sure sign that the glycol feed was punctured, the coolant spraying into the cool air and back onto the cockpit, covering it in green liquid, blinding the pilot. With fortune, it was all the damage necessary. The Macchi dropped, heading towards the ground in spirals, wings going over and over. Billy followed him but didn't plan on firing again unless somehow the guy cleared the glycol and went back into the attack. The Eyetie was finished, Billy was pretty certain. But he owed it to his comrades to make sure.

He passed within four hundred feet of the Spit he'd saved, which was now pulling out of its escaping dive. He saw the number and knew who it was. Jake Dent. The boy gave him a thank-you wave. Billy knew his name now only because the other brother, Jimmy, was dead. He waved back.

Something flashed past him, passing within twelve feet. A canopy, he realized, only because he looked ahead again and saw that the Italian he'd hit had levelled his plane and was now climbing out onto its wing. He clutched the cockpit sill with one hand, looked at Billy, waved with the other—and hurled himself into the air. Glancing back, Billy saw the white mushroom unfold. He nodded, pleased. When they were in their birds, gunning for his comrades, it was his duty to take the enemy out. Yet if he knew the pilot had survived, Billy was happy. He may not have cared to talk with the enemy in a Mess, but he was always glad to know he hadn't killed anyone else.

He'd followed him down. The kid had a long way to fall. But Billy needed to go the opposite way, because a quick glimpse showed him that the dogfight was taking place perhaps two thousand feet above him. He did a half-roll and, pulling the stick back, began to climb.

He was halfway there when he saw the black crosses on the underside of wings.

Krauts. Krauts flying Messerschmitt 109s. Billy smiled. Hunting Germans always made him smile.

The smile went when his radio burst into life with a shout. An American shout.

"Two 109s on your tail, Cokey. Get out of there!" yelled Franklin.

Goofballs, as they called the cannon shells, passing him on both sides, over both wings, confirmed the warning.

His mirror showed them straddling him. A bank and roll, another steep dive, might lose one, but not two. What he needed was speed. Reaching, Billy flicked the switch of the supercharger. His bird surged forward, the Messerschmitts receding into specks in his mirror.

The mechanic in him had been fascinated by the development, the 100-octane fuel from the U.S. allowing for the amazing boost. Now it had saved his life.

For now. He couldn't run on it for long. The negative Gs made his eyes bulge, the controls worked less well, there was a danger that any manoeuvre at this speed would cause him to black out. Just long enough to outdistance the foe, switch off, climb, then drop on them again like vengeance from on high.

He flicked the switch. The pain in his head eased, the roar of the engine lowered, the sound of wind whistling through the Perspex returned. He checked the mirror, saw the specks growing larger again. They'd sped up to try to keep up, but 109s didn't have a super-charger. Time for the climb . . .

The one place he hadn't checked was ahead. Something made him now.

A veteran in his first squadron—he could see his face, couldn't remember his name, so long dead Billy had forgotten it—had told him once, when he'd been a rookie, that you could see the bullet that was meant for you. He hadn't believed him. But he did now, because he saw the goofball coming for him, like a giant snowflake floating into the windscreen of a car in a winter storm. Beyond it, the black shape of a 109.

He fired as well on instinct, even as the cannon shell punched a neat hole in his canopy and exploded just above his left hip. Metal entered him like a dozen red-hot pokers into his flesh. But he had other things to consider than pain—another goofball must have pierced his engine, punctured his coolant line, because now there was blue-dyed glycol pouring in through the neat starburst hole before him, ribbons of it slapping his face, covering his goggles, blinding him instantly. He whipped his goggles off, stripped off a gauntlet, shoved it into the hole in front of him. It blocked the flow, enough to let him wipe the stinging coolant from his eyes.

A shape passed above him, the guy who'd shot him. He'd turn, come in again, join his two Kameraden in the kill. But not today. Instinct again—Billy banked and put his bird into a steep dive. He didn't know how much power he had, or how long it would last. As long as the glycol probably. When that was gone, the engine would overheat fast, and instinct wouldn't matter anymore.

He knew what the Huns would be doing. Laughing. A 109 was smoother and faster in a dive than a Spit. They'd assume he was a scared rookie, knowing no better, just wanting to get away. He let them laugh, let them think that. All his gauges were busted now but he counted the seconds, guessed the speed—at what he thought was about one thousand feet he made a sharp port turn, played the ailerons, pulled the beer tap way back, hit the throttle and soared back up the way he'd come.

If his eyes weren't still slick with coolant, he might have been able to see the Germans, passing close, no longer laughing as they tried to turn and follow him up. He heard that same dead veteran—Wilfridson, that was his name; a Brit who, like Billy, had been an actor—declare, "They may beat us in a dive, old boy—but we thumb our noses at them in a turn-and-climb."

Billy couldn't thumb his nose. He wasn't even sure he could raise an arm. But he could get the fuck out of there before his engine quit. The glycol was no longer pouring onto his windshield, which might be good or bad. Perhaps it was all gone. Perhaps it had suddenly healed its own tear. Miracles happened. He didn't know a pilot who didn't believe in miracles, who didn't pray for them. There were no atheists in a cockpit. He levelled. And then something came at him again, as fast and as slow as the goofball had before, like that snowflake in that storm on that windshield. Also white, but bigger, much, much bigger. Slow enough that he saw a boy's face, dark against the whiteness of his spread para- chute. Close enough that he could see the eyes widen in terror . . . the moment before he hit Billy's propeller and it tore him to pieces.

It had to be part of the body that smashed into the windshield, the bang loud, even louder than Billy's scream, and red shot through the blue in liquid streaks. Yelping, Billy spun the bird onto its back, dove again. The 109s would have followed him up and might follow him down again but he had no choice. The engine was shutting down, he could hear it in its stutter, in the way his stick, his rudder, his ailerons were getting more and more sluggish. He had to land and land fast. He couldn't bail out, couldn't raise his right arm above his head, so couldn't pull back the canopy. He would have to crash-land and get low enough, fast enough, to choose a suitable field before he lost all power; low enough to be able to glide.

He tipped a wing and saw it: water. At first, he thought the fight must have taken him some way out over the sea. But then he saw land, a headland. It looked kind of like a man diving into the blue. Recognized it.

He was about a thousand feet above the Lago di Lentini.

He swung southeast, dropped, though he wasn't sure if he was dropping the plane so much as it was doing that all by itself. As he hit what he thought had to be about five hundred feet, he looked down and ahead to the airdrome on the ridge, and saw the goofballs passing him again, on either side.

His rudder wouldn't swing him, his ailerons were shot, he

couldn't turn, climb, weave. Could only go on dropping into his glide. He felt his tail struck again, saw metal ripped up in jagged spires on his wings. But the runway was dead ahead and he was heading into the wind— always better for a landing. He lowered his wheels, thanked God that they weren't jammed, pulled back a little on the stick. As he flew over the ack-ack battery he could hear it open up. The goofballs immediately ceased passing him. The two Huns had to know he was done. No doubt they were soaring high into the air now, weaving to avoid the flak that chased them away.

He was perhaps thirty feet up on the edge of the runway, gliding now, the engine giving its final coughs. Still, he closed off the throttle, moved the stick gently back, breaking the glide.

The engine died the moment before his wheels touched the ground. It didn't matter, he had enough power left to coast the length of the runway and bring the bird to a gentle halt, just beside another plane that must have landed before him. Through the cracked windshield, the red and blue and black streaks that covered it, he saw the pilot slumped on the ground beneath his wing. His face was in his hands, his shoulders were shaking, he was weeping. It was Jake Dent. Billy knew that he should go to him, comfort him. But when he tried to raise his arms to unbuckle his safety harness they simply wouldn't cooperate. He could move his head, that was something, and he turned it now to see ground crew running towards him; felt the thump as some scrambled up onto his port wing; heard the fire extinguisher spraying into his engine, the hiss of steam; heard grunts as someone tried to open his canopy; understood that it was stuck, which would have screwed things up, parachute-wise, had he even had that option.

"Look away, sir. Look away now." It was Corporal Dunald who was commanding him. Billy obeyed, looking down. Though he couldn't see so much now, because everything was growing ever darker, he could see his flying jacket, his trousers, see that both were soaked in blue and red, like his windshield. And seeing the blood reminded him of the goofball he'd seen coming at him like a snowflake, and the Italian pilot's face, and he suddenly felt pain, pain like he'd never felt before, everywhere, all at once, and as the windshield fell in, smashed in with crowbars, as chunks of Perspex tumbled onto him, the darkness came for him and took him totally. Though just before it did, he heard it: Dunald's favourite word, spoken in horror, in awe.

"Fuck," the corporal said, as Billy went away.

EMERGING from a morphine haze was rarely pleasant. It usually meant that the drug had worn off. So waking meant pain, one that would grow and grow, with no guarantee that it would end anytime soon, because the nurses were overworked since the last big push had happened. Billy, in his twice-daily shuffle to the latrines, had seen how the rows of beds went on and on into the distance, under the spread tarpaulins of the field hospital. Waking also meant the return of the cacophony, the babel of voices, rising up, crying out, as his had risen and cried so many times in the last two weeks. English in all its varieties, regional, colonial; French, Czech, Polish, Danish, Afrikaans, Urdu and Hindi. And those were just the Allies. German voices called out too, Italian. The enemies were equal here. Equally agonized, equally demanding, more or less equally treated. All ranks as well. Billy had always felt himself a member of the proletariat, a worker with brothers in whatever country they were from. But he knew that, when he'd first come in and the pain was at its worst, he had invoked the Coke name and its ancient, noble privileges. Now he was relieved that it had gained him no favours, that no one around him seemed to recall his bleating. Back then, though, he would have given up world revolution for an extra vial of sweet surcease.

Yet he realized that it wasn't the diminishing drug that had woken him. He could feel, or rather couldn't feel, the parts of himself that would have woken him had they been in pain. His left hip and thigh, which both still had metal buried deep within them. His left arm, broken at both wrist and elbow by God knows what flying pieces of steel. The feeling that every muscle in his back had been twisted hard and suddenly against the grain. None of that hurt so much, for now. What had woken him was the voice. Not a scream in a foreign language. A whisper in his own. "Cokey," the voice said. "Wake up, pal, will ya? Just for a second? We've come to say cheer ho."

Cheer ho. Au revoir. No one said goodbye. It was too final. Why was Hot Dog Darby saying cheer ho? Was he off on a Ramrod? Another Rhubarb? Had Billy missed the briefing? Well, he'd catch the boys when they got back. This snooze was too peaceful to give up just yet.

"Nurse?" he heard Franklin say. "Any chance you could rouse him? Just for a minute?"

"Certainly not!" It was Staff Nurse Winley, a big denier of immediate relief, who spoke. "We don't wake patients unless absolutely necessary. Wake up, they make demands. We're quite busy enough, thank you." She must have walked away because her last words faded. "Let him sleep."

"Never mind, sir. Let 'im fuckin' sleep." It was Dunald who spoke now. "I'm glad he can. Never thought he'd wake up again, to be honest, when we pulled him from his fuckin' Spit. Never seen one so shot up, and I've seen a few. Talk about a wing and a fuckin' prayer."

"Come on, Hot Dog, truck's waiting." A different voice again, Aussie. Chips Woods. "We'll leave him a note and hoist a pint for him back in Valletta."

"Well, shee-it. OK, yeah. Anyone got a pen?"

"In my pack, under the cot," Billy said, and opened his eyes.

"Cokey!"

Aside from the three who'd spoken there were several others also there—Kowalski, Carrington-Jones, Flight Sergeant Jenkins. The one that surprised him most was Jake Dent, his red hair a pyramid atop his head, his flying cap skewed across it. The sight of him made Coke frown. He wondered why he was still there. He shouldn't be flying again, not as the only remaining son of the Dents of Three Hills,

Alberta. But he was finding it hard to put that thought into words. Besides, Hot Dog was babbling.

"Buddy, so pleased you woke up. We're out of here today. Heading back to Malta."

"Malta?" It didn't make sense. "Did we lose the battle of Sicily?"

"Hell no, sir." It was Jake who spoke now. "That finished two weeks ago. We're just about to invade Italy, and—"

The others hushed him, looked around. There were plenty of enemy prisoners lying on cots nearby. They may not have been going anywhere, but you never knew in war.

"So we won? Here?"

Kowalski nodded. "Those Irish boys took Centuripe in two days. The Krauts tried to hold on around Mount Etna, but then gave it up and evacuated to mainland Italy." He frowned. "Too many of the fuckers got away."

"So if," Billy lowered his voice to a whisper and the men leaned in, "Italy is next, how come you're going back to Malta? Wrong way, isn't it?"

"Repairs, sir." Jenkins joined in. "And some rest. Plenty of new squadrons coming in. Flying the new Mk IX. We'll retrain on that, then get back out there."

"A new Spit, Billy." Franklin's eyes gleamed. "If it's an improvement on the VIII, imagine what it can do!" He grinned. "We'll keep your seat warm for you."

Billy asked the question he needed to ask. "How many got back from the bounce at Centuripe?"

They all looked at each other. "All of us," replied Kowalski. "All except . . ." He reached to tousle the red hair of Jake Dent, knocking off his cap.

Billy felt exhilaration and terrible sadness at the same time. "Why is he here?" he said, forcing himself to sit up, staring angrily at Jake. "His brother's dead, right? He should be on his way home, to the farm, to the fucking farm."

"I ain't going," replied Jake softly. "Why should I? My brother's alive, you said. You said you saw him crash-land." His jaw set. "He's a prisoner, and I'm staying. I'm staying till he's free."

Billy looked at Franklin, who shrugged. He knew the truth. Everyone there knew it. But they'd decided to keep Jake anyway and fuck the rules. Sometimes it happened; a kid became like a mascot. They'd keep him, and tousle his hair, like you'd kiss a rabbit's foot for luck.

Billy sighed. He wasn't strong enough to argue. Besides, something puzzled him. "How did we all get back? They bounced us, they were good flyers. 109s and Macchis. How?"

"You, Billy. You distracted them."

Billy frowned. He shook his head. It hurt. Now he knew the morphine in his bloodstream was running low. "What do you mean?" he said, falling back onto the pillow. "So two 109s followed me away. That's not many. The rest—"

"Four. Four 109s."

"What?"

"It was four, sir." It was Dunald who took up the tale from Franklin. "Fuckers were chasing you from the lake. Fired so many fucking shots we thought you was a goner. Your plane—" He broke off, shook his head.

"Why'd they follow me?" Billy started to laugh, which also hurt, but he kept going anyway. "What had I ever done to them?"

"You shot down their leader."

"I got a Macchi. One Italian."

"I saw that. It's confirmed. But the guy who got you?" Franklin grinned wide. "You got him too."

"How?" Billy closed his eyes. Everything in the last weeks was a morphine muddle. He remembered seeing the goofball bound for him, the one that had caused him all this damage. But had he fired at the same time? He couldn't remember.

"Don't know how, pal. But he went down, and the rest went apeshit. The Germans, anyway." Hot Dog shifted his gum to the other corner of his mouth, crouched, resting his palms on the bed.

"Some Sappers found his body. Major Ernst Schimmel. Battle of Britain, Tobruk. Thirty-five kills. He was some kind of Nazi hero." He laughed. "When you headed for Lentini, all the Krauts followed you. Eyeties headed for home when the Germans left. We met them coming back, and Jake here"—he reached out and again pulled at the thick thatch of hair—"got one of them. His first." He grinned. "See why we can't let him go?"

From somewhere in the distance, a truck's horn sounded, playing a rough approximation of the start of Glenn Miller's "American Patrol."

"Sir," said Jenkins, "we do 'ave to go."

"Sure thing. Can't keep the new Squadron Bleeder waiting."

"New CO?"

"Yup. The Walrus has been kicked upstairs, thank God. Got a new guy and, guess what? This one's even a Canuck." He smiled. "So between you, Jake and him—hell, we might even properly qualify as RCAF!" He rose from his crouch. "See you, buddy."

Billy was starting to hurt again. Others were murmuring their farewells too but he didn't want to show them his pain as their last look at him, so he took a deep breath. "See you boys in Valletta. First round at Ciappara's is on me."

Franklin frowned. "Pal, didn't they tell you? You bought a Blighty ticket. The surgeons here have done all they can. We were told you need a specialist." He reached down and touched Billy's shoulder. "You give my love to Piccadilly Circus, and I'll give your love to, what was her name? Martene, eh? Oh, and before I forget." He reached into his breast pocket and pulled out a battered playing card. "Those two confirmed over Centuripe mean that you've overtaken Kowalski again. That's twelve kills, pal. Get back to us fast so no one overtakes you, eh?" When Billy just stared at the card, didn't take it, Franklin laid it face up on his chest. Then he stood up straight and saluted. All the men followed suit, then, as one, they turned and left the tent.

Billy squinted down at the card, black and stark against the white sheet. It was the Ace of Spades. A death card. He'd have liked to have flicked it off. But he knew that as soon as he moved the pain would double. So he closed his eyes—but opened them again fast. Because a face had appeared, dark against an expanse of white silk. A face he'd seen for less than a second.

Billy began to cry.

TWELVE
ALLIES

Oslo. December 21, 1943

KLAUS STOPPED SUDDENLY JUST inside the exit of
Majorstuen station. Other passengers jostled him, some cursed him,
until they noticed the peaked Luftwaffe cap, with its eagle carrying a
swastika. Then they lowered their eyes, moved past, no doubt still
muttering, some likely even expanding their insults. He didn't care.
In his three months in the country, he'd learned not to. It had
annoyed Klaus when he'd learned that insolence towards the occupation was proscribed and penalized by the occupiers. It made them
look petty. "You will smile at us, you will not leave your seat if we sit
near you, you will . . ." He was sure that if a Norwegian officer stood
at a U-Bahn exit in Berlin blocking the way, he'd have insulted
him too.

It was the snow that had halted him. He was unprepared for its
sudden ferocity. When he'd looked out of his office window at Klingenberggata, there had been only a few flakes drifting down. When
he'd realized the time, how late he was, he'd rushed out, forgetting to

grab his scarf, his single glove, from the radiator where they'd been drying. Then he'd been in the tunnel from the National Theatre station to Majorstuen. Only here, now, staring at the huge snowflakes falling so fast they dazed him, did he realize the error he'd made.

He stepped through the entrance and fumbled with the top button of his greatcoat. Though he'd had the slits widened to accommodate his disability, it was still a struggle, made worse by the wind that accompanied the snow, blowing it almost parallel to the ground. He closed his eyes, finally got the horn button through. Pulling the peak of his cap down, he shrugged into the storm; took it carefully, aware of the peril of the packed snow and old ice under the new slick fall. When he eventually reached the third crossroads, at which Fru Boren said the church would stand, he stopped.

He'd met her the week before at a cocktail party she'd hosted for her organization—the women's wing of the NS, the Nasjonal Samling, the Norwegian Nazi Party. She was quite high up in it, responsible for many of its cultural activities. Once she'd learned of his passion for music, she'd invited him to this event.

What she had failed to do was tell him which way to go from the junction. Cursing, he thought about why he was late to begin with— the report that had come just as he'd been about to leave. The good Fru had boasted that "her" concert would offer some of the finest professional players in Oslo. Now he'd missed at least half of it; all because the agent he'd managed to smuggle into England with a party of Norwegian refugees had obviously been captured. He was almost certainly already dead, executed by the British. But the dead man kept sending messages, albeit without the requisite confirmation code. Klaus had lost two hours, absorbed in trying to figure out what his rival spy agency, SOE, wanted him to think and why.

Turning back and forth, unsure which way to go, suddenly he heard a flute. He followed the sound, stumbled off a curbstone, crossed the street. There was darkness ahead but his feet found steps leading up to a tall wooden door, ajar. The flute was much clearer here, and louder still when he stepped into the lobby.

"Major von Ronnenberg! You made it!"

The voice, just above a whisper, was Fru Boren's.

"Let me help you, Major." Fru Boren was a forceful woman of considerable size, a head taller than Klaus, so he was unable to prevent her unbuttoning his coat then whipping it off him. He managed to take off his own cap, which she seized, placing it on a hook above his greatcoat. Her only hesitation came when she was trying to decide whether to fill his one hand with a program or a glass of aquavit. Happily for Klaus she decided on the latter, and he gratefully sipped the caraway- flavoured Norwegian liquor he'd already developed a taste for. He felt instantly warmer.

"You have missed so much marvellous music, Herr Major," she reprimanded him. "However there is yet some—"

From the end of a pew nearby, an older man in round spectacles turned and hissed at her. Frowning, she took Klaus by his half-sleeve — truly, the woman was brazen!—and guided him to a pew that seemed full at first, but a space rapidly cleared at its end when she leaned forward and glared.

He squeezed in, she returned to her post, and he was able to focus on the music. It was an Adagio in B Minor that he knew, but he couldn't remember the composer. There was a harp accompanying the solo flute. The harpist, a man in his forties, was bespectacled, with thinning hair over a high forehead, pinched cheeks. He couldn't see the flautist's face, as she was leaning towards the harpist and her long hair fell in a blonde veil past her shoulder.

Klaus looked above the frescoed walls to the church's wooden vaulted ceiling and closed his eyes. The acoustics were rather fine. Sighing, he relaxed his shoulders and slumped back into his seat. Fru Boren had been correct to say that her ensemble contained some fine musicians. The harpist was good, but the flautist's playing was absolutely exquisite. Some old experienced professional, no doubt.

The Adagio ended, the clapping began, he opened his eyes. The flautist was facing forward now, acknowledging the applause with a faint smile. Not an old professional at all. Perhaps early twenties and quite, quite stunningly beautiful.

Klaus sat up for the rest of the performance and did not take his eyes off her.

They went on to play Corelli's *Christmas Concerto*. Watching the young violinist, Klaus felt something he rarely did these days, three years after the crash—his missing arm. Could almost feel those lost fingers moving over the strings. Shaking his head, he put memory aside, focused on music—and on the flautist, unused in this string concerto. She was sitting back too, eyes intent on the first violinist, who was around her own age and . . . was there love in the look she gave him? Klaus was suddenly jealous—of the boy's playing, of the girl's look. Of them. They looked . . . innocent of the world. Of dead agents, bombed cities, missing limbs. Alright, they were in a nation occupied by another. But Norway was a backwater of war and they still looked like he had done when he was their age, when he thought only to play music. Great God, he thought, perhaps all of five years ago.

He settled back again, closed his eyes, lost himself in Corelli's swooping arpeggios. The second violinist, a middle-aged woman, was not quite as good as the first. The cellist was adequate and the guitar player rather wonderful. Then he gave up judging, just received. The music filled him, soothed him, took him away. If he wasn't enjoying it so much, he might have slept.

He didn't open his eyes when the flute began playing "O Tannen-baum." Even a pretty girl couldn't compete with what went on behind his lids—his family gathered around the huge fir tree in the hunting lodge at Gehrden.

Klaus jerked up. He *had* fallen asleep for a moment! Applause for "O Tannenbaum" had woken him. Sitting up, he rubbed his eyes as a single trumpet sounded the opening bars of perhaps the most famous Christmas song of all. The trumpeter played solo to begin with, until someone else rose to join him, took a deep breath, and began to sing.

It was the flautist. She was not a trained classical singer, but the song sounded all the better for that, her voice sweet and pure, her German impeccable. She sang with her eyes closed but Klaus kept his on her all through the hymn, found it hard to look elsewhere even when the whole ensemble concluded the evening with Bach's rousing Magnificat in D Major, though without the choir.

Loud applause. He wanted to jump to his feet, but it appeared not to be the Norwegian way. Clapping was denied him, of course, but he uttered several "bravos." One of several men doing so, but perhaps he was the loudest because the flautist's eyes came to him for a moment—and did he imagine that she appeared to give him a personal smile?

People rose, started talking, gathering coats and bags. He felt a touch on his shoulder and turned to the beaming face of Fru Boren. "Did you enjoy that, Herr Major?"

"Very much. Yes, very much indeed." He swallowed, glanced at the flautist laughing with the violinist as they put their instruments away. Then he realized that Fru Boren was speaking again.

". . . in an apartment nearby. Not as lavish as I would have liked but we have a few Norwegian festive treats, and thanks to the generosity of our German friends—"

"I am sorry, dear lady. What are you asking?"

She frowned at him. "A little reception for a few special guests. I hoped you would join us."

Klaus decided not to look at the flautist again. "Are the musicians coming? I would like . . . like to congratulate them on their playing."

"Some of them, yes." She leaned in, lowering her voice. "Between you and me, we suspect that some of them are Jews. But we have asked a select few." Perhaps she sensed something. "The charming Frøken Magnusson for one. The reception is being held in her father's apartment."

"Frøken . . . ?"

"The flautist?"

"Ah." He'd meant to return to his office, work into the night on the latest decoded reports from England. That, he decided, could wait. His spy was dead, after all. He smiled. "I accept your invitation with gratitude, dear Fru Boren."

"Excellent. I will fetch your coat and be your guide."

She swept off to the door. Klaus looked again. But the musicians had gone.

THE RECEPTION WAS in a first-floor apartment in a block on the same street Klaus had struggled up from the station. It had not been such a hard return as the snow had dwindled again to a few flakes, and Fru Boren kept a firm grip on his arm to prevent any falling. Hers, he suspected, not his.

The first room he entered was book-lined, and held a table with food and drinks on it. There was a Norwegian equivalent of Glüh-wein, but after a glass was handed to him, Klaus found it a bit thin and moved onto aquavit. There was salmon, both poached in dill and cured as gravlax, various cheeses, and some foul-smelling cod dish that the Norwegians seemed most excited about, each newcomer crying "Lutefisk!" when they saw it and tucking in. The spread was excellent for a city during wartime, but Fru Boren and perhaps the host obviously had German connections to supply them.

Unlike the others, Klaus could not fill a plate and carry it into the one of the two larger reception rooms, where the main party was taking place, so he put a plate on the table and ate a little right there. Not too much. He had other plans.

In the corner of the second room was a Norway spruce. It wasn't as tall as the trees back home, but was decorated like them with candles, plaster globes, tinsel and strings of flags—the red, white and blue of Norway intertwined with the red and black Swastika. An angel played a trumpet at its apex. When he moved to stand beside it he could see into both rooms.

She was in the far corner of the last room, sitting cross-legged on the edge of a sofa. She had an empty plate balanced on her thigh, a drink in one hand, a cigarette in the other. Standing before her was the young violinist. He was waving his own cigarette around like a conductor's baton and he said something that made them both laugh.

"So. We have another victim for the ice princess."

Klaus, lost to his thoughts, started, turned. Behind him, looking where he'd just looked, was a tall officer in the black uniform of an SS major. The man shot his right hand up. "Heil Hitler."

"Major." Klaus noted the man's eyes narrow slightly when he didn't echo the salute. He knew he shouldn't do it, shouldn't bait the Nazis. He cleared his throat. "Excuse me, but what did you just say?"

The man shrugged, then grinned. "I saw you staring at the delectable Fräulein Magnusson. So I thought I should come and warn you. She has turned down half the Kriegsmarine, most of the Heer, and all"—he glanced at Klaus's eagle—"the Luftwaffe."

"All the SS too, I assume?"

"Everyone. Some say she does not like men. I mean, she even turned me down."

Klaus studied the face before him. He didn't see irony in it. The man was sharp of cheekbone and jaw, had thick blond hair slightly longer than regulation, expensive teeth, eyes the pale blue of a finch's egg. He was handsome in a very direct way. Confident too. The flautist's rejection would have been a rare insult to this man, he thought.

"Klaus von Ronnenberg," he said, clicking his heels lightly together.

The officer stared at him. "'Von'? And that perfect heel click? Prussian, I take it?"

"Yes. You?"

"Baden-Württemberg. Karlsruhe." He inclined his head. "Major Erich Striegler."

Klaus recognized the name and glanced again at the uniform. "I thought you were in the Sicherheitsdienst?"

"Seconded to them. But intelligence servicemen tend to wear suits." He gave a short bark of laughter. "I paid a fortune for my uniform on the Kurfürstendamm, and I'm damned if I won't show it off."

Klaus studied the man more closely. Part of his work in military intelligence required him to make swift assessments of people, consider their use, their potential, their . . . danger. Major Striegler's uniform would indeed have cost a small fortune, so he had money or, more likely at his age, came from it. The face, the teeth, the bearing all spoke to privilege. But the slight colour he'd given the words *von* and *Prussian* indicated perhaps a resentment of the class above his. Industrialist's son, he thought. Then he saw something else. "Are you a pilot as well?" he said, pointing to a badge the man wore on his left breast pocket. "The Eagle means flyer, but I do not recognize the symbols here."

Striegler nodded. "Was a pilot. This badge shows I was wounded while I was with the Condor Legion."

"You fought in Spain?"

"Yes."

"And were wounded there?" The man grunted and Klaus continued. "And so had to retire from the air?"

"No." Striegler ran his tongue around his mouth, as if he'd just tasted something nasty there. "I carried on after . . . after the wounds. I got this one"—he raised a hand, in the middle of which was a small scar— "later. In France." He glanced at the empty sleeve pinned to Klaus's jacket. "You?"

"A raid on England. A crash on return."

"Also the face?" He gestured with his chin to the shiny skin on Klaus's forehead and nose.

"Yes. Some burns."

"I see." He glanced up at the ceiling. "I flew against England too. Bombed the shit out of them. Nearly burned their fucking London down one night."

"December 29, 1940."

"Yes!" The blue eyes swivelled back to Klaus, excitement in them. "Where you there?"

"It was on the return from there that this happened."

"Fucking rain that night! Bombers?"

"Pathfinders. I lit the way for the bombers."

Striegler whistled. "One of the fucking glory boys, eh?" When Klaus just shrugged, he continued. "Well, comrades of the air, eh?"

"Both on the ground now." He took a sip of aquavit. "I believe we were meant to have met by now, Major Striegler." Klaus dipped his head. "I am recently arrived in Oslo. Transferred to the Abwehr."

The blue eyes narrowed. "Which Abteilung?"

"Three."

"Ah, counter-espionage. My field too."

"Indeed. And don't recent directives state that we should liaise more closely, Abwehr and Sicherheitsdienst? I left a message yesterday with your orderly."

"I was away. Further north, near Trondheim. Assisting in razzias." He licked his lips. "Caught lots of the little resistance bastards, some almost with their fingers on the Morse keys. Lots of their families too."

"Congratulations."

"Yes, it is good. We'll get plenty of information out of them . . . later . . . or sooner. And speaking of liaison . . ." He put his glass down on a table beside them. "You should come with me. Attend the interrogation."

Klaus kept the distaste from his face, his voice. He knew what went on. He had always managed to avoid it. "I don't think that will be necessary."

"No? I am sure those same directives spoke of the need for Abwehr agents to attend such occasions to put, uh, pertinent questions. Did they not?" He shrugged. "Look, tonight actually won't be so interesting, and I'd hate to drag you away from the party. But I've got a bigger fish arriving tomorrow from the north. Come and meet him."

Klaus nodded. He had to seem to acquiesce but there was probably still a way out of it. "Where? When?"

"Victoria Terrasse, of course. Intelligence headquarters. When? Hmm." He chewed at his lips. "Let us work on him for a couple of days. Even the tough ones usually crack on the third day."

"Three days? But that would be, uh, Christmas Eve, no?"

"I forgot! A holiday for Germans and Norwegians alike. And I am being entertained by a very sweet tyskertøs who, as a matter of fact, I met at one of Fru Boren's parties. A few extra days with no clothes in a freezing cell with cold water thrown on him every few hours to keep him awake will make him even more receptive, hmm?"

Klaus swallowed. "'Tyskertøs'?"

"Ah, I forgot. You have only just arrived. It is what the Norwegians call the kind ladies who offer themselves to us. 'German fancies.'" He brushed some crumbs from his sleeve. "Shall we say the 26th then?"

He bowed his head slightly. "Major."

The hand snapped up. "Heil Hitler."

This time Klaus threw up a limp wrist. "Heil Hitler . . . But one last thing." Klaus's words halted Striegler, and he turned back. "You described how no one in our forces has made any headway with Miss . . . Miss Magnusson, was it? Could it be that she simply doesn't like Germans? Many don't. Many don't want to be a . . . tyskertøs."

"Oh no. She may be a frigid bitch, but she loves Germans and Germany. See that man?" He pointed to the corner opposite the flautist, a tall man there, reciting some poem to a half-circle of admirers. "That's Wilhelm Magnusson. Her father. A famous writer and one of the leading Norwegian Nazis. He is a skilled propagandist for us here. And his daughter, Ilse?" He swung his arm back to her. "She was studying music in America and took a boat to Sweden after our invasion of her homeland. Escaped from internment in Stockholm, skied across the border, all to help her father and his cause." He sighed. "Pity she likes women, eh? Though if she'd care to bring a friend to *that* party . . ." He laughed, then walked away.

Klaus watched him go, before looking again at the woman the major had called Ilse, saw her finish the dark red liquid in her glass.

Moving swiftly, he went and filled a fresh glass with Glühwein, his own with aquavit, and, with the dexterity of practice, picked both up in his one hand and moved into the next room.

———

ILSE WATCHED the German with the smart Luftwaffe uniform and the missing arm cross towards her. She'd noticed him at the concert. His was a new face in Oslo and one of her tasks—one of her few tasks—was to report on important arrivals, shifts in personnel. Fru Boren's parties were good for that. The old Nazi bitch had contacts deep into the occupying establishment. Anyone of importance would show up at one of her parties sooner or later, and the woman liked using Ilse's father's apartment—hers now too, since Ilse had given up her own little attic room and moved in three months before.

She glanced over at Wilhelm, towering over his audience who were rapt over the poem he was declaiming, Goethe or Schiller no doubt. Then she looked again at the approaching officer. He was definitely making his way to her, and she felt a little shiver of anticipation. She may have been frustrated by how little she was allowed to do to fight the enemy, but she would do that little well.

The room was crowded and the German polite. He halted, asked for passage, squeezed through. She had a few moments to focus—she really shouldn't have had that third glass of Glühwein—on the checklist of questions SOE had prepared for her and updated on her monthly radio messages. Name, rank, service, reason for the German's posting to Norway mainly, together with as much recent history as possible.

She also used some of those remaining moments to consider the man in front of her, who'd been making her laugh. She hadn't seen Torvald Linström since high school, when they'd played together in the school orchestra. He'd been gawky then, stalk-thin with glasses and braced teeth. She'd barely recognized him when they'd met to rehearse the Christmas concert the week before in the Church of the Priests. The glasses were gone, the teeth were perfect, he'd put on muscle in all the right places—an avid skier and climber, he'd told her. He'd been away, living on an uncle's farm in Gudbrandsdalen. Returned to Oslo because he missed playing music with other people. Glad he had, he'd said, with special emphasis, looking into her eyes.

She'd thought she might sleep with him. She ached for that close contact with someone. Letting go for once, in that area at least, because always holding on, always pretending to be what she wasn't —loving daughter, dutiful Nazi—was a strain from the moment she awoke until she went to sleep. She was only free in dreams, and even those had lately been tormented: running or skiing away from someone who pursued her, whom she couldn't see.

Besides, SOE had advised her to find ways to relax, for stress led to anxiety and on to carelessness. And yet, despite the many offers— Norwegian offers, German offers—she hadn't made love since . . .

. . . since Billy Coke.

Close to three years? After an affair that had lasted . . . three days? Was she crazy? Neither had promised the other that they would remain faithful. Both had gone to war, in their own ways. And Billy, a fighter pilot, might well be dead by now—though she had an odd feeling she'd somehow know if he was. And her? Most of the time it didn't feel like she was at war at all. Just living where she'd always lived, doing what she'd always done, on poorer rations.

But now it is time to fight again, in my own small way, she thought, watching as the German cleared the final obstacles. He was four paces away. She looked up at Torvald. He smiled down at her. Hope in the smile, and a promise. It would keep. There was another concert in two days, on the 23rd, Little Christmas Eve. After three years, she could wait two more days to decide.

"Frøken Magnusson?"

He'd made it through, this slight German with the pinned sleeve and skin that caught the lamplight on parts of his face. Burned, she saw. There was some grey in his short hair, at the temples. Grey in his eyes too. These smiled at her, along with his mouth, which was a little lopsided, a small white scar trailing from its left side.

"Yes?"

"I . . . I noticed that your glass was empty." He proffered the Glühwein, then glanced up at the tall young Norwegian. "I am sorry I could only carry—"

"I am sure Torvald here can fetch his own drink." Ilse rose from the sofa arm as she spoke, placing her glass and plate on the mantel behind her. She took the glass from the German, scanning his collar tabs. "Thank you, Major . . . ?"

"Von Ronnenberg. Klaus, please."

He put out a hand. She took it. "Ilse Magnusson."

"Torvald Linström." The young man shook his hand also, giving a small head-bow.

"I must tell you, Mr. Linström, that your playing tonight, especially on the Corelli, was exceptionally fine. That Allegro is fiendish."

Torvald smiled. "You know the violin, sir?"

"Not as well as you. An amateur but a keen one, nevertheless. No more, alas." He gave a slight shrug which jiggled his empty sleeve. "But I appreciate it even more now, hearing it played so excellently." As Torvald flushed with pleasure, Klaus turned back to Ilse. "Matched by your exquisite flute, my dear lady. And your voice, of course. For a few moments I was back in my homeland. Remembering . . . better times."

The memory of better times paused the conversation for a moment. Ilse saw it in the slight blush that came to the German's face. He'd introduced the war, which they'd all managed to briefly escape. And though the war was what she wanted to talk about, and his work in it, she knew she should not approach that directly. "Your Norwegian is excellent, Major . . ."

"Klaus!"

"Major Klaus." They both smiled and she continued. "But are you not a newcomer here? I have certainly not seen you at one of these things."

"I have been in Norway for three weeks. Back in Norway, I should say. I was here a lot in my teenage years."

"Ah yes," said Torvald. "You Germans came here on holiday in your thousands, did you not?"

It was said without colour, and Torvald still smiled.

"Indeed," replied Klaus. "There were travel companies in Germany that extolled the beauties of your land. They undersold it, I may say. And once I knew I was to be posted here, I got some Norwegian colleagues to help me to . . . brush up. Is that the term?"

"Where were you before?" she asked, sipping wine, glancing away, around the room.

"Russia," he replied.

Her eyes moved briefly to his pinned sleeve, then up again. "Flying? Is that where—?"

"Oh, no, I was wounded before. Elsewhere. Now I am, ah, in military intelligence."

"Abwehr?" On his nod she continued, enthusiastically. "So you are a spy? How thrilling!"

Klaus laughed. "I assure you, I am not. I push papers around a desk, make lists." He shrugged. "No cloak, no dagger, I am afraid."

"Pity. When I am sure you look so good in a cloak." Her eyes widened. "Wait. Russia, you say?" She switched to German. "My brother is there! With the Standarte Nordland. Trygve Magnusson? Were you at Leningrad?"

"For a while."

"Perhaps you met him? Looks like me, but taller?"

"I do not think—"

"We have not heard from him for a while, neither my father nor I." She glanced over at Wilhelm in his corner, no longer reciting poetry but listening intently to a German army colonel, then looked back at Klaus. "We are concerned."

"I could make some enquiries, if you like," said Klaus. "The Standarte has just disbanded. Many Norwegian volunteers are coming home. Others I believe have formed the core of a new regiment."

"Trygve will be one of those!" she said. "He is a great believer in the fight against Bolshevism. As we all are."

"Yes, well, I can ask if you like."

Ilse reached out, touched his hand. "It would be a great favour. To my father. To me."

Klaus looked at her hand, resting on his. Her touch was light. Thrilling. "Then I will do so," he mumbled.

There was a silence, broken by Torvald. "I must go." He drank off the last of his aquavit, put the glass on the mantel.

"A rendezvous, Torvald?"

He shook his head. "Not the way you ask it, Ilse." He smiled. "You know I only have eyes for you." He lifted and kissed the hand she'd withdrawn from Klaus, then turned to him. "Major, it was a pleasure to meet such a . . . connoisseur. We play again on Little Christmas Eve. At the same church. I hope you will come."

He held out his hand. Klaus took it, shook it, retained it. "I was hoping to form a smaller ensemble, Mr. Linström. A quartet or quintet perhaps? I may not play anymore, but I love to conduct. Would you consider . . . ?"

"I would. Let me know, let me know." Torvald took his hand back, bowed to Ilse and wove his way through the crowd.

"A talented fellow," Klaus said.

"He is."

"And would you also consider joining my quartet, Miss . . . Ilse?"

She looked at him. What was he asking her? For her musical skills? Not only, she could sense. Well, she'd flirted with the invaders for several years now. It was one way she fought her war. One more, who loved the music she loved? Who had gentle eyes? Why not? she thought and said, "As long as I am not always playing . . . second fiddle."

"Never," he said. "I would feature you, of course. Mozart. I love his quartet in D Major."

What we played that night in London, she thought. When the

incendiaries fell. When I met Billy Coke. "Then I would be delighted," she replied. Looking at one man, thinking of another.

"I am so pleased."

"As am I."

"Ilse!" A voice boomed beside them, ending the moment.

"Father."

Wilhelm Magnusson loomed over them, using all his near-two-metre height. "You must come and speak to Oberst Klingen. He has been sharing fascinating tales of the Leningrad front. He says Trygve's regiment are outstanding fighters. He—" It was as if he had only just noticed Klaus. "Who are you?" he demanded bluntly.

"This is Major von Ronnenberg, Father. We were also just discussing Lenin . . ."

"Major! A wounded hero, I see." His gaze had wandered over Klaus's uniform and now he vigorously shook his extended hand. "Excuse me, but I must borrow my daughter." He called across the room. "I am bringing her, Oberst." His arm around Ilse, his size, neither could be resisted. "I tell you, according to the Oberst, your brother and his boys gave those Bolshies one hell of a licking! Come!"

He swept her away. Yet in her last backward glance, she managed to convey one word to the major.

Later.

ERICH STRIEGLER SAT in the back of the Mercedes as the streets of Oslo, swathed with new snow, passed by. He was not seeing them, though. His mind was still at the party.

This new Abwehr man. This Klaus von Ronnenberg. *Von.* With all the arrogance the title gave him. Combined with the arrogance of a branch of army intelligence that considered themselves superior to all others. Who considered espionage a kind of game, a football match played against their English opposition, the SOE. Von Ronnenberg would be the type of man who, when the final whistle went, would go into the bar and toast his opponent's health in steins of foaming beer.

Striegler snorted. And the man's half-hearted Hitler salute? Another Prussian officer who no doubt resented taking orders from someone who'd only risen to the rank of corporal in the first war. Failing to understand the nature of genius. That rank—his, the Führer's—meant nothing anymore. Hitler had changed all that. Bent even the most stubborn aristocrat to his will. His iron will. Transformed the Fatherland, raised it from its abject state, shattered its enemies within its borders and without. Restored Germany to its proper place, not just as the foremost country in Europe. In the world! Restored men like himself. No more grovelling to aristocrats. No more grovelling to Jews for handouts like his father had to do.

His father. Striegler swallowed. He rarely thought of him. Because when he did, he saw him as he'd last seen him: hanging from the beam in the garage of the house he'd just been forced to sell to pay off the Jews. Striegler had cut him down. Too late, much too late. And then, two weeks later, the Nuremberg Laws were passed and all debts to Jews were cancelled. His elder brother had taken over the business, raised it up again.

Too late. "Herr Major?"

Striegler looked up. His driver's eyes were reflected in the mirror. "Yes?"

"We are here, sir."

They were at the front entrance of Victoria Terrasse. "Good. No, I'll get it," he said, as the driver moved to step out from behind the wheel and opened his door. "Goodnight."

The car drove off. Striegler stood on the pavement, in that wonderful silence of new snow. He closed his eyes, tipped his head to the sky, put out his tongue to catch one of the few still-falling flakes.

One landed. He opened his eyes, looked at the main entrance. Upstairs was his office. His orderly would have laid a fire in the grate. There was a bottle of schnapps from his last visit home in a drawer. Maybe he should begin up there?

No, he thought, and went down the stairs to the cellar. At the iron gates, he rang the bell beside them.

He wouldn't say he enjoyed the work he did in the basement of Victoria Terrasse. It was messy, noisy and . . . well, he was not a sadist. But it was necessary. Unlike for that von Ronnenberg fellow, war was never a game to him. He would never drink beer with his enemies, for they were the enemies of progress, of the better world the Führer was striving to create. They were only barriers to be broken down, obstacles to be surmounted.

As he waited for the guard to come and admit him, Striegler knew it was not cruelty he was going to practise this night in the cold, stone room down the corridor. It was not revenge either.

It was duty.

The guard saluted, then opened the gate. As he walked down the corridor, Striegler remembered when he'd truly witnessed cruelty. When he'd seen revenge—in Spain, six years before, when his friend Gootsie had been executed by a man he'd very much like to have in the room ahead someday.

His corporal, Behmer, was standing outside cell number 5. The former army boxing champion was wearing his usual singlet vest, his hairy shoulders bare. Looking at him, Striegler shivered, despite his own greatcoat.

"Heil Hitler!"

"Heil Hitler!" Striegler glanced at the cell door. "Softened up?"

The corporal grinned. "Oh yes, Herr Major. Very soft."

"Good." Striegler nodded, reaching for his coat's collar button. "Then we'll begin."

THIRTEEN

MESSAGES

Oslo. December 22, 1943

THE TRAM JUDDERED TO a stop at Holmenkollen station. It was 2:30 already, and would be dark by 4 p.m. Thus there were many more people waiting to board to return to Oslo at the end of their day's skiing than there were setting out.

Ilse stepped onto the platform and went to the fence, out of the way of those heading home. There were a few Germans among the skiers, distinguished by their winter whites, and by the space around each of them. The Norwegians may have been ordered not to shun the occupier, but it was a hard rule to enforce and most Germans didn't attempt it. They stacked their skis in the external racks and boarded the tram like everyone else.

It pulled away, leaving the few late skiers, breath pluming the air. Ilse dawdled, pretending to check her bindings. The others put on their skis and took off along the nearest trails—a young couple, three youths, two middle-aged men together, two men on their own. Ilse gave them five minutes, looking down towards the city though it was mostly obscured by low clouds; looking too at the huge ski jump that gave the station its name. It was one of the biggest in the world, and Norway was proud of it and the jumpers that used it. Her brother had been one of them, and she had spent many an afternoon here before the war watching him hurl himself into the air.

Satisfied that she was alone, she set off, following the main trail away from the station. The temperature was probably minus five—the snow not clumpy, not icy yet—but it would be dropping fast. The place she needed to reach was about fifteen minutes away if she skied hard. With fortune, the conditions would be good for transmitting and receiving, here above the clouds. She could be done and back at Holmenkollen station within the hour, before darkness was full.

She took a side trail, a little less used, but with ruts she slipped into easily. She just hoped that they had not been made by any of those who had just preceded her from the station. At the next turn she paused, took a deep breath. The going had gotten harder, and there were no ruts here, just snow from the previous night's fall. No one had come this way today. She exhaled, consciously lowering her shoulders. Digging her pole tips into the snow, she pushed herself on.

Despite her attention she missed the hidden trail the first time. She cursed the wasted minutes, doubled back, looked more carefully. There! Between two firs, their lowest branches intertwined, she saw the sign she'd left on her last visit: a casual array of sticks, their ends just poking up above the surface in a V. Ducking low, she pushed between the branches, which sprang back behind her. The base of her skis grated on loose stones under the trees, then she was back in knee-deep snow that was hard to push through. Soon she came to a slope that steepened immediately. When she'd been here a month before, she'd walked to the summit up a small elk trail that still had some autumn to it. Now she herringboned her skis up the steep, white slope.

It took her two minutes to reach the summit and her breath was coming hard by the time she did. There were no marks on the virgin snow under the rocky outcrop; no one had been there. Still, she paused to listen, in case she'd been followed. After a moment or two she was satisfied and walked on her skis around the rock.

It was only the third time she'd transmitted from this place. She liked it, but she knew that she might only have one more chance here before she'd have to move again. The Germans in their DF stations listened to every broadcast, and each time she sent they got closer to pinpointing her. In the late summer, at her previous spot in a forest on the western shore of Oslofjord, the enemy had sent up a Fieseler Storch, the plane circling uncomfortably near. She'd moved that same day, brought her gear home, then moved it again the next day, brought it . . . here.

She shivered. The next few months were only going to get colder, especially up at Holmenkollen. She'd need to move her gear to a spot lower down anyway, so she could still use her fingers on the key.

Leaning her poles against the rock face, she unbuckled her skis, leaned them there too. Then she took off her haversack, reached in and pulled out the folding shovel. The blown snow had banked against the rock face, so she dug that away first. The ground was frozen, but the transmitter wasn't down deep. She'd fashioned a covering from withies woven together, placed fir branches across that, then a layer of earth. Stripped away, she pulled the suitcase from its hole, sprang the catches. Her Type B Mk II radio filled the space within.

It was only a matter of minutes to set up. The rock face before her was a good reflector for her signal; one of the advantages of the place. She took a battery from her sack, attached it—she always brought a fresh one as buried batteries corroded easily. After plugging in her headphones she slipped them over her ears and turned on the machine. It gave its usual alarming clicks and whirs, then settled to a low hum. It was already set to the frequency she used, but there were two other powerful frequencies very close by, including a German one. She adjusted the dial slightly and the static faded. Now it was a matter of luck and atmospherics. She was largely above the clouds here, and the night was clear—though that might not be the same in Scotland. Plugging in the Morse key, she took off her watch. Pinned it to the lid before her on the hook she'd put there. It was 2:58, and her sked time was 3 p.m. She waited. When the second hand hit 2:59:50, she blew on her hands, rubbed them hard together, then sent her signal. It was the home station's one-off call sign, for this day only.

BZY. BZY. BZY . . .

She sent it for exactly one minute. Waited for one minute. Nothing came. She blew, rubbed, sent.

BZY. BZY. BZY . . .

One minute send, one listen. Still nothing. She would do it seven more times. If there was still no contact after nine, she would send her message anyway, blind, and hope.

She tapped but her mind was elsewhere. If they didn't acknowledge, or even receive her message, did it matter? She didn't believe her news was very important. She had no way of knowing for sure, but she suspected that reporting on military personnel arrivals in Oslo could hardly be as vital as what others were surely doing. Though, since coming to Norway, she had been allowed no contact with any resistance group. "Too porous," Cholmondeley-Warren had told her. "Keep yourself to yourself and you'll keep safe."

BZY. BZY. BZY . . .

She felt almost safe. She also felt angry and frustrated. Most of all she felt bored.

She sighed. Fifteen seconds till her fourth call. She blew, rubbed . . . Her ear set crackled. The Morse came clear. *PSO. PSO. PSO.*

It was her call sign for the day. If anything other than PSO had come, she might have been speaking to Germans.

The next letters came: *QRU.* So they had nothing for her.

Then came: *QRU?* Did she have something for them? Yes, she did, for what it was worth. One message, so she sent out *QTC1.*

She flexed her fingers. Waited. Security first. At the other end they might still suspect she had been caught, turned. So she sent her readiness: *QRV.*

The test question came. Number 4. She knew what that was: What colour lipstick was she wearing today?

Ilse smiled. It was one of six test questions she and her "god-mother" had worked out. She'd met Trina Slingsby at Fawley Court, where she'd been sent for her training. Trina was a FANY—a nurse working for the First Aid Nursing Yeomanry from which so many godmothers were drawn. All those English terms still made her smile. A godmother was responsible for receiving the messages from their assigned "children." Everyone had their own style when they trans-mitted—the way they tapped, the lightness or heaviness of their touch. It was called a "fist" for some reason, and Ilse was a "pianist."

They'd needed to get to know each other quickly—and had, over nights in the Fawley Court Mess. They could hardly have been more different, the classical flautist and the farmer's daughter from York-shire. Yet they got on famously. Ilse could still hear Trina's bray of a laugh that could bring a bar to a shocked silence. One night, when they'd been allowed out to see a show in London, Trina had been much taken with Ilse's lipstick, which had come with her from New York, the latest from Tangee: Red Majesty, it was called. Such a thing was unseen in England since the war began. On their last night together, Ilse had given Trina the tube.

She imagined her wearing it now as she encoded her reply, sent the scrambled letters back: *My ski boats are tight, and I have blisters.*

Trina wouldn't only know it was Ilse replying because of her fist and because she had the answer right—Ilse could have given that to the Germans under torture. She had also included her "true check" by misspelling the eighth letter of her message: *boats* not *boots.*

Ilse waited. She was holding her breath. If Trina doubted her, she might send her a new key number in the form of the first words of a nursery rhyme—or something. She would have to decode it, create a new crib. It would take time, and it was getting darker, and she colder, by the minute.

The reply came. *OK.* Simple as that. Then, *QRV.*

Ilse looked at the paper she'd encrypted earlier. Smiled, remembering the reactions of her two handlers, Major Cholmondeley-Warren and Lieutenant McBride, when she'd told them the poem she'd selected to be her "poem code." Her trainers at Fawley Court had offered their usual English selections—something from Shakespeare, Tennyson, Keats . . . But her offer of a favourite childhood rhyme had been accepted.

"*Sånn rider damene med nesen i sky'n,*" she'd recited.

The major's eyebrows, the only hair on his head aside from his pencil moustache, had contracted when she'd quoted it. "What the devil does that mean?"

But the Irishman, McBride, had laughed. "My Norwegian nanny in Ålesund used to bounce me on her knee to that poem. I think I might still have the bruises on my . . . posterior." He smiled at the major's perplexed expression. "It's a bouncing game: 'This is how the lady rides, with her nose in the air. This . . .'"

"But we have the same nursery rhyme," Cholmondeley-Warren interrupted. "Ends with 'This is how the farmer rides . . . gallopy gallopy gallopy gall—'" He broke off, as if suddenly embarrassed. "Why not use the English one?"

"Because I am Norwegian, sir," she replied softly.

McBride leaned forward. "I think it's a wonderful idea. But translate it directly into English. Without all the Norwegian umlauts and curlicues, I think. Make it easy for your godmother."

She had. Trina had liked it.

Now Ilse tapped. The first group of five letters—GSIUD—showed which words in her poem she was using for the coded message. Then she sent the message itself in groups of five letters.

GSIUD ETANN EEERO NENON LEIMA RAAOX HSPNL
TGAKE MTRNN UERVU EOLPN GIYGR SMWAW SBEUI
NLWAE TLOOS ABYRE IREPB EETEB TTHNW LNEAG
SORDE RELAR FBUSN

EOLLH

She sat back, imagining Trina transcribing, looking for Ilse's final check—she wrote *futher* for "father" and *Uslo* for "Oslo"—that would prove it was indeed her without Germans standing over her. Once confirmed, her godmother would read: "Father to Berlin to meet Goebbels early New Year with all European propaganda men. Klaus von Ronnenberg new Abwehr in Oslo."

The signal came: *QRN3*. They'd missed something because of static. Static was poor at 3 but not terrible. QRN1 was not bad, QRN5 the worst. She waited.

GR? 9 10

They were asking her to resend the ninth and tenth groups of letters.

She did.

A pause. Then: *QSL*. They acknowledged receipt of her message.

She sent: *VA*. Her message, such as it was, was over. Now she wanted to be away.

VA came back. And then a further short burst. This uncoded, in plain text: *Stay safe*.

She sighed. I'm in no true danger, she thought. Still, she packed up fast, though carefully. All actions reversed, and the transmitter safely stowed and concealed. She would return for it in a few days and decide where to set up next.

***

ILSE SURVEYED the wreckage on the dining room table, the plates glistening with congealing pig fat and gravy, the beer glasses with their dregs of juleøl, the empty shot glasses, the overflowing ashtrays. She knew she should start to tidy up, take the dirties to the kitchen, wash everything. Wilhelm was sitting in his chair, a fat cigar in one hand, his other fiddling with the radio dials. He would not help. He'd been proud to cook the feast, especially the meat. His German connections had provided the ribbe, the pork belly roast that was the centrepiece of every Christmas Eve feast—though she knew that very few households in the rationed city would have it this year. He'd also shot three grouse in a recent hunt; hung, plucked, gutted and cooked them himself. That was all man's work. Cleaning up after was what women did. Her two aunts, Turid and Boggen, her cousins Sidsel and Line, had all offered to stay and help, but Ilse had shooed them away. They were anxious to get back to their own apartments before curfew.

Two things held Ilse in her chair. Her tiredness—she'd drunk much more than she usually did, joining in every "Skål" shooting back the aquavit, taking gulps of the strong Christmas ale. She'd hoped it would take away her malaise—the excitement of transmitting her recent message two days before had quickly passed, leaving her again discontented, bored of her work, her pathetic contribution. The liquor had indeed worked for a while. She'd joined the circle to dance around the tree, sang the song. Sang others, the drinking ones, as more aquavit was raised, relations pledged. There was one—"Helan Går"—she especially loved, even if it was Swedish. But now the alcohol had left her lethargic, and the task before her was so vast.

The second reason she waited was more interesting and had to do with her father's fiddling at the radio in the next room. He was trying to tune into the BBC World Service, the Norwegian broadcasts. This was forbidden. Indeed, all radios had been confiscated in 1941 to try to prevent Norwegians from hearing anything but Nazi propaganda. Imprisonment was the consequence—or worse. But the rules did not apply to members of the Nazi Party and especially not to Wilhelm Magnusson. Indeed, part of his job was to listen to English lies, then counter them with writings and broadcasts of his own.

She would listen with him, exclaim with him against "perfidious Albion." What was more interesting to her though were the messages that would be broadcast before the news: coded messages to resistance groups. Only once had one been for her—to let her know that a new Morse code book had been hidden in a dead-letter drop in a tree in a forest to the north. That had been two years ago.

Yet earlier today she'd taken her daily stroll to Frognerparken, Gustav Vigeland's great sculpture park. And there, on the third toe of the left foot of a sculpture of a huge naked wrestler throwing another man, was a second tiny scratched cross beside the now-faded first one from two years before.

It was an order to listen. So she would. Perhaps SOE wanted to change her poem code. Perhaps, more excitingly, they would have a new transmitter for her. Hers was old; she'd brought it with her when she'd skied across the border from Sweden to Norway in March '41. She'd been trained in basic repairs, but she was reaching the limits of her skills in keeping it alive.

"Damn!" her father exclaimed, throwing himself back in his chair. "I think my clumsy fingers are too big for this work."

She got up, joined him in the other room. "Or did those last three shots swell them, Pappa?"

"Nonsense!" Wilhelm took a deep pull at his cigar and exhaled the plume at his daughter. "I was as moderate as I always am." He squinted at her through the smoke. "And you sound just like your mother."

"I hope so. Someone has to keep an eye on you." She smiled. "Do you miss her?"

His eyes moistened. "Every day. And that's a lot of days in thirteen years. You?"

Ilse saw her for a moment—her mother. Not as she'd been when the cancer had wasted her. Not in that last moment when her hand had gone cold in Ilse's—but before, at a feast like this, teasing her father, making him roar with outrage and laughter. "Every day as well."

"Is that why you were a little sad tonight? Thinking of her?"

"Maybe."

He leaned out of the chair, put a hand on her shoulder, rubbed. "I also." He sat back. "At least that last pledge of aquavit was to her. I could hardly refuse it, eh?" He sighed, turned back to the radio, struck the top of it. "Damn thing! I know I can listen to the recordings at the office. But I like to hear what lies the damned Britishers are telling when they tell them."

Ilse glanced at the clock on the mantel. Eight fifty-eight. Two minutes, and unlike her father she would not be able to hear them later, though he would bring the transcripts home. "Let me, Pappa."

He grunted, got out of the chair. She sat, reached for the dial. She'd toasted her dead mother too, but her fingers were more delicate. In a moment the static faded, music came. Shortly afterwards, a voice.

"This is the BBC Home and Forces Programme. This is the news, and this is Peter Forster reading it. Before we begin, we have some personal messages for our friends in Norway." Then came the famous four notes from Beethoven's Fifth. But Ilse always heard the code now. Heard also the echo of a truck's horn in front of her hostel in London, summoning her for a trip to the countryside.

Dot-dot-dot-dash. V. V for Victory.

"Victory? You can dream it, Englender," Wilhelm muttered, as he always did.

Ilse rested a hand on the mantel as her father leaned forward. A different man began to speak in Norwegian. The usual nonsense came, repeated once. "Ferrets keep their burrows warm"; "Unusually the heather blooms all December"; "Poker is a better game than bridge for four." She didn't understand any of it, of course. But all over Norway there would be men and women who did and who would act on the instructions. Go and wait on a snowy field at a set time for dropped men, munitions, food. Focus on an area of surveillance, sending back new coordinates for Nazi U-boat bases, perhaps. Sometimes, more rarely, blow something up. Sabotage had decreased in the last two years. The reprisals were too savage, and many innocent Norwegians had been murdered by the Nazis.

She sensed that the messages were coming to an end. There had been nothing for her. Perhaps the scratch marks on the discus thrower's toe had been a mistake?

Then it came. "Don't steal the eggs from the plovers' nest. Don't steal the eggs from the plovers' nest."

Ilse didn't hear the final message. That wasn't for her. And she was glad that she'd been holding on to the mantel because her knees had gone weak when she'd heard the words.

"I'll go and start the dishes, Father," she murmured.

He grunted at her as the English newscaster came back on and began talking of the war's progress. He had his pad out, a pencil poised. Aquavit or not, he'd write a column for *Aftenposten* that night, to appear in the newspaper's second edition. It would be a skillful parody of the BBC news, full of Norse humour. He knew his job.

She did the dishes slowly, even enjoying the mindless work, which gave her a chance to think. When she was finally done, she returned to the living room. Wilhelm was at his desk now, sitting in cigar smoke, typing away.

"Pappa," she said, sitting on a chair arm.

"Hmm?" he grunted, a little annoyed.

"You noticed my . . . sadness tonight."

He didn't stop typing. "Yes?"

"I think . . . I think I need a little time away."

He hit an emphatic full stop, then turned to her. "Away you say? Where?"

"The hytte. You know how I love it there. I can ski, play my flute, read. Also, Tante Leni was not well last summer. I would like to see her."

"Leni! I haven't seen her in, ah, must be a year. When I went there last summer, she came here." He lowered his voice. "I think she does not approve of"—he gestured to his typewriter—"my work. She is like your mother. Never liked Germans very much." He sighed. "But January in Rondane? It will be cold."

"True. But you cut so much wood for us back in May."

"Will you have enough food?"

"You left lots of tins. Leni will start baking the moment she sees me. I will be fine."

"How long?"

She could not know. "A month?" she guessed.

"Hmm. I'll miss you."

"And I you. But—"

He nodded. "You must do what you wish, min kjære." He struck his forehead. "Damn! I haven't told you. That meeting at the Propaganda Ministry in Berlin I must attend?"

"The one with your fellow correspondents from all over Europe? Mid-January you were going."

"That one. Except now Goebbels wants us all there much earlier. Apparently we are too"—he glanced down at his typewriter—"varied in our messages. He wants uniformity." He laughed. "Germans, eh?"

"How long will you be gone?"

He shrugged. "Probably the same as you. A month? When will you leave?"

"I thought . . . soon. Maybe the 26th?"

"The same day as me." He grunted. "OK."

OK, she thought. End of message. She rose. "I'll leave you to your work."

He dove in straight away, fingers furious on the keys. She stopped in the doorway between rooms to watch him. "Pappa," she whispered, not loud enough for him to hear.

There were times—nights like tonight—when she could forget what had come between them for a while. When she could just enjoy the man he was. He had raised her and her brother Trygve solo since their mother's death, put aside his own terrible grief to help them get through theirs. She loved him for that, for everything, always would. It was only when her duty intruded, as it had this night, that she remembered: he was her enemy. Then she was sad, as she lied to this man she loved, betrayed him daily, as she would go on doing until he and his cause were defeated.

And when it was? Norway would not forgive those it considered traitors. He would be punished, imprisoned certainly—at the least. Well, she thought, reaching up to wipe away a tear, then I will show him the love he showed me. Even if that just means visiting him every day in his prison cell.

She went to the bathroom, got ready for bed. Once she lay down, and despite the aquavit, her mind would not rest. She started packing mentally. What she would need to prove to the Germans that she was permitted to spend a month in the countryside. What she would need to get across the border into Sweden.

What she would need for England.

KLAUS VON RONNENBERG stared at the papers on his desk. There were too many, on too many different subjects, and his new orderly was still using the system of his former boss and taking too long to implement Klaus's preferred methods. He would have to be firmer with him.

Yet it was not the work that he had to finish by midnight that had most of his attention. That was focused on two other pieces of paper.

The first was a note from the flautist, Ilse Magnusson. The day after the concert he'd sent her an invitation for supper on the 26th and she'd sent a swift acceptance back. Now this note told him that, due to the sudden illness of her mother's sister, she would be gone for a time to nurse her in the countryside. She would be in touch when she returned to Oslo. She hoped it would only be a couple of weeks but it could be a month.

He was disappointed. But it wasn't a petty excuse and so that left him with some hope. No, it was the other piece of paper that disturbed him. It had come in a folder of documents from Berlin, sealed with the imprint of Abwehr headquarters there. He was glad now that his orderly had reported sick this morning—hungover almost certainly, the man's purple nose betrayed his passion—so Klaus had been forced to go through the file himself. Most were standard official papers— field agents' reports, economic updates, new directives on inter-service cooperation. The usual stuff. The paper in the middle wasn't usual.

A photograph. Two words written on it.

It was a photograph of his cousin. His first lover. The second word was her name: "Remember Gretchen."

Sometimes photos came of foreign nationals who might be useful to contact, exploit, turn. His orderly would have thought this photo was one of those. Klaus had searched the papers again, but there were none connected to the photograph.

He picked it up once more. There was his cousin, in the garden at Gehrden, a wreath of summer flowers in her hair, that soft smile. Taken when she was perhaps sixteen, a few years before they'd become lovers.

Did the anonymous sender know that she and Klaus had been more than cousins? Was he asking him to remember her life? Or her death from typhoid in Sachsenhausen concentration camp?

In their week of love they'd had only one disagreement. He was no Nazi, had refused to join the Party when so many did to get ahead. But he was a patriot, determined to fight for Germany. She had said that if he fought for the Nazis, he was their accomplice in all the terrible things they did, some of which she detailed. He had kissed her out of her humour. Now, looking at her smiling face, he suddenly wished he hadn't.

There was one other thing about the photograph that set it apart from all the others he'd been sent. Perhaps the most disturbing thing.

The words were a statement, not a question.

Why was someone at Abwehr Berlin wanting him to remember a woman the Nazis had caused to die? And who was it? Hans Messer himself, the deputy chief who'd visited Klaus in France and offered him the job?

Klaus lifted the photo again, held it at arm's length. Why had he been sent this? So that he could immediately repudiate her, as he'd failed to do before? It was the one black mark in his career: the letters he'd sent to every senior Nazi he knew, trying to get her freed. But if that's what the sender wanted, who was he supposed to send such a *mea culpa* to? The file the photo had arrived in contained papers from a dozen different departments, had twice that many counter-signatures. He was lowering the photograph in front of his desk lamp when he noticed something. It was almost as if his imagination took over because, for a moment, it looked like Gretchen's eyes sparkled. He raised the picture again—and saw that, in her left eye, at several other places on her body, and in two of the leaves of the bush she stood before, light shone through the paper. Holding it closer, he saw that this light came through tiny pinholes. Eight in all.

Someone had to have made them. The sender. But why?

The photo had been blown up to the standard German letter size. There were a dozen letters in the file. He took them out, one by one, and placed the photo onto each in turn, using paper clips to hold it in place. The pinholes fit over letters in three cases. He wrote down each set of eight letters revealed. All were gobbledygook.

rtpysmtn vcrlipbb ykvaelir

Then he saw it, because he'd always liked crossword puzzles. The one that was an anagram. The last one.

"Valkyrie," he murmured, writing it out. He stared at the word for a long time. It meant nothing to him, aside from bringing memories of the time his parents had taken him to Bayreuth at eleven years old to see the Ring cycle. He was pretty sure that the sender of this simple message—it was barely a code—was not trying to remind him of Wagner.

Of only one thing was he certain. He'd been contacted. For what purpose, he did not know. The Abwehr was one secret organization, subordinate to the Oberkommando der Wehrmacht within the whole German intelligence organization, the Sicherheitsdienst. All its separate arms—the Geheime Feldpolizei, Gestapo, the SS, the SA, each different branch responsible for their own areas—were meant to coordinate, pool all information for the greater cause of the Party and especially of the Führer. Though, in practice, there was great rivalry and secrecy between them. Was this communication from a superior running his own covert operation that he didn't want one of the other branches to know about? He could find no answer staring at the unscrambled word because there wasn't one. This was an introduction only. The conversation proper would begin later. Meanwhile . . .

It was always difficult with one hand, but with the aid of a paperweight and a book Klaus placed the photo exactly over a blank letter-sized piece of paper, then used a tiny paper clip to punch holes where the original holes were. Then he put a tiny pencil mark in the top right corner of that paper and put it back into the middle of the sheaf he'd taken it from. Replacing that in his desk drawer, he drew out his lighter, put a cigarette between his lips, lit it and burned the three sets of letters and the paper with the anagram solution, then the three blank pages that had been under it in the sheaf, laying them one by one in the large glass ashtray on his desk. Then, squinting through the rising smoke, he raised the photo by its top, and stared again at Gretchen for a long moment before holding its bottom edge to the flames in the glass. It caught, crisped, black rolling up towards her face, taking that just as it became too hot for him to keep holding the photo. He laid it down to become ash with the rest.

He finished his cigarette, letting his mind drift. It went, as it always did, to music; then, as it often did, to Schubert's *Death and the Maiden*. Finally, stubbing out the cigarette, he carried the ashtray to the window, put it down, slid the window up and tipped the ashes out onto the street below.

FOURTEEN
THE PLACE

January 16, 1944

ONE MOMENT THE STORM TROOPER was looking at her papers, the next he'd dropped them and had lunged at her, reaching his long arms around her back, pulling her close, so close she could see the smile in his eyes as he banged his groin into hers.

Ilse moved her head to the left side of his and bit his ear. He yelped, bent away from the pain, which freed her arm that was pinned against her side. He was taller than her, so her hand was in the right spot. Pushing it forward, she gripped him by the testicles and squeezed, hard.

He cried out again, though he still didn't let her go. But now he was a little off balance, so she jerked her left forearm free then dropped it hard down onto his gripping right arm, keeping up the push. As soon as the man started to dip, she grabbed his right wrist with her left, twisting it as she pulled it up even as she continued driving his forearm down. Now he could only let her go as he bent over, his right arm straight up, his face heading towards her knee, which she snapped up—to stop perhaps half an inch from his nose.

"*Aufgeben, Kamerad?*" she asked, still twisting the wrist.

"*Ja! Ja, sicher. Ich gebe auf !* " Still she didn't let him go, so he peered up to the man standing against the wall and continued. "Bleedin' 'ell, Sarge! Get 'er off me, will ya?"

Sergeant Grimes laughed, as did Ilse when she finally released the man and shoved him away. Only the soldier didn't seem to find it very amusing. He knelt and regarded Ilse morosely. "Did you 'ave to squeeze me knackers so 'ard, love?" He reached into his trousers and pulled out a groin protector cup. "Look at this! Bent all out of shape, it is." Then he put his hand to his bitten ear and removed the tape there. "Am I bleeding?" he asked.

"Stop bellyaching, Widmer, or I'll make you do it again. You can grab her from behind this time—and we all know where that ends up."

The private stood up fast. "No, no, that's OK, Sarge," he said, rubbing his ear. "I'm sure she knows what she's doin'."

"Right, Private. Off you go."

"Sarge." He saluted, then turned to Ilse. "And good luck to you, miss. I reckon those Nazis got their hands full with you."

"Thank you, Widmer, for all your help."

"Well, I'd like to say it was a pleasure, miss, but . . ." He raised the bent groin protector, grimaced, then grinned. "Cheerio," he said.

They watched him leave the stables. Then Grimes turned to her. "You did do well, miss. That private doesn't cut anyone any slack. We had a Frenchman in 'ere last week, a captain in their security service. Big tough bloke. Widmer kept putting him on the deck. He wasn't 'alf pissed off." He nodded. "I think you'll be able to handle yourself back there—wherever *there* is. Just wish I had a little more time with you." He grinned. "I'd love to show you what you can do to a bloke *without* a groin protector."

"Yes, well, that little pleasure will have to wait till next time, I'm afraid." The man who spoke stepped out of the shadows beside the barn door.

"Major Cholmondeley-Warren. How good to see you again."

Sergeant Grimes snapped a salute, which the major returned.

"Good to see you too, miss," he said. "And in such, ah, fighting trim." He turned. "You can leave her with me now, Sergeant. I look forward to reading your report."

"Sir!" Grimes saluted again, then nodded at Ilse. "Good hunting, miss."

Ilse stepped forward, held out her hand. "Thank you again, Sergeant. For everything."

Grimes looked at the hand for a moment, then shook it briefly, nodded, swivelled, and marched out.

"Will he really write a report about me?" Ilse asked.

"Of course. All your tutors in the last three weeks have submitted them. Very gratifying. Apparently, you are the second-best pistol shot ever to pass through Aston House."

"Second?"

Her tone made the major laugh. "Well, the first was a former Texas Ranger. We called him Dead-Eye Dick."

Ilse smiled. "My father had me shooting pistols at targets when I was four years old."

"It shows. So, top marks in everyone's estimation."

Ilse raised an eyebrow. "Everyone's?"

The major shrugged. "Alright, your Morse gets a little blurry under pressure . . ."

"I don't expect men will be shouting in my ear when I send."

"And your parachute skills are not perhaps of the very finest."

"I am terrified of heights, so—"

"Fortunately that is not going to matter."

Ilse stiffened. "You *are* still putting me back in?"

"We are. Just not that way. We'd love to keep you longer but," Cholmondeley-Warren ran his finger along his thin reddish moustache, "needs must when the devil drives, eh?"

Another strange English expression she'd not entirely got to grips with. But she knew it meant matters were pressing. "Are you going to tell me about it?"

"Indeed I am. But why don't you go and have a clean-up first, what? Then we'll have a bite in the Mess and discuss it over a Scotch afterwards. The chap from Six will arrive soon. Got some quite interesting new information for us, I gather."

As he gestured to the exit, Ilse picked up her small towel from a stall, wiped her face. "Six?" she asked, as she moved towards the door.

"Ah yes, sorry. Newish designation. Another wing of the Secret Intelligence Service. These chaps deal specifically with counter-espionage. Their opposite numbers might be, ooh, Abwehr Abteilung Three, say. Which I believe, in this case, might be the actual point."

He'd been looking at Ilse all the while he spoke, as they walked from the stables to the main building of Aston House—one of many "spy schools" she'd attended in the last few weeks. And though Ilse was careful to show nothing on her face, her heart gave a little flutter.

Klaus von Ronnenberg worked for Abwehr Abteilung Three. And though no one, in the three weeks since she'd flown into Leuchars in Scotland from Sweden, had said anything at all about him, she knew that it was the message she'd sent about his arrival in Oslo that had led to her summons back.

"Well," she said, pausing at the door that the major was holding open for her, "I look forward to meeting this . . . chap."

———————

"I LOVE COMING HAR," said "the chap," enthusiastically spooning Eton mess from the serving dish onto his plate. "Betht bally food in the whole of eth-o-ee. Apparently, the head cook used to be a chef at the Thavoy Gwill."

Ilse regarded the man who had been introduced to her as Angus. She knew it wasn't his name because he'd failed to respond to it, twice. She'd seen the major's eyes narrow the second time, and some less-than-subtle eye rolls further down the table from the ten men assembled. Whatever his name was, he wasn't military. He slouched over his food and had a wodge of floppy auburn hair that dropped over each eye in turn, depending on which way he was facing. His accent was so posh he lisped. He had what her father would call, when deriding the Brits—whom he loathed both for their imperial arrogance and for what he called their serial betrayals of Norway— "a cousin-fucking accent." According to Wilhelm, it had been developed by centuries of inbreeding.

He set to on the Eton mess—another strange Englishism, a concoction of tinned strawberries, custard and meringue. Ilse had taken one bite then shoved it aside. However, that was partly because the rest of the food had indeed been excellent, and she'd enjoyed the game pie, potato galette and roasted vegetables. She knew she'd lost weight in Oslo, partly from nerves, mainly because rations were short there, even for a Nazi's daughter. Not so, apparently, in England's Secret Intelligence Service establishments.

After a concentrated minute of silent wolfing, Angus threw down his spoon and sat back smiling. He pulled out a watch—on a fob, no less, Ilse noted—and said, "Betht get down to it, eh, Major? Got to be back in London by midnight. Meeting a lovely young WAAF for a bit of a dance and—" He broke off, then grinned at Ilse. "Do you dance, Miss, ah, Gustavsen?"

"I do. Though I haven't found much occasion since the Germans occupied my homeland."

Perhaps it came out a little harsher and louder than she'd intended. It brought a silence to the table, as all the men looked at her. Yet it didn't faze Angus a jot. "Quite. Quite!" he declared. "Can't be danthing with the invader, eh? Unless . . ." He beamed at her, then at Cholmondeley-Warren. "Forgo the cheese, shall we, Chumley? Take our thscotch to some little nook?"

"That's Chumley-*Warren*. And why don't we stay here and let everyone else go? There's a snooker tournament, and cards I believe." The major glared around, and everyone, still eating or not, put down glasses and cutlery, then rose and left without a word. She'd been at Aston House a week, knew some of the others, if only a little. All men and all, like her, had false names. Only two were British, most were from other occupied countries, and no one spoke in more than generalities about themselves.

The major went to the sideboard, took up three crystal tumblers with one hand, and lifted a decanter of whisky with the other. He came back, put the glasses down, raised a thin eyebrow at her. She hadn't drunk all meal—hadn't touched the wines Angus had been so enthusiastic about. Partly because she wanted to be absolutely clear about what was said to her. Partly because, one night at the parachute school near Manchester, a visiting officer had insisted Ilse drink most of a bottle of Scotch with him. Ordered her to, actually. Part of the training was to see if she could hold her tongue while inebriated. She had—but it had taken her two days to fully shake the hangover.

Now she nodded, indicated a small tot with her finger and thumb. "Excellent, excellent," Angus murmured as Cholmondeley-Warren poured. Then, raising his glass, he said, "To dancing with the enemy."

He sipped, Ilse didn't. "Is that what you wish me to do?"

"It is a part of what we wish you to do, yes." Angus put down his glass. His eyes, which had been filled with mischief and somewhat glazed during dinner, were now keen and somewhat cold. "The rest we will now discuss. I am sure you are keen to know our plans for you, eh?"

The lisp had also gone. Ilse studied him for a moment, took a sip, sat back. He looked like he wished her to ask some questions. She thought she'd wait to see what he volunteered.

The no-longer-rheumy eyes appraised her. Then he nodded, spoke. "Tell me, what do you know of Valkyrie?"

"Norse mythology. Wotan's maidens. They fetch the glorious dead from the battlefield. Take them to Valhalla for an eternity of feasting."

"Anything else?"

"Plenty. But I assume you don't want a lecture on Wagnerian opera, do you?"

"Indeed I do not. Wagner is—" He broke off, glanced at the major, continued. "Did you discuss Wagner with Major Klaus von Ronnenberg?"

She thought back. "No," she replied. "We talked only generally about music. He admired my playing. He asked if I would care to join a quartet he was forming. He used to play himself before—"

"Before he lost his arm, yes," Angus interrupted. "I apologize, do go on. What else did you learn about Herr Major Klaus von Ronnenberg?"

He pronounced it as the Germans would, not like the rank of the man sitting beside them. Hearing the precision, Ilse switched to German. "It was one brief meeting at a Christmas party. I am sure you read my report."

"I did. I am more interested in what was not in the report. He asked you out for dinner, did he not?"

She'd guessed right. His German was the equal of hers. "He did. But I did mention that in the report."

"But you didn't go?"

"No. I was summoned back here. I sent a message."

"As you wrote. But what was also not in the report . . ." He glanced again at Cholmondeley-Warren and reverted to English. "I am sorry, Major, but do you—?"

Cholmondeley-Warren shrugged. "I was a prisoner of the Boche for two years in the first show. I picked up some, but I would prefer . . . do you mind?"

"Not at all." Angus continued in English. "I was asking our friend here what was not in the report." He turned back to Ilse. "Was the invitation purely, how would I put this, professional?"

"What do you mean?"

"Come, Miss . . ." He looked around the now empty room, then lowered his voice. "Miss Magnusson. Was he only interested in your . . . flute playing?"

"Young man," growled Cholmondeley-Warren, "you can steer right away from such smutty schoolboy innuendo, thank you very much. This is one of my most valued agents you are talking to here."

"I am sorry," said Angus, not looking sorry at all. "I was just wondering if Miss Magnusson got the sense that the major desired her."

"Of course he desired her, boy. Look at her."

Ilse put her hand on Cholmondeley-Warren's arm. "It's alright, my friend. I am quite capable of handling . . . what did you call it, 'school-boy innuendo'? But I appreciate the gallantry." She squeezed the arm then looked again at Angus. "Yes, I got the impression he liked me. For more than my flute playing."

"Well, there we are." Angus drummed the table with his fingers in a brief staccato, then bent to lift a scuffed satchel from beneath his chair. Flicking the clasp, he delved and drew out a file folder. "I wonder, Miss . . . may I call you Ilse? I wonder, Ilse, if I could tax your excellent German a little further." He extracted a page from the folder and handed it across.

It was a photograph of a typed document. The title of it was *Unternehmen Walküre*—or "Operation Valkyrie." The preamble to the document stated that it was to be an emergency plan issued to the Territorial Reserve Army of Germany for the "continuity of operations in case of a civil breakdown of order, caused by some unforeseen event." It was only when Ilse had carefully read the introduction in full that she saw what such an event might be.

The Führer Adolf Hitler is dead.

Those words stopped her breath for a moment. But she didn't raise her eyes, knowing that Angus was regarding her so intently. She took a deeper breath and carefully read to the end. Only when she'd finished did she place it on the table in front of her and look up.

Angus was swirling his whisky beneath his nose. "So, is the Führer dead, Ilse?"

"Since this document is dated last November, I believe I might have heard if he was."

Angus nodded. "Observant." He pointed at the paper. "This is a, uh, fallback plan. There are now, and have always been, plots to kill Hitler. If one were to succeed—and after he was, no doubt, spirited away by Valkyrie to the home of the glorious dead—he would want to assure continuity for his thousand-year Reich. 'The King is dead, long live the King,' that sort of thing." He glanced at the major. "I suspect Winston has something similar set up, wouldn't you say, Cholmonde-ley-Warren?"

"I couldn't possibly comment," came the murmured reply.

"Quite." Angus turned back to Ilse. "But this is different, anyway. It's a revision to an original document—one that didn't talk specifi-cally about Hitler's death so much as about a breakdown in order; an internal revolt of the millions of foreign slave labourers in German factories, for example. But this"—he leaned forward, tapped the page —"is a recent, and secret, revision. As you read, it states that the commander of the Reserve Forces in Germany—one Colonel-General Friedrich Fromm, on the news of der Führer's death, would take control of everything, military and civilian. All organs of state, every police force, the whole Nazi Party. The Waffen-SS, hitherto a separate military force with its own command structures, would be immediately absorbed into the Wehrmacht. So Fromm would essen-tially have the same supreme power that Hitler does now—but every-thing would now be under Wehrmacht control. *Wehrmacht control,*" he repeated, taking another pull at his whisky. "So, for the first time since the war began, generals would be in charge of all the armed forces and the overall direction of the war. Not a former corporal. And not the Nazi Party."

"Which some of them might like?"

"Which, indeed, many of them *would* like, Ilse." He sat back, swirled the whisky again, sniffed it, didn't drink. "Do you have any other questions about this document?"

"How did you get it?"

"We have someone in Abwehr headquarters in Berlin. Someone virulently anti-Nazi and in such deep cover he makes you look as obvious in Oslo as . . ." he reached into the bowl still on the table in front of him and snatched up a single piece of mushy fruit, "the last strawberry in an Eton mess." He popped it in his mouth, spoke while chewing. "Anything else?"

"You say this is a secret revision. Secret even from Hitler, unlike the original?"

"Oh, most certainly. You see, Operation Valkyrie has changed. It is no longer about maintaining the power of the state in the event of some calamity. It is about *provoking* such a calamity in order to seize power *from* the state. The calamity being"—he broke off to stare above him at the hall's high, vaulted ceiling—"the assassination of Adolf Hitler."

This time Ilse didn't restrain her gasp. "Who would do that? And why? I thought the Germans were fanatical in their devotion—"

"'Who'?" Angus interrupted. "So many people. Most believe that there is almost no opposition to Hitler and his mad dreams. It is not true. There is strong opposition, men and women who hate his policies, his treatment of the Jews, the destruction being meted out daily on their land. They're necessarily covert, of course—students with leaflets, priests in their pulpits, trade unionists in factories. Above all, lots in the army. Old Prussians who resent a house painter's commands. Gifted and experienced field commanders who are forced to act on a corporal's military whim." He shook his head. "They know that the war is essentially lost. And that Hitler's rants about preferring to destroy Germany rather than see her beaten in war for the second time in twenty-five years are his absolute determination. They also know that Hitler has enough power and loyalty to prolong the war for some time to come. Many in the Wehrmacht want to seize control and negotiate a separate peace with the Western Allies. Because what they truly fear, what they have always feared, is the Slav. Our esteemed ally, Joe Stalin." He pointed at the paper again. "Valkyrie, this revised Valkyrie, is their starting point."

He stared at her again, eyebrows raised for her further questions. She had so many, of course. And it was a thrill to her to hear someone declare with such certainty that the Nazis would be beaten in the end. She had never doubted that herself. Knew in her heart that such evil could not triumph. But that was all to think about later. Because, in the end, there was only one question that was vital to her. So she took a sip of whisky, put down her glass, and asked it.

"Why are you showing this to *me*?"

"It is my question as well." The major leaned closer to the man opposite him. "Since it is my operative you obviously want something from. What is it, man?"

Angus looked from one to the other, licked his lips. "You will both have noticed how Fromm, the reserve commander, having assumed control, will immediately delegate it to other commanders in their own spheres. On every front line—Russia, Italy. And in every occupied country." He looked directly at Ilse. "If this coup is to succeed—and a coup is what we are talking about here—once Hitler is dead it will require a near-simultaneous seizing of power everywhere that the Wehrmacht operates." He nodded. "Including, as stated clearly in the document, in Norway."

She'd seen her country's name written there. And even though it wasn't actually written down, she now saw another name on the page. A name that had been spoken at the very beginning of the conversation. "I see," she said.

"Damned if I do!" the major slammed his fist upon the table. "What do you want of her, Angus—or whatever your real bloody name is?"

"Would you explain it to the major, my dear? Before he pops a vein."

Ilse spoke over Cholmondeley-Warren's renewed growling. "He believes that Klaus von Ronnenberg is part of Operation Valkyrie. That he will be helping to seize control in Norway when this coup is launched. Is that not correct?"

"Almost. You see, we are not certain how deeply he is committed. But our friend in Berlin believes he could be . . . most important."

Angus stared directly into Ilse's eyes. "Now, if only we could be certain of him in some way . . ."

He left the question in the air. The major looked up, as if seeing it there, and frowned. "How is Ilse to make certain of—" He broke off. "Now wait a bloody minute here, are you asking her to—"

"We are asking nothing of her, Major." Angus switched his gaze to Cholmondeley-Warren. His eyes were cold. "We need her to get information. How she does that is up to her. Using whatever method she considers most . . . effective." The other man spluttered in outrage, full sentences not quite coming. Using the interlude, Angus reached across, snagged the paper, shoved it into his briefcase and stood. "Must be going," he said, the loose smile back on his face. "Our gallant lasses in the Women's Air Auxiliary simply can't be kept waiting. Too many bloody Yanks waiting to cut in." As Ilse stood, he reached out a hand and she took it. "It's been delightful, Miss . . . Gustavsen. Are you with us for much longer?"

"None of your business, matey." The major also stood. "She'll be going back . . . soon. Meantime, we want to give her a brief respite, starting tomorrow—"

"A holiday? How delightful! Do wish I could squire you round a bit. Since you like to dance." He laughed at Cholmondeley-Warren's grumble, then shook his head. "Best not though, given the, uh, connections, what?" He looked coldly at the other man. "However, I think you'll find it *is* my business, Major." The smile came back as he turned back to her. "I do wish you all the very best with your, ah, endeavours to help end this war so much sooner." His eyes hardened. "Like any soldier in a trench, any sacrifices you make will be most appreciated." Before Cholmondeley-Warren could muster coherent outrage, Angus said, "Thanks for the top-notch grub, Major. Compliments to the chef, eh?"

With a returned lisp and a wide smile, he walked from the room.

It took some time to calm Cholmondeley-Warren down, basically by agreeing to all he said about the limits of her "sacrifices," and how any work she did for SOE was "vital to the cause." In the end she had to plead exhaustion, which was not untrue. They started at dawn and worked her hard at Aston House.

However, when she lay down in her bed, sleep would not come. Her mind ran over all she'd heard, what had been said—and what had not. She could make no decision there, in a safe house in England, about what "sacrifices" she was prepared to make back in Norway. But she did remember how, so often during the two and a half years she'd been back in Oslo, she'd craved a deeper involvement. Something to make her think she was fighting and helping to win the war, to free her country, free the world.

Her eyelids drooped. Sleep was coming. Yet Klaus von Ronnenberg— his wounded eyes, his soft voice—was not the last man she thought of just before it took her.

That was Billy Coke. She wondered, as she often did, but especially either side of the veil of sleep, where he was. If he was even alive. Yet now she also wondered something else: if he was alive, what sacrifices had he made, was he still making?

BILLY COKE WAITED till the 38 bus had pulled in and fully stopped at the bottom end of Piccadilly before he lowered himself down from the platform. No more for him the joys of leaping off the platform of a double-decker while it still moved, using the momentum to sprint along the pavement. The surgeon had warned him that if he wanted all those pins in his thigh to hold, he must not attempt sudden speedy movements. "Walking's most efficacious, though. Confine yourself to plenty of that. No sprints or hurdles just yet, eh?"

It was why he'd got off where he had. The pub he wanted to drink in was about half a mile away. The walk would indeed be "efficacious." He set out at a good clip, using the walking stick—its silver top engraved in an elaborate "WC"—to aid the swing of his left leg. He'd purloined it from Coke House, where he was convalescing. He'd never been made welcome there from the moment he'd arrived as an orphan from Canada at the age of seven. And in adulthood, his "unsavoury politics" had meant he was essentially banned. But since his cousin Sir Gervase Coke was now in India with the 1st Battalion of the Devonshires, the family regiment, there was no one to say him nay. One of that regiment's founders in the seventeenth century had been Sir William Coke—the very WC whose initials decorated the silver. The man Billy's father had named him for.

The crowded pavements slowed him. It was a rare sunny January day in what had been the coldest winter of the war so far—so the citizens were out taking advantage of it. Quite different, he thought, as he weaved through the throng, from the last time he'd spent any time in the city, exactly three years before. Then the Blitz had been at its height, and citizens cowered in their Anderson shelters at home, or in Tube stations. Then, if you walked along Piccadilly, you crunched shattered glass and stepped over tumbled brick, with the stench of leaking gas mains in your nostrils. But the German bombers rarely came now, and when they did it was in far smaller numbers than they used to. Many people didn't even shelter from them anymore, regarding the sirens as an auditory irritant more than anything else. Struck buildings had either been repaired or were hidden behind scaffolding and dark builders' cloths.

The crowds he threaded through were different too. For a start there were children about. In '40, '41, most of them had been evacuated to the country to avoid the bombs. But though the government had urged parents to keep them there, many—perhaps most—had disobeyed. They were mostly with their mothers, their fathers being away at war. Which did not mean there were not men about; there were, in great number, and nearly all in uniform, providing much of the colour on the streets—maroon berets for the paratroopers, green for commandos, blue for Polish troops. Not many of the soldiers were British. Many more were Yanks. And a sizeable number of those were Black.

Billy kept his head up, taking in all the sights and sounds of the great metropolis. He wasn't a Londoner by birth and had spent time here only sporadically over the years. But it thrilled him still, especially after three years stationed mainly under canvas in North Africa, the Middle East and around the Mediterranean. The cold got into his knitting bones some. But the desert could be cold too. What he was looking forward to today was the reward for his doctor-prescribed exercise—a cellar-cooled pint or two in one of his favourite pubs, the Red Lion in Duke of York Street.

Outside one building he pulled his hat brim further over his eyes, turned his face to the passing trams and buses: 128 Piccadilly. It was the RAF Club. He'd paused before it the week before, looked up—and his stripes were noticed, his Canada shoulder badge, and two young officers had dragged him inside. Though he had loved much of the camaraderie of the Mess, after three years of it he was relishing his time alone. Also he'd always been out of step with the English public schoolboys who mainly officered the RAF. Had been when he'd arrived as a boy from British Columbia, became more so when he learned about politics and began his march ever leftwards. So when his nice young kidnappers had begun "A Malta Song"—"We're flying fucking Hurricanes with fucking long-range tanks . . ."—Billy had slipped quietly away.

He'd flown fucking Hurricanes out of Malta in '41, unlike these boys, and had no wish to dwell on the place or the time.

No one hailed him today, and twenty paces on he raised his head again, took in the sights. Just past the Ritz Hotel he turned down St. James's Street, then took a left onto Jermyn Street. By the time he turned right again, onto Duke of York Street, he was happy to see both his destination ahead, because his leg was beginning to ache, and that it was open. There'd been beer shortages that winter, and many pubs were closed until supplies came in.

The Red Lion was an old Georgian pub, with gorgeous tall mirrors lining its inside. The landlord had refused to take them down during the Blitz and afterwards. Superstition, he'd said: "Take 'em down, Adolf's bound to score a direct 'it, in't ee." The Luftwaffe *had* scored a direct hit three doors to the right, four to the left, and right opposite. But the Red Lion stood proud and unscathed. And so Billy was able, as he sat and drank off his first pint, to survey the clientele in the beautiful glass on either side of his little snug's wooden walls, without appearing to do so. Survey and . . . enjoy.

It was another big difference of war: there were lots of women in the pubs—frequently without husbands or any other male escorts. This had not been the case before 1939 and it was still frowned upon by many now. He'd read several outraged letters to the *Times* decrying the change—the combination of solo women, liquor and lusty soldiers had led to the "English rose's rampant promiscuity . . . even with Negroes," wailed one incensed retired judge from the safety of Sevenoaks. But in uniform and in civvies, the women often outnumbered the male customers—as they did this lunchtime.

Billy sipped, looked around—and met a reflected pair of eyes. Dark, in a setting almond-shaped. Curly brown hair spilled from under a cap; he couldn't see which badge. Military, probably WAAF or WRNS.

He held the look for a moment, long enough to convey a degree of interest before looking away, down, to study the peaks and troughs in the creamy head of his brown ale. Was he interested though? It had been a while since . . . Martene, in Malta. Christ, he'd almost forgotten her name! It hadn't been love, far from it. It was only just short of a financial transaction truly, the local girls hanging around the base, skinny from their island's long siege, liking the food, the stockings and lipstick the pilots could get, the attention. She'd been . . . a nice enough girl, and he'd been lonely. There hadn't been many before, the opportunities in North Africa very few and very far between. Since Sicily, his shooting down, the pain of his wounds had stopped him focusing on much else. Now he was recovering, though, he felt once again able to seek company, should he want to. But did he? Would his doctor also consider a little sex "efficacious"?

"Got a light, uh, sir?"

He looked up. She'd seen the two stripes on his sleeves. He now noticed the propeller on hers. She was a leading aircraftwoman—and prettier face-on than she'd been reflected. "Billy, please," he replied, "and . . . of course." He reached for the Swan Vestas he'd laid on the bar before him, then noticed she didn't have a cigarette ready for lighting. "Would you care for one of mine?" he asked, holding out the packet.

"Wouldn't say no," she said, adding: "Ooh, Camels, eh? You must have American friends."

"I do."

They both extracted cigarettes. When he struck a match, held it out to her, she took his hand, leaned in to light hers. Her fingers were cool on his and he thought, oh hello, at the shiver that passed through him. She peered up at him, through wreathing smoke. "I'm Deirdre, by the way. My friends and I"—she indicated their reflections with a wave; two other WAAFs still sitting at the table, who waved when he looked— "were wondering where you was from? Canada it says by your flash. But you don't sound Canadian."

"I am and I'm not." He shrugged. "It's a long story."

"Well, it's a lovely voice, whatever the accent. And I love a story. Longer the better." She squeezed onto the other stool. The snug was small, and their knees touched. "Want to tell us?"

Her accent was London, working-class. Her eyes, closer to, were more auburn than black. There was some red in the curls that spilled from her hat, as there was in the freckles that ran over her nose from both cheeks. She was . . . cute, no other word for it. And once again Billy got that tingle he hadn't felt for a while. "Drink?" he said.

"Don't mind if I do. Gin and it, please."

As Billy signalled the bartender he said, "Would your friends care for one?"

"I am sure they would."

"Would you like us to join them?"

"What, and share you? No bleedin' thanks!" She gave a trill of a laugh that ran half a scale. "You can send 'em over a couple of gins though, if you like."

Billy gave the orders, including another pint for himself. The "it" was water, and he asked the barman to carry a small jug and the two gins over to the table. Whatever the barman said there made the girls laugh, and they raised their glasses and waved again at Billy.

"Good health," Billy said, raising and toasting with his beer.

"Chin-chin," Deirdre said, clinking his pint pot. They sipped and she continued. "I noticed you as soon as you come in. You got a bit of a limp. A stick." She frowned. "Wounded, eh? Shot down?"

A flash came—a snowflake shell puncturing his windshield, hot metal in his body. He swallowed. "Something like that."

"Sorry, don't mean to pry. We don't need to talk about that. Bloody war!" She took another pull at her gin. "Tell me about your English-Canadian thing. Your voice is ever so nice. Like off the BBC."

"Before the war I was an actor."

"You never! I love the movies, me. Tell me about that. You ever work with Leslie Howard?"

He didn't actually get to tell her much about anything. One of her questions would lead to another, and then to her opinions on the questions asked. He was happy about that, letting her talk, prompting her a bit, enjoying her openness, hearing in quite extensive and revealing detail how much fun the war had been for her. His own past didn't interest him so much. It opened too many doors onto corridors he had no wish to walk down.

Yet, as she talked, he found himself paying less attention, his mind drifting. His leg was aching a bit; perhaps the walk had been too much. Also, there was something about her, delightful and fresh and open as she was, that disturbed him. It took him the rest of the pint to figure out what that was.

She was the opposite of Ilse.

There were not many days that he didn't think of her. Wondered if she was alive and, if so, where. The frequency of his memories had dropped. In the first year after they'd parted, he'd thought of her almost every hour. In the second, certainly every day. Latterly, often . . . but not always? Yet in the company of another woman he did. In their attributes, he thought of hers. For if Deirdre was a fast-flowing river, Ilse was a gentle brook. If Deirdre was flame, Ilse was a fire, banked, ready to break out with the right blown breath. If Deirdre could make him tingle, the memory of Ilse still made him shake. If Deirdre was cute, with her open face and freckles, Ilse was simply, utterly, beautiful. And he realized now why he'd chosen this pub to walk to, to drink in. It wasn't his destination. It was a stop along the way.

"Hark at me, rabbiting on!" Deirdre laughed and reached across him, snagging another cigarette, lifting it to her mouth, her pencil-painted eyebrows rising, inviting him to light it. " 'Aven't let you get a word in edgewise. Your turn."

He struck a match, lit her cigarette, dropped it in the ashtray. "Have to be another time, I'm afraid." He drained his pint, rose.

"You're not leavin'?" Her eyes went wide. "I thought we might, you know, make a day of it?"

"I'd love to, but"—he pulled on his coat—"duty calls."

Her lower lip came out. "If I give you my number, will you call me?"

"Sure. I'd like that."

He must have said it with enough conviction—ever the actor—because she excitedly dug out a pad and pencil from her purse, scribbled a number, drew a heart around it, held it out. "You promise now?"

"Cross my heart," he replied, tucking it in his pocket. He put on his hat, picked up his stick, limped a few steps, his leg always stiff after a little rest.

" 'Ere, Fly Boy," she called, and he turned. The pout had gone, the sparkle was back. "What's my name?"

"Deirdre," he replied. "You think I could ever forget?"

He heard a gust of women's laughter as he stepped out of the pub. The closing door cut it off.

He'd realized where he needed to go. Where he'd put off going in his week back in London, since his discharge from the hospital. He didn't even know if he'd get an answer, if the person he'd ask it of was even still there. But it came to him clearly now—what Ilse had told him just before they'd parted three years before.

My friend, Kirsten Larsen . . . She works in Norwegian naval intelligence. She will perhaps know . . . something.

He hadn't a clue where Norwegian naval intelligence would have their headquarters. It might not even be in London. But there was a place he'd seen before, walking across Trafalgar Square. It was on the south side, on Cockspur Street, and it had elaborate decor, a statue of some warrior saint and its name above the door: Norway House. When he'd first seen it, he'd asked a passing copper what the place was. He'd said it housed departments of the Norwegian government in exile.

A good place to begin.

He'd met Kirsten Larsen once. He'd been on a three-day furlough just before shipping out for North Africa, six months after parting from Ilse. He'd called the number he'd been given, and they met at a Lyons Corner House, the one opposite Charing Cross station, for a cup of tea. But the short, full-faced, dark-haired woman had told him nothing. Hadn't known where Ilse was, how she was. Even if she was still alive. "She is not one of us, you know," she'd said, tapping the words *KGL Norsk Marine*, which formed the band of the hat she'd laid on the table beside her gloves. "She works directly for the British."

Billy had frowned. "Which outfit?" he'd asked.

"I cannot say," she'd replied, in a way that meant she could, but wouldn't.

He'd tried the number from the hospital in Portsmouth, post-surgery, when still half-delirious on morphine. It was disconnected. Now he stood before the tall door, with its rectangular wooden panels lined with gilt, the stone frame around them decorated with heraldic shields. On the lintel, the words *Norway House* were divided by a larger shield bearing the axe-clutching Lion of Norway, a red crown above him.

The huge doors swung open and closed as people entered and

left. In glimpses he didn't see a reception desk, someone to ask, just a wrought-iron elevator shaft, a stone stairwell beside it. He was standing out of the way to the side, but people still gave him quizzical looks as they passed. Finally, one of them, a young man going out, stopped. "May I help you"—he glanced down—"Flight Lieutenant?"

His accent was almost flawless. He was wearing a charcoal suit, beautifully cut. The only hint of the military came from that same red lion in a pin on his college—Billy suspected Oxford—tie. "I hope so," Billy replied. "I've been . . . away." He waved his stick as if that might explain it. "Just got back and was hoping to find a . . . friend. But her number's disconnected."

"I see." The young man smiled. "And what is the name of this friend?"

"Kirsten Larsen."

"I see," the young man said again, without betraying any recognition.

"Do you know her?"

"I might." He grinned. "I might be her fiancé. Then I might wonder what such a handsome young pilot would be wanting with her, hmm?"

"Are you her fiancé?"

"I might be."

"Well, I don't want to speak to her . . . in that way. We have a, uh, mutual friend. I wanted to find out how *she* was."

"I see," he said again, in a manner that was beginning to annoy Billy.

"Look, pal," he said, coming off the stick stepping closer, "there's nothing sinister here. I just want to see if this friend of ours is OK."

"This woman friend. What is her name?"

"I think I'll just keep that to myself, if you don't mind. Do you know Kirsten, or should I pop in to Norway House and make my enquiries there?"

The young man's eyes glinted for a moment, before he smiled again. "I'll tell you what, Flight Lieutenant. You see that canteen over there?" He pointed to the other side of Trafalgar Square where, in front of South Africa House, people in a truck with an awning over its open side were dispensing mugs of tea. Billy nodded. "You wait over there for a little bit and I'll see if my, ah, fiancée cares to join you for a cuppa, yes?"

"So you do know her?"

"Yah." He said it the same way Billy had noticed Ilse reply to some questions, and how Norwegian airmen he'd met did too—barely vocalizing the word, saying it on an indrawn breath.

"My name is Billy Coke."

"And your mutual friend?"

It was Billy's turn to smile. "She'll know my name."

"Very well."

The young man turned and made his way west along Cockspur Street towards Pall Mall. Billy went the other way, dodged traffic across to the square, crossed it under Nelson's horizon gaze, and arrived at the canteen. He didn't join the queue, however. His leg was truly starting to ache now, so he lowered himself onto an artillery-shell-shaped stone bollard to wait.

He didn't wait long. In about ten minutes he noticed the young man in the suit and a woman in a dark blue naval uniform cross from the northwest corner of the square. They stopped about thirty feet away, saw that he'd seen them. The man said something to her. She nodded, squeezed his arm. He gave Billy a little head-bow, then walked back the way he'd come.

She came to him, stretched out her hand. He rose, took it. "Flight Lieutenant Coke," she said. "How nice to see you again."

She was different than he remembered. Thinner of face, and hair. War and worries had done that. "And you. Did you want a cup of tea?"

"It is the worst tea in London, and that says quite a lot."

"I couldn't . . . I couldn't buy you a drink, could I? I would like to sit down."

She looked at the stick, the way his leg was angled. "The war, of course?"

If she looked different, he was sure he did too. "Yes. Shot down. Sicily." He shrugged. "Getting better by the day though."

"I see," she said. Maybe it was a Norwegian thing. Then she looked away briefly, looked back. "I cannot come for a drink. I am expecting . . . something important at my office. But I wanted to see you, to tell you . . ."

She trailed off, and his throat seized. "She's not dead, is she?"

"No, she is—"

"In Norway. About her . . . work?"

"About her work, yes, but not in Norway." She looked around again, then up at him. "She is here."

"Here?" He gasped. "In England?"

"In London. Not for long. She—" She broke off again. "I cannot tell you anything; she cannot tell you anything. But she told me once—"

"What?" He saw hesitation in her eyes. "Please!"

She swallowed. "She told me that if ever you were to get in touch, I should let you know how she was. That you were the only man in the world that I should." Her face, concerned up to now, broke into a smile. "I have known Ilse Magnusson since kindergarten. She would not say that unless she really meant it." Once more she glanced around, then slipped a piece of paper into his hand. "Will you please learn what is written here very quickly then give me the paper back, Flight Lieutenant?"

"Billy. And . . ." He turned the paper over, saw the address, memorized it, handed her the paper back. "Is she there now?"

"Perhaps."

"For how long?"

"I do not know. Not long, I think." She smiled again. "But it is on the Northern line, yes? And you can get that right here," she nodded over his shoulder, "from Charing Cross, can't you?"

"I can." He reached out his hand. "Thank you. I cannot tell you how grateful I am."

"It is OK. Good luck."

She squeezed his hand, walked away. He called after her. "Is he?"

She stopped, swivelled. "Is he what?"

"Your fiancé? He said he was."

"Magnus?" She laughed. "He wishes. And he told me he was very jealous of this handsome young pilot who was looking for me. Men, eh?"

The blue coat merged into the grey crowd. Billy went the other way, to Charing Cross station. After buying a ticket, he made for the escalators descending to the Northbound platform. Edgware branch. His leg didn't hurt any longer. All the pain was in his heart, beating as fast as if a 109 was on his tail.

ILSE STOOD at the kitchen sink, drying her lunch plates, gazing out onto Hampstead Heath. It was only a garden's length away from the first-floor flat in the SOE-run house where they'd placed her. There wasn't even a fence to stop her from entering the London parkland because, according to the houseowner, Mrs. Phillips, who lived on the ground floor, the railings had long since been "melted and transformed into bombs to drop on that bloody Hitler's head."

Crows swooped and squabbled over branches on the winter-bare trees. But their black silhouettes moved against a clear blue sky, the first she'd seen in the three days she'd been there. She had five more days before they returned her to Norway, retracing the route she'd taken to arrive: a flight to Stockholm, a train to the border, her cross-country skis awaiting her in the rural station's lock-up. A bus to a crossroads, and then a ski into the wilds of Femundsmarka, a truly rugged place of which this "wild" English heath was only an imitation. Her family hut was another long bus ride and then a three-hour hard ski away. She'd arrive near dawn, rest up, and then ski into Otta for lunchtime. Another bus, another train; barring accidents, she'd be back in Oslo by late evening.

She realized that the plate in her hands could not be any dryer. She placed it in the cupboard with the others, then leaned on the sink edge and looked out. The major had said she should take a holiday, had even suggested a few places. "I know you feel you have not been doing much for us in Norway," he'd said. "But do not underestimate the steady strain that all secret work confers. Get out, breathe some fresh air, is what I'd do. Ever been to the Lake District? Marvellous, the hills!"

But she'd decided that just the luxury of being alone, of not always thinking about how she was presenting herself, what she could learn, was holiday enough. And she could breathe some hill air right in front of her—Parliament Hill, from which, Mrs. Phillips had told her, she could see the whole of London spread out. After days of freezing fogs, today was sunny, so she'd walk up and take in that view. Maybe keep walking, right across the Heath to Kenwood at its apex, and eat supper in an old coaching pub that had been recommended to her, the Spaniards Inn.

There were clothes in the flat that fitted her, worn by other operatives that had passed through. She wondered about them as she pulled on some fleece-lined boots that fitted remarkably well, a thick Shetland sweater, a woollen headscarf: the women who had worn these items, setting off across the Heath as she was about to do, before returning to their countries, their war. Was she alive, in France, in Belgium, in Greece, the woman whose perfume—Caron's Le Tabac Blond, one Ilse herself had worn in New York—faintly lingered in the wool? Was she making her own choices, her own compromises, as Ilse must?

As Ilse would.

She was at the door, holding up a waxed coat that looked a little too large for her, when the knock came. Mrs. Phillips no doubt, always popping up with baked treats. Rationing didn't seem to affect her at all—the advantage of running a safe house for SOE, surely.

Part of her duties seemed to be fattening up operatives. Ilse felt she'd put on several pounds already in the three days she'd been here.

She opened the door. It was Mrs. Phillips. But she was not alone.

The man standing behind her was instantly familiar, and different too. "Oh," she said, her hand rising to her mouth, as she saw the changes that three years of war had wrought in Billy Coke. Though he'd been through much even then, at twenty-three the boy had still been clear. That boy was gone. But one thing had not changed, and she wondered why she only remembered it so clearly right now. The way he was looking at her, as he had looked at her when they'd parted.

All this, in that same moment, while Mrs. Phillips spoke. "He says he knows you, my dear," she said, her voice tight, with all the clipped vowels of her private-school education. "But I told him that I would have to make sure that was true."

Ilse had no words, barely any air, had to look down—and saw, in the housekeeper's wrinkled left hand, a small automatic pistol. A Beretta, she thought, and that word gave her others, and breath again. "He does, Mrs. Phillips, thank you. We are . . . old friends."

The Beretta was vanished into a cardigan pocket. A smile came to the older woman's face. "Now, isn't that nice?" she said. "Put the kettle on and I'll fetch you up some jam tarts, shall I? Just baked a batch."

Ilse looked into Billy's eyes again. "I think we'll be OK, Mrs. Phillips, but thank you." She lifted the jacket in her hands. "I was just going out for a walk."

"The young man has a cane, you'll notice. And has already walked from Belsize Park station. Don't you tire him out." She looked between the two of them and nodded. "There you are, then. Do let me know if you need anything."

She went to the stairs. Her slow footfall faded. He did not move. "Hello, Ilse," he said.

"Hello, Billy."

He limped towards her. One step. Two. Until he was close. "Do," he said.

"Do what?" she replied.

"Do tire me out."

HIS SHOULDER HURT, even more than his leg. But he wasn't going to move it. Ilse was tucked into him, her soft, sleeping breath tickling the skin of his chest. He felt he must have held other women there. He couldn't remember a single one. This felt like her . . . place. Moulded for her. Or like they were two puzzle pieces, fitted together.

Is that what we are, he wondered? Two . . . *puzzled* pieces, finding their match. It had been three years. He knew what he had been through. He could only guess at what she had. Yet there she was, in her place, in their place, and it felt like no time had passed at all.

He sighed. Watched his breath plume the air. Realized only then how cold the room was, despite the wintry sun still in the sky, fading beyond the window. He tried to pull the down comforter up over both of them without waking her. But she took a sudden breath, and her eyes shot open. He saw a moment's confusion in them as she looked up at him, as if he were not real, only the last image of the dream she'd been having. He knew the feeling, and he'd not slept, had only held her while she did.

"Billy Coke," he offered. "Nice to meet you."

She laughed, tucked her head in again. Said, after a moment, "Am I killing your arm?"

"Nope. That died a while back." She made to shift, and he squeezed her tight. "Don't you dare."

She laughed again, settled in again. Ran her fingernails back and forth across his chest. "It's getting late, isn't it?"

"Yeah, I'd say around three thirty. I guess I've put paid to your walk."

"I'll forgive you."

He let her stroke, listened to her soft breath. Felt himself start to tire. It had been quite the day. But as his eyes fluttered, he opened them wide. He didn't know how much time they had. He'd sleep none of it away. "Hey," he said. "Got any plans?"

"Maybe," she said, suddenly pinching a nipple.

"Ouch," he cried, then laughed. "I mean, later, after . . . Which I am completely OK with, by the way. I—"

"Really?" She rose, rested her arms on his chest, looked down at him. "I would never have guessed."

"No?"

Her hands started to rove again, and he reached down, took one in each of his. "But later, after . . . how long are you here?"

He saw it, the world coming back into her eyes. Regretted putting it there—but suddenly he had to know. Time might be suspended for a while, but it would return, as it always did. "How long do we have?"

She shook her white-gold hair, and it danced on her shoulders. "I have . . . a few days. Five days, before I . . . before I must work. You?"

"I've got longer. Convalescing, you know. Getting stronger. Another month at least before I get sent to a new squadron."

She ran her fingers under the covers to his left leg, to the vivid pink ladder made by stitches only recently removed, that earlier she'd carefully traced with her tongue. "Do you wish to tell me, Billy? Tell me about this?"

"Not really, no." He reached and grabbed her hand, brought it to his lips, kissed her palm. "I'd like to know if you need to do anything in those . . . five days." He faltered slightly on the time limit. "Or if you might like to go somewhere. Get away."

"A holiday? I've been told to take a holiday." Her eyes were glowing now. "Where would we go? How would we get there?"

"I have a thought as to where." He grinned. "As to how? By car, of course!"

"You borrow that lorry again?"

"Mac's? No, no. I don't even know if the Globe is still standing, haven't been yet. Anyway, I didn't say 'lorry,' I said 'car.'"

"You have a car?"

"I can get one."

"And petrol? I thought that was impossible to all but the army."

"I'm in the army. Well, air force. And this is important military business. I'll requisition some petrol."

"What military business?"

"Um, 'liaising with allies'?"

Ilse grinned and tapped his chest three times. "This you have already done."

"More . . . liaising. Right," he said, sitting up. "I'll go get that car."

"Now?" She laughed. "You are like a little boy again. You want to be up and doing."

He chuckled. "OK, maybe not now. In the morning. First thing."

"Maybe not *first* thing," she said, then drew his head down for a kiss.

―――――――――――

"I DO NOT FEEL your cousin would approve, sir."

"I'm damn sure he wouldn't!" Billy looked at the other man and laughed. "Another good reason to do it, eh?"

Jeffers sighed. The old butler often did when Billy was at Coke House. Though one night a week before, over a cognac Billy had insisted he sit down and take, he'd also confessed that Billy's father had been his favourite Coke in his three generations of service to the family. Intimated that the son did remind him of the father. Billy had taken the opportunity to learn more about his dad. How William Coke Senior had always been a rebel too. How he'd won a medal for gallantry at Ypres, been shot by a sniper, and then refused to rejoin the regiment, instead taking himself off to Canada.

"Besides, Jeffers," Billy continued, "he's not going to know, is he? Where is Gervase now anyway? Rawalpindi?"

"It's where I last heard from him. The Devonshires could be anywhere now. War's hotting up down there. Burma, perhaps?" He harrumphed, as if he had suddenly been caught revealing military secrets.

"Far enough away not to hear of a little excursion, anyway. I promise I'll have it back in three days without a betraying scratch on it."

"Yes, sir." The older man sighed. "It's just that your father said the same thing to me in 1911 when he borrowed Sir Geoffrey's Rolls-Royce. He returned two weeks later, in clothes I hadn't packed for him, and without the Silver Ghost."

Billy laughed. That was another story he'd like to hear more of. But it was one for another day. It was already 9 a.m.; he'd told Ilse he'd be back to pick her up by noon. And there were many things he had to do first.

He stared again at the sky-blue Bentley on blocks before him. It truly was a fabulous machine. "When was she last run out, Jeffers?"

"March 1941, sir. Just before your cousin shipped out." He shook his head. "I'm not even sure the car will start after all this time."

"Oh, she'll start. After I've given her a little love and attention." He took off his jacket, which the butler immediately came to collect. Billy looked around the small mews garage. "I see the tires and the pump. Get those on first. I assume you have petrol, oil and lubricant?"

"In that cupboard over there, sir. Some may have evaporated."

"Tools?"

"There's a full set in that drawer, I believe." Jeffers folded the jacket carefully and hung it over one arm. "Will you be requiring any help, sir?"

"I'd love a flask of coffee and a roll, if Mrs. Jacobs can spare them."

"Certainly, sir. Anything else?"

"Can't think of anything," Billy replied, rolling up his sleeves. "Though I suppose I could use a bath, and I do need to pack—"

"I will draw one on your signal, sir, and pack some clothes for three days motoring in the country. I'll also ask Mrs. Jacobs to put a hamper together."

"Excellent. With some wine, perhaps?"

"Of course. I believe you have found the 1929 Rhône to be acceptable."

"Most acceptable, thanks."

As Billy limped over to the tool drawer, Jeffers watched him. "May I say, sir, it is good to have someone to look after in the house again. Actually," he cleared his throat, "it is wonderful to see you back and, well, alive."

Billy dipped his head. "Thank you, Jeffers. This morning it feels especially good to be so."

As the old butler left, Billy looked again at the magnificent vehicle before him. "Now, my old beauty," he murmured, and reached into the drawer.

AT NOON ON THE DOT, Billy pulled up outside 42 Tanza Road, Hampstead, and tooted the Bentley's horn. Mrs. Phillips was the first to appear and immediately went back inside, her place taken by a dozen kids who sprang as if by magic from the surrounding houses. They gawked, chattered, and ran their fingers over the paintwork which Jeffers had insisted on polishing up.

Billy was in civvies—the suit he'd had made for him and last worn in 1941 had required an extra hole to be awled in the belt. He stood at the rear door of the car, blue against its blue, beaming.

Ilse appeared, dressed for travel in a lavender wool coat that was a little large for her, and a beret that was perhaps a little small. She looked stunning.

Billy opened the rear door. "My lady," he said, reaching to take her small valise.

She released it to him, but didn't climb in. "I'm going to ride in front with you, yes?"

"You are," he whispered, gesturing to the wide-eyed kids, "but let's give them a bit of a show first, eh?"

"Ah!" Smiling herself now, Ilse accepted his hand, stooping as he passed her into the deep seat. "My God," she said, running her hand over the soft, pliable leather, "wherever did you find this?"

He closed the door, went around to the driver's side, sat, turned the key. The engine came to life with a purr it had taken him near an hour to perfect. "Sometimes," he said, "and with all apologies to my comrades in the proletariat . . . it's good to be a Coke." He looked at her in his rear-view mirror. "Where to, milady?" he asked.

She laughed. "Don't you know?"

"I do, indeed. And I'm going to surprise you."

He wound the window down. "Clear orf, you bleedin' mites!" he yelled.

They followed him, laughing and yelling abuse, halfway down the road. When he turned right, out of their sight, he pulled over and Ilse joined him in the front. She kissed him, then seized his arm, laying her head on his shoulder.

Not quite in her place but close, Billy thought, as he stepped on the accelerator.

FIFTEEN
CONFESSIONS

Oslo. January 21, 1944

KLAUS VON RONNENBERG laid the paper down on the desk; then, his hand still shaking, he reached and pulled a cigarette from the silver box above his blotter. Placing it between his lips, he lifted the large tabletop lighter and pressed. The flame wobbled as much as the paper had done, and he had to focus on getting it to the cigarette's end. He sucked, sat back and inhaled deeply.

Christ, he thought, exhaling, crinkling his eyes against the rising smoke. It has begun.

He looked down again at the paper that had given him the shakes. He had seen something like this document before. It had been another emergency "government continuity plan," orders to be followed in the event of some unspecified breakdown of civil order in German society. Those orders had passed across his desk and soon out of his mind. They were specifically concerned with Germany itself, and he had not been stationed there for many years.

These orders were different. Firstly, they concerned not just

Germany but all of the Greater Reich, the Eastern and Italian fronts as well as France, Denmark and Norway. Secondly, they stated that it was to be the Wehrmacht specifically that would establish and hold control if and when the plan was implemented, and not—and this was very clear—the Nazi Party or any of the army units connected with it, such as the SS.

But it was the third and final difference that had made his hand shake. Because the trigger for the implementation of the continuity plan was no longer a somewhat vague breakdown of civil order. This potential event was very specific.

The Führer Adolf Hitler is dead.

Klaus turned to gaze out the window. Another night had stolen upon him without him realizing it. When he'd sat down it had still been daytime. Now it was dark out there—and his blackout curtains were not even closed. He was surprised that the building's superintendent had not already been up to shout at him.

He rose and pulled the heavy canvas cloths one by one across the frame. Yet he wasn't thinking of them, or of bombs falling.

He was thinking of Adolf Hitler.

Thinking how, like almost everyone he knew, he had hailed Hitler's accession. How he had believed in the man who promised to restore German honour, especially German military honour, after the humiliating peace that had been forced by politicians onto an army that had not lost the war upon the battlefield. How Hitler had kept that promise and more. How the Wehrmacht had swept through country after country, all-conquering. And how Klaus had proudly worn his pilot's wings and done his duty for his people, for his country, for its inspirational leader . . . who he was now joining a conspiracy to kill.

He knew that was what this paper meant. The Führer was not dead. Not yet. He was safe in Berlin, or in his Wolf's Lair in East Prussia, leading his country to a disaster far greater than the humiliations of 1918. Disaster for the army too, for Hitler had made it complicit in his terrible crimes. Killing enemy soldiers was a soldier's duty, part of any war. Rounding up and slaughtering civilians, Jews, Poles, Slavs, Gypsies? Anyone the Nazis condemned as lesser breeds, as *Untermenschen?* Less than fully human? No—these actions turned every soldier into a murderer, a criminal of the very worst kind, whether he was shooting a peasant in the back of the head on the rim of a pit the victim had been forced to dig or . . .

. . . or drawing blinds across a window in Oslo.

Klaus returned to his desk, sat, picked up the cigarette he had put down. The tobacco was of such poor quality, supplemented with so many other things, that it had gone out. He didn't relight it, just stared ahead at the door to his office. Thought again about the message that had come with this continuity plan: "Await further orders."

It had come from the same source as several accompanying it: Abteilung Z, Berlin. Abwehr headquarters. And though there wasn't anything that positively identified the sender, Klaus had little doubt who he was. A man he admired, who had visited him in his hospital bed in France three years before, recruited him there, and whom he had worked under and alongside ever since—Generalmajor Hans Messer. With whom he had discussed Gretchen, and how they'd both failed to save her. It had to have been Messer who sent the photograph of her, that had first alerted Klaus that something was happening. And if Messer was involved, Klaus had little doubt that the old man must be too— Konteradmiral Wilhelm Canaris, the boss of the Abwehr.

Honourable men. German patriots. Soldiers who could see where this war was heading. The army may not have been defeated in 1918, but they were being defeated everywhere now. Driven from North Africa, from Sicily. Italy invaded, with the Allies building up to the invasion of France and a second front in the West. The heartland of the Reich itself destroyed day and night by British and American bombers. Above all, the Eastern Front crumbling. The Russians were coming, Germany's oldest enemies, set for revenge. The disaster at Stalingrad had clearly been the beginning of the end: a German field marshal forced to surrender along with all his forces to the Russians. The people back home only heard of the victorious armies. But Abwehr intelligence knew, because they had to prepare for all eventualities.

Operation Valkyrie had changed. It was no longer a contingency plan depending on events. It was a precipitator of those events. It would begin with the reality of the first line in the document before him: the death of the Führer. It would end with the army again in control, an honourable peace found. And Klaus von Ronnenberg would be a part of it. His role had not yet been specified. It had to do with where he was, what he did there, that much was clear. Nothing else was, not yet. So like the good soldier, the good German, he was, he would await those further orders.

The footsteps came suddenly and crisply down the corridor, steel heels clacking on the parquet floor. They halted outside his door, and he saw the outline of a man there who knocked three times.

"Who is it?" Klaus called.

"Stürmführer Richter," came the reply.

Slipping the papers back into the stack they'd come from, Klaus called, "Come."

The door opened. The young man in the smart black uniform of the SS entered, halted, and gave a sharp salute. "Heil Hitler," he called.

There was a time, even at the Christmas party, when Klaus would deliberately still give the army version of the salute, a somewhat different arm movement, no mention of the Führer. Many in the Wehrmacht did, maintaining their separation from the Nazi Party and its leader. Given what was now hidden before him on his desk, that time had passed. He would give no opportunity to anyone to question his loyalty to the supreme commander.

He rose. "Heil Hitler," he snapped back, clicking his heels. "You have a message for me?"

"Yes, Herr Major."

"Stand easy and give it to me."

The Leutnant—Stürmführer was a separate title used by the SS—looked about fourteen years old once he removed his peaked cap. "Major Striegler sends his best wishes and asks that I accompany you to Victoria Terrasse."

Klaus stiffened at the address, the headquarters of much of the secret services. Like everyone, he knew what went on there and had seen no reason to visit. Except, dammit, he remembered now that Major Striegler, at that Christmas party where they'd met, had suggested that he attend one of his interrogations. That interdepartmental cooperation was not only useful—it was a sign of devotion to the cause. A memo had come from on high ordering such meetings. Klaus had found ways of avoiding direct contact, just reading reports. But Striegler had stated that there would be times when only someone with specialized counter-espionage experience would know exactly what questions to put to a prisoner. And if a member of the resistance had been caught and was offering information of a military nature, that was Abwehr territory and so part of Klaus's duties.

It appeared that, in the major's judgement, that time had come.

Klaus had already used up all his excuses to avoid this. Besides, that time had passed—for the same reason he could no longer refuse the Hitler salute.

"If you would wait outside for a moment, Stürmführer," he said, "I need to finish with a few matters. Please close the door."

"Sir!"

The officer saluted, swivelled and left, firmly pulling the door shut. Klaus put all the papers on his desk into his small safe and spun its dials. He stood, shrugged into his greatcoat—always hard with one arm—buttoned it up, put on his cap. Picking up his cigarette, he bent to the table lighter and lit it. Taking several deep drags, he stared at the blackout curtains, not seeing them. Then he crushed the butt in the glass ashtray and went to the door.

Outside the building, a sleek black Mercedes limousine was drawn up, the uniformed chauffeur smoking a cigarette by its front wheel. He dropped it in the gutter, then opened the rear passenger door. Klaus looked up, at a sky where, for once in this freezing Norwegian winter, he could actually see stars.

"What is it, a three-minute walk? It's a pleasant night." It was crisp, but the temperature was only around zero, and he had been in his office all day.

The Stürmführer stiffened. "Major Striegler asked for you immediately."

"Yes, and he did not know how much work I needed to finish before I could accompany you." He said it sharply, saw the officer wince. He reached out and patted the young man's arm. "I take full responsibility, ah, Richter, wasn't it?" he added, with a smile.

"Sir," replied the younger man, not looking happy. But he snapped a command at the driver, who reached into the glove compartment of the car and produced a flashlight. Richter took it, turned it on, and pointed the beam along the street. "Please," he said.

They set out. Maybe the prisoner will have died by the time we get there, thought Klaus. The thought made him shake again, and he decided to concentrate his mind on not slipping on the icy pavement. Very little light stole out of apartment block porticos, and a moon not far off full glimmered silver on banked snow and ice. There were few people out, and even fewer cars. Behind its blackout blinds, Oslo brooded.

They had to wait to cross Karl Johan, the city's wide central thoroughfare, halted by a column of trucks crammed with troops and preceded by motorcycles and a limousine on which swastikas fluttered. The whole column turned down towards the harbour. "Reinforcements for the Eastern Front," Richter commented. Klaus heard it in the young man's voice, turned to see it also in his blue eyes: yearning. The Stürmführer wished to be in the action, killing for the Fatherland.

The last truck rounded the corner. Staring at them out of the flaps at the back was a private no older than Richter. His eyes had yearning in them too. All he wanted to do was to stay in Norway.

Across the street, Victoria Terrasse gleamed in the moonlight. A long, three-storey building, studded with domes and cupolas and faced in whitened brick, it contained elegant, tall-windowed apartments that had housed some of Oslo's wealthiest citizens before the war. The owners were gone, no doubt to the country cabins—the hytter—such folk possessed. The choicest homes in the capital had been commandeered by senior Nazi officers.

"Herr Major?"

Klaus looked at the Stürmführer. He was gesturing that the street was now empty, that they should cross. Klaus had deliberately delayed to admire the architecture, contemplate an elegant life that had all but gone. Though most of the building was no longer even lived in. It had been taken over by the security services. It housed their offices, behind those glorious tall windows. But Klaus knew that the part of the building he was headed for was windowless and, as far as was possible, soundproofed. Cellars often were.

He nodded and crossed swiftly, Richter a step behind. The flashlight beam proceeded them, pointing their way. Not to the recessed main doors with the marbled atrium beyond. To a flight of stairs at the side. "Careful here, Herr Major," the Stürmführer said. "The stairs are icy."

Clutching a metal rail to the side, Klaus descended into the dark.

As his eyes adjusted, his other senses took over. He clearly heard echoey laughter ahead—raucous, male. Then his nostrils filled with smells. The strongest was chlorine—acrid, distinct. But that had been used to cover other scents, not chemical at all. Human.

Shit. Piss. Vomit. Blood.

Klaus passed through an open brick entrance into light. The flashlight clicked off behind him. "Left, Herr Major," the young man said.

The corridor he turned into was long. He halted a few paces in, at an iron-railing fence that reached to the arched ceiling; the corridor continued, a turn forty metres ahead.

Richter was beside him, jangling keys. "Excuse me, sir," he said, and inserted a long, heavy one into the lock. It needed some force to turn it. The gate was solid and whined as he pushed it in. "After you," he said.

As Klaus stepped through, louder laughter came from beyond the turn. He walked towards it, and Richter locked the gate behind him. Every ten paces there was a low-wattage bulb shedding scant light over several doors. These were solid wood, and each had a grille at head height in the middle. At the third door he passed he heard something— a soft, high-pitched whimper. He couldn't tell whether it was a man or a woman who'd made it.

"So she told me she'd never done that before," came a voice from around the corner Klaus had almost reached, "but for such a handsome young officer she was willing to give it a try!"

Another roar of laughter. He recognized the voice, even though he'd only met the man once. There was a distinct accent in Karlsruhe, as in most other places in Germany. Softer than his own, from the heart of Prussia.

He turned the corner—and there he was: Erich Striegler. The tall, lean man was dressed for the cold, his black trench coat buttoned up, a woollen scarf around his neck, wearing his black peaked hat, the SS insignia of the skull in its middle gleaming even in that corridor's poor light.

The man standing opposite him, with one foot on a stool, was a vivid contrast. Squat and hefty, dressed for heat in a singlet vest. He was sweating, lines of moisture running from his shaven skull down a boxer's broken nose. He was looking up at Striegler, laughing with him.

Klaus and Richter halted a few paces away. The Stürmführer snapped a salute. "Heil Hitler," he called.

A chorus followed, salutes accompanying them, Klaus's as impeccable as anyone's. He wondered if Striegler remembered his other Wehrmacht salute at the Christmas party, its implied reluctance. If so, he gave no sign. "Herr Major," he cried, arms opening wide, "how good to see you here! At last." One hand dropped onto Klaus's shoulder. "I wouldn't have asked you to join us if I didn't think you would find it most interesting. And if we didn't need the help of the special skills of the Abwehr in these matters. Matters of military counter-espionage, no?" He tapped the side of his nose, then gestured to the sweating man. "And speaking of special skills, may I present SS Rottenführer Heinz Behmer?"

The man stood to attention, gave a sharp head-bow. "Major," he said. The SS, as a separate force, had their own names for their ranks. In the Wehrmacht it would have been a corporal standing before him now in a vest. Stained, Klaus saw, with trails of blood. Some vivid and scarlet, still glistening; some dried, rust brown. Behmer held a metal rod across one shoulder, made from what looked like a small cannon shell, a long fat screw emerging from it, ending in some thick, flexible rubber. This, Klaus saw, had metal barbs in it. He'd been told the instrument's name once, on an interrogation course. He'd forgotten it.

Klaus acknowledged the bow with a slight one of his own as Striegler continued. "It took us a while because the subject in here proved very, ah, resilient. And quite a remarkable liar. But Behmer persevered, and I was able to suggest some, ah, modest improve-ments." He shrugged, not modestly at all. "Then, as always happens, when the subject talked, there was a lot of it. Some of it even truthful, we suspect. We picked this person up because we thought they might be part of Sivorg, the civilian resistance group. But then they let slip something that led us to believe they might be military."

"Milorg?" Klaus sensed a way to extricate himself here, perhaps. "That would make them Norwegian military resistance, which is still your field and not mine, Major."

"Ah, but what they let slip led us to believe they are with *Special Operations Executive.*" He said the full name in English. "Trained by the Brits. I know we have learned that the two groups are working together much more closely these days. But SOE and Milorg are still rivals in some ways, are they not?"

"Like the SS and the Abwehr, Sturmbannführer?"

"Ah, surely not like us. At least no longer." Striegler's smile widened. "We are all now simply loyal followers of the Führer, no?

But them? We believe they still have separate operatives, yes." He nodded towards the door. "And we think we have one of them in there."

Klaus sucked at his upper lip. If whoever was inside was SOE, it was indeed very much Abwehr territory, his territory. In the game of counter-espionage, the two organizations, English and German, were almost perfect opposing teams. "And so why wasn't I sent for earlier?"

He asked it coldly. But his tone didn't cool the SS man. "It is only in the last hour we made the discovery. There was," he glanced at Behmer, "a deal of noise before the revelation. Then a lot of names yelled after it. Familiar names—to both of us, I think. Because of this, uh, noise, it seemed to be the perfect time to involve you. We think we would lose them to unconsciousness if we carried on in our way. Waste time. So perhaps now, a new technique. A friendlier face? One that our subject might remember?"

Klaus started and looked again at the door. He knew the person beyond it? Suddenly he felt a sharp pain in his stomach and, for no reason he could think of, thought of Ilse. Perhaps it was because Striegler had said that the names would be familiar to both of them. The two officers had only met once before, at that party, where Klaus had also met Ilse. And Striegler hadn't said if "they" were man or woman. Breathing out slowly, he said, "This man says he knows me?"

"He says he has met you." Klaus relaxed slightly at the pronoun. "And when he was asking us to stop what we were doing, you were one of the names he appealed to."

"Who is he?"

"Oh, Major," replied Striegler, grinning again, "why would I spoil that surprise?"

"Very well." Klaus took another deep breath and nodded at the three SS men. "Let me talk with him."

Striegler moved to the door and grasped the bolt, which was not shot. Klaus took a step towards it, and the corporal took his foot off the stool to follow. "No, no, Behmer. Let the major go in alone. For some reason, the young man doesn't seem to like you very much. Here," he said, handing Klaus a tall, steel flask, "he may be thirsty."

Striegler opened the door. Klaus entered and it closed behind him to more laughter.

It took him long moments of blinking to be able to see. The cell was much better lit than the corridor, with a huge arc light shining harshly down on its centre. On the chair there, and on the man chained to it. He was the source of much of the stench that Klaus had smelled as he'd entered the building, so strong here that Klaus retched and put a hand to his mouth, fighting to control his stomach. He didn't need to add more vomit to the room; there was enough there already, along with all the other fluids he'd smelled before and did again now, much more distinctly.

The man was a wreck. His chest, back and thighs were gouged with long jagged wounds, leaking blood. Totenschläger, Klaus thought, remembering the name of the instrument Behmer had held. A cross between a whip and a club, the barbed end was slammed into flesh, the whip jerked down. It had wreaked this havoc on the young man's flesh. Between those lines there were what looked like burn marks, made by cigarettes.

When Klaus had mastered his stomach, enough to take a step closer, the head jerked up and a moan escaped from between shredded lips. The face was a mask of blood. One eye was a purple swollen ball, the other clear—and filled with the light of terror. "Please," the man whispered in German. "Please, no more. No more!"

"Shh," Klaus said, bending close, studying him. Striegler had said that he knew this man. There was nothing he recognized in the ravaged face. "I have water."

He spoke in Norwegian, and the man answered in the same. "Water?" he asked, as if he didn't know what the word meant. Klaus took the lid from the flask, held the rim to those ruined lips. The man gulped, choked, spilled. Water ran onto his chest and diluted the blood there, rivulets running into his naked lap.

"Easy now. Easy."

The man slowed, sipped. When the flask was nearly drained, he sat back. "Thank you," he sighed, slumping down.

"Would you like a cigarette?"

"I don't smoke. Bad for the wind. I am a skier." He gave a bark of a laugh, then choked on it. "Yes," he managed finally, "yes, give me a cigarette."

Klaus withdrew his packet from his breast pocket and shook it till one filter popped out. The man took the cigarette into his mouth and Klaus lit it.

The man inhaled, and immediately began coughing. "Christ," he said, "it truly is a filthy habit."

"Do you want me to take it away?"

"No. It is . . . the best thing I have tasted for a while."

It was then that Klaus recognized him. "Torvald Linström," he gasped.

The one clear eye rose to him. "Yes. You all know my name."

"No, I . . . we met before. The concert. You play the violin."

The man's one eye scanned his face. "Ha! The musical major. You wanted me to join a consort." He coughed again, his eye tearing up from the smoke. "I don't think I'll be fit to play for you anytime soon, Herr Major."

He rattled the handcuffs that held his hands behind his back. Klaus glanced—and saw another mass of congealing blood. The three fingertips he could see didn't have nails.

Klaus averted his eyes. There were many ways to get information from a prisoner and he was versed in several. None of them involved this kind of . . . desecration. He had never trusted the information he got from it. If a man was subjected to this much pain, he would do anything to make it stop. Betray anyone, whether innocent or guilty. Klaus had always felt that in his interrogations, he got more reliable information than the Gestapo or the SS, with their . . . Totenschläger.

He looked into the young man's eye. Remembered now its vivid blue. Remembered whose eyes he'd spent far more time noticing that night. "Who have you given up, Torvald?" he asked, his voice gentle.

"Oh, everyone." He tried to say it breezily, but he choked on the word, spat the cigarette to the floor on a sob. "Everyone I know! I had to make them stop. I couldn't—"

"Were any of them true?"

"Yes, I think so. Some, perhaps. They were just . . . names." He choked. "Names to make the pain stop."

"Was Ilse Magnusson one of the names?"

"Ilse?" The eye swivelled up to him again. "I don't remember." He sniffed. "Maybe."

Klaus lifted his gaze to the whitewashed wall behind the chair. Christ, there were even splatter stains on that. When had his countrymen become *these* people? Like those he'd been thinking about at his desk earlier. Patriots in field grey, obeying their orders. Putting guns to the backs of children's heads over a ditch.

He shook his head to clear the vision, took a deeper breath, another. There'd been something else on his desk. It was in his safe now. Something that could perhaps be the beginning of the end to . . . all this. Thinking it through, he suddenly knew what he had to do. And it began here.

He gently placed a hand on Torvald's shoulder. The man winced, but Klaus held the touch. "Tell me this, young man—was it a lie when you told my . . . colleagues that you were not Milorg but SOE?"

There was an extended silence. Finally the man spoke. "It was no lie. I am a soldier, a sergeant in the Norwegian Free Forces, trained in England." His voice rose slightly. "For God's sake, can't you treat me like a soldier?"

"Perhaps." He patted the shoulder once, then stepped away. "I may be able to help."

He moved towards the door. "You fuck . . . you fucking bastard," Torvald sobbed. "You're sending them back in again, aren't you? Aren't you?" he screamed.

Klaus didn't answer him. Pulling the door open, he stepped

outside. The three men were smoking. Striegler, now sitting on the stool, rose, ground the butt out with his heel. "He's making a lot of noise again. Well done, Herr Major. Was I right to send for you?" he asked.

"You were." Klaus took Striegler's arm and led him a little way down the corridor, then stopped. "Sturmbannführer," he said softly, "I don't think you realize quite what a wonderful job you have done here."

"I have?" Striegler blinked at him. "What job?"

"You have exposed one of their main operatives in Norway. If this goes as I think it will"—he let his eyes shine—"you'll soon have a pip where there isn't one now."

He tapped the centre of the epaulette on the left shoulder of the other man's coat. Striegler gasped. "You think so? I have been passed over before for Obersturmbannführer. Others with better connections—"

"You will not be this time, my friend, I can tell you that." He laid his hand on the shoulder he'd just tapped. "Not when they read my report on you in Berlin."

Striegler, who'd always seemed so superior in all their dealings, now actually blushed. "I . . . I would be most . . . most grateful, of course."

"No gratitude required . . . may I call you Erich? A just reward, Erich. And a promotion for your corporal too, I think. Another fine job." He squeezed the shoulder, then moved past the man, heading away down the corridor. "I will have a car sent for the prisoner."

"What?" Striegler came after him fast, took him by the empty sleeve. Embarrassed, he dropped it. "But he is a prisoner of the SS."

"Not anymore, Major. Thanks to your identification of him as SOE, he is now a prisoner of the Abwehr. My prisoner, in fact." He smiled. "But your promotion? I suspect our glorious leader may wish to confer that upon you personally."

For a moment, Klaus wondered if he'd gone too far. Then

Striegler spoke. There was no doubt in his voice now. Only awe. "The Führer himself?"

Never underestimate the power of worship, Klaus thought. "Why not? Also, is he not always looking for trustworthy men for his personal guard? Drawn from the ranks of the SS?"

That actually silenced Striegler for a moment, long enough for Klaus to almost reach the junction of the corridor. "But Major von Ronnenberg," the man called. "The names he has given us. We were going to organize a razzia, arrest them all. His family. That beauty he played music with at the party. His uncle—"

Klaus stopped, turned, his mask in place. "Compile the full list and send it to my office. Many of the names will have been given to halt your interrogation, as you know. I will vet them all and contact you so we can together arrest all who seem possible. Now, give the prisoner something to eat, a blanket, then let him sleep. An Abwehr car will collect him at dawn." He snapped into the best salute he'd ever given. "Heil Hitler!" he cried.

"Heil Hitler!" came the reply, from all three men down the corridor. Klaus rounded the corner. Out of sight, he slowed slightly. He had pulled it off. He knew what made men like Striegler tick. Klaus didn't outrank him; but in the ordered hierarchies of the German military this was now his—the Abwehr's—field.

Footsteps came, Richter hurrying after him. They reached the gate, and the young man opened it. "A car, Herr Major?" he asked.

"Thank you, no. It is still a nice night, and I will walk. Goodnight."

"Goodnight, sir. Oh, you will need this." Richter held out the flashlight.

Klaus retraced his route to his office under the light snow that had begun to fall. Back at his desk, he slipped out of his coat, poured himself an aquavit, lit a cigarette. On the blackout curtains he no longer saw soldiers or prisoners. He saw her, Ilse Magnusson, nursing her aunt in some snowy wasteland. Perhaps Torvald had only reached for her name, one among many to spare himself agony, just before he named his own mother and his sister, no doubt. Still, it did mean that Klaus would have to see Ilse, for more than personal reasons.

I am a loyal soldier of the Reich, he thought, taking a deep drag. I must do my duty.

SIXTEEN
CHALK GIANT

Dorset. January 21, 1944

ILSE STARED AT the passing countryside, the churned winter-bare fields and grassy downs of southern England. She could tell by the sun, pale in a largely cloudless sky, that they were now heading more south than west. The roads were still unnamed, unmarked. Even if there was no longer a possibility of invasion, low-flying German pilots would not be aided in their search for their targets. Not that there were many of them now. She'd learned, in her brief stay in London, that air raids had diminished to a few a month, and often those were just single or pairs of planes. Shelters across England were covered in cobwebs.

She looked at Billy, one hand on the steering wheel, one on the rounded ebony tip of the Bentley's stick shift. He'd had a smile on his face from the moment he'd picked her up. The further south they drove, the more rolling the roads became—hills to be surmounted with a clutch-and-drop of gears, obstacles to be slowed before and accelerated around. Not much in the way of other vehicles. They'd left those, mainly army convoys, behind on the major road out of London. On these narrower lanes there was the occasional tractor, several carts pulled by horses, other livestock—herds of black-and-white cattle, flocks of sheep, one of geese. He'd grin, slow down, speed when he could. Speed was his default. When she asked him to go more slowly on one straight stretch so she could study the land, he promised he'd try, and forgot quickly that he had.

They'd stopped once for a late picnic at Stonehenge. Ilse was amazed that anyone could just wander up to the huge standing stones, shoo away the resident sheep, crack open bottles of brown ale, leave crumbs and beer froth on the cropped grass. "They'll never fence this off," Billy had said. "It's an Englishman's ancient right, to come here."

"For someone who so loudly and often proclaims the cause of the international proletariat, you seem most fond of English traditions and privilege."

He'd laughed, put on some Hollywood actor voice. "What can I say, baby?" he'd declared, in flawless American. "I'm a contradiction, wrapped in an enigma."

She'd laughed too, and studied his profile. He truly is a handsome man, she'd thought, even with the new lines on his thinner face, carved by events he wouldn't talk about. She remembered how hard it had been to get him to talk, three years before on that other trip, in that other part of England, about one of the sources of his sorrow. About what had happened to him, and what he'd done, in Spain. But once he had, it had opened everything up for them. Still, she had no thought of making him talk now of what had happened since. It made her happy to see him happy. That other world, his and hers, the memories of their recent past, didn't have a place here. A holiday was meant to be an escape from everything, memory included, future plans included.

Wasn't it?

She turned to look again out the window. Now, though, she didn't take in any details of the passing countryside, only her own reflection in the glass. What worries are now etched on *this* face? she wondered. What does he see here when he looks at me? She knew how . . . *ardent*, was that the English word? How ardent he was for her. As she was for him. She'd never had a lover like him, though she hadn't had so many. But she knew that they had something different, recognized something she'd never known before. It wasn't only the physical, the way he touched her, the way she wanted to touch him back. "Making love" was what it was called. She'd never understood the term before. Now she did.

She wouldn't make love with Klaus von Ronnenberg. But she would fuck him.

The harshness of that word, the thought, a decision not made until that very moment. Its suddenness made her gasp.

In the reflection, she saw movement behind her, Billy turning. "See something?" he asked.

"Something. Some bird, yes. Amazing colours," she lied.

"Pheasant probably." He licked his lips. "I would love to eat a pheasant. More common than chicken in Coke House at certain times of the year." He shifted down a gear, and the car slowed. "Oh, and we are here."

"Where?" she said faintly, still in the future, in what she now knew she must do.

"Here," he said, pulling onto the verge. He cut the engine. "Come on."

"Is this the pub you told me about?"

"No. That's later. This first." He grinned, left the car, came around to her side, opened her door. He was still grinning. "You're going to love this," he added.

She stepped out, looked up—and saw it immediately. On the slope of a steep hill stood a huge man, impossible to gauge how tall at first, at least ten storeys of a building, she thought. Above his head, he held a huge, knobbed club. But that wasn't what really drew the eye. What drew the eye was his enormous penis. Flagrantly erect, it rose halfway up his belly.

Billy laughed. It must have been her face. "May I introduce you to the Cerne Abbas Giant?" he said.

Ilse laughed too. " 'Giant' is right. How? When?"

"How? The hill is a chalk down, so the people who made it would have removed the turf from above the chalk, which lies not very deep. When?" Billy scratched his head. "Dunno. I think I heard someone say it was carved just after the Romans left. Someone else said it was much more recent, seventeenth century perhaps. But who really knows?" He reached out a hand. "Let's go say hello."

"We can climb on it?"

"Of course."

"Ancient English privilege?"

"Of course." He flexed his stretched fingers. "Come on. We can actually do more than climb on it. You see the phallus?"

"It's, uh, hard to miss."

"Fertility symbol, surprise surprise. They say that if a couple is, ah, having difficulty in that area . . . you know, getting pregnant . . . they come here at night, make love within the phallus . . ." He stepped closer and snatched up the hand she still hadn't held out to him. "So let's go."

He tried to take a step, but she didn't move. "I cannot get pregnant, Billy," she said.

He frowned. "I know that. It's why we've been taking prec—"

"And it is cold."

"Could warm you up."

He tried to pull her towards him again. Still she resisted. "No, Billy. Let us go to this pub you talked about. Get a room."

"OK." He dropped her hand. "Quite the sight though, eh?"

"Yes," she replied, looking away from it, opening her door, slipping inside. It was still warm in the car, but she shivered nonetheless.

It was the talk of getting pregnant. For the first time in her life, she had met a man she might actually consider doing that with. But her decision about the German officer, the one she'd made only moments before . . . it had changed everything. Would have to, from now on. She'd accepted, in that moment, that it was the best way for her to fight the war. She had sacrificed so little when people everywhere were sacrificing so much. But it was not something she could tell the man beside her, not a hint of it. It would devastate him. It hurt her just thinking how much. And Billy Coke had been hurt enough in this life.

"What's up?" he asked, climbing in.

"Nothing. I'm just cold." She turned to him. "We can go?"

"As my lady desires," he said, and started the car.

They drove in silence now. She looked at him, just once. He was no longer smiling.

BILLY COULDN'T KEEP the polite smile on his face any longer. "You're not serious," he said.

"I certainly am," replied the publican, her lips only unpursing from their disapproval to speak. "I told you, The Marquis of Lorne is a God-fearing establishment."

"And I told you, madam"—Billy inhaled deeply through his nose, trying to keep his temper—"that I forgot our marriage licence in London."

"Nothing I can do about that," she said, running fingers through her grey helmet of hair. "My husband, God bless 'im, left me strict instructions when 'e marched off to war. 'Elsie,' he said, 'you keep this 'ouse respectable. Allow no sin under its thatch while I am away fighting.' "

"He probably meant no sin for you!"

Ilse took his arm. "Billy, don't—"

"How dare you?" The landlady drew herself up. "I am as true as 'e. And while 'e is giving his all for his country in Italy, I will not—"

"Look, you," Billy barked. "I have just come back from fighting in Italy. Was wounded there." He raised his walking cane, slammed it down on the wooden bar, making her jump. "While this lady is . . . is also fighting. We have a few short days to enjoy a rest. Then it's back to it."

"That is no excuse for loose ways," she said. "Not 'ere. Not under my roof. Get over to Bournemouth. With those Americans at their base there, they allow anything I'm told." She shuddered. "There are English girls, drunk as you please . . . Negroes, the lot!"

"You . . ."

"Billy!" This time Ilse pulled him away. "Let's go."

"But it's dark now. We're hungry, tired—"

"We'll find somewhere. We cannot stay here. Come."

When Billy snatched up his cane, the woman flinched. He stomped out the front door of the inn, leaving the few locals in the bar gazing at him with glasses half-raised to mouths. At the car he stopped, kicked gravel. "Jesus H. Christ," he shouted back through the door he'd left open. "Don't they know it's 1944?"

"Billy, it's OK. We'll go. How far is Bournemouth?"

"I don't know, an hour? More, probably, with the blackout. We'll have to go slow."

"Then we will. We still have some of Mrs. Jacobs's sandwiches, yes? We'll take it slow." She tried to meet his eyes which he'd kept on the ground. "Would you like me to drive?"

"I'll drive," he said, moving around to the other side of the car.

For the first time, he'd forgotten to open her door. She let herself in. "Billy," she began.

"It's OK. I'm OK," he grunted, turning the key, taking off the hand- brake, switching on the lights, which were hooded, of course, for the blackout, illuminating very little. He eased out of the inn's driveway, turned left onto the road. By the car's clock it was 5 p.m. and only the faintest light was in the sky. Lanes so narrow the Bentley's sides grazed the barren hedgerows eventually disgorged them onto an A road. He turned left onto that, increased his speed.

"Billy," she warned.

He slowed, a little. There was more light now, as a moon a day off of full had just risen, silvering the rolling hills. Neither of them spoke.

Fuck, thought Billy, has my luck just turned? What is happening here?

"Look at that," Ilse said, and he followed her pointing finger to the right. "What is it?"

Billy glanced. Turf ramparts rose in rows up a slope. "Some ancient hill fort," he replied. "Bronze or Iron Age. There's a lot of them about, especially around here."

"Fort? So people were at war then too?"

"People are always at war," he muttered. "It's what people do."

"Billy," she said again, the fifth different way she'd said it in the last half-hour. Slightly mockingly this time. And it did what she'd meant it to. Jerked him from his mood. Reminded him of her and . . . and suddenly made him realize that he didn't ever need to feel like he just had ever again. Not for that reason, anyway.

He pulled over onto a verge, cut the engine. "Let's go."

"What? Where?"

"The fort," he said.

"I thought you were hungry. Tired."

"Not anymore." He leaned into her, so he could see her eyes. "And I don't want to say what I have to say to you in a car. Come on!"

Before she could protest further, say his name differently again, he had opened the door and was gone. She shook her head, stepped out.

He was quite far ahead, moving fast in that loping, limping stride of his, up a track, faint in the moon's light. "Hey, wait for me!" she called. But he didn't, just kept going. Sighing, she followed.

She caught up with him at the highest point. Breathless, she still managed a gasp. "Amazing," she said, looking at the landscape, the slope falling away on each side. Below them, the way he was facing, and far away, moonspill glimmered on the sea.

He turned to face her. "I love you," he said.

"And I love you," she said.

"You do?" His eyes went wide. "I didn't know."

"How could you not know, Billy? After everything we've been through?"

"After so many years apart?"

"Doesn't change anything. Not for us." She stepped into him, put her arms around him. "Not for us."

"I guess I'm not very good at recognizing love," he said. "But now I do. Which makes this next bit easier."

He came out of her arms and, using his stick to lower himself to one knee, looked up at her and said, "Marry me."

"What? Billy!"

"Marry me," he repeated. "You love me. I love you. I've never loved anyone before. I never will again. Marry me," he smiled, "and we'll never be refused a bed in any pub in England." He threw his arms wide, laughing. "In the whole, wide world!"

He looked up. She'd turned her face full into the moonlight and he saw it there. Saw instantly what she was about to say. He forced himself up, to block the words with a kiss. But his bad leg made him too slow.

"I can't."

"Yes. You can."

"I am going back to war."

"So am I." He leaned closer to her. "We'll both be at war until it's over. But this way, we'll know someone's waiting for us. It will make it easier. It will give us something to look forward to. To fight all the harder for. So it all ends quicker. So we can get back to . . . us!" He seized a hand, kissed it. "Marry me!"

"No."

It was so brutal, the short, hard word. It shocked him. "You're not . . . you're not already married?"

There was no hesitation. "No."

A sudden fear squeezed his heart. "There isn't . . . isn't someone else, is there?"

This time there was a pause. "There . . . It's complicated, Billy."

"No." He backed away from her. "No, oh no," he cried, turning to look over the rampart, towards the sea.

"Listen to me," she said, touching his shoulder. "There's something I must explain. As much as I can. I—"

"No," he said, shrugging her hand off, his voice calm now. "There's nothing to explain. It's all perfectly clear now."

"It isn't! You see," she said, "back in Oslo, my work—" She grabbed his shoulder, tried to turn him. He shrugged her hand off. "Billy, look at me, will you? Listen to me."

"Fuck," he said softly, but not to her. He was looking out to sea.

Where she looked now too, saw what he saw.

Hundreds of planes flying low over the water.

She placed a hand on his shoulder again, and this time he didn't move it. "Ours?"

"Theirs."

"How do you know?"

"I know." He nodded at them. "Heading to London from France, I suspect. The Blitz is back." He shook himself, turned. "And we should be getting back there too."

"No, come on! We have four more days." She struck him lightly on the shoulder. "Billy, you *know* what it is I do. We agreed when we first met . . ." Suddenly she was the one shaking. "What the hell do you expect of me? After three years?"

"Nothing," he said. "I expect nothing . . . anymore." He shook his head. "I was just thinking of . . . thinking of this man I knew . . . this young man. Italian. I . . . I only knew him for a moment. Thinking how maybe he stood on a cliff one night, looking over the Bay of Naples perhaps, asking someone to marry him. Did she say no? Did she say n—?"

He choked on the word, then pushed past her. She reached for him, missed, stumbled. When she got her balance, he was gone, moving fast. She didn't follow, looked up, at the planes beginning to pass over, further down the coast. She suddenly realized they were vanishing into cloud, that the moon was disappearing, that winter was back, that war was back . . . and that love, which had so briefly come, had gone.

"Billy," she said, in a way she never had before. All love, all sorrow, all hope, all despair in a name. When she looked he was already far down the path. She suddenly thought, what if I say yes? Say no to the German? Major Cholmondeley-Warren said I needn't, indeed mustn't. Told me that there were still other ways to fight. And Billy? she thought, seeing him reach the car, wrench the door open, fall inside, slam the door. It will make him so happy. It would make me so happy too. Four more nights of happiness before . . . before . . .

A louder roar made her look up again. Another wing of planes coming, passing closer, directly above her this time. She saw the bomb bays, pregnant with their loads. They didn't carry life within them though, only death. Mothers, wives, lovers who would die this night, were waiting for them in London, not knowing they only had moments left. While back in Oslo, mothers, wives and lovers would be dying soon as well, shoved against walls and shot, taken to cellars, tortured, murdered. She had committed to fighting it all, to the limits of her courage and her ingenuity and her strength. So what would she do? Go back to Norway, refuse Klaus? Go back to sending messages about new Nazi arrivals and other little bits of information her bosses at SOE might find perhaps a little useful? Do that until the war was over?

The last planes passed her; engine noise faded into the distance. Close to, another engine started up, Billy in the Bentley. Ilse raised her hands above her head, fists clenched, eyes shut. "Ahhhh!" she cried into the sky, stretching the sound to the limits of her breath. Slowly she let her fists drop to her forehead, spread her fingers, wiped away the tears, then started back down the hill.

THEY BARELY SPOKE on the way back to London. The return took much longer, even though the roads were still largely clear, because on the outskirts of the city they were sent on long diversions around the damage that the air raid had already caused. By the time they finally pulled up outside the house in Tanza Road, the sky was lightening again though it was hard to tell that day had come because the freezing fogs that had held the city for weeks and had briefly gone were back, along with German bombers.

He didn't park or turn off the engine. She had to try. "Billy," she said, turning to him. "It doesn't have to be like this."

"Doesn't it?" He drew the last cigarette from a packet, crumpled that, wound down the window and threw it out. Pushed in the lighter on the dash. Without looking at her, he asked, "Are you going to marry me?" She didn't answer. "Thought not," he said quietly. After a moment the lighter popped, and he raised its glowing coil to the cigarette tip.

Ilse got out of the car, not closing the door, then opened the back door, pulled out her valise. She leaned in again at the front. "Are you going to wish me good luck?" she asked.

"We never wish an actor good luck in the theatre, you know. That's bad luck."

"But I am not an actor."

"Aren't you?" he whispered, as he finally looked at her. He stared for a long moment, his face unreadable. Then he spoke. "Break a leg, Ilse," he said.

She shut the door, and he accelerated away. The rear lights, already blackout-muffled, were swiftly lost to fog. She watched for a while, hoping that he would realize, that he would turn around, come back, come inside. But when, after a minute, he didn't, she picked up her bag and slowly climbed the few stone steps to the front door.

PART 4

SCHERZO

SEVENTEEN

THE CHOICE

Oslo. February 15, 1944

IT WAS THEIR ONLY disagreement so far. Sitting at Blom's, the café where he'd first brought Ilse two weeks before, after her return from nursing her aunt, Klaus was shocked to hear her opinion.

"You cannot mean it," he said, lowering the glass of wine he'd half raised to his lips.

"I do."

"But . . . Mozart changed everything."

"So did Bach."

"He . . . improved everything. A sublime composer, no question about that. But he was, ah, restricted, shall we say, by his operating almost entirely within church music. Everything he wrote was ultimately for God. For cathedrals. Wolfgang Amadeus wrote for the people—for concert halls, for salons, for the theatre—"

"Opera? I despise opera."

Klaus went white. He had to set his glass down. "You *despise*—"

"It is too strong a word." Ilse smiled at the expression on his face, took a big sip of wine. "I have been amused by it, even moved by it on a rare occasion. Nothing like the feeling when I hear Bach played though, or when I play him."

"A feeling you don't get playing Mozart?"

"Not," Ilse tipped her head to the side, considering, "in quite the same way."

"But Bach wrote, what, four sonatas for the flute?"

"Six."

"Mozart—"

"Also six. But it's not the quantity anyway, as you know. It's . . ." She held up her glass, showing him. "This wine, it is . . . average."

"It is poor. And the best they sell here." He took a sip, frowned. "The rumour is that it is Algerian."

"Not the best. I happen to know my father keeps some French wine here. Bordeaux. Delivered three cases before the war and, of course, he has connections with your people. Blom's has always been the place where artists, writers and their ilk go." She pointed to one of the many heraldic shields that decorated the walls above and between the Corinthian columns. "That's his shield there."

Klaus looked. A griffin held a quill. "And your point?"

"We would know the difference between his wine and this wine."

"Are you saying"—Klaus pushed his chair back—"that Bach is French and Mozart . . . Algerian?"

Ilse shrugged. "Maybe he is Italian. Thank God he is not one of your terrible Rieslings." She laughed over his protests, continued. "But, for me, he is not Bordeaux."

Klaus sighed. "Frøken Magnusson, that sound you hear is my heart breaking."

"Oh dear," she said, reaching to lay a hand on his arm. "However could I repair it?"

He looked down at her hand, then up at her face. Studied it, though he'd already memorized every contour. The light in Blom's cellar was low, and mainly supplied by candles. But he knew she would look just as beautiful in a tropical sun. "You could try and prove it to me."

"Oh yes? And how would I do that?"

"A challenge. You could play both, one after the other. Bach's Sonata in B Minor. Mozart's in D Major."

"All of them? Unaccompanied?"

"Perhaps just the Andante of each. We could maybe find someone—" A vision of Torvald came to Klaus, the young man he'd pulled from the SS cell and sent to the prison at Grini. He was getting better. But you didn't take prisoners from their cells to play music. Besides, his nails were... "Or—"

"Or?"

"I could provide a very simple accompaniment." He raised his single hand. "I practise most days. I learned that I cannot be completely without music."

"You have a piano in your apartment?"

"I do. Upright, small. Old."

"My father has a baby grand. And my flute is there, of course." She sipped her wine, grimaced. "I think he might also have a bottle of Bordeaux." She squeezed his arm. "We can go there."

His heart, not broken at all, skipped. He had never been anywhere with her except Blom's. "Will your father not mind the company?"

"My father is still in Berlin. Minister Goebbels does not wish to let him go, it seems." She raised her half-full wineglass, thought better of it, put it down. Stood, took her coat from the back of the spare chair, picked up her gloves and hat. "Shall we?"

Klaus rose, opened his wallet, left more than enough kroner for the overpriced swill they'd been drinking. Though he'd grown deft at it, Ilse came around and helped him with his coat, as she'd done the first time he'd brought her here. "There you are," she said, pressing his shoulder.

They walked towards the stairs leading up and out. Blom's was not busy that night and most of the tables were empty. But close to the door a corpulent older man sat at one. He wore tweed, a bow tie. Ilse recognized him, though couldn't remember his name. Helmer something. He'd been a well-known actor before the war, a masterful exponent of Strindberg and Ibsen. Now he was drunk, his glassy-eyed gaze fixed on the empty schnapps glass he tilted, its bottom edge on the wood before him.

As Ilse moved past him, without looking up, he hissed a single word.

"Tyskertøs."

Klaus halted. "What did you say?"

"Klaus, never mind. Leave him."

"No. I wish to know." He glared down. "Repeat what you just said."

At last, the filmed eyes rose from his glass. They took in Klaus, his one sleeve pinned to his coat, his epaulettes. "Say, Major? I just said what a pretty, pretty girlfriend you have. A regular Oslo Princess, no?"

"It was not the term you used." Klaus cleared his throat, which had become thick with anger. "You will apologize to the lady, immediately."

"He's drunk," said Ilse, pulling his arm. "It doesn't matter."

"Pardon me, sir, is there a problem here?"

The manager had joined them, rubbing his hands, fear on his thin face. Klaus ignored him. Looking straight into the sitting man's eyes, he said, "You know I could have you dragged out of here for insulting a German officer. There are laws—"

"Fuck your laws! And fuck her!" The man thrust himself up from the table, swayed, gripped it, pushed his heated, red face forward. "Which no doubt you are, huh?"

The man was a good half-metre taller than Klaus, twice as wide. But Klaus doubted he'd studied any jujitsu, as Klaus had before the war. He didn't need two arms for that. He just put one foot between the man's two, grabbed a handful of tweed, jerked him forward to throw him off balance, then shoved him back.

The man fell hard, dragging his own table with him, falling on the one behind, where two men sat who now jumped up, cursing at the spilled wine, the shattering glass. Klaus watched to see if the man was going to get up again, but he didn't, only flopped there with the grace of a sea lion on land. So Klaus turned, followed the tugging hand.

On reaching the street, they both stood for a moment, taking in gulps of cold air. "Are you alright?" he said.

"Are you? You didn't have to do that."

"I know."

"You hear it. All the time." She shrugged. "It is a small price to pay for believing in something."

"Something?"

"The cause of the Germanic peoples."

He looked at her closer then. In all their times together they had never discussed politics, and, only glancingly, the war. But he knew of her father, a half-German journalist and writer. Had read several of his articles. A skilled propagandist. In one interview he'd written of how proud he was of his musician daughter, what a support she'd been since his dear wife had died.

"Come," she said, taking his arm. "Let us go and forget all this, in music."

"We could walk to my office, get a driver."

"The train is just over there, by the National Theatre. It is five minutes to Majorstuen."

Majorstuen. The station he'd got out at in a snowstorm to walk to the church where he'd first heard her play. "Yes," he said. "Let's take the train."

"And no more fights, eh?" she said and laughed. "No wonder you like opera. Maybe I should play you some Wagner. Should I call you Siegfried?"

At last, he laughed too, and they set off along the road.

Tyskertøs

The word that the man in the café had hissed at her kept sounding in her head. It hadn't been the first time she'd been called it —on a tram, coming out of a store, at the theatre, spoken by someone she'd immediately look for and never see. Any woman associated with Germans in whatever way—as she was because of her father, and the various musical consorts she belonged to—would be called it sooner or later. But it had hit her hard that night. If that actor had stood and spat in her face, he couldn't have sickened her more.

Now she could deny it to herself no longer. Because of the man now lying beside her, who'd finally fallen asleep. His breath came so softly, his bare, pink, curiously hairless chest scarcely rising and falling.

German fancy. German . . . *whore.* That's what she would be now, fully and finally, in many people's eyes. And there wasn't a way she could tell any accuser the truth of the matter. Why she'd accepted the title. What she planned on doing with it.

The first step was taken. Now she needed to take the next one. Get back in touch with her handlers at SOE. Let them know what she'd . . . achieved. Find out exactly what they needed her to do next.

They'd turned off the light and opened the blackout blinds when they went to bed. A little moonlight fell now on the softly breathing form beside her. He'd suggested the dark—his scars, he said, the stump of an arm. She wouldn't have minded them. Hadn't, nor any of the ways he'd touched her. He was gentle, tentative. It had been a long time, he'd told her. And though it hadn't been that long for her, she hadn't thought of Billy Coke while she made love to this new man. Only now she did, remembering the last time she'd seen him, also by moonlight. So, about a month ago, she realized.

Such a little amount of time for a world to change.

She felt it again now, lying there, just as she'd felt it standing on that English hill—as if someone had wrapped a hand around her heart and squeezed it. Saw again the devastation in his eyes, caused by a single word.

No.

She writhed, pressing her hand against the ache in her chest. Could she have said yes? Married him, the man she loved yet barely knew? Become his wife and immediately betrayed him? Because she'd known, even then, what she would do, what she had to do; knew that she would be lying beside another man before much time had passed.

Billy—she thought his name as if she were speaking it aloud. *I love you*, she added. *I love you, and now, I think, I will never see you again.*

Klaus murmured something. She swallowed down her pain. Wasn't this her job, to hear the enemy's words, spoken in their sleep or in the afterglow of lovemaking? Pillow talk, it was called, a man relaxed enough to speak freely about things he otherwise wouldn't and shouldn't. It was faintly absurd, the idea that an Abwehr officer would reveal something of importance while he slept. Still, she leaned in to listen.

It wasn't a state secret, what he said then, unless it was in code. It was only a single word. A name.

"Gretchen," Klaus von Ronnenberg murmured, then began to softly snore.

Since he had said a name aloud, she felt she could too. "Billy," she whispered, then turned onto her side, wiped a tear away, and sought sleep.

AS THE JEEP sped away from the CO's hut, where he'd reported to his new commander, Squadron Leader McRae, Billy shrugged deeper into his greatcoat and pulled the brim of his hat lower over his eyes so he could see through the sleet that was slanting across the tarmac.

It was the latest variation in the foul weather the winter of '43/'44 had thrown at him. On the far side of RAF Hendon's runway were the main hangars, some dark, some lit with ground crews swarming across the wings and under the bellies of the birds. He could make out an Auster, an Anson, two Lysanders and four Dominies—the standard planes for a communications squadron. He hadn't flown the first two, but prior to coming to Hendon he'd spent a week training on the Dominie. The big biplane was very different to a Spit. For a start, it carried passengers, not cannons and sometimes bombs. But in his years of flying, from Spain to Sicily, he had flown so many different types of aircraft at short notice that he felt he could step into one and figure it out in fifteen minutes. Enough to get airborne, anyway. Landing he'd work out when he came to it.

A plane is just a plane, he thought. Like a kiss is just a kiss? Where had he heard that? As the barrier lifted to allow the jeep off base, he remembered. It was a line in a song from that movie he'd watched in Malta. Except now he knew that wasn't true.

Five minutes later the jeep stopped long enough to disgorge Billy and his suitcase in front of his new digs in Hendon Central: 48 Crespigny Road, a nice-enough-looking detached house in a row of them. The landlady, Mrs. Speerwell, was out shopping—according to the maid, who kept wiping a steadily running nose as she showed Billy to his room. It was spacious, well-furnished and the sheets were linen. It may not have been Coke House, but he had not fallen too far down the social rankings, it seemed.

It didn't take him long to unpack into the tall wardrobe and matching armoire. He didn't have much. After he took his shoes off, he lay on the bed but kept his coat on because the room was cold. He smoked. Tea, as the maid called it, would be served when Madam got back, around six.

Lighting a second Camel from the butt of his first, he reached into his coat pocket and pulled out the two letters. The first he'd had for a while; the second—a note really—had arrived only that morning. It had caught up with him just as he was about to leave the training base. He laid that one down and read for the tenth time the one Hot Dog Darby had sent "from somewhere over Italy!!!" with the three exclamation marks. These were in keeping with Franklin's excited style. Short on specifics, of course, and where he'd over-expanded, a censor's black rectangle ran through words—probably town names and squadron numbers. It appeared that the new "Squadron Bleeder," after the Walrus had been kicked upstairs, was a real flyer who looked after his pilots like they were his kids—of which he already had six back home in Ottawa. He had adopted as his seventh the remaining Dent twin, now nicknamed "The Red Baron" because of his hair and because he'd added to his first score in Sicily with five more kills since. "Get back here, compadre," Franklin advised. "He's gonna take your record real soon, mark my words!"

Billy shoved the letter back in the envelope, laid it on the bedside table. Stared through the rising smoke for a moment, then took a deep drag before stubbing out the fag and lifting the second letter from the bed.

The notepaper was headed "Norway House, SW1." It was not dated. Not many words followed. Maybe a quarter of what Franklin had written. Somehow, they said so much more.

Flight Lieutenant Coke,

I believe I told you before that I am unable to tell you anything about our friend's activities unless she is close by. She went into the countryside recently and I have no clue as to where, nor what she is doing. That will not change, so please don't leave any more messages for me.

Only this will I say. I believe I told you that I have known our friend since a very long time . . . I do not believe I have ever seen her as angry or as sad as when I last saw her.

Good luck with your own war. For all of us, for the world, may it end soon.

Yours, Kirsten

A *k* was crossed out after *since*, Billy could see. She'd told him the two girls had been in kindergarten together.

This letter needed no censor's ink. But he knew that the countryside she wrote of was not England's but Norway's.

Ilse had gone back to her war.

Which was she more, angry or sad? he wondered. There was perhaps some hope in one, little in the other.

"What did I do?" he said out loud. "What the fuck did I do?" Screwing up the note, he threw it into the corner of the room. Then, putting his arm over his eyes, he pressed them into the rough blue wool and tried to think of something, someone else.

Failed.

EIGHTEEN
SPIDER'S WEB

Oslo. April 15, 1944

CIGARETTE SMOKE FILLED the sitting room of the cozy little apartment he'd never been to before. Through wafting blue clouds, Klaus watched the three other men as they studied the paper he'd just handed them. They represented the three Wehrmacht branches: the Luftwaffe, Kriegsmarine and Heer. The fourth man in the room, Rudolf Heine, was the senior lawyer for Generaloberst von Falkenhorst, commander of all German forces in Norway. He was the only one looking at Klaus now. He'd seen the paper before, because he and Klaus had arrived early to set up the meeting.

"Jesus fucking Christ," whispered the army man, Burgdorf.

The government continuity plan, with its startling opening line — "The Führer, Adolf Hitler, is dead" — produced the same reaction in everyone there that it had in Klaus when he'd first seen it. Being a Christian, though, he'd left out the blasphemy.

As the men read the details, Heine explained the law: that on news of Hitler's death, the commander of the Reserve Army in

Germany, Colonel-General Fromm, would take control of the country by first bringing all the armed forces under his one central command and then delegating command to individual supreme leaders in every sphere of the war: at home, in every occupied territory, on every front line. "Furthermore," he added, "none of them will need to have been involved in, nor even know about, this conspiracy . . . which is called, gentlemen, 'Operation Valkyrie.' They would simply be doing their duty in the event of the new situation: that Hitler is dead, and it is the army that now takes command."

"But will Hitler be dead? How many times have people tried to kill him before?" The two other men muttered agreement with the navy man Udet's statement.

Like them all, Klaus knew it was Hitler's death that was the key to everything that must follow, what he and these men had to do. He also knew of the numerous failed attempts. But he had to believe that this time would be different. That the last short, encoded message he'd received from Berlin was true. He repeated it now.

"No one from the innermost circle has had this chance before. A hero has volunteered. Hitler will die."

He spoke the words quietly, with all the confidence he had forced himself to muster. It appeared to work on them. "Yet the jackals close to Hitler? Won't they try to assume command themselves?" It was the Luftwaffe man, Brüning, who asked the question.

"Yes." Burgdorf leaned forward. "Himmler, Göring, even that little shit Goebbels. They will all have something to say about this, won't they?"

"Kameraden," said Klaus, "we can only presume that contingencies have been made to, ah, deal with these people too. In Germany. Also, the continuity plan states quite clearly who is to take command —and who is not to."

Burgdorf, who held the paper, suddenly let out an oath. "Shit! This is what I was most wondering—how those black-uniformed bastards, the Waffen-SS and their ilk, with their separate structures outside the Wehrmacht control, would react. Especially since they have almost become Himmler's private army." He tapped the paper, low down. "But it says here that once Hitler dies, 'the entire Waffen-SS is to be integrated into the army with immediate effect.'"

Udet gasped, reached, and Burgdorf handed the paper to him. "So they are supposed to suddenly accept orders from the regular army?"

"That is what the paper says," Heine replied.

"And will they?"

"Many will," Klaus said, "because they are as conditioned to obey as any soldier of the Reich. Remember, with Hitler dead, their personal oath of allegiance to him dies too. Still, many won't obey, will look to their own leaders, obey them instead. Which would mean civil war. Which would not help us to hold off the Allied armies while we negotiate a peace with them. Which is why," Klaus delved again into his briefcase and pulled out the second piece of paper, "here and everywhere in the Greater Reich—Italy, France, Poland, and at every battlefront—orders like these have been prepared, for patriots like you to follow." He held the paper out but didn't hand it over yet. "On it is the list of all the places that must be taken throughout Norway as soon as the word that Hitler is dead reaches us. It is the list you would expect: every military base, all communication facilities and the like. But also listed are the places where, uh, resistance might be found. Here in Oslo, that is the headquarters of the Gestapo at Møllergata and the rest of the intelligence services at Victoria Terrasse. And here is the list of those who must be arrested immediately."

He passed the paper to the nearest reaching hand, Burgdorf's. "Ha! That fucker Striegler. Arrogant shit! Who gets to arrest him? Can I? I'd like to see his face when I do."

For a moment, Klaus's eyes gleamed. "I do," he said quietly, then pointed again to the paper. "On the reverse of the paper, you will see the assignments for each of your branches of the Wehrmacht." Burgdorf flipped the page and the others moved to peer at it. "When the moment is right, you must brief your commanders as to what they need to do."

"Do we each get a copy of this?" asked Brüning.

"I am sorry, Herr Oberst, but no. Nor the continuity plan, I am afraid," Klaus replied. "Indeed, for obvious reasons, all copies of everything must be kept to a minimum. These are, in fact, the only ones in Norway." He shrugged. "So I am afraid, gentlemen, I must ask you to commit your assignments to memory."

The men crowded around. Muttering began, fingers were poked. Heine took Klaus by his arm, pulled him aside to stand by a cabinet of drinks in the corner, though neither man reached for a bottle. "There are two other things I must discuss with you, von Ronnenberg," he said in a low voice. "The Abwehr has been dissolved, am I correct?"

Klaus nodded. "One month ago. Hitler had had enough of real intelligence, and perhaps of questionable army loyalty from our boss, Canaris, down. He'd rather hear the SS tell him glorious fantasies." He shook his head. "But the SS still needs to know what we knew, so I have been undergoing debriefing."

"How long will that take?"

"I can prolong it for quite a while. I have been slow at supplying the required reports." He smiled. "It drives Striegler and the others crazy."

The lawyer inclined his head. "Quite a while?"

"At least until . . ." Klaus nodded back to the three men muttering over the paper.

"You'll remain at Victoria Terrasse? Which is why you will be the one to arrest Striegler and his subordinates?"

"Correct."

"Good."

The lawyer hesitated, peering at him over his wire-rimmed spectacles. Klaus smiled. "And the other thing, Herr Major?"

Heine glanced back at the others, then leaned even closer. "Do you have any contacts with, uh, the other side?"

"You mean the Allies?" Klaus considered for a moment, then said,

"I do." He looked above the other man, focusing on the ceiling. "There are always . . . ways. There are times, even in war, when some things need to be, hmm, discussed, shall we say?" He looked directly at the man again. "Why do you ask?"

"I ask for others. In Germany." He ran his tongue over his lips. "You mentioned to the Obersten here that a vital part of Valkyrie is putting ourselves into a position to negotiate with the enemy. To strive for an acceptable peace. But at Casablanca in January, did not the Allies call for the unconditional surrender of Germany? That we just lay down our arms and accept any terms they choose to impose?"

"They did." Klaus nodded. "But many believe that, were Hitler dead and the worst Nazis dealt with, there would be enormous pressure for the Allies to change that position. We know they are preparing a seaborne invasion of France. It is hugely risky, and they may fail. They know also that Hitler is developing secret weapons—rockets capable of delivering terrible destruction upon their cities. If we can keep the war going longer, the price may just be too high for them to pay. But if we negotiate a just peace? Maybe split the Brits and the Americans from the Russians, whose ambitions for conquest some of them fear almost as much as we do?" Klaus shrugged. "We think there is room to talk."

"Which is my point—what channels do we talk through?" The law- yer put an arm around Klaus's shoulders, leaned into his ear. "My people in Berlin are saying it is hard to get through to the Allies from there; they are all under such scrutiny. Many who have tried are dead, or in the camps." He swallowed. "They asked if I knew anyone with . . . contacts." He pulled back, looked into Klaus's eyes. "I told them I'd ask . . . someone who might be able to help."

Klaus returned the look but gave nothing away. Over the years he had had some contacts with both the resistance and SOE. He'd turned an agent, Kaspar Jensen, fed false information to the British, gained knowledge; but the man had killed himself a year before. Torvald Linström, the violinist he'd saved from Striegler's dungeon by transferring him to Grini had, with Klaus's more subtle interrogation, revealed more about SOE's work in Norway than he'd betrayed under torture. But once Klaus had learned that the Abwehr was about to be dissolved and he would lose all power, one of his last acts was to transfer the young man to a military prison hospital in Germany. Not a holiday by any means—but better than Striegler getting him back.

Now he thought about what Linström had said, and not said. He hadn't given away any more names under interrogation. But he'd shouted many at Victoria Terrasse. Most had since been discounted, put down to a man trying to stop the agony. But one had stuck in Klaus's mind. For obvious reasons.

He realized he'd been silent, that Heine's eyes were still querying. "I . . . will see what I can do," he said, at last.

The two majors returned to the others. Questions were asked and answered, where possible. Some could not be—especially regarding the date. They must be ready to act fast on what they needed to do; brief a very few men in their turn. And then they must wait.

Act fast, then wait—the life of any soldier.

They left, separately and a few minutes apart. Klaus was second to last, with Heine remaining behind to lock up.

The Oslo night was bitterly cold again, despite being well into April, with a freezing rain falling slantwise, hammering his coat and cap. Not a night for a long walk. So he moved briskly the two streets over to Klingenberggata. He didn't go up to his office—there wasn't much there anymore, now he was clearing out. But for the moment, he still had use of a car. He woke the driver, climbed in, and ordered him to drive to Ilse's place at Majorstuen.

He watched Oslo pass, didn't really see it. His eyes were on their reflections in the rain-streaked window, asking himself the questions. Could the woman he was in love with be what Linström had named her—only once and while in great pain? Ilse always spoke of her love, not for Nazism but for the Pan-Germanic identity that their two countries shared, that ideal of Volk, of the Northern Races, bastions against the barbarism coming from the east. It was the same cause her beloved father wrote about so extensively, and she spoke about it as passionately as she spoke about Bach.

As any spy would.

She never asked him about his work . . . No, that was not true. She rarely did, and only casually.

As any spy would.

On one hand, it would break his heart if she had betrayed him. On the other, it would be useful, so useful, especially now.

But this he also knew—she would have to be the greatest actress in Norway to have pretended all this time to fall in love with him, to be in love with him. He still believed she was. He knew he was.

Perhaps love *and* loyalty to a cause do not have to be mutually exclusive, he thought.

As the car passed before the tram station and through empty, ill-lit Majorstuen, Klaus looked away from his reflection and ahead through the windscreen. He felt the familiar tightening around his heart that he always did when he was about to see her again. It had been three days. Yet maybe, this time, part of that tightening was fear too. Of what he must find out. Of what he would need to do if he did.

Well, he thought, as the car turned into Harald Hårfagres gate and then swept up to her door. I will do what must be done.

As any spy must.

ILSE STOOD at her kitchen sink, staring through the heavy rain into the communal garden of their block, cleaning the cabbage she'd just dug up from her patch out there. It was a monster, greeny-white and very dirty. It was also the last of what she had put in the previous autumn. It had survived frosts, being buried under three feet of snow, the predations of rats, and the covetousness of neighbours whose own patches had yielded all they could. Everyone, including her, had already planted onions, carrots, radishes and, of course, potatoes. It was said that a Norwegian without a potato on his dinner plate was no Norwegian at all.

Ilse glanced at the sheep bones in the bubbling pot making a good broth, and the cubes of mutton on a plate, which would join the cabbage in the cauldron. Torment for those who lived nearby. Before the war, when everyone in this middle-class apartment block lived well, she'd never noticed anyone else's cooking. But deprivation sharpened all the senses. She'd had nights when there was only a bowl of thin soup on her table, a slice of bread adulterated with sawdust, and she had sniffed the air when a neighbour had more, better.

Not tonight though, she thought, looking at the ingredients. Tonight she would make a family favourite: fårikål. It was literally that: mutton and cabbage. Though each cook had their own touch, many just poured water onto the cabbage and meat and boiled away. Her father, a great cook himself, always insisted on adding both juniper and caraway seeds. She'd picked and dried both the previous summer. He also said the flavour was far better with bone broth. And the shoulder of lamb, delivered the day before by a young German private on behalf of Major von Ronnenberg, had been bone-in, so she'd cut that out, simmered it for hours. Fårikål was usually an autumn dish, but it was delicious anytime.

Cabbage clean, she cut away the outer leaves and stalk, setting them aside for boiling later. What would have been thrown away before the war was the source of several meals now. God, she suddenly thought, when this war is over I shall never eat cabbage again.

When this war is over . . .

Shaking herself, she lit the stove with a match, then put a large pot on, pouring in a splash of cooking oil. She sliced the cabbage into quarters, then those into thick half-moons, put a quarter in, waited till it had fried a bit, then added some meat and scattered some seasoned flour on mixed with black peppercorns, the caraway and juniper. More cabbage, more meat, more flour, building the layers. When everything was used up—apart from two half-moons she'd add much later so there would be some crunch—she poured in the hot broth, brought it to a boil, then a simmer, and put a lid on it. Then she washed her hands, wiped them, glanced again into the garden. Remembered.

It hadn't, of course, been envy that she'd seen in her neighbour Fru Kroken's eyes when she'd dug out this cabbage beside her. It had been disdain. Many in the apartments knew that Ilse was often visited by a German officer. That the smells that tormented them from her kitchen were made by meat that the nation's occupier had brought.

Klaus von Ronnenberg. She was his tyskertøs, he was her Nazi. Except, of course, he wasn't. It had been hard, to begin with, to get him to discuss much beyond music, poetry, art. Gradually, and at certain times when he was most relaxed, he'd talk of other things. His love for his family, his country. His . . . distaste for many things that had been done in its name. She had drawn him out by always taking the other side, excusing what the Nazis had done in terms of the ends justifying the means: the defeat of the Slav, of Bolshevism, of English imperialism. Forcing him to talk about some of the "means" he had seen. Things that sometimes brought the dreams that had him crying out in the night.

As she listened to the gentle bubbling, she thought now about the three times she'd had contact with SOE since she'd returned to Norway. The first when she'd taken a train to the town of Drammen and, at a deserted barn an hour's hike from the station, had sent a message on the radio she had hidden in an old chopping block that she'd spent two days hollowing out the week before. That time she'd confirmed that she had contacted von Ronnenberg. On the second visit, she'd told them that she and the German major had become lovers. SOE had sent an immediate "stand by" and she'd waited, shivering in the March cold for half a day, before she'd received the message back which, decoded, told her that there would be no more messages. A man would contact her, speaking a sentence to which she would have to reply in a certain way.

She got up, used a cloth to lift the lid, gave the stew a stir, thought of that man, their meeting at a ruined church on the eastern outskirts of Oslo. How he'd spoken his strange sentence, "The berries in the valley are not yet ripe," and she'd replied with hers, "They are best when picked young." They'd walked, he'd informed her of what she needed to know in excellent Norwegian that even had a touch of a Bergen accent— though she knew that still disguised an Englishman.

He'd been very clear. As "Angus" had stated at Aston House, "Valkyrie" was a plot to kill Hitler. There were conspirators across occupied Europe as, for the coup to succeed, it would need to take place everywhere simultaneously. Von Ronnenberg was involved but SOE didn't know how deeply. They needed to. If she thought the time was right, and they hoped it was, she needed to find out. Find out how the plotters in Norway could be aided.

She realized she'd been stirring for a while and that there was no need to continue. She put down the spoon, replaced the lid, sat. Thought about another man, who she was making the stew for. And then another, who she also loved.

Is it possible to love two people at the same time, she wondered — as she often did. It appeared to be. Because she still loved Billy Coke, even though he had hurt her so, even though she would never see him again. Yet she'd also discovered that she loved Klaus von Ronnenberg. Discovered that slowly, incrementally, like the layering of ingredients in a stew pot, building up. Billy was fire, passion; it was how he loved her, in all the ways. Klaus was coolness, gentleness, caring; it was how he was in everything, how he loved, made love.

She'd been shocked the moment she realized she loved him. Dismissed it, thinking it absurd, a reaction to Billy and how they'd ended. Denied it, thought she was merely getting fully into her role, like the actress she'd been forced to become. Had argued with herself that it was not possible to love a man and still betray him, every moment of every day, because of the secret she kept from him. And then she remembered that she'd done that with her father, for years.

She'd found it was possible. Both to betray and to hold two men in her heart equally and at the same time.

The one was gone, probably forever. The other would be with her tonight. Tonight, when she would have to tell him her secret, and hope that he would also believe that love could live within betrayal, and that what she believed him to be—a good German—would prove true. True enough for both to act and then reach that time...*when this war is over.*

She stood up. "And never eat cabbage again," she said aloud, and took a step to the stove to stir once more.

The doorbell rang. She took off her pinny and went to the front door. Her heart was beating fast as she walked.

She opened the door to her apartment, left it ajar, walked down the short flight of stairs to the street door, opened that. He was facing away, watching a black Mercedes drive off.

He turned, lifted his one hand. "I haven't brought wine," he said, smiling in apology.

"You sent meat," she replied, reaching out, drawing him in by that hand, closing the door behind him. "And my father has said we can take one last Bordeaux. After that, we are on our own."

She led him by the hand up the stairs. When she closed the door behind him, he stood a moment, sniffing deep. "That smells wonderful," he said.

"And will be even better when it's ready. An hour yet. Come." She helped him off with his coat, hung that and his hat on the hall's hooks. "We can drink wine by the fire while we wait."

He leaned in, kissed her on her cheek. "That will be lovely," he said.

IT WAS ONLY after he'd mopped up the last of the stew with his bread, eaten that slowly, and taken a large sip of his wine, that he felt he was ready. Then he looked across the table at Ilse and spoke the words.

She thought she must have misheard. "Pardon?"

He cleared his throat. "I said, 'Will you marry me?'"

Ilse stared at him, trying to separate out the jumble of thoughts that flooded her mind. The first, strongest image was of Billy at that ancient fort, kneeling in the moonlight, asking her the same question. Two men, two pilots, two enemies, both asking that she become their wife. When was that? Three months ago? She thought she might laugh—at the absurdity, at this world she'd got herself caught up in. But she forced the urge down.

Was this another moment to play the spy? Lead him on with a promise she had no intention of keeping? To begin with, and though the situation was different, she would not become a wife while the war continued and perhaps be a widow before it ended. She had gone as far as she was willing, for SOE, for the cause. However, she also recognized the opportunity here.

She would say no. But she did not need to say it straight away.

She reached across the table, gesturing for his hand. Took it, bent to it, kissed it. "Oh Klaus," she said, "we can't get married. You know we can't."

He swallowed. "Because you don't love me?"

"No. No, it is not that. It is . . ." She shook the hand she held, fixing him with her eyes. "What kind of life would we have? Where would we have it? You know what I am called. What that actor called me at Blom's. The term that is hissed at me in the street." She sighed. "In Norway I will forever be a German whore. I cannot live here with that title."

"Then . . . Germany?"

"Klaus . . ." She shook her head. "You know, I know, that Germany will lose this war."

He stared at her. "*You* say this? You who have always talked as if we cannot be beaten?"

"I am the daughter of a journalist. My father's job is to raise people's spirits. Play up the few small triumphs. Play down the steady drip of defeats." She pointed at the sofa behind them. "But he sits there, and he tells me the truth. How bombers are day and night reducing the Fatherland to a ruin. How the Russians are coming. The Americans are coming. The Brits are coming. While in every country Germany occupies, there are secret armies waiting to rise. In France, Greece, Italy, Denmark . . . here." She squeezed his hand again. "What life would there be in a ruined Germany for a former officer and his whore?"

He pulled his hand away. "Stop that. You know that is not what you are. You know I love you."

"I know that." She smiled. "And I love you as well."

"You do?"

"Of course I do. Can you doubt it?"

"I can. I must." He smiled. "I am a spy after all. Trained to doubt everything." He took a deep breath, exhaled it slowly. "And because of that, I have a question for you." He leaned closer, stared deep into her eyes. "Are you also a spy?"

"What?" She laughed, looked away. "Of course not."

And Klaus knew the lie. Years of interrogations had made him quick to recognize one. His stomach turned . . . but his mind also cleared. There were many things to consider here. For himself, yes. But for his country too. That was where he must begin, and only return to himself later.

"That is not what Torvald Linström told me."

She looked quickly back at him, her eyes widening. "Torvald? I heard he was arrested."

"He was. Held at Victoria Terrasse."

Her face flushed. "And we know what happens there."

"We do. I was able to, ah, intervene. Save him perhaps from the worst of it."

"Why?"

"Why did I intervene?"

"Yes."

He looked above her. "Perhaps because I remembered how beautifully he played the violin. Perhaps because . . ." He looked straight at her again. "We are not all monsters, Ilse. Some of us are—" He shook his head. Later for that too, he thought. "Besides," he continued, "I do not believe that information gained in this manner is always . . . accurate."

"Such as the information that I might be a spy?"

"Such as."

"Well, I am not, so . . ." She picked up her wineglass, sipped.

"Which is a great pity," he said, lowering his voice. "Because right now what I really need is a British spy."

She looked back. Her glance, which had been unfocused, was keen now. "Why?"

It was the moment—for both of them, he knew, he recognized it—that moment when someone must break cover and tell the truth. Not all of it, never that. But enough. So he lifted his glass, finished the wine in it, set it back down, and spoke again.

He told her . . . enough. No names, of course, not even the name of the operation. Some of the plan. His part in it: the seizing of Victoria Terrasse and the arrest of the senior SS officers. She listened to it all without comment, until he appeared to reach a conclusion. Then she spoke.

"So why do you need an enemy spy?"

"Because of what you talked of before: to prevent a ruined Germany. To halt the Russians. We believe there are many amongst the Americans and the Brits who fear them almost as much as they hate us. If we could enter negotiations, achieve a just peace, then . . ." He sighed. "Also, I think of all the lives that will be saved."

She regarded him for another long moment. "I see," she said at last. "I need to ask you one thing before I say anything more." She took his hand again. "Did you mean what you said before?"

"Which part?"

"Do you want to marry me?"

"Yes," he said, squeezing back. "Oh, yes."

"And any answer I give you will not change that?"

"Only one." He swallowed. "That you are a spy for SOE and your love for me was simply a ruse."

She smiled, then lifted his hand and kissed it. "Then I say two things to you, Klaus von Ronnenberg. I love you and . . . and I am a spy." She stood, still holding his hand, moved around the table till she stood before him, looking down at him. "We have talked enough. Later, we will need to talk more, much more. There will be . . . there will be someone I need to introduce you to. But for now"—she tugged, and he rose to her pull—"now we need something else."

THEY DIDN'T TALK LATER, not much anyway. Between the wine, and the relief of the telling, and the lovemaking, they both fell asleep fast. But Ilse woke soon after, and lay there for a time, staring up at the dim ceiling.

It wasn't anxiety that kept her awake. She had done exactly what her bosses required of her. They had pointed her at Klaus. They'd been right about him. Now all the waiting, all the frustration at feeling she was making no contribution to the fight, was behind her. There was much she still had to do, with many risks still to take. They would begin with the new day.

No. What kept her awake was unconnected with war. It had to do with love. With the men she loved. The one sleeping beside her. The one sleeping across the North Sea. Or not.

Am I keeping *you* awake, Billy Coke? she wondered. Then she rolled over onto her side and closed her eyes.

NINETEEN

LANDINGS BY MOONLIGHT

Tempsford Airfield, April 17, 1944

IT WAS LATE AFTERNOON by the time Billy dropped his Lysander down towards the Tempsford turf. As ever with the Lizzie, it was easy to land—in fact, he sometimes felt when flying one that he could put his feet up and take a nap! The automatic slats kicked in at eighty-five miles per hour and triggered the automatic flaps. Once he saw that on his dial, he did all that he truly needed to do: lowered a lever, locked them in. The descent was steep—so steep to a pilot used to Hurries and Spits. They needed a long runway. The Lizzie could stop in seventy-five yards. McRae, his CO in the communications squadron, and the man who'd first shown him over one, had said, "It may not go down like a lift—but you'll feel like you're on an escalator."

Billy let the plane descend, only raising the nose at the last moment. He barely felt the ground as it met his tires. To keep it interesting he tried to cut the landing distance by twenty yards. But the bird did balk a little at that, and he lurched slightly forward as he stopped and cut the engines.

"Fuck!"

The curse came from his passenger in the rear cockpit. "Sorry about that, sir," he called. "Bloody rabbits!"

"Yes, well, never mind. Can you get me out, please? I am having some difficulty."

The voice was lightly accented, and curt. "Certainly, sir." Billy unbuckled himself, then leaned over his seat and fiddled with the passenger cockpit hood. It was a little stiff but gave after a few sharp tugs. The man immediately pulled it back, climbed out onto the wing, lowered himself to the ground, and walked briskly towards a long hut to the left of the control tower. "You're welcome," Billy called none too softly after him, then added, because he'd seen the man's shoulder badge, "Ha det bra," one of the Norwegian phrases he'd picked up over the years.

He was still ignored. The man had been impatient and in a hurry from the moment Billy had been assigned the flight. He wasn't even meant to be flying today, having done the long haul to Scotland and back the day before. But everyone else was out, and this man had to be gotten to Tempsford fast.

Billy looked around. The aerodrome was reputed to be the most secret in England. It was certainly heavily disguised from the air, looking like a series of barns around a farmhouse. Billy knew it, could recognize it, because he'd dropped men here fairly regularly. Often, foreigners like the surly Norwegian. Tempsford was where the clandestine flights left for occupied Europe, dropping supplies and agents. Mostly France, Belgium. Occasionally, he'd heard, to Norway. The man had been in uniform, not civvies, so Billy assumed he wasn't going in. Briefing, probably, for someone who was.

Norway, he thought. Ilse.

He was startled from his reverie by a voice. "You comin' in, sir?"

He peered over the cockpit rim. A ground crew corporal was standing forward of his wing, hand raised against the glare of the sun, bright in a cloudless sky. Billy recognized him from previous flights. "Not sure, Corporal Oakley. Might just wait here for my return orders."

"That's Oakfield, sir. And it might be a while. Bit of a flap." He jerked a thumb over his shoulder at the control tower. "We got a brew on, and Mrs. Wingfield managed to get some eggs, so she made us her famous scones. Fancy one?"

Billy shrugged. "Why not? I'll be over in 'alf a mo'."

Shutting everything down, Billy climbed out. He had his satchel, with the book he was reading, the new one from Somerset Maugham, *The Razor's Edge*. With his nose in a book he might be able to avoid pilot chit-chat if anyone was about. He wasn't feeling very sociable.

The Tempsford Mess was a long, tall-roofed room converted from a barn. The bar was a trestle at one end, behind which some beer barrels rested and over which a few optics hung. Mrs. Wingfield poured him a cuppa, plated a scone. Billy went to a table in the opposite corner to a group of men, heads close together, one of which belonged to his passenger. He settled, took a bite of the scone. The corporal had been right, it was good—much better than those Mrs. Bishop had made in the shelter she'd run in London. Where he'd taken Ilse the night they met.

Jesus, he thought, and shook his head. It annoyed him that most things today reminded him of her—his passenger, Tempsford's occasional flight destination, this bloody scone. He put it down, took a sip of tea, opened the book. It was a little hard to concentrate as the barn was cavernous, and the men at the far end were now arguing fiercely. The topic was intermittently audible, despite several hisses which reduced the volume for a few sentences before it rose again.

He read one paragraph three times, then gave up. The topic the men were discussing was clear. It centred on Norway—again! And it appeared that they had a serious problem. After a few more minutes, when he realized what that was, Billy rose and walked the length of the barn. As he reached the table, the men fell silent, glaring up at him. Three of them were in civilian clothes. The man he'd brought was Norwegian army. The last man wore the stripes of an RAF group captain, and it was him Billy saluted.

He didn't return the salute. "Can we help you, Flight Lieutenant? Rather busy here."

"Yes, sir. I can see that. Or rather I heard it. And I am thinking that in fact *I* may be able to help *you*."

"How so?" It was the Norwegian, his passenger, who spoke. Billy had not paid him much attention before and now saw a man—a major — perhaps in his mid-thirties, though his blond hair was so heavily shot through with grey he could have been older. He looked at the others. "This is the pilot who brought me here."

"Flight Lieutenant Coke. With 24 Squadron, out of Hendon."

"You didn't win your DFC with a communications squadron." The group captain's gaze rose from the ribbons on Billy's chest.

"No, sir. Hurricanes. North Africa."

"And the two bars?"

"Spits. Malta. Sicily."

"Good show." The man's frostiness thawed somewhat. "So. How exactly do you believe you can help us?"

"As I say, I couldn't help overhearing—"

One of the civilians, a man with black hair and slightly crossed eyes, interrupted. "I told you all to keep your fucking voices down."

Billy ignored him, carried on. "And I heard—may I?" He pulled out a spare chair and, without waiting for permission, sat. "Heard that you were suddenly short a pilot."

"Fucker's got food poisoning," said that same civilian.

"This mission is, uh, urgent by nature, is it?"

"Most urgent." It was the second civilian who spoke now, an older, chubbier man with a thin moustache and dandruff on the shoulders of his black suit. "We need to get this fellow, um, somewhere." He indicated the last civilian, who was fair-haired and blue-eyed, easily the youngest there and dressed quite differently, in brown canvas trousers and a Shetland Isle sweater. "And we need to, um, extract another fellow at the same time."

The young man leaned forward. Spoke in, as Billy had suspected he would, a distinct Norwegian accent. "It is my last chance to go in this way. In one month the sun will not go down in Norway much at all. Planes cannot fly there in the light." He glanced at the RAF man. "But the captain here says that it will take too long to get another pilot here to fly to . . . where we must go . . . for it still must be dark when we get there."

"Much too long. By the time one reaches us here at Tempsford, it would be too late." The group captain shook his head. "It's bad enough that we must fly in five days either side of a full moon. Sky's already bright enough for Jerry to spot us. But near dawn. No, sir."

"I am prepared to take the risk," said the young man.

"Whilst I am not prepared to risk the life of my pilot!"

"Group Captain," said the chubby civilian, "the man we are trying to get out is, um, very senior in our organization there. That may make the risk worthwhile."

"I tell you, I cannot—"

The argument erupted all around again, with no attempt now to be quiet. Billy let it proceed until all the men simultaneously took a pause to draw breath. Then he said, "I could fly the plane."

Men about to shout exhaled instead. All looked at him. "It's a specialist plane, a Lysander," said the group captain.

"I just arrived in a Lizzie."

"But . . ." The man scratched his head. "You have to fly by dead reckoning, compass and map."

"I got top marks in navigation. I could show you my logbook." He grinned. "Though of course, that is back at Hendon."

"I cannot possibly allow something so irregular. Pilots who do this run are specially trained and—"

"Group Captain Whittaker." It was the Norwegian in uniform who interrupted. "You noted yourself this pilot's medals. They speak to his courage, no? And while we all understand the risk, we also understand that if we do not take it, the man we need back here will die, and our work in my country may be compromised because of that." He looked around at the others, all of whom nodded at him. "I know ultimately you must make the decision on the actual flight. But I ask you, sir, do you not think this pilot's sudden appearance is a sign?"

"A sign? From whom?"

"From God."

"Oh, God?" The RAF man said, as if the Almighty were another general to be annoyed at. He stared at each of them in turn, before finally fixing on Billy. "You understand you are volunteering for something extremely dangerous. Why would you do this?"

Billy shrugged. "I was thinking of my former Spitfire squadron, fighting their way up Italy right now. I suppose I feel that if this mission is as important as these gentlemen make it out to be, then this may be a way for me to help bring my friends home a little sooner."

He decided not to mention Ilse. How touching down in Norway might connect him with her, if only for a few moments. That, he thought, will make them think me mad. And they'd be right.

"Very well," Whittaker said, and everyone else at the table let out held breaths. "This gentleman here," he pointed to Billy's passenger, "will explain the where of it. This one," he waved at the chubby civilian, "the how. While I"—he stood—"need to inform you of all the special things to do with the Lizzie you will fly. It's a Mk III, not a II like yours. Specially adapted for this work. Let's to it." He looked around, gave a swift smile. "Well, gentlemen, it appears the game is once more afoot!"

———

WHEN HE FIRST SAW THE outline of the coast ahead, Billy felt several things at once: relief that he had found the country at least, after two hours of seeing nothing but the waves he skimmed. Euphoria when he noted the landmark he'd been told to watch for: moonlight glimmering on two bodies of water just inland from the North Sea, the one below long and thin leading up to one that was bigger, bulkier. "Like a cloud of smoke coming from its cigarette," his young Norwegian passenger had said— who tapped him on the shoulder now from the seat behind him and gave him the thumbs-up. But the feeling that made his stomach jump was seeing the place he'd been trying not to think about and always did. The place where she was.

You bloody idiot, he thought. What the hell are you doing? Seeking some momentary link to her? As if a current will run through the grass to wherever she is for the ninety seconds I'm supposed to be on the ground?

Would she feel that? Would she care if she did?

He shook his head. Time to focus now. Later he'd try not to think of her again. Fail again.

He pulled a lever and felt, in the slight lift of the plane, the Lizzie's relief as the long-distance fuel tank dropped away to the sea. He checked his gauge. It would be a thing of fine margins, but he had enough gas to do what he needed to do and get back to the forward station he'd taken off from, Felixstowe.

He dropped the plane to two hundred feet, checked the map wrapped in plastic on his lap, looked at the land, seeking. The moon, three days past full, reflected in long, narrow bodies of water that, in the main, pointed him the way he wanted to go. Nor'-nor'-east.

He glanced up and around, reflexively. It was a hunter's moon. If the Germans had any night fighters up, he was fucked. The only things he could do, he had done: fly under the radar over the water, count on the muffled engine over land, and pray. He hadn't done that even once since Sicily. Ferrying passengers didn't require it. Christ, he thought, I am a believer once again.

He'd over-egged his navigation skills back at Tempsford. The word written in his logbook was *proficient*, not *exemplary*. So he was especially pleased when, fifteen minutes after crossing the coast, another tap on his shoulder confirmed what he'd also just seen: a lake that took a sudden right-turn north. Flying half a mile due east from that junction, he passed over another body of water. And then . . .

The taps came hard. "Seen them," he murmured, as four powerful flashlights snapped on briefly, demarcating a rough rectangle. Billy swung the Lizzie north, banked around. Didn't go very far, didn't need to, with this bird's landing abilities. He eased the throttle, and when his speedometer read eighty-five miles per hour, he felt the automatic slats kick in. At eighty, the flaps did, and he pressed the lever, locked them. The plane dropped sharply, like the escalator McRae had talked about. When those flashlights came on again, he corrected slightly to place himself right in the centre of the triangulation and put the bird down. It bumped, lifted again, bumped. It was a field he was landing on, and not even a tended one like his bases back in England. But he closed the throttle and the bird settled.

He was in Norway.

He had nothing to do now. It was the man behind him who did, together with those who'd turned their flashlights off, who Billy could now see running towards the plane. Two men were carrying a stretcher— he'd been told that the agent he was bringing out was "not well," his ailment or wounds unspecified. Again, it was the lad behind him, and those approaching, who would deal with all that. He was just the pilot, and he did all he needed to: kept the engine idling.

As the man behind him opened the side hatch, as Norwegian words were harshly whispered, Billy took the moment he'd anticipated, the one he'd come for. "Do you feel me, Ilse?" he murmured, eyes shut. "And if you do, can you ever forgive—"

"Nei!" The man's scream was shockingly loud, then echoed by a half-dozen more voices as car headlights flashed on, centred on the bird, illuminating everything, dazzling Billy. The voice came immediately, harsh and amplified.

"*Aufgeben! Hände hoch! Hände hoch!*"

Billy whipped his head around. His passenger was on the ground, but two other men were trying to pass a fourth man, obviously the wounded one, up into the cockpit. They each yelled, tried to lift him faster. He screamed, throwing back his head in pain. And then the first shots came, one of the lifting men twisted, fell back. The other dropped the man they'd held, then turned and ran.

More shots. Some hit his fuselage. Gunning the throttle, Billy set off fast down the runway. The sounds of shot and screams fading behind him, he was aware of vehicles racing in from each side, trying to get ahead of him. But the Lizzie could take off in as short a space as she could land. He was off the ground in thirty yards, and fifty feet off the deck five seconds later. He felt shots hit his underbelly, like punches to his gut. But moments later he was banking over trees that bordered the east side of the field, and the punches ceased.

He tipped his wing, snatched a glance back. Saw headlights zigzagging across the field, red flashes from muzzles. Focusing forward again, he set the plane in the only direction he could think of . . . home.

Then he checked his gauges.

He was not going home. He didn't know the size of the bullet hole in his petrol tank, but the way his gauge was falling it was big enough. He hadn't had time to even curse. He didn't have long now, but he did. "Fuck!" he shouted, tipping his wings each way, seeking left, right and ahead for any piece of flattish land where he might put down and have a chance of not killing himself. The land below him now appeared to be all water, or all wood. Neither were good options —but he began to steel himself for a swim.

The gauge kept dropping. It was at a quarter; the rate it was falling he reckoned he had no more than two minutes. He called on God again. Made the latest vow in a series he had broken in Spain, North Africa, Malta, Sicily. He tipped his wing—and saw it. A shallow hill, moorland probably. Its summit looked barren and flat, and no more than three hundred yards long.

He banked around, dropped his speed. But neither the strats nor the flaps kicked in this time when he reached eighty-five. Fucked like his tank, he thought. Just as well.

He felt the engine shudder, cough, then die, but since it was just as he reached his stalling speed of sixty-five miles per hour it didn't matter anymore. The engine stalled, he was gliding, but the moon-light was flattening the land, making it hard to gauge his height, which he had to do with his eyes since his altimeter was also fucked.

He looked ahead, above the engine. He was going to overshoot! Kicking the rudder right, and left, he began to fishtail, slowing himself as his tail swung from side to side. The ground grew closer, fast, so fast. There were so many things he'd love to know, so he could compensate for them: where the wind was coming from, for one; was he landing uphill or downhill, for two. But he had no time for any of that. He was making a dead-stick landing by the light of the moon on unknown terrain. So really, all he could do was what he had been doing: pull the stick slowly back. And pray.

Then, when he knew he was mere feet off the ground, he remembered what his first flying instructor in Spain had told him in the event of such a crash. "Side-slip," Miguel had said. "Let the wing take it first."

So that was the very last thing Billy did—applied the right aileron and put his starboard wingtip into the ground.

The Lizzie turned from bird to threshing machine. Flung up, flung right, flung left, lifted, dropped, his safety straps buffeting the air from his lungs. He took in a breath, released it on a yelp. His arms, which he'd tried to brace against the dash, were thrown about as if disconnected from his body. The plane was spinning round and round, like on some fairground ride, and the liver sausage sandwich he'd eaten an hour before ejected from him. The sound was a cacophony—screaming metals torn apart, Perspex cockpit disintegrating.

And then, and then . . . everything slowed. Slowed and spun to a stop. Sounds continued for a while—metal contracting within sudden stillness, wires that had been stretched to the limits suddenly snapping. Gradually all that faded to nothing, until the only thing Billy could hear was his heart, thumping wildly, and the wind making varied whistles through the holes torn in his canopy.

He checked himself. Moved arms and legs, torso. All was

strained, especially his neck, which felt like he'd turned it a complete 360 degrees. Other than that . . . he was OK. He was OK! "Thanks, God," he said. "I'll make it up to you next time."

He started to laugh, cut himself off sharply. There were things he had to do. Get the hell away from here was one. But not before he'd destroyed his bird. Group Captain Whittaker had been very clear on that point. "Jerry hates us flying Lizzies in and out and would love to get his hands on one. Crash it in water if you must. Don't let him have it. It's worth more than your life!"

"Easy for you to say, pal," Billy muttered, as he slipped out of his straps. The cockpit lock was jammed; of course he'd forgotten to open it before impact. But since the Perspex was already shredded it didn't take him long to kick his way out. Before he left though, he reached back for two things: his satchel, and the petrol can behind his seat. That was not kept to top up his engine. It was kept for the purpose he put it to now.

When he'd emptied it over the whole bird, saving most, as Whittaker had taught him, for its innovations—its strats, flaps, cockpit and engine—he stepped away and regarded it. "Shit!" he said. The bullets had been fired from a 20mm cannon; holes punched all along the belly. How the balls had missed him he couldn't figure. The wing he'd landed on had done the job he'd intended, absorbed a lot of the shock, snapped in half. The propeller had been bent back almost flush along the engine housing.

Shaking his head, he reached into the satchel, pulled out a packet of cigarettes and his Zippo. He lit himself a fag, and stared towards the plane, not really seeing it. Took three deep drags then said, "Thanks, baby," and flicked the glowing butt up into the cockpit, before turning and limping rapidly downhill.

There was a whoosh when he was about fifty yards away. Flames threw his shadow onto the low gorse before him. He didn't turn back, didn't need to, didn't want to see it. He had done all he could, and the bird would either burn or it wouldn't. At least there would be no explosion. It was out of gas.

He hadn't chosen a direction; he had just gone. But when the land dipped, and the guiding flamelight was lost to him, he stopped, sat down on a rock, surveyed the valley below. It wasn't a very high hill, and the moon, though getting lower in the west, was still quite bright. He could make out darker shapes that had to be farmhouses or barns. To the northwest and quite far away there was a longer, deeper patch—a town, perhaps, or even a city. He knew Stavanger was that-away, he'd seen it on his map.

Map, he thought. Fuck. He even turned around. But of course it was far, far too late. A glow came from over the hilltop.

He looked ahead again. The city was out; it was a major German naval base and would be crawling with Krauts, even if he could reach it. He had to assume that the enemy would already be looking for him. If they didn't know how badly he was shot up, fighters would even now be near the coast to cut off his escape to England. If they had guessed that his was a wounded bird, they'd already have patrols out.

He heard it even as he thought it—the hum of an engine, getting closer fast. He lowered himself into the shadows of the rock he'd sat on, drawing his knees up to his chest.

The plane came over low, maybe three hundred feet up. Swept over the hilltop and Billy recognized it—a Fieseler Storch, a German reconnaissance craft. Brilliant, Billy, he thought. He'd lit a beacon for them to follow. Hey fellas—here I am!

But he'd had his orders. The plane circled the hill twice, then flew off north, towards Stavanger. Radioing coordinates, no doubt.

He suddenly felt very tired. He'd like to curl up here, despite the sharp wind, and have a kip. But he knew he couldn't. Surrender wasn't even an option. It was one of the last things Whittaker had told him; another reason the group captain had been so reluctant to let him go. Hitler, furious at the raids taking place throughout Europe, had personally ordered that anyone caught during clandestine ops was to be treated as a spy—and immediately shot. Even if they were in uniform.

Billy forced himself up, groaned as his body reminded him of all the places where he'd wronged it. His odds, he had to admit, were not good. But he'd discovered over the course of a somewhat eventful life that they rarely were. Luck would always play a huge part, and he'd need a bucketful of it now if he was to slip the noose that was already tightening. He'd have to hope that any farmhouse he approached held patriots—*jøssings*, he knew they were called—and not quislings, those traitorous German allies, of which there were far too many. Most, however, would probably be people just trying to get by: attempting to keep their families alive, and unwilling to risk anything that might threaten them—such as sheltering an Allied airman on the lam.

Billy could already see a lightening in the land ahead. This far north, in April, dawn came early. He looked down, and in one of those squat brown shapes a light briefly flared before disappearing behind some pulled curtain. Time for all good farmers to be waking, he thought, so time for me to be moving.

That light was as good a sign from God as any, so he began to walk towards it. He'd only gone about fifty yards when another thought came. "Ilse," he said. He'd wondered if she could feel him through the rubber of his plane's wheels. Now he wondered if she could feel him through the leather soles of his boots.

GUNNAR SOLBAKKEN STOOD at the living room window of his farmhouse, one hand pulling back his heavy curtain, staring out. It was still too dark to see much, but the sky was lightening over Ljosådalen, the valley where he'd spent his life. It was four in the morning, the hour he'd got up every day since he was eleven years old. First on his father's farm, then here, on his own. Sixty years of early rising because, as his father always said, the cows would not milk themselves. But three months earlier the Germans had taken his last cow, leaving only her calf, who had sickened and died three days later. Of a fever, the vet had said. Of loneliness, Gunnar knew.

Still, he rose. Stood at this window and watched, sometimes for an hour, he did not know what for. Perhaps for his son, Per, who had gone "på skauen" two years ago when the Germans had tried to force-recruit all the young men to be shipped to Germany to work in their factories. Most had not waited for the trucks to collect them but had gone off in the night, like Per, shepherded away by the resistance. Per could be anywhere now—in a skauen camp, deep in the woods. Across the border in Sweden, where the Swedes, instead of interning Norwegian refugees as they had done earlier in the war, were now allowing them to train as policemen, to return when the war was over. Or he could even have made it to England, have joined the exiles' army, be in uniform, marching up and down, shooting guns.

Gunnar smiled. He couldn't see his boy with a gun. He was short-sighted and more than a little clumsy. And he hated killing things, which was a drawback for a farmer's son. Gunnar had never been able to persuade Per to put a bullet through an elk's heart so they would have meat for the winter. Though he'd deny it, the lad always aimed high.

Gunnar's smile went. It had been hard going on the farm since they'd taken his last cow. He'd sold milk, butter, cream, or traded it for things he needed. Now all he had were chickens, some ducks and geese. But he'd seen the German quartermaster eye them up before he left with the cow. If they came back . . . he did not know what he would do. The scraps of paper they left "in payment" bought almost nothing.

Unlike many of his neighbours, he had never hated the occupiers. Unlike some others, he did not love them either, nor seek to help them, nor hinder them. That was work for braver souls. He was a farmer. He got up at four, he worked the land. But the war did impact him, of course it did. His son gone . . . and his wife, Hilde, who couldn't get the medicine she needed for her chest and who had died three months after Per fled.

Maybe, like the calf, what had really killed her was the loneliness. He looked again now to the summit of Nasefjell. The glow had died. Someone had lit a fire up there; he couldn't understand why. He'd heard a plane earlier—it was what had woken him a little before his normal time. Strange, because planes flew over all the time, out of the big German base near Stavanger.

"Yuh," he said, speaking the word on the inhalation. "Time to move." He would get the fire going, heat a pot, make some tea from dried dandelion roots. He'd saved a bread roll from the batch Fru Øve down the valley had given him when he'd mended one of her fences. It was perhaps a little past its best, but dipped in the tea . . .

He shrugged, was about to let the curtain fall, when he saw it— movement on the lower slope of Nasefjell. An elk or . . . ? No, it was a man, walking downhill. Away from that glow. He had a strange gait, as if one of his legs was much longer than the other. He wore dark clothes, no hat. There was not yet enough light to see his face, though Gunnar felt that he was young. He was also sure he was not local. No local would be lighting a fire on top of that hill in April.

The man reached the valley floor, climbed a gate, dropped to the ground, leaned against it. Then he looked up and down the road, the 9, which ran south along Setesdal all the way to Kristiansand and north to Hovden. He must have seen something, or heard something, because suddenly he was moving fast, still in that shambling way, straight across the road, straight along the track . . . towards the farmhouse.

Gunnar let the curtain fall. Stood holding it, shaking his head. When the man crossed the road, Gunnar, who still had a hunter's eyesight, had seen the colour of the man's short jacket. Blue. The Germans wore grey. The Germans—whose engines he now heard, as the man must have heard them, on the road. Many engines and getting close fast. But beneath them he now heard swift, slightly drag-ging footsteps in his yard. Then the clump up the steps. He held his breath. After a moment there came a soft knock.

He shook, went to the door. "Yah?" he called.

There was silence—but not in the distance, where engines grew noisier. Then words. It took Gunnar a few seconds to make sense of them because he'd left school at thirteen and only the first ones were in Norwegian.

"*God dag.* I'm sorry, but I need some help."

Gunnar shook his head again—then pulled back the top and bottom bolts and opened the door.

A young man stood there in a uniform that was indeed blue, dark blue, and on the jacket's left breast was a badge of spread white wings, a crown between them . . . and the letters *RCAF*.

"I'm awfully sorry," said the man, running a hand through a mop of thick black hair, pushing it off his forehead, glancing down the road, before looking back, "but unless you let me in the Germans are going to shoot me on your front porch."

Gunnar didn't understand most of what the young man said. But "Germans" and "shoot" were at least clear, as was the fear behind the calmness of the Englishman's words. Gunnar frowned. He didn't take sides. But the young man was not much older than Per, and those same Germans had taken his last cow. So he said, "*Kom inn da,*" which he thought was probably similar in English. Certainly the firm hand on the young man's shoulder, and the tug, were clear.

He closed the door behind the youth, bolted it. Sounds came through it, of engines, most of these suddenly cut off. Shouting followed. He took the man's arm, led him down the hall through the kitchen and out into the yard, and straight to the chicken shed. He pulled up the door. Chickens rushed them, squawking for handouts. He pointed and the other man did not hesitate, just dropped to his knees and crawled up the short ramp. The door was a squeeze, but he pushed himself through. Then Gunnar spent a few moments throwing hens in after him before pulling the slat down.

He went to his bedroom, took off his clothes, put on his pyjamas. Then he went again to the front window, parted the curtains, just a crack. German vehicles had stopped along the road—two motorcycles with machine-gun sidecars, two trucks, soldiers spilling out of one of them, and a car. There was an officer standing up in the front seat, pointing and shouting. Immediately, a troop climbed the fence and began walking quickly up the hill. One of the motorcycles headed north at speed, the second truck following. The officer took time to point directly at the farm before sitting down again, the car setting off as he did. The village of Nausen was less than half a kilometre up the road. Gunnar assumed that was where they were heading.

He let the curtain fall, stood there and listened as the second motorcycle roared closer, then screeched to a stop. Boots pounded on the three steps, then a fist on the door. The German was a lot louder than the Englishman had been.

"*Aufmachen!*" The door was shaken hard against the bolts. "*Schnell! Schnell!*"

Gunnar stood still, counting to twenty, which he thought was the right amount of time for a man who rose later than he himself did to get to the front door. This was threatening to come off its hinges, as something wooden had replaced flesh being hammered on it.

"*Ja da, ja da! Jeg kommer,*" he said, shooting the bolts, stepping away as the door flew in.

The German soldier was even younger than the Englishman. Not as polite. He screamed something in his own language, which Gunnar had studied even less than he had English, and both so long ago. When he just shrugged, the man shoved him hard to the side, and yelled at his colleague still sitting on the motorcycle seat—an older man, who sighed, got off and climbed the stairs.

The younger soldier—he had a triangle on one sleeve, Gunnar noticed, which he thought made him a corporal—gave some sort of order. The older man sighed again, took Gunnar's arm, and led him through the kitchen and out into the backyard. The sound of chairs being thrown around followed them.

The chickens flocked them, and the German laughed, moving them gently aside with his boots as he went first into the empty cowshed, poking at a pile of straw there, then emerged and, after peering over the walls to the pasture beyond, crossed to the chicken shed. Gunnar stiffened when the man bent to the latch, pulled the door up. But then the soldier reeled back, as six chickens came charging out, running to join the rest of the flock as if they'd received food that the newcomers hadn't.

The German laughed again. "Jaerhøns?" he asked.

It was the breed, the common Norwegian breed, and Gunnar nodded. "I have . . ." the German said in Norwegian, using the muzzle of his short machine gun to scratch his forehead, "Chickens. Many. In home. Type Augsburg."

He bent, snatched one up that had been pecking at his boot. Gunnar looked past him, to the entrance of the hutch. Another chicken emerged, dragging some sort of coloured cloth—a blue ribbon perhaps, which should not have been there. Gunnar looked up at the German, now nose to beak with the chicken. "You take," he said, in what he thought might be German.

The man looked up. "Me?"

"Yes." Gunnar nodded, then remembered another phrase he'd heard in German when he'd visited Stavanger for supplies. Street kids had yelled it at soldiers. He said it now. "You give me chocolate?"

The man's eyebrows came together. "Chocolate for chicken?" When Gunnar nodded, the man beamed, put his gun on the roof of the chicken shed, opened his coat's breast pocket, and pulled out a chocolate bar. He handed it over, then unbuttoned the coat enough to slip the chicken inside. "Thank you," he said.

Shouts came from inside. The soldier sighed. "*Wir gehen. Schnell! Schnell!*" He said it in a mockery of how the other soldier had spoken it through Gunnar's front door.

Gunnar followed the German back through the house. The corporal was already in the motorcycle sidecar. "*Schnell! Schnell!*" he yelled.

The older man winked at Gunnar then went down the steps, mounted the machine, kicked the engine into life. There was a brief argument about the chicken, with the young man finally throwing up his hands and pointing forward. They drove to the road, where another soldier bent down and said something, gesturing back up the hill. The corporal nodded, then issued some command. The motorcycle took off up the road, where the rest of the force had gone.

Gunnar watched the one left behind turn and begin to trudge up the hill. He waited till he was halfway up before he went back to the yard and over to the chicken hut. "Hallo," he called in English, "is good."

There was a shuffling, and then a face appeared. It was streaked in shit and had a large yellow patch of yolk above the left eyebrow.

"Chocolate?" Gunnar said, holding out his prize.

TWENTY

FRIENDS

Oslo. July 17, 1944

ILSE STILL FOUND IT STRANGE. After years in Oslo doing nothing except sending a monthly message with little to report, not feeling that she was really helping in the fight, not seeing anyone, certainly not having contact with the local resistance, now she was engaged every day. Now she was meeting people, new people, from all the different organizations. Somehow she had become the coordinator of these groups, just as Klaus was on the German side of the operation. They'd talked about that, how they were outranked by those they effectively gave commands to. Yet both had to do so without appearing to do so. Men—it was always men she met, very few women held high positions in the resistance—were too proud to directly obey anyone they felt was a rank below them, or inexperienced. They had to be . . . cajoled. Placated. Beefed up, as the English said. Well, she had been doing that all her life with proud men. Conductors of orchestras, tutors. Her father. He had trained her well.

Like these men, she thought, staring at the three of them gathered in the small front room of the safe house, an apartment on Niels Juels gate. She didn't know their real names. They were "Tore," "Anders" and "Karl." To them she was "Marie." The men were each there on behalf of the main Norwegian resistance organizations. Tore was the Milorg man, the long-established military wing. Anders was his civilian equivalent with Sivorg, who were responsible for fake IDs, underground newspapers, and the transport of agents in and out of the country. Whereas Karl . . .

He was the only one she hadn't met before. He was with the communists, who had disagreed so ardently with the other groups earlier in the war and had indulged in attacks and acts of sabotage that had brought savage reprisals down upon the civilian population, with so many innocents shot. They had reluctantly stopped such acts, focused on labour disruptions, halting German war effort production when they could. But they always wanted to push for a harder line, a more aggressive action. Restraint irked them. And before the war they'd been more anti-English than anti-German. Like her father had many times, Karl—the nickname no doubt chosen out of love for his movement's founder—had earlier in the meeting gone on a long and distracting rant about British imperialism.

Their organizations might be rivals, but they were all Norwegian —and thus they all resented SOE, which Ilse represented. She'd soothed them on that also, saying she was merely a coordinator, a conduit for what SOE knew of the German plot against Hitler. When she felt they were ready, she briefed them on what they needed to know of the Norwegian side of Valkyrie. Finally she pulled the three copies of single sheet paper from her bag, the instructions from SOE, which had taken her so long to transcribe, decode.

She held them out. "Please read these. They are the tasks London wishes each of your organizations to undertake in the event of our German"—she nearly said *friends*, decided against it—"conspirators' success." She handed a page to each man. "I know I needn't tell you to memorize the instructions before giving them back to me."

"Instructions from the imperialist Brits," muttered the communist. But he said it almost as if it was a rote response, as the priest might in a back-and-forth with his congregation in church. Because he also took the paper and read as avidly as the other two.

Managed men, Ilse thought, sitting back, looking at them. Then she closed her eyes for a moment, thought of another man she'd managed. An honourable man, a patriot, a peacemaker. A lover of Mozart. Klaus von Ronnenberg . . . who would get no chance to negotiate a peace. She knew the truth of what SOE had told her to pass on to these men, which she could not pass on to him: that the Allies had no intention of backing away from what had been decided at the Casablanca conference. Hitler or no Hitler, there would be no negotiated peace with Germany, only unconditional surrender.

While the tea in the cups before them cooled, the men read, asked for some clarifications, learned their roles. And when they were done, Ilse took their pages to the hearth and burned them. She watched them flare, blacken, finally dissolve, before turning back. "Keep someone always on lookout for the sign," she said. "When the Norwegian flag hangs upside down outside the Elisenberg post office, Hitler is dead . . . and our time has come."

The divided men were united by her words. Even Karl shook her hand as he left the apartment. Its owner, a woman who went by "Lotte," emerged from the kitchen on Ilse's soft call. "I need somewhere to, uh, change," she said, and was shown into a small bedroom. Ilse had her copy of the orders she'd burned. One had to be preserved in case amendments were made, or even full changes. For a moment she was tempted to simply put it into her handbag—she was heading straight home after all. But remembering her training, she decided against it, and took off her blouse, then her brassiere. Smiled as she remembered how red the SOE major, Cholmondeley-Warren, had turned when he'd asked for her bra size. She'd gone down two sizes since the German invasion, but a branch of SOE had made one for her that was only one size smaller in order to accommodate the pouches where secret documents could be hidden.

Folding her papers carefully, she shoved them in, then closed the silk flaps over them.

Lotte let her out of the apartment and Ilse descended the three flights to the street. It was ten o'clock at night and as bright as midday on Niels Juels gate. She turned left, crossed Bygdøy allé. As she neared Frognerveien she heard a tram, probably the one she'd catch for Majorstuen. But she didn't run for it, deciding instead to enjoy the summer evening and the walk. Enjoy her thoughts too.

She couldn't help it. She was proud of herself. She was really doing something here, something that could affect the war, save thousands of lives, free her people. Besides, there was nothing much awaiting her at home. Some cold potato pancakes—and her father, fresh back from another trip to meet Joseph Goebbels in Berlin, full of the stories that the Reich minister had fed him, stories about secret rockets being developed that would destroy London, New York, Moscow. Stories she had passed on to SOE. Wilhelm was not well, a stomach ailment that did not respond to any treatment. But his eyes were bright with the drugs they had him on, and he talked fast, constantly, of the great Pan-Germanic future that was to come: the defeat of Bolshevism, the Nazi triumph.

She stopped beneath a beautiful cherry tree and looked at her wristwatch. Ten after ten. The other thing that was not awaiting her at home was Klaus. She hadn't seen him for two weeks. For one, he mainly slept in his office, awaiting words that must be instantly acted upon. For another, he had decided that the game they played was too risky—doubly so since she had revealed who she truly was—for them to see each other. "When this is over," he'd told her, "and not just this operation but the war itself, I promise you I will never leave you alone again."

She'd protested, even as she was secretly glad. When at least some of their truths were out, he had grown fonder of her. She, conversely, had felt her fondness diminish, like tea cooling in a cup. She couldn't explain it to herself. Had she needed to believe in love to do what she'd had to do? Her duty. Her duty to get close, closer, to him. Now she had? Strangely, as her love for the German faded, she began to think more and more of the Canadian, Billy Coke. The man she would never see again. She started walking again, turned the corner. Too lost in her thoughts, she looked up . . . too late.

They were across both sidewalks and had halted the tram in the road. Germans, in the black uniforms of the SS, others clearly Gestapo in their long leather trench coats. The shock was so sudden, such a contrast to what she'd been thinking about, that she didn't do what she should have done—kept walking. Instead, she turned around and took three steps back down Niels Juels gate.

It was exactly what the Gestapo were watching for.

She heard the shouts. The first thing she thought was: How strange! Because the German words could be English too.

"*Stopp! Halt!*"

The pounding of boots on pavement. Louder as the chasers rounded the corner. Then the first clearly German word.

"*Stillgestanden! Sie! Frau!*"

Ilse obeyed, stood still. Took a deep breath - which was immediately expelled as someone shoved her hard in the back. She stumbled, nearly fell, half turned. Saw the black uniform coming at her, too close to see his face. The storm trooper grabbed her by the shoulder, spun her, shoved her again. She shot her hands out before her, just preventing her face hitting brick.

"Why did you run away?" the man shouted at her. "What are you hiding?"

"I didn't. I . . . nothing!"

She tried to turn to protest, but his hand was still holding her dress at the shoulder. Twisting the fabric, he didn't let her.

She eyed the wall, heard footsteps; a different voice, a lighter register, spoke. "Papers!" the man snapped.

"Yes! Yes, of course. In my bag—"

She realized she'd dropped it when the thug threw her at the wall. "There," she said, jerking her chin down.

The bag was dragged out of her sight. She heard the clasp snap open, the clink of lipstick, compact and purse against each other. Then the man spoke again, in heavily accented Norwegian. "Your name is Frøken Magnusson?"

"Y-yes."

"Turn her."

The hand at her shoulder twisted her again, spun her around, then shoved her so her back struck the wall. She gave a little cry, saw the soldier—young, dark eyes set close together—smile. There was another, equally young, beside him. Both held Schmeisser sub-machine guns.

The man who held her ID card was older. He had stubble, a pencil moustache and wore the long trench coat and fedora hat of the Gestapo. He stared at her face, then at the card. "Name!" he barked.

"Il-Ilse—"

"I cannot hear you."

She breathed deeper. "Ilse Magnusson."

"Address?"

"I live in Harald Hårfagres gate. Number—"

"Profession?"

"I . . . I am a musician."

It was what it said on the card. He nodded. He folded it, dropped it back in the handbag, seemed disappointed that there was nothing else of interest within. Then his eyes lit up as he remembered. "But why were you running away from us, Frøken?"

"I wasn't, I . . . I didn't even see you. I'm sorry. I . . . I forgot that I was meant to go to a konditori. In the other direction."

"Meeting someone?"

She realized that if she said yes, they would take her there, check, discover she was lying. "No, they make good lefse there. My father likes them. He is Wilhelm Magnusson, a great friend of—"

"Sht!" He made a sound like paper tearing. He wasn't really listening. He was looking down instead and Ilse realized that the other German, in pulling her by her summer dress, had ripped two buttons away. The fabric gaped, and her right breast was three-quarters exposed.

The man now smiled, revealing uneven teeth. "I think we need to search you, Frøken Mag-nus-son." He drew out the name like it was false, suspicious. "*Soldat!*"

He gestured, and the man who'd grabbed her also smiled and handed his Schmeisser to his grinning comrade. There was an alley just beside the wall, and he pushed her down it.

Ilse looked behind him. There was a small crowd gathered, but other Germans were already moving them away. As she stumbled forward she thought: They can't plan to rape me, not here, not in daylight in central Oslo? Then she realized that they could; she would put nothing past them. Yet even as terror warred with defiance, she thought it was equally likely that they would just enjoy "searching" her: taking her clothes off, feeling inside each one, touching her everywhere as they did. But if they did that, if they looked carefully, they'd find the papers in her bra. Then not only was she finished. Operation Valkyrie, at least in Oslo, was too. The smiling soldier—he still had acne, could be no more than eighteen—stepped closer and went straight to his desire. He thrust his hand hard into her left breast, groping inside her bra.

"Enjoying yourself, soldier?"

It was a different German voice, smoother, more cultured.

The young soldier stepped away, snapped to attention. "Major!"

His move revealed the man standing behind him. She had seen him somewhere before, this officer in the beautifully tailored SS uniform, but she couldn't remember where.

His memory was obviously better. "Ilse Magnusson," purred Major Erich Striegler, as if they'd just met for tea. "What are you doing here?"

"She ran away from the checkpoint, Herr Major. Said she was going to a konditori." It was the Gestapo man speaking now. "You were busy with another suspect, so we began—"

"Oh yes. I see what you began. But am I going to let you finish?"

Striegler sucked at his upper lip. "No. I don't think so. Mainly because you'd be wasting your time. Frøken Magnusson is a great patriot, a great . . . *quisling*." He breathed out the word most Norwegians hated. "She is also the . . . *special friend* of a colleague of mine. So, back to your duties. I will deal with this."

"But Herr Major . . ." the Gestapo man began.

The look Striegler gave him halted his words. Instead he came out with others. "*Jawohl*," he said, and "Heil Hitler!" A chorus of that followed, then he and the two soldiers moved out of the alley. Ilse saw the one who'd assaulted her look back, as disappointed as a dog that'd had its fresh bone taken away.

Striegler watched them go, then said, gesturing, "Please, Ilse, tidy yourself."

He watched as she did, expressionless. When she bent to her bag, which the other man had dropped, she stumbled. He picked it up, handed it to her, put a hand under her elbow, steadied her. "This konditori," he said, "shall I accompany you there? Perhaps we should take a cup of coffee together, hmm?"

She'd taken enough breaths to steady herself too, at least a little. "Please, Major. I think now I'd rather go home."

"Of course. And anyway, I really should be about my duties here." He led her back to the street. "Do you still live in that charming apartment near Majorstuen? Yes? Good? I asked for the tram to be held while I investigated what all the fuss was about."

He kept hold of her arm as he guided her up to the corner of Frognerveien, around it, all the way to the tram, even stepped with her up onto its platform. When he finally released his grip, he held her instead with soft words. "I think my colleague von Ronnenberg will be happy that I helped you, no? Perhaps that will make him more helpful to me. He's a bit of a stiff old Prussian, isn't he? What's left of him." He leaned in, placed his lips close to her ear, whispered, "So if ever you feel grateful about today, Ilse, and decide you want a real man, a whole man, you know where to find me, yes?"

He kissed her ear then, before stepping swiftly off the platform.

"Go!" he called, slapping the tram's wooden side. The driver pushed his handle and the vehicle moved swiftly away.

Ilse sat, heard whispers around her, didn't look up at anyone. Tears slipped from her eyes, but she found she hadn't the strength to even raise a hand to brush them away. Her palms hurt where she'd tried to stop herself falling against the wall; her breast hurt where the soldier had groped her. But she found that it was her ear that discomfited her most— the one the Nazi's lips had touched.

TWENTY-ONE
LAST MOMENTS

Oslo. July 19, 1944

KLAUS HAD ONLY RETURNED to his apartment to change his shirt and underwear, to collect a further change of clothes, his razor and soap. He would take them to Victoria Terrasse, and he would not leave his office, tiny though it was, until it was over. Until he was either victorious or dead.

His hand lingered on the razor—a cutthroat that had belonged to his father. It was a beautiful item, the ivory handle gloriously yellowed with age, the lightly curved Solingen blade gleaming bright. He felt his scratchy chin. He had let himself slip. He was tempted to stay longer, tidy himself. Reluctantly he decided he could not. The midday-like sun outside was deceptive. It was night in Oslo, as it was in Berlin. As it was at the Wolf's Lair, which Hitler rarely left these days.

There was no car waiting for Klaus downstairs. Since the dissolution of the Abwehr a few months before, he had lost many things—like transport, and his huge, comfortable office in Klingenberggata.

But that, especially, was an advantage now. He'd been assigned to an outsized closet in the building on Victoria Terrasse, while he slowly, so slowly, wrote reports for the Sicherheitsdienst's various departments on everything they would need to know to take over the intelligence his force had handled. He only had a tiny desk but he had paid some guards to bring his armchair from the old place. Wing-backed pliant leather, he could sleep in it. And did. Most importantly, he still had a phone. That would ring when the coup was launched. It had rung the day before. When he'd picked it up, one word was spoken.

"Soon."

Victoria Terrasse was exactly where he needed to be. There he would meet the soldiers von Falkenhorst dispatched and then he'd arrest all the SS men on the premises. He knew where they all were, had dropped by every one of their offices and said hello. For those not there, he also knew where they lived.

The two black-clad Waffen-SS guards at the main door snapped their guns up in a salute, clicked their heels. "Heil Hitler," he called as he passed between them. The marbled entrance hall was always busy, but today it was even more so. Soldiers, both officers and men, were running up the stairs or past him, out the door. He paused, a still centre to the furor. Which is when he heard the familiar voice, its accent heavy and from the south.

"Lost again, Herr Major?"

Klaus turned to see Erich Striegler striding down the ground-floor corridor. It was the direction his new office was in, and the previous week Klaus had pretended he'd taken a wrong turn to end up at the SS man's door. "No, no," he said. "Just wondering what all the excitement is about."

Striegler halted beside him. He was pulling on gauntlets. "Excitement indeed! I'm flying with a squad up to the west coast right now. Place called Skipevige, on the Austfjorden. Know it?"

"Uh, no."

"Why would you? It's just another shit village where families fuck their cows and each other." He laughed. "It's not far north of

Bergen. There's an air base about ten kilometres away, which is where we'll land. More men will meet us there, we'll motor over . . . kebam!"

He was in excellent spirits, even clapped Klaus on the shoulder—and they were not the best of friends. "Ke . . . bam?"

"A razzia, Herr Major. A little canary sang us such a nice song just now." He jabbed a finger downwards, to where Klaus knew the dungeons were. "I haven't done a swoop in three months, and that was nothing but herring in our net. Small fish! This one's song tells of salmon! Resistance leaders. Maybe even an Allied airman or two."

A junior officer ran up, snapped a salute. "The car is outside, Herr Major."

"Good. I come." As the man sprinted away, Striegler turned back to Klaus. "I meant to tell you—I rescued your little tyskertøs a couple of nights ago."

Klaus caught his breath. "You mean—"

"Frøken Magnusson, yes. She caused some suspicion at a surprise checkpoint I was at."

"'Suspicion'?" Considering what Striegler could mean, Klaus was relieved his voice was even on the repeated word.

"Yes. Walked away from the checkpoint, silly girl. Still, I sorted it out. Rescued her from a, uh, thorough search, eh?"

With the lascivious way he said it, Klaus knew exactly what he meant. "Thank you."

"Yes. You owe me now, von Ronnenberg." He ran his tongue over his lips. "She really is a peach, isn't she? I envy you. Such breasts."

Klaus felt his anger surge. He'd like to have punched the man. But it would not do him, nor Ilse, any good. "As I said, thank you."

"Oh, you are so welcome." Striegler stared at him a moment longer. His contempt could not be clearer.

He turned to go, but Klaus halted him with words. "How long will you be gone?"

"The raid is at dawn tomorrow. But with the sun up nearly twenty-four hours a day in this fucking country I don't know why we wait. I'd like to bring the prisoners back here by tomorrow night at the latest." His eyes narrowed slightly. "Why do you ask?"

"Oh, no reason. Simply in awe at how efficient SS men are."

"More than the Abwehr, obviously." Striegler's voice had lost any geniality. "Which is why I am leading razzias and you are writing reports." When Klaus said nothing, he continued. "And speaking of reports, did you truly send that recommendation to Berlin after my interrogation of that Linström fellow? For my promotion?"

"I did. I showed you the copy, remember?"

"I saw a copy. Doesn't mean the original was sent." Striegler took his lower lip between his teeth, sucked. "I also found that you'd sent the fellow to Germany."

"For further interrogation, yes."

"I wanted to interrogate him here. Here!" he suddenly shouted, colour flushing his cheeks. "I have applied to have him sent back. No word yet."

"Well, you will be busy with other interrogations very soon, won't you?"

"Yes. Yes, I will." He smiled again. "Much bigger . . . salmon. So perhaps I won't need your help for my promotion, eh?"

"I am sure not, Herr Major." Klaus noticed something on the man's gleaming cheek. It was something he'd been thinking about a little while before. "Did you cut yourself shaving?"

"What?"

Klaus pointed. "There's blood on your cheek."

"Eh?" Striegler reached up, rubbed a finger, looked at the fleck on it. Barked a laugh. "It's not mine," he said, and strode out the front door.

Klaus watched him until his car had driven off. Damn, he thought. He hoped the Nazi did make it back tomorrow, if the word he'd heard on the phone was true. Striegler was high up in the SS in Norway, one of its great fanatics. He needed to be locked up in a cell below. Or, Klaus thought, he needed to be dead.

The vision of that cheered him up a bit, and he whistled some lieder as he walked the five flights up to his cubicle. He looked, as he always did, to the right corner of his desk. It was where transcribed messages were left for him. He'd often walked into his old office to find twenty or more there. Today there was only one.

He closed the door, squeezed around the desk, dropped into his chair. The memo was about some stationery supplies he'd ordered from Berlin. It regretted their lack of availability, due to "transport disruptions."

He took the small book from his inside pocket. Gretchen had long been supplanted as a method of communication. It was Stefan George's turn now, a collection of his poetry.

It didn't take him much time to figure it out. The message wasn't long.

"C 2 Wolf. 20J."

The killer was going into the Wolf's Lair . . . tomorrow. July 20.

Klaus burned the paper, using it to light a cigarette, before swirling the remains in an ashtray. He inhaled deeply, blew out a series of rings. It was happening. After all the false starts, it was time.

On July 20, Adolf Hitler would die—and a new Germany would be born. If men like him, throughout the Fatherland, throughout Europe, did their duty.

TWENTY-TWO
RAZZIA

Skipevige. July 19, 1944

"THE END," BILLY SAID, and closed the book. A couple of men in the hut sighed. Most just nodded. Even those who didn't speak English that well enjoyed his readings from *The Razor's Edge*. These were often accompanied by whispers, as better-educated men helped their friends through the more difficult passages. The story itself, for all its layers, was fairly simple: a young man, traumatized by a war, travelled the world in search of meaning. Every young man who listened—and this was the fifth time in three months that Billy had read the novel through, as he was passed from group to group—dreamed of the time after the war, when they could again travel. The Norwegians, Billy had learned, were great travellers. He'd been told —more than once!—that before the war they'd had the third-largest merchant fleet in the world. From the time of the Vikings to today, Norwegians set out in ships to see the world.

He'd sung them songs from his days in the theatre. Recited

Shakespeare, those speeches he could remember. But it was Somerset Maugham's novel he was always beseeched to return to. He never minded. As he moved from place to place across the country, from Gunnar Solbakken's chicken shed to this fishing hut, he too had enjoyed the escape the novel gave. Saw himself, alone, travelling to the high Himalayas to seek enlightenment from a guru, then living in a hut on a mountaintop, as Larry Darrell had done. That was his favourite part, that vision of solitude, after three months of being crammed in, cheek by jowl, with assorted Norwegians and the odd Brit fleeing like him. He could recite several of those passages verbatim.

As he closed the book, tucking it carefully away in his satchel—wartime books were printed on cheap paper between thin covers, and his copy had long since come away from its binding—he felt excitement again at knowing that freedom was getting closer by the minute. By the end of today, he would be on his way to Scotland—by bus! The Shetland Bus. He'd heard of them, of course, the famous ships that brought supplies and resistance spies into Norway, ferried refugees and would-be fighters out. Never thought he'd be on one. He'd been happy to hear from Leif Nordal, in charge of the group getting him out, that the old "buses," trawlers, had been replaced by fast Royal Norwegian Navy submarine chasers. The less time he spent at sea, the better. There was something about the motion, quite different than when he was in the air, that always made him puke.

Billy stood up, swung his body around, loosening. It had taken him two months to shake off the effects of his crash, and truly only in the last three weeks had he been completely free of pain. *Latest* crash, he thought, shaking his head, and not just to ease his neck. How many more can I limp away from? This cat is down to his ninth life!

He joined a man at the door of the hut—Hovard, youngest in the group of fighters that Billy had been passed to three weeks before. The kid was perhaps seventeen. "Beautiful, eh?" he said, gesturing to the view.

Billy looked at it. Before him, in the half-light that passed for dawn in Norway at this time of year, was the inevitable fjord, with its green-grey water, rocky promontories pushing into it, bare hills rising steeply from it, and only small patches of grass and moss breaking the monotony of granite. They'd been moving him along the coast every few days, and it all looked like this. And though he'd been born on a farm in Canada, he was a city boy now. Give him a vista of rooftop and steeple any day.

"If I see one more fucking fjord in this life," he said.

Hovard laughed and patted his shoulder. "It is not the Côte d'Azur perhaps."

"That it is not."

"Of all the places you read to us about, that is where I most want to go after the war." The boy stared out, no longer seeing Norway. "I wish to wear a dinner jacket and play cards in casinos. I wish to sleep with many beautiful French women."

"Then I am sure you will."

"Have you been there, Billy? The Côte?"

"Nope."

"Let us go together. We would make a good team, yes? You with your voice and me with my . . . hair!" He laughed, shaking a blond mane that was longer than anyone else's, and gloriously thick. "How could pretty Francine and Amélie resist us, huh?"

Billy laughed too, then looked quickly away to the water so the boy wouldn't see his change of expression. Let him have his fantasy. Billy had his own, and the woman he wanted wasn't in the south of France but in the south of Norway. And today he would be leaving her. Again. He shook his head. When he woke in the middle of the night from dreams of her, his immediate thought was always that he should slip away from the group, make his way to Oslo, find Ilse. Daylight brought reality. Though he had made sure he picked up some Norwegian in his time with the different groups, he certainly couldn't pass for a local. Besides, he was a soldier, and he had his duty: to escape back to England and continue fighting the war. To do anything else would be . . . desertion.

"Heya!" It was Leif who called, pointing at the hilltop directly opposite the little fishing station. A man was up there with a view out along the Fensfjorden to the sea. He was waving a flashlight, back and forth, then snapped it off. "*De kommer. Ta tak i tingene dine.*"

It was a Norwegian phrase Billy knew; he'd heard it a lot in the previous three months. There'd never been a lot of things for him to grab—he had one change of donated clothes, a sweater, trousers, underwear. He had the one much-patched jacket and his fisherman's knitted hat. Those and his satchel, which contained a pair of socks and his book, were his only possessions. His uniform and cap were long since burned and he didn't need shaving tackle the Norwegians offered since he'd decided to grow a beard—which he thought suited him, even though it had surprised him by coming in so streaked with grey. Around him, the passengers made ready. There were ten catching the bus. Eight men and two women. The latter were the mother and sister of a senior resistance fighter who'd been taken in a razzia. As always, the Germans were seeking the family—if the man wouldn't break under interrogation, torturing his relations in front of him often made him. So they were being got out. The men were a mix of boys off to train with the Norwegian forces in exile, and agents.

Leif called out, keeping his voice low, speaking English for Billy's sake, while a lieutenant murmured the translation in Norwegian. "It is quite simple. As soon as my man signals again, the bus will be coming fast into the bay here. We all move quite quickly to the boat at the jetty. It will be crowded, yes, but it is only a short ride." He nodded. "Safe travels—and God save the King!"

He was echoed here, in Norwegian. *Gud bevare kongen* was another phrase Billy had heard often. He couldn't quite bring himself to say it. I am an anarchist, after all, he thought, smiling. But he appreciated the people's love for their monarch, how it focused them for the fight. The king's symbol, "H7," with the royal crown above it, was painted on walls across the land. Strictly forbidden, it drove the occupier crazy.

Billy held his bag before him, watched the hill across the bay. He was going, if not home—he had no clue where that was—then at least back to the fight. He felt the land beneath his feet. "Goodbye, Ilse," he murmured.

The light flashed from the hill. "Now!" called Leif, and the group moved, out of the fishing hut, fast towards the jetty and its boat, one man in its stern, blue smoke rising from its engine.

They were halfway to it when he heard a familiar roar.

Messerschmitt, he thought—confirmed when the plane swept over them, coming in fast and low from behind, from the east. A 110, it soared out towards the open water, dropped from sight beyond the headland. Almost immediately, the sound of cannon fire came. Moments later, a different cannon responded.

The group had frozen, halfway to the dock. The sudden sounds had disguised others for a moment. Billy now heard them, clearly: engines, not a plane's. Heard gravel spitting, the shriek of brakes hit hard. Followed by an amplified voice, distorted, monstrous, clear.

German. The same words that had been shouted at the plane when he'd landed in Norway.

"*Aufgeben! Hände hoch! Hände hoch!*"

Machine-gun fire came, a Schmeisser. Billy had heard that slow staccato burst first in Spain. No bullets hit anywhere; they were firing high. The Germans wanted everyone alive.

"Run!" yelled Leif, and some did, after a fashion. Some just gave up, raised hands as ordered, especially as more shots came, these striking close, driving into the wood of the hut. Others made for the boat, the man in it shouting for them to come, come! But even as he took a step that way, Billy looked to the water—and saw the two E-boats speeding in, heading straight towards the jetty.

He was not the only one to run left, to the side, parallel to the water, along a faint hillside path. Twenty paces and it dipped towards the shingle, a small stretch of narrow beach, small rowing boats drawn up there. "Halt! Halt or you die," came that amplified voice, followed by another burst of gunfire, more than one Schmeisser now, bullets bouncing off the face of the rock that stood like a sentinel on the shore. One of the runners cried out, fell, clutching his face. Just four men ran on now, two ahead of Billy, one a pace behind.

That was Hovard. "Come!" he cried. "Not the boats. Not the boats!" He grabbed Billy by the satchel strap, jerked hard. It broke, the bag fell, but before Billy could stoop to pick it up, he was shoved forward, to the left, to a gap between rocks that he hadn't seen. Just before he passed through, he saw the other two reach the upturned skiffs. Saw bullets tear the wood. Saw a man cry out, arms flailing high as he tumbled. In a last glimpse Billy saw the last man throw up his arms in surrender.

There was another path leading between the rocks and Billy followed Hovard fast along it, keeping low. Most of the rocks were head height or taller, but there was the occasional gap, and bullets flew near, striking shards off stone. His German was much better than his Norwegian and he heard someone shout, "Alive! I want them alive!" as the path suddenly started to climb. It was rough, made up of jagged ledges and small, rain-filled pools. Billy fell, took skin off his hands; Hovard stooped, yanked him up, stumbled in turn; Billy grabbed him, pushed him on.

The slope, which had been steep, became less so. The boulders got smaller, and then there was an open space between two, like an exit. Beyond it, treetops. Linden, he thought, knew, as their scent hit him: honey, lemon peel. As the sudden flatness of the ground made him stumble, he saw a host of them twenty paces ahead.

"Forest, Billy!" gasped Hovard. "We . . . hide!"

They'd crossed half that distance when the soldier stepped out from behind a trunk. "Stop!" he yelled, levelling his Schmeisser.

Hovard did stop. He also pulled out a pistol. Both men shot. Both fell.

Billy stooped to the young Norwegian. The machine-gun burst had taken off half his head, the glorious hair suddenly lank with blood and death. There was nothing he could do, so he turned and stumbled on towards the tree-line, to the German soldier writhing on the ground.

He made it. But he didn't see the second German, only movement, as the man appeared from behind another linden, raised his gun and drove its stock into Billy's forehead. Then there was a kind of grey nothing, and the stench of honey.

––––––––––

HE DIDN'T KNOW what woke him. Perhaps it was the sharp stone pressing into his cheek. Perhaps it was the sound of women weeping. He didn't think he'd been unconscious very long.

He groaned and immediately heard boots approaching. Then there were hands on his shoulders, jerking him up to sit. His head swirled, he thought he was going to puke, and he tried to fall back down. But someone kicked him in the ribs, so he forced himself upright. Before he put his head to his raised knees—fuck, that hurt!—he glanced around. He was towards the end of a line of seven people, sitting like him in front of the fishing hut. They faced the sea. Between it and them were three bodies, all in the odd contractions of death. Hovard was one of them, with Leif beside him, his face towards them, a single bullet hole in the middle of his forehead, centred above his eyes, which were open. He looked strangely amused.

Glancing right, Billy saw the source of the weeping—the two women holding each other, both sobbing, tears and snot running down their faces. He looked left, saw the other men he'd read to only a little while before. He wondered where his satchel was, his book—wondered for a moment if the Germans would let him keep it.

No, you clot, he thought. They're going to shoot you.

He looked ahead, down to the jetty. An E-boat was pulled up there, a naval officer was on it, one foot up on the gunnels, talking to an SS officer on the dock. As Billy watched, the E-boat captain stood straight, snapped a salute that the other man returned. "Heil Hitler," both men called. Then a command was shouted, sailors threw off restraining ropes and jumped aboard. In a puff of blue smoke, the vessel pulled away and was halfway to the bay's entrance before the officer left behind had walked to the land end of the dock and started up the slope. His face was raised, eyes already appraising the prisoners. He was smiling and Billy immediately realized that the last time he'd seen this man he had not been doing so. Because then, like the women beside him now, he'd been weeping.

He supposed there were faces you never forgot, especially in certain ways that you'd seen them. Ilse's, of course, below him, above him, as they'd made love. Andoni's, his eyes crossed over his recorder. His father's under the tree that killed him. The young Italian pilot's, which he had seen for less than a second before his Spitfire's propeller shredded him. The German navigator's whose brains he had blown out in Guernica seven years earlier. And the other German's as he'd blubbered and begged and soiled his trousers, and whom Billy had only failed to kill because his gun had jammed. That man, going to the far end of the line now. The pilot who had strafed the Basque town and killed Andoni, with his corn-blond hair and eyes dark as any Italian's. That man had been Luftwaffe then. He was SS now. Billy knew he'd never forget his name, either.

Erich Striegler.

Billy lowered his head again onto his knees, listened as Striegler made his way down the line, stopping before each prisoner, asking their name in Norwegian, their nationality. Hitting prisoners with the baton he carried, when he didn't like their answers because they were mumbled, or too slow, or just because he wanted to. When he reached Billy, he used the stick to raise his face by the chin. "Name?" he asked. "Nationality?"

He'd been thinking the words, as the man got closer. Of all the Norwegian Billy had practised, these were the words he'd worked on most. "Einar Helland. From Norway," he said.

He made himself look straight back at Striegler. Saw his eyes contract a little, as if something about Billy puzzled him. Suddenly Billy wondered if he appeared in this man's dreams, as this man did in his. Billy took a breath, held it. Striegler stared. Then his eyes moved on, and then his feet, and he stood before the two women, so Billy lowered his head again.

"Name? Nationality?"

"I am . . . I am Fru Johansen. Irmi Johansen. From Drammen. And this is my daughter—"

"Tch," the German snapped. "I am asking her, not you, Frau." Billy turned a little to see Striegler put his baton tip under the younger woman's chin, lift her head. "Name? Nationality?"

But the daughter couldn't speak. Tried, but choked as she did on her sobs.

"Hmm," said Striegler. "I like my questions answered promptly. Perhaps I should let my men take her into this stinking fish hut and see if she'll answer better in there, hmm?"

"No! No, please, sir! Please!" Fru Johansen rose to her knees, clutching the shiny boots before her. "I answer anything. Anything!"

"Anything?" Striegler looked from her, back along the line. "Then answer this. A little bird told me that not everyone here would be Norwegian, as you all have said. That perhaps you were also trying to get an Allied airman away. An Englishman. And then I found this!" Billy saw that he held *The Razor's Edge*. Striegler bent and slapped the older woman across the face with it. Pages broke loose and fell to the churned ground. "So if you tell me who the Englishman is here, my men will not go and play with your daughter."

Billy was watching the woman's eyes. He saw them flick towards him—caught the barest hint of sorrow in them. He couldn't blame her. If he'd had a child, he assumed he would do the same.

"Him," she said.

"*Raus!* " Striegler barked, and two men came and grabbed Billy, one on each arm, dragging him backwards, throwing him against the hut wall. The Nazi officer followed, taking a Schmeisser from his sergeant as he did. "Englishman, eh?"

Billy shrugged. It didn't seem the time to discuss his birthplace. "You speak German?"

Billy nodded.

"Pilot? Or SOE?"

"Does it matter?"

"Yes, it matters. SOE, we keep you alive. Talk a little with you." Striegler grinned. "Pilot . . . and we shoot you here, as our Führer has commanded for any airman dropping agents in Norway."

Billy looked straight at him. "I'm SOE."

"Truly?" Without taking his eyes off Billy, he said, "Bring the old woman." She was dragged forward, and Striegler continued. "Is this man a pilot or spy? Be careful how you answer. My men are still hungry."

"I think he . . . the others s-s-say he," she stuttered, "is a pilot."

"Good. And a pity too, of course." He gestured with his head and the sobbing woman was dragged back. Striegler hefted the gun, flicking off the safety. "Any last words, Englishman?"

He'd said this last in English. So Billy thought he'd reply in the same. He was so very, very tired suddenly, and his head hurt. "Fuck you," he said.

Striegler smiled, raised the gun . . . then stopped. That same look of puzzlement that had briefly appeared before returned now, stayed, grew. The man swallowed, then stepped closer, peered harder. "Shit," he murmured, reverting to German, shaking his head. "I do not believe... you . . . you are Billy Coke!"

He shouted this, shouted some other things, most of them foul. But Billy only heard a few words before Striegler's shiny right jackboot swung back and then sharply forward, into his head.

This was an even deeper darkness than before. He sank into it, gratefully.

STRIEGLER STARED down at the man he'd just kicked, and tried to get enough breath into his lungs to lift his foot and kick him again . . . everywhere. Bust his ribs, stamp on his head, watch his brains pour out like . . . like Gootsie's had poured out onto that Spanish wheat field.

But when he raised his jackboot straight up, someone screamed—man, woman, he couldn't tell. Maybe it was him. Whoever it was deflected him, and he drove his iron-shod heel down, not onto flesh but onto the dock, hard enough to crack one of the planks. He swayed, saw pale splintered wood gouged from the creosote—then looked up into his Feldwebel's startled eyes. Beyond Grosz, soldiers and prisoners stared. The older woman wrapped her arms around her child, burying her head in her daughter's hair.

He turned and marched off the platform to the water's edge. He prided himself on what the French—another conquered people—called *froideur*. He had that, was always cool, never needed to shout to establish authority. His bearing, his uniform, did that.

He had let himself down. He looked out at the water, to the headland opposite. Sea, rock, patchy grass, he saw none of it. Only the face of Billy Coke. He'd seen it in nightmares, and in daydreams of revenge. But Billy Coke had always been a fantasy.

Until now.

How was it possible he was here? It was a question the Englishman would have to answer. What would he do with him then? That Striegler must answer for himself.

A throat was cleared behind him. He turned. Grosz stood there. For a man who always had as much froideur as his commander, he was looking uneasy.

"Yes?"

"Uh, the prisoners, Herr Major?"

"What about them?"

"The usual? Norwegians to the base, then shipped to Trondheim for processing?"

"Of course. See to it immediately."

"Yes, sir." Grosz swallowed. "And the, uh, pilot? The Englishman? The usual for him too?"

Striegler opened his mouth. Words didn't come. Perhaps that was the answer. The simple one, as it was for most things: obey orders. The Führer had decreed that any enemy combatant caught in the occupied territories was to be executed immediately. Erich had done it himself numerous times: pilots caught after a spying mission, commandos before or after a raid. He'd been about to obey his Führer, kill another man. Until he'd recognized him.

It would be simpler. Billy Coke for Gootsie. A bullet in the head. Perhaps then a sleep without seeing either of their faces.

He rubbed his eyes. "Put him in the car."

The sergeant's own eyes widened. "Alive?"

"Of course alive. Why would I want a dead prisoner in my car?" Striegler smiled. His froideur was back. "Manacle him. You will accompany us."

"Yes, Herr Major." Grosz glanced behind him. "And the place?"

"You know the drill, Feldwebel. Torch it."

Grosz snapped a salute, turned and walked off, shouting orders. As the usual sounds came from behind him—petrol sloshing, women crying, blows falling on prisoners who moved too slowly—Erich crouched, took off his peaked cap, dipped his hand in the sea water and splashed his face.

Victoria Terrasse, he thought. I'll take him to the cellar. Behmer will know what to do with him. Behmer always knows . . .

A flash came. A young man broken on a stone floor. One of his eyes was halfway down his cheek.

There was nothing he could do. When it surged up from his stomach, Striegler leaned forward and puked into the fjord.

IT WAS HARDER THIS TIME, swimming up from the dark. Billy thought that if this was death, it was alright. Dull, perhaps, but he'd had a busy life. He could do with some quiet.

He must have groaned or given some indication that he was not quite out still, because he heard someone say something and then he was pulled upright, which hurt like hell—in his head, which had been doubly battered, and at his wrists, which he now realized were held tightly together. Manacles, he saw, looking down. Looking up, he saw Erich Striegler.

He was only a couple of feet away—the length of the car seat they sat on. They were both in the back, Billy behind the driver. A sergeant, by the stripes on his sleeve, was in the other front seat. He must have been the one who had pulled Billy upright. Now he sat back but did not face front again, the muzzle of his Luger resting on the seat back, a slight smile on his face.

Striegler was smiling too, differently. The sort of smile a cat might give, if a cat could smile, and if it had a mouse wriggling under its claws.

"Billy Coke," he breathed, and shook his head. "It is almost enough to make me believe in God. That he brought you to me. But if I do not believe in him, I do in fate. Do you, Billy Coke? Do you think that we were fated to meet again, one day?"

Billy stared back. It was the face he remembered, though older, of course. He suspected they were about the same age. What had they been in 1937, when they'd met so briefly at Guernica? Twenty? Little more than boys, really.

He ran a tongue over his lips. His mouth was a cold hearth. "Water?" He thought he might be refused. But Striegler nodded to the sergeant in the front seat, who lowered his pistol, bent down and then produced a flask. He unscrewed the lid, reached it across the seat, tipped it for Billy to lap at the liquid. It helped.

He looked around. It was still light, but that could mean it was any hour of the day at this time of the year. They were in a limousine of some kind, a staff car, meant for officers, its seats plush leather, its engine a purr. The loudest noise came from the windscreen wipers, moving fast, struggling to disperse the pelting rain. "Where are we going?" he asked.

"Oslo. We were supposed to fly but this weather suddenly came and . . . oh well." Striegler patted the seat beside him. "Still, comfortable, no? I had to commandeer it from the local army captain up in Hordaland. He wasn't happy. Fortunately I outranked him. Also, the Wehrmacht doesn't fuck around with the Waffen-SS."

"And why are you taking me to Oslo?"

"Why?" Striegler's smile widened. "Because there's someone there I want you to meet. His name is Behmer." He leaned towards the driver. "How long?"

"Hard to say with this rain, Herr Major. Less than two hours?"

The car suddenly swung sharply to the side and everyone in the car lurched hard. "Careful, you fool!" Striegler barked.

"Sorry, Herr Major. The roads are difficult. If I might go slower?"

"No. I wish to be in Oslo as soon as possible. By 4 p.m. at the latest. Just drive more carefully."

"Major!"

Billy looked out the window, saw a town sign flash by. Bagn. He sank back, closed his eyes, listened to the beat of the wipers, the cascading rain. There was no question he could ask that would give him a relieving answer. It was obvious what was going to happen to him in Oslo. Perhaps it was fate, like the German had said. Or what had Larry Darrell called it in *The Razor's Edge*? Karma. That was it. Not fate exactly. More like . . . payback. For his sins. He had so many. This payback was for one sin specifically. The one he'd committed in a Basque town, seven years before.

"It may not mean anything to you," he said softly, "but I regret it."

Striegler turned to him. "Regret? Regret what?"

"What I did. In Guernica." Billy swallowed. "Not a day has gone by since that I have not regretted it."

Striegler stared for a long moment. Finally, he whispered, "You are right. It means nothing to me at all." Suddenly he looked tired, older. "Sleep," he said, rubbing his eyes. "You may as well." It looked like he was going to add something more. But then he just shook his head, closed his eyes, settled back into his corner.

But Billy couldn't sleep. It wasn't only the ache in his head where Nazi blows had fallen, from gun stock and boot. He didn't want to. He suspected he didn't have much time left. So why waste it, he thought. He stared through the windscreen, at the rain which seemed to be getting heavier, and thought again about fate. Was it fate that was bringing him to the place he most wanted to be, where she was? Or was it simply irony? He would die within a few miles of Ilse, and she would never know.

It was because he was staring out, watching the rain, the speeding wipers, that he saw it, probably at the same time as the driver. The truck around the corner that had swung wide to avoid something ahead of it, a pothole perhaps, and crossed a little onto the wrong side of the road, their side, with no distance for their driver to do much more than spin the wheel hard away, screaming as he did. Which was just time enough for Billy to do the last thing he would do in a plane, if it were crashing: put his head and arms against the back of the seat in front of him, and brace.

The truck had tried to swerve as well and the car clipped its wheel arch, plunged on, away, brakes making no difference to its speed, wheels failing to bite on the slick roadway. It left the asphalt, bounced high onto a verge, seemed to accelerate past that, veering twenty metres at least into the brush before it smashed into a tree.

Billy was lifted off his seat. His forehead struck the driver's shoulder, but not too hard because the driver was also shooting forward, the force of the sudden stop smashing him into the wheel, chest bones cracking with a sound like gunshots. It was different for the man beside him, the sergeant, no wheel before him, nothing but the windscreen which did not stop him but gave out from his velocity, smashing as he went through it. Striegler replaced him in the front seat, falling over that into the well.

From total noise to near silence. Billy could hear a wheel spinning for a while, but the engine coughed then died, and the wipers stopped halfway across the screen. The driver began to moan, clutching at his shattered chest, blood running from his lips. Then he must have fainted, or died, because he went quiet.

The passenger door beside him had buckled, so Billy put his back against it, and kicked Striegler's door hard. It burst out. Billy slid across and dropped to the wet forest floor.

He lay there for a moment, taking huge breaths, checking himself. He didn't feel that anything was broken or too badly twisted—confirmed that when he stood, rolling his neck, shaking his limbs. When he was ready, he grabbed the front passenger door handle and, after a few hard tugs, wrenched the door open.

Striegler was where the crash had sent him, still face down in the footwell. He was not moving at all and at first Billy thought he was dead. Then he saw a pulse in the man's neck. He bent and hauled the German from the car, laying him on his back on the ground. He still didn't wake, there was blood pouring from his nose, from his mouth. One of his eyes was smashed from where he'd collided with the dash.

I suppose I should kill him, Billy thought. Kill the enemy who was planning on killing me so slowly.

He considered it for a moment. Then, instead, he turned Striegler onto his side so he would not drown in his own blood.

He went to the sergeant. He *was* dead; when Billy part lifted him, his head lolled because the neck had snapped. Billy laid him on his back, went through his pockets. In one he found a set of keys, at least twenty on the ring. The fifth one opened the manacles, which Billy dropped to the ground, following them down, resting his hands on them, kneeling there. Trying to figure out what the hell he was going to do now.

The voice was not loud, but it still shocked Billy when the only other sounds had been the clicks of cooling engine, the spatter of ceaseless rain. "Stand up," Erich Striegler said.

Billy rose, slowly, lifting the manacles as he did. The man was now standing where Billy had left him lying, ten feet away—swaying there, like a drunk. Peering through the one eye that worked, his left one. In his right hand was a Luger.

"Come here," Striegler said, beckoning with the muzzle. "Come closer."

Billy didn't move. "You're hurt, Major. We should send for help."

"Help?" The German shook his head as if trying to clear it, clear his sight. He reached up, touched his eye, the smashed one, shuddered. "No one can help," he said.

Billy took one step nearer, and the gun barrel swung to him again. "The road," Billy said, his voice low, soothing, as he took another step. "Someone will come. Let's go wait for them."

"No!" Striegler shouted, his stance suddenly more solid, the gun not wavering so much. "We do not go anywhere. You are my prisoner. You come here. Now. Now! Or I will—"

Billy bent at the knees and threw the manacles as hard as he could, uncoiling his arms from his left hip, hoping he could get enough spin. The Luger went off as the metal flew towards the German, and Billy felt something like a needle jab his right arm. But there was no time to think about that, no time to do anything but rush at the man who had taken the manacles in the face and neck, who was tumbling backwards, who Billy knocked off his feet as he barrelled into him.

Striegler screamed, in agony, in fury. He tried to swing the muzzle into Billy's side, but Billy had a hand on his wrist, twisted it hard away, banging it onto the ground. But the Nazi didn't let the gun go, instead he roared, found strength to somehow raise himself up, throw off Billy, who landed on his knees two feet away.

Billy looked at the muzzle swinging back towards him. Looked at the man, at his one smashed eye, at the other now streaming tears and blood from where the flung manacles had caught it. And he realized he had one second, only one, so he used it, springing forward again, arms wide. His left one caught Striegler's right and he jerked the bigger man towards himself.

The gun went off again. This time Billy felt no sting. He was holding Striegler as close as a dance partner, a wrestler, a lover. So close he could see into the ruined eyes. See the light in them, fading, fading.

The gun dropped. Billy kicked it away, then lowered the man to the ground. The light was almost gone when he bent over him. He was trying to speak. Billy leaned down.

"Billy Coke," Erich Striegler whispered, and died.

Billy sat beside him for a short time. Only a little. He assumed this was a main road they'd come down, and other traffic would be along it soon. Most would not be friendly. His arm hurt, and he looked at it to see a tear in the cloth near his bicep, some blood beneath, still running. He'd been clipped, but only just. It made him think of his father, suddenly, the scar the sniper's bullet had made at Ypres. Like father like son, he thought, taking a handkerchief from his pocket, wrapping it around the wound, using his teeth to tie it off. It would do, for now. He had other priorities.

He picked up the Luger, shoved it into his belt, then returned to the wrecked car, found the flask of water, drank it down. Found a paper-wrapped package of sandwiches in the glove compartment and tucked them inside his sweater. Then he went up to the road.

The truck was there, its engine still running though it too had smashed into a tree. The driver—Norwegian, not German—was still in the cab. He was breathing but unconscious, blood streaming from his nose. There was little Billy could do for him. He had to get away. But he leaned the man against the door so he would not fall and perhaps choke. Billy reached into the man's jacket and pulled out his ID papers and ration card. They didn't look much alike, but any papers were better than none. He was about to step away when he had a thought. He reached down and sprang the latch on the glove compartment. "Gotcha," he said, and pulled the map out.

He opened it, looked for a bit, found the village whose sign he'd seen earlier: Bagn. Then he heard an engine approaching from the way they'd come. Folding the map as he went, he moved fast the other way, till after fifty yards he noticed a trail that went into the forest, and took it.

He thrust the map into his belt beside the Luger. He remembered again how he'd lied to Group Captain Whittaker back at Tempsford three months earlier, when he'd said he was excellent at navigation. He was merely proficient. But he felt he could find Oslo, even so. Just before the crash, the driver had said they were about two hours from the city.

What would that be, thought Billy. A day's walk?

TWENTY-THREE

VALKYRIE

Victoria Terrasse. July 20, 1944, 4 p.m.

KLAUS STARED AT the phone on his desk, willing it to ring. The last time it had done so had been four hours before. A man, who did not identify himself, had said two words—"She flies"—and then hung up. It was what Klaus had been waiting to hear.

Operation Valkyrie was on.

He didn't know the how of it. Brave men in Germany did, and they would be acting. By bullet or bomb, Hitler would die this day.

He looked up at his wall clock. The big hand moved to one minute past the hour. How could time move so slowly? He had occupied himself by doing all he could: shuffling the envelopes that held the commands, changing their order slightly each time, changing them back. Truly it made no difference—the envelopes would be dispatched by messenger near simultaneously anyway. But it passed the time, a little. Then, an hour before, he had stopped doing even that. Just sat there, tried to think of some musical piece he used to play in the days when he had two arms. But he found he could not remember more than a few bars of each. He couldn't even remember the key of the sonata Ilse had played for him, the Bach. It was a minor of course. But E Minor? D?

Everything made him think of Ilse. He'd tried calling her, twice. The first time no one had answered; the second, yesterday, her father did, and told him a long tale of the article he was researching, how he was off in an hour to spend a day and night at a Hitler Youth Camp in the forests of Telemark. "Marvellous young people. True believers," Wilhelm had informed him. Klaus had rung off as soon as simple politeness allowed. He'd left a message, one he knew she would understand: "Tomorrow, perhaps we'll listen to Wagner." When the Valkyrie ride, he added, but only to himself.

He sighed. Thought of what Wilhelm had said. He had been a true believer once. No more.

I would like to hear her voice, he thought. Just for a moment.

He reached for the phone, even rested his hand on it this time. But he took it away again. Even a few seconds, he might miss the call from Berlin. When he received it, he would act, do what he had planned. He calculated that he'd know if the plot had succeeded, in Oslo at least, within an hour. Then he would call her, say something simple about Valkyrie. After Odin's maidens had flown, he'd have plenty of time to hear her voice. Perhaps for the rest of his life?

And yet?

It had to be his nerves, the lack of sleep. He was questioning everything. Everything! Even love. He had no doubts about his for her. But did she truly love him? It had been cooler, their last time together. She had demurred when he'd tried to take her to the bedroom. A bad time, she'd said with a half-smile. A bad time for a kiss too, he'd wondered as he left, her lips cold on his.

He shook his head. Her nerves, perhaps. The strain she was under. Beyond putting him in touch with a contact at SOE she had not discussed her work with the resistance any further. What did she do for them, he'd wondered. Still did. Was she sitting at home now, shuffling envelopes?

Was she thinking of him?

He looked at his watch. It told him the same dismal story as the clock. Two minutes past four. He looked at the envelopes. Maybe check the order of them again?

The phone rang, so suddenly, so loud, reverberating off the walls of his tiny office. He took a breath to steady himself, so he wouldn't pick up the receiver and drop it. Lifting it to his ear, he said, "Yes."

The line had a lot of crackle on it. The voice sounded very far away. But the words were clear, simple.

"He is dead. Proceed," a man said, and hung up.

Klaus looked at the receiver for a long moment, as if it would tell him something else. Then he replaced it in its cradle, stood, put on his cap, checked, for the tenth time, that his Luger was loaded, then tucked the stack of envelopes under his arm and left his office.

He walked down the stairs. There were frequent power cuts in Oslo and some people he knew had been stuck in the elevator for three hours last week.

When he reached the ground floor, he hurried to the front desk. The dispatcher, a small corporal named Wülfstein, with the thick lenses of the very short-sighted, put down a crossword puzzle he was doing and peered up at him. "Herr Major, how can I help?" he queried.

"Heil Hitler," Klaus declared, hand rising, heels clicking.

The formality, when there usually wasn't any between them, made the man sit up, then stand. "Heil Hitler!" he replied, struggling to do up his opened top button.

"I need riders. These are to go out with the utmost urgency." He laid the envelopes down on the man's counter.

"How many, Herr Major?"

"Ten."

"Oh." The man swallowed, a large Adam's apple bobbing within a scrawny throat. "We are just changing shifts. The five new men are just starting and—"

"Then retain the other shift and use them too." He tapped the papers. "These orders have come straight from Berlin. Something has happened that requires—" He broke off. Nerves were making him explain what he needn't to a subordinate. "See to it immediately," he snapped, "or you may find yourself transferred someplace where there would be no time for crossword puzzles."

Wülfstein's eyes shot wide. "Yes, sir!" He reached below the counter, pressed some button Klaus could not see but could hear the result of: a bell sounding three times down the corridor.

"Is Major Striegler back?" he asked.

"Not yet, sir. We heard that he had to change plans, as the rain wouldn't allow his plane to take off. He is driving. Should be here soon though." He smiled. "With a prisoner."

"Very good," Klaus said, though it wasn't. "And is the meeting of the SS still taking place upstairs?"

"Yes, sir. Scheduled to end"—he glanced up at the clock behind him—"at five o'clock."

Dispatch riders were now arriving at the desk. Wülfstein snapped at one of them to go back to their waiting room and summon the others whose shift had just ended. While he did, the corporal handed the first four envelopes to the others. They all checked the addresses and ran out the door, tightening the chin straps on their helmets. In moments, the roar of engines was heard, followed by the whine as they moved fast away.

"Good." Klaus now smiled at the corporal. "Well done."

He walked out the main door. The rain was still falling heavily, and he took shelter in the portico, delved into his breast coat pocket, pulled out a cigarette, put it in his mouth, reached again for a lighter, struck it. He smoked, squinting at the rain through the cloud. His hand was now on his holster. Through the leather he felt the stock of his Luger. He resisted the urge to pull it out and check it again. Even in the portico rain was splashing around, heavy drops bouncing in off the paving stones. He didn't want to get the gun wet.

If the messenger who'd taken the first envelope was fast but safe, he should be at army headquarters within fifteen minutes. There,

Oberst Burgdorf would be waiting for the envelope to take to his commander—the commander of all German forces in Norway, Niko-laus von Falkenhorst. Two pieces of paper were inside: the first was a copy of the document Klaus had shown the colonels at that first meeting three months before, with its striking opening line—"The Führer Adolf Hitler is dead"—and its further orders to immediately seize all the places of power in Oslo, as well as every SS barracks. The second held detailed orders that were more specific: to send a platoon of Panzergrenadiers to Victoria Terrasse where, under Major von Ronnenberg's command, they would arrest the leaders of the Waffen-SS, now in their meeting on the second floor.

He took his hand away from the revolver butt. I hope I don't even have to draw it, he thought. I am a pilot, not a storm trooper, after all.

Surprisingly, now it was happening, all his tension was gone. Things would proceed now, or they wouldn't. He had done all he could—as, no doubt, had the conspirators in every occupied capital city in Europe, on every front line and, most especially, in Berlin.

He flicked the cigarette butt into the gutter, started to hum. Of course, he thought, that Bach flute sonata Ilse had played for him— B Minor. That's the key.

ILSE STOOD at the front window of her apartment, looking at the street. Looking at the rain, truly, because it obscured everything, blur-ring all the hard edges—the car that was parked outside that belonged to one of Quisling's henchmen, visiting his mother in the apartment block opposite; the garbage cans, crammed with refuse, added to every day because the civic workers who were meant to empty them had not shown up for two weeks. She was amazed that anyone had things to throw out in Oslo, four years into a war. But this was an area for the well-off, and they always had something to get rid of.

Some scavengers were out there—what rich people threw away, poor people would live on. But she could barely see them, they were water people, their edges also blurred. It reminded her of a painting she'd once seen by Edvard Munch—A Kiss? The Kiss? Something like that. Like the one of the same name by Klimt, which she'd seen when she'd visited Vienna with her father. Through her window she saw a Norwegian version now; dark, not golden, set against wood, the lovers dissolving into the bark of a tree.

Another form joined the two by the cans. His outline was different— he was taller, and she thought that a beard elongated his face. He had no hat, no coat—which meant he must have been very wet, like the poor often were.

She stepped away. But she did not again try to sit. She couldn't stay in one place and sitting was worse than pacing the apartment. If it weren't for the rain, she might have gone out. Except, of course, she couldn't. Not on this day. She had to wait for Klaus's call telling her that the Valkyrie were flying. Then she would make her own calls—to the communist, Milorg and Sivorg men.

She looked at the clock above her mantel. Four twenty-five. Dear God, hadn't it said that ten minutes ago?

A bell rang. But it wasn't the phone. It was the front door.

She went back to the window, looked along the building to the block's entrance. Under its little jutting roof, less rain was falling, and she could see him—the shape of him anyway—the man she'd only guessed at. He was facing away, looking down the street towards the station. She could see an outline of that beard.

They came sometimes. Men seeking work, or beggars simply after a handout. Her father had told her not to give any of them anything; the house would be marked for ever after. But she had, of course—the little boy was so skinny, and she had just made a batch of potato pancakes. They came fairly regularly after that, at least once a fortnight. She couldn't spot any mark on her front wall. It would be inconspicuous, like the scratch on the toe of the statue in Frognerparken that used to advise her to listen to the messages on the BBC.

At least she now had a purpose! She hurried to the kitchen. Her father had been hunting the week before—hare, his favourite quarry.

She'd hung the beast for a week and had stewed it only that morning with juniper berries and carrots. Scooping a few ladlefuls into a small earthenware pot, she put some cheesecloth on top, tied it off with ribbon. Then she went to the door of her apartment, left that ajar, descended the one flight of stairs, opened the door.

The man was still half-turned away, looking down the street. He was indeed hatless, his thick black hair was long, a little like the Bohemians her father so despised. And it was soaked, of course, as was the beard, full of raindrops that could not penetrate the thick hair. They glistened there; those, and the grey streaks, the only light.

"It is not very much," she said. "But it's still warm and—"

The man turned. He stared for a moment before he spoke. "Hello, Ilse," he said.

She knew it was impossible, impossible that this man was standing there. Still, she dropped the pot. It bounced, didn't break, well made that it was, though it ended up on its side with the stew leaking out. She couldn't do anything about that though, because she found that she was leaning against the doorframe, her legs too weak to hold her up on their own. Speech was as wobbly as her knees. She made sounds that sounded like questions.

"May I come in?" He didn't wait for an answer, just bent and scooped up the pot, tucked a hand under her elbow, lifted her a little, moved her back into the hall, letting the heavy door fall closed by itself behind him. "Where?" he asked and, wordless still, she pointed with her chin to the open apartment door. He led her up the steps, the pressure constant under her arm. But in her hall, with her door shut behind them, and Billy Coke standing in a growing puddle on her wooden floor, she found her voice again.

"What the hell?"

He put the pot down on a chair, licked his fingers clean of stew. "Sorry if it's a shock."

"A . . . shock?" The word was so paltry, so . . . inadequate, she actually laughed. "Billy, you can't be here."

"I can go if you want," he replied, that sparkle in his eyes she remembered so well, that she'd thought she'd never see again.

"Go? Where?"

He shrugged. "I am sure there are lots of Germans looking for me. Shall I see if I can find one?"

He stepped towards the door. But he'd spoken with that same twinkle and her hand on his chest was not necessary to stop him.

"I do not understand this. How . . . how *can* you be here?"

"Ah, thereby hangs a tale!" He laughed. "It's quite a good one, actually. Although"—his eyes lost some of their light for a moment—"it is not entirely a comedy."

"Tell me!"

"I will. Everything. But . . ." He gestured down to his soaked clothes and the smile came back. "Can I not tell you in a hall, with, uh . . ."

"Of course. Of course. We must get you out of those wet clothes. Into some dry ones."

She was already moving past him, towards her brother Trygve's bedroom. He was still away, fighting for the Germans. He and Billy were about the same size.

Billy caught a trailing hand. His voice came low. "There is an obvious need to get me out of these. Though not such an obvious one to get me into others."

Ilse stared at him a moment . . . then laughed. She'd forgotten—or had tried to forget perhaps—how easily this man could make her laugh. "Are you saying that you have come here, through everything, only because you wish to—"

He pulled her a step closer. "Not only. But since I *am* here . . ."

"Oh, Billy," she murmured, and closed the distance between them. Didn't care that the wool dress she wore soaked up his water like blotting paper as soon as she touched him. Didn't care about anything much, except the kiss. The way he kissed her, the way she kissed him back! Something else she'd tried to forget.

She stepped away. "Come then," she said. "Later for explanations. Everything else can wait."

She pulled, but he did not follow. "One thing can't," he said. "The first thing I knew I would have to say to you, if God, or fate, or karma, or whatever the hell rules us gave me the chance. Listen." He took a deep breath. "I am so, so sorry for how I behaved the last time we were together. My stupid temper. My refusal to understand why you had to say no." He swallowed. "Will you forgive me? *Can* you ever forgive me?" His eyes that had been clear and bright now misted.

"Oh, my man," she whispered, lifting a hand to his cheek. "Of course I forgive you."

The tears spilled, ran down both his cheeks. But he was smiling now. He took her hand, turned it, kissed the palm. "Thank you."

"Don't thank me yet," she said, startling herself with how husky her voice had gone. "Thank me later."

She pulled him again. This time there was no resistance.

IT WAS when he saw the three army trucks approaching, saw who was in them, that he knew it was over. Whether Hitler was dead or not, whether Berlin was now in control of the army or not, the part of the coup that was to take place in Oslo had failed.

The men in black uniforms, with the death's head skulls on their hats and victory runes at their collars, meant exactly that. Von Falkenhorst, the German supreme commander in Norway, had not sent regular Wehrmacht soldiers to arrest the SS. He'd sent the SS to arrest the conspirators. As Klaus turned and walked quickly, but not too quickly, away from the front entrance of Victoria Terrasse, he heard the Waffen-SS soldiers spilling from their trucks behind him. Heard the orders sharply called. Heard boots on the stairs. Not coming after him. Not yet. Soon, for sure. But not yet.

He did not know how much time he had. He'd been careful not to leave any papers in his office that would incriminate him. But someone would name him soon enough, in one of those rooms in the basement of the building, or more likely just in an office, as one of those colonels tried to deflect the blame away from themselves. "It was von Ronnenberg, of course. He organized it all. I simply led him on."

It would take a little time—the breaking, or the gut-spilling. Not much perhaps. Maybe a day? He doubted anyway that anything would happen before morning. If Hitler was dead, there were many men who would be striving to take his place. Himmler, Göring, Goebbels. Others. If he lived, it would take time to start arresting the plotters.

He'd walked away from Victoria Terrasse without a destination in mind. Now he found he was standing before the station at the National Theatre. He entered, descended the stairs. A train was at the platform, and he shouted for a man, in the uniform of the Norwegian Hirden, to keep a door open for him. He did, and Klaus stumbled into the carriage. The train lurched forward and Klaus's legs gave. Fortunately there was a seat, and he fell into it. It's over, he thought. I . . . am over. Finished. Suddenly, in the blur of the tunnel walls speeding past, he saw a face. Gretchen's. His cousin was telling him again that supporting Hitler was wrong. That he should oppose him now. Not later. Not when it was too late.

Why didn't I listen to you? he wondered. Why?

His vision swam. He thought he might be sick. But then he took one deep breath, another. No, he commanded himself. Think of a living love, not a dead one. Think!

Ilse. Striegler, others, they knew of her. She was in the same terrible danger that he himself was. So he would go to her now. That's why he was on this train. He would help her pack while she contacted her resistance friends. They would get her out of the city, out of the country. Over the border, to Sweden.

Though maybe they will get us both out, he thought. I tried, didn't I? And a traitor was one of the most useful types of spy. Then he shook his head. No. He was not going anywhere. He needed to stay behind to make sure she was safe.

———————

FOR ONCE, Billy did not make a movie out of his tale. Only their love-making had been allowed to be slow, both agreeing wordlessly that there was time for that, at least; that the rest of the world could go hang while they did. But when they lay there afterwards, time pressed again. He told her the gist. The crash landing, the months on the run. His capture. The luck of the escape. The luck of finding a man with a truck, after three hours of walking, who was smuggling contraband into Oslo and who, for the trade of his Luger, was willing to smuggle him too. The man had an Oslo phonebook with him. Wilhelm Magnusson's address wasn't far out of his way.

He talked about how he'd gotten his bruised face, but he didn't mention Striegler by name, their connection. That was a story for another time. Especially when she told him that there were things happening in Oslo that would affect them. "My father is also due back tonight," she said, throwing him some clothes. "We must find you, swiftly, a place to hide. I know some people."

While she went to the phone, he dressed, first exchanging the handkerchief around his arm, which was aching now, for another, having washed the gummed blood away. Her brother was a little taller than Billy, wider too, but a belt and braces took care of that. If it wasn't his suit from Savile Row, it would do.

He was just knotting a tie when she returned. She was in a silk dressing gown. He paused, studying her. "I wonder if you realize quite how beautiful you are," he whispered.

"Enough of that, Flight Lieutenant," she said, drawing the gown tighter around her. "There is someone coming to meet you shortly. In front of the station in the square around the corner. The man is a priest— the collar, you know? He will ask you if you are a Catholic. You will tell him you are not, but you're willing to learn."

"I might even be. Way my life has been going." He swallowed. "And then?"

"I do not know. It is not part of my work here. I assume there are methods for getting Allied airmen out. The coast? Sweden perhaps?"

"I don't mean that." He stood, came to her, took her by the shoulders. "I meant what for us?"

"Billy." She looked up at him. "You are not going to propose again, are you?"

"I wouldn't dare. Though I hope it's something you'll consider . . . after."

"After the war?" She smiled. "I think, perhaps, I might consider it then."

"You will? Gee whiz!" he said, in his best American GI twang, grabbing her hand, spinning her in a jitterbug move. They both laughed and then he pulled her near. "Ilse, it can't last much longer. Hitler and his goons are on the run, everywhere. They are going to liberate Paris any day now. Maybe Oslo is next." He pulled her even closer. "It's going to give soon, I feel it."

"I do too. Maybe sooner than you think."

He heard it in her tone. "Do you know something?"

"Nothing that I can talk about."

"Will you always have secrets?"

"Maybe not always." She put a hand around his neck, drew him down, kissed him, and he kissed her back. Then she pulled away, said, "Are you ready?"

"I think so, yes? Though I am very hungry. Got more of that stew you threw at me outside?"

"In the kitchen. Come."

They had just reached it when the doorbell rang. "Your father?"

She frowned. "No, he has his key. I do not know." There was a door on the other side of the kitchen. She crossed to it, opened the two bolts. "Here," she said, pointing to some stairs. "These lead to the cellar. There is a wooden door facing you. Here is its key." She handed it to him. "Lock it behind you and drop it there. Take the stair up into the garden. Cross that, there is a gate in the opposite wall. Turn right. The station is just there." She pressed the second key into his hand. "This is for the garden gate. Throw it back through the grate. I'll collect it later."

The bell rang again. She pushed him. "What about my food?" he said.

"The priest will have to give you some!"

"But the priest can't give me this." He bent, snatched a kiss. She laughed, then tried to close the door but he had one foot across the jamb. He spoke, his voice soft now. "Do you remember when I told you, that first time we parted, how someday I'd find you again?"

"Of course I do. But Billy, please, you must go."

She put a hand on his chest, shoved. Still he didn't budge.

"And I did, didn't I? Despite everything Hitler and the world could throw at us." He leaned closer, looking deep into her eyes. "So I say it again now. I will find you, Ilse. Someday."

The bell rang again. Longer, louder. But now she was the one who couldn't move. "Or I will find you," she said, "someday." She kissed him, fast, then shoved him. "Now go!"

This time he went. She shot the bolts, tied the gown cord tighter around her, then walked slowly to her front door, opened it, descended the flight of stairs, looked through the viewer. When she saw who it was, she mumbled a curse, then opened the door.

"Klaus," she said. "What has happened?"

He didn't answer, didn't wait, just pushed past her, reaching back to shut the door. He took her arm, led her up the stairs.

This is absurd, she thought. It reminded her of a play her friend Kirsten had taken her to in London. A farce, it was called. A lover leaving by the back door, another coming in the front. Except there was no humour here, and none in Klaus von Ronnenberg's face when he shut her apartment door behind them. "What has happened?" she asked again.

"It has failed. Whatever has happened in Germany, the army has not taken control of Oslo. We are both in great danger. You must leave immediately. Pack a suitcase." He looked down, frowned at her dressing gown. "Have you been in bed?"

"A, uh, nap. A headache."

She resisted his tug towards the bedroom, so he stopped, his voice rising. "Listen to me. They will be coming for me—sooner, rather than later. As soon as one of the colonels cracks." He swallowed. "They will all run for cover, squeal about everything to save their own necks."

"But you can do that too. Save yours."

He shook his head. "No, my dear," he said, his voice sad. "I think the only one I can save now is you. If you hurry."

She let him pull her to the bedroom, where she immediately began to dress. He frowned at the crumpled sheets, as he had frowned at the gown at the door. But he just reached up to the top of the wardrobe, grabbed her suitcase, opened it, threw it onto the bed. "What will you do though, Klaus? How can you protect me?" she asked, slipping a sweater over her head.

"By giving you time. If they think you are just my mistress, my *tyskertøs*," he spat the horrid word out, "they may not hunt for you too hard. At least to start with. And every hour I stay strong in the cellar of Victoria Terrasse is another hour that you can use to get away."

Her hand froze on the button of the slacks she'd pulled on. One night she'd made him tell her what caused him to sometimes wake screaming in the night. So he'd told her of what went on in those cells. A little of it, anyway. "No," she said, doing up the button, taking his one arm. "You can't do that. There must be another way."

"Yes. I could shoot myself." He tapped the holster at his hip. "I did think of that. But if I do, they'll round up anyone associated with me. They will hunt everywhere for you. So if I can keep my lies good? If I last for a day, two days? Remember I am as trained in interrogation techniques as they are. Better trained, truly. For they are merely thugs."

She stared at him, not wanting to believe this. "But," she said at last, "you told me that everyone talks in the end."

He nodded. "They do. They can't help it. They can only lie for a while. I will see how long I can lie for."

Another thought came to her, sending a chill up her spine. Klaus had met the three resistance leaders once, to coordinate this day; while SOE had insisted that Klaus talk to two other SOE officers, Brits in disguise. She had been furious, as if SOE didn't trust a mere woman enough. But she'd obeyed orders. "So you will give up everyone I introduced you to?"

He shrugged. "I will have to. They will make me. But believe me, yours will be the last name I give them. And by then, with God's good grace, you'll be safe."

They stared at each other. She didn't want to believe anything he was telling her, yet she did—all of it. And she did not know what to do. Here, at last, she did not know.

The siren had nagged at them like the distant whine of a mosquito, unimportant compared to all they were saying. In a city at war, there were always sirens. Yet in their silence now they heard it again. But not just one. Many. Getting louder, louder, louder—then suddenly cutting off nearby.

"My God," Klaus whispered, his face white. "I was wrong. They have already come." The hammering on the front door of the building began immediately. At the same time they heard the smash of the iron outer garden gate as it was flung against the inside wall. From the window they saw, pouring into the garden from Kirkeveien, squads of black-uniformed men.

"Go," he said.

"Go?" she echoed, her voice quavering. "Where? They have us."

"Me, not you. They want me first. You are only my . . . tyskertøs." As the shouts rose, as people in nearby apartments began to scream, he dragged her from the bedroom, ran her to the back, to the kitchen door. Through it they could hear men already hammering at the building's garden gate. He jerked open the bolts. "You say you have an attic. Go up there. It's a chance. Take it. Go!" he yelled.

She'd stood there, less than ten minutes before, with another man.

They had kissed. She loved him. She'd thought she loved this man too. In a way, perhaps, she still did. He was a good man.

She kissed him on the cheek. "Goodbye," she said, and ran up the stairs, her bare feet cold on the stone. She heard the gate downstairs smash in finally under German blows, then the sound of German boots coming immediately, followed by a shouted command: "Break it down." She heard her back door shattering as she reached the top-floor landing. There was a trapdoor set into the ceiling directly above her, a metal loop on one edge. She grabbed the rod with the hook that was in the corner and snagged the loop, pulled the trapdoor down, and used the hook again to pull down the folded ladder. She released its lower half, climbed it quickly, then leaned from the trapdoor and reversed her actions, pulling up the ladder, folding in the door. She had done it often as a child; the attic was her special place where she could hide from adults, live out fantasies. It ran along the building's four sides.

The roof was high-ceilinged and she could move upright down the attic's centre, passing on both sides the things the building's inhabitants had chosen to store: children's pushchairs, worn sofas, chests of drawers crammed with old clothes or papers. She and her father had an area, not directly above their apartment but further on, halfway along the north side of the building. She turned the corner, moved swiftly to their place.

First, she slipped on an old pair of hiking boots, then took a coat off a hanger and put it on, shoved a headscarf into its pocket before bending towards her father's old desk, covered by a cloth. She threw that back, reached into a pigeonhole on the right, found the catch, pulled it. The secret drawer sprang out.

She'd added some things to it during the war years. Old code books, fake IDs. If the Germans had found them, she was either in their hands, dead or gone. She pulled two IDs out now, tucked them into her coat pocket. Then she delved a little deeper and pulled out the gun and a box of bullets.

It was wrapped in a blue cloth, which she tore off before laying the weapon on the desk. It was a Webley Mk IV, the same kind of weapon she'd used back at Aston House a few months before. She had not fired it since, hadn't thought she'd need to again. Now she pressed the break-top lever and opened up the cylinder, swiftly filling the six chambers with .38 bullets from the box. This took a little more time than it usually would, as she kept having to stop to wipe away her tears.

She snapped the cylinder back into place and moved to the attic window at the front of the building, which looked over the main street in Majorstuen. There had been several razzias on their block over the years and the Germans always did the same thing—brought their prisoners out onto Kirkeveien. They could assemble more forces there, rather than in narrow Harald Hårfagres at the back. Though Ilse knew it was just as much about demonstrating German might to a cowed people.

She tipped the window up, took a swift glance out. She'd been right. Three armoured cars had pulled up in front of the building's main arched entrance, along with half a dozen motorcycles with side-cars, and two army limousines. A truck with barred windows on its rear doors was directly beneath her. A dozen soldiers in the black uniforms of the Waffen-SS stood with submachine guns raised, looking up and down the street. A few citizens stood in doorways or leaned from windows, watching the show.

She sat down beneath the window, her back to the wall. Thought about all she'd learned at Aston House from the weapons instructor. But there'd been a reason she'd been the top shot of any female graduate there and better than all but one man: her target-shooting father had put a pistol in her hand when she was four years old.

She took steady breaths, wiped away the last of the tears. This must be done, she thought. For all the people who are in danger now. And truly, for him.

It grew suddenly louder below. She lifted her head just over the window's ledge. All the men in the street, every soldier, every civilian, were now looking to her right, where the main entrance to the building was. Apart from the throb of engines, the world was quiet, and she was able to clearly hear the gasp that came from the civilians as they saw whatever was making the dragging sound that came now.

"*Schnell! Schnell!* " someone shouted, harsh and guttural.

All eyes would be elsewhere now, she knew, so she raised her head higher above the sill to see what had caused the gasp, made the dragging sound.

Klaus. He was held by a single storm trooper by his one arm, which was bent back behind him. They had stripped him, the first stage of his breaking, leaving him in only his undershorts. The stump where his left arm had been stood out pink and mottled against his chest. Everything about him looked fragile, a naked child being dragged along by some grinning troll. Blood was streaming from his nose. One of his eyes was swelling.

More shouts as an officer yelled for the truck's rear door to be opened. The storm trooper threw Klaus hard against the door, and the driver scurried from his cab to open it. But Klaus didn't fall. For just a moment, he was standing alone, free, and he used the moment to look up into the sun.

Ilse wiped her eyes, lifted the pistol, put one hand into the other, rested both on the sill, aimed, breathed out, and put two bullets into Klaus's pink chest.

She dropped the gun, was already moving away, when the screams and the Schmeisser fire began. None were aimed at the window where she'd been. The Germans would be trying to figure out where the shots had come from.

There was another trapdoor ten paces back. She lowered it, then the ladder; but when she put her foot on the third rung, she slipped, dropping to the floor, yelping as her ankle rolled over. But she didn't stop, just limped fast to the stairwell. It led down to a door to a side street, which was up near the corner with Kirkeveien, away from the gates. She figured that most of the Germans would be swarming by those or looking up at all the windows. She had to hope so anyway, because her only chance was to leave the building fast and unobserved.

She leaned against the door, bent to look at her ankle. It was already swelling. She'd have to ice it, elevate her foot. Not now though. Now she had to walk away, up the road.

Taking a deep breath, she opened the door.

BILLY STOOD in the main square in front of the station, resisting the tug of the priest on his arm. He couldn't leave, wouldn't. As soon as the trucks and cars of the SS pulled up and storm troopers rushed into Ilse's building, he knew he had to stay. Somehow, he must have led the Germans to her. The smuggler who'd dropped him off? That was it. The man had betrayed him. He must make amends, offer himself.

"I will leave you if you do not come now," hissed the priest in his ear, pulling hard.

"Then go," Billy answered, jerking his arm free. The priest mumbled something, but he only stepped back, didn't leave.

Among a small crowd now, behind a line of storm troopers who were preventing anyone from getting closer, Billy stared up the street. At the armoured vehicles pulling up, the soldiers, the building he'd just left. He knew that this had to be about Ilse. Realized, with his stomach twisting, that there was nothing he could do if she was dragged out through those gates—except watch, except perhaps give her a glimpse of him. A glimpse of love.

But it wasn't Ilse who was dragged out. It was a man, nearly naked, shoved forward by a huge guard. Like everyone, Billy winced when the man was hurled against the prison truck's steel door. The small man stood tall though, looking up into the sun.

The shots came, two of them, high-pitched cracks. The naked man fell and, like anyone who had ever been around flying bullets, Billy dropped to the ground fast. Others did too, as the line of soldiers turned back, hefted their guns. Some began firing, up into the windows. Glass shattered; people screamed.

He got up, crawled to the edge of a fruit stall, got behind it, went onto one knee, peered—and saw her.

She could be any woman in a coat and headscarf, limping away up the road, away from the turmoil. But he knew it was her, and he was up on his feet, slipping between the soldiers whose attention was elsewhere. He didn't know what he was doing. But he had found her again, had to protect her from these men . . . one of whom up ahead had also seen her, was lowering his gun, shouting at her to halt. When she didn't, the man flicked off the safety on his Schmeisser.

Billy was twenty feet from him, but he thought he might have made it if the priest hadn't wrapped his arms around his chest and pulled them both to the ground.

One burst, that's all it was. The woman—Ilse—fell.

"No!" Billy screamed. Kept screaming. But he was only one of many. Then a hand went around his mouth.

The priest's voice came, soft but firm. "If she is alive and you run to her, you will both die, because you are a Brit. If she is dead, you can only join her in death."

Billy thought that would be best. But he found he had no strength to resist when he was lifted, pulled away. Still, he looked back as long as he could, at the soldiers rushing to the fallen woman, then lost sight of her as the priest dragged him into the station, down the slope to the platform, onto a waiting train.

EPILOGUE

London. May 8, 1945, VE Day

THE CLOSER BILLY GOT to Norway House, the thicker the press of people. It was on the edge of Trafalgar Square, after all, which was one of the great gathering points in the city. Piccadilly Circus was another, and it took him five minutes to squeeze through that. Sometimes his progress was blocked entirely and he just had to wait till another slight alley opened for him to slip down. Twice he was jammed so tight he was actually lifted off the ground and carried a few paces. At last, when he'd passed Eros and stood at the top of Haymarket, it eased a little, as most people were coming from the other end, making their way up to the Circus. He'd discovered that if he had the chance he should just march swiftly, let others get out of *his* way. It worked, most of the time, though twice he was bumped quite hard, jarring the hip with the metal in it, making his limp a little more pronounced.

Finally he stood where he'd stood twice before, in front of that great granite doorway, the statue of some king at its apex, the Lion of

Norway in a shield below him. The great wooden doors were wide open, so he stepped into the marbled hall. The roar from outside—horns, trumpets, endless singing—dropped a little, to his relief. But there were celebratory noises ahead too, up the stairs.

He checked his watch. 6:15 p.m. An hour late for the rendezvous his contact had reluctantly agreed to that morning. He could only hope she was still there. She'd been away on honeymoon, he'd been told, when he'd called on his return to London two weeks before. This was her first day back.

Quite the day.

He climbed the stairs. The party was on the first floor, a crowd spilling from a large office too small to contain the throng. A cloud of cigarette smoke swirled blue above people who were dancing to Glenn Miller on the wireless. There were glasses in everybody's hands. As he came through the door and paused, scanning for her, he heard murmured endearments next to him. A couple were leaning against each other, saying the same thing over and over while contradicting each other.

"*Jeg elsker deg.*"

"*Nei, jeg elsker deg.*"

"*Nei, jeg elsker deg.*"

It was some of the little Norwegian he knew. Because Ilse had said it to him.

I love you.

The young man noticed him staring, turned eyes that were glazed with booze and happiness towards him. "You need help, soldier?" he asked.

"Kirsten Larsen?"

"Kirsten?" The man threw his bleary gaze over the room. Then his eyes narrowed. "There. Far corner. With Harald."

Billy looked. He didn't know who Harald was but he glimpsed Kirsten through the shifting bodies. "Thank you," he said, but the couple were facing each other again.

"*Jeg elsker deg.*"

"*Nei, jeg elsker deg.*"

Kirsten noticed him when he was halfway across the room. She said something to the man she was with, who looked over as well, and nodded.

"Hello, Flight Lieutenant," she said, when he reached her.

"Hello."

"You remember Harald?"

"I don't think—"

"I was the one who sent Kirsten to you that day you came here."

"Oh." A vague memory came. "Her fiancé?"

She laughed. "He wanted to be then. He wore me down." She raised her right hand. Two rings glittered on her fourth finger.

"Congratulations. You are a lucky man."

"Oh, I know. Drink?"

"No thanks." Billy faced her again. "You said on the phone you might know where Ilse is?"

She shook her head. "I did not. All I said was that I knew something but could not talk on the phone."

Billy swallowed. It was like him these days to make up something that wasn't there. "Can you talk here?"

Kirsten looked at Harald, who shrugged. "It is so little I can tell you, I am afraid. You know that Ilse . . . Ilse was not with Norwegian intelligence. She worked for the British. SOE."

"I spoke to someone there. They wouldn't even pass me on to anyone who might know anything." He tried to keep his voice level, but it rose a little. "Can you just tell me if she's alive?"

"We do not know." On Billy's exhale she continued. "But she was. We only know this because some of our people"—she glanced at the man again—"escaped from the hospital where she and they were being kept. After Valkyrie failed . . ."

"Valkyrie?"

Another glance. "It was a plot to kill Hitler. But the bomb didn't get him and most of the conspirators, German, Norwegian . . . everywhere, were arrested."

"And Ilse was . . . a conspirator?"

"We cannot know. Not one of ours, yes? But we think so. And we know that when our people escaped from the hospital, they took her with them. Even though she was quite badly hurt."

Badly, he thought, but said, "She didn't stay with them?"

"Everyone separated almost immediately. For safety. No one has heard of her since." She reached up and squeezed his arm. "I am sorry. It is as much, and all, that I know. But I think . . ." She glanced at Harald a third time and he nodded at her. It seemed to steel her, because when she continued, her voice was firmer. "I think that, if she was alive, then somehow . . . somehow I would know. Would have heard. So I say to you now that maybe," she sighed, "maybe you should let her go."

On the far side of the room, someone started shouting. Billy turned and saw the drunk lover. He was yelling in Norwegian to the crowd, nothing that Billy could understand but lots of people cheered it. "Yes, it is time," Kirsten said. She drained the glass she was holding. "We are going to join the street party, Flight Lieutenant. Will you come with us? We are heading down to the palace to see the king and queen."

"It's kind of you. But no, no thank you." He tried a smile. "I'm not much on kings and queens."

"Very well." She let go of the arm she was still holding. "Perhaps we will see you again?"

"I doubt it. But thank you for all . . . all you have tried to do."

EVERYTHING, everywhere, everyone reminded him of her.

Mob surge pushed him to the far side of Trafalgar Square—and there was the bollard he'd sat on a year and a half before, waiting for Kirsten, who'd told him that Ilse was there, in London, a Tube ride away. He sank onto it again, stared about. The crowd reminded him of her, singing songs they'd heard together at Mrs. Bishop's tea house, like "Roll Out the Barrel"—a different one every twenty yards. In a space cleared by their dancing, GIs jitterbugged with their English girlfriends and he recalled spinning Ilse in her Oslo apartment almost a year ago when she'd told him she forgave him, that she loved him still. That she might even marry him one day. And, of course, everywhere people were kissing—lovers, and strangers who would become lovers on this night perhaps, when most rules would be set aside, because five years of fear had ended, and no bombs would be falling from this clear May sky to claim them.

He'd never felt as lonely in his life as he did in that vast crowd.

He shook his head, stood, began to move, anywhere to get away. But he was soon forced to stop again before the steps of St. Martin-in-the-Fields, halted this time by a huge conga line—men and women, in uniform and not, hands on the hips of the one before them, making their own music, shooting out their legs.

"Dah-dah-dah-dah-dah . . . DUH! Dah-dah-dah-dah-dah . . .DUH!"

He waited to let them pass, eyes lowered, unseeing. Until he realized that someone was standing right in front of him, not moving. He glimpsed a red dress, red lips. "'Ere," the woman exclaimed, "I know you!"

He looked at her. It was the WAAF from the Red Lion. He'd met her just before he'd learned that Ilse was back in London. "Deirdre," he said.

"You remember me!"

Billy slipped on a mask. "I told you I always would," he said, matinee-idol smooth.

She pouted, taking in her lower lip. "But you never called me."

"Well, you know." He shrugged. "The war."

"Over now, eh?" She looked around, then tipped her head back and yelled. "Over!"

A man appeared beside her, with a boxer's nose and wearing the uniform of the American navy. "Hey, sweetheart," he said, "you're losing the line."

"Don't care," she said.

The sailor looked at Billy, taking in his uniform, his stripes, his RCAF shoulder badge. "Hey, Johnny Canuck," he growled, "you ain't cutting in on my gal here, are ya?"

"Your gal? Chance 'ud be a fine thing." She slipped her arm around Billy's. "This is my 'usband, Yank. So you can piss off."

"Husband. Like fuck!" The man glared, and when Billy saw the man's hands bunch into fists, he took a slight step back to give himself room. But then some other laughing sailor came up and grabbed his shipmate by his arm, dragging him away. With one last snarl, he was gone, back into the line.

"Bloody cheek! Buy you a gin and think they own you for the night!" She looked up again. "But you could be."

"Could be what?"

"My 'usband. Only for the night, like." She winked. "Until the real one comes 'ome."

She laughed, and he couldn't help laughing too. He *did* remember her. Not just the name. A smile that went all the way through her, a sparkle in the eye. So, he thought, why not? Why bloody not? Drink enough, lose myself, celebrate like everyone else is celebrating. What he'd fought for longer than most of them had fought, because he'd fought since Spain: fascism, beaten at last. Peace, perhaps even for him.

But even as the thought came, it left. Because he knew why bloody not. "I can't, Deirdre. I'm sorry."

"Someone else, is there?"

There was, but not in the way she meant. "Yes." The conga line was still passing. He nodded. "Don't miss your train."

She looked, then looked back, lunged up and planted a big kiss on Billy's lips, before cutting in and grabbing the hips in front of her. "You're the one 'oo missed it, love," she cried. "Yahoo!" And with that, she was gone.

The end of the line came quickly. The crowd was thinning a little now but Billy didn't move. He had no idea where to go, what to do.

Coke House? He'd been in residence there since he'd gotten back, having eventually been smuggled from Norway to Sweden, waiting in Stockholm for one of the few precious seats on the biweekly flights. The RCAF had put him straight on "convalescence." He'd sat with the servants, Jeffers and Mrs. Jacobs, that afternoon and listened to Churchill's 3 p.m. broadcast announcing Victory in Europe Day. They were warm, kind people, but no matter how he tried, they always treated him as a master, a son of the ancient family they served. No one from his squadron would be at the Mess in Hendon. Like everyone, they'd be here.

Then he remembered somewhere with people he liked, who liked him. A place where he could sing for his supper.

That's what I need, he thought, setting off towards the Strand. I need a song.

SOME OF THE Globe's clientele were no doubt dead. Others were still out on the streets. But by 10 p.m. on VE Day, many had found their way back. And those who recognized him were delighted that "their Billy" had returned and was still in good voice. Both McGovern brothers were there, Don and wife having made their way up from the country for the celebrations. They stood behind the bar with Mac and Molly, dispensing pints and wisecracks. The rumour was that many pubs in London had run out of beer hours before. Not so the Globe. The McGoverns would always find a way.

Their mother was there too, in a corner, putting away half-pints of Mackeson. She may have been nearly deaf, but Billy mostly sang songs everyone could sing, and they did, loudly, so even she could hear and tap her feet.

But it *was* 10 p.m., and many there had drunk themselves from happy to melancholy. It was the time for the toasts to "absent friends," to those who had "gone on before"—taken by bombs, felled by bullets, vanished into air, into unmarked graves, into no graves at all. Everyone there had lost someone, several more than one. It was for them that Molly wanted Billy to sing now. "One last one, love," she said, as she placed another full pint before him.

There was a song that he'd avoided all evening, even though it was one of the most popular. Because it was hers, the one he'd sung to her in Mrs. Bishop's cellar the night they met. Now, finally, he was ready for it. Ready to say goodbye.

He stood. Both McGoverns yelled, "Quiet now, please," and Billy closed his eyes. I have to sing it for them, not for me, he thought. Let them cry, not me. I am a professional, after all. Dammit. *Damn* it.

He took a deep breath.

If you were the only girl in the world
And I were the only boy
Nothing else would matter in the world today
We could go on loving in the same old way
A garden of Eden just made for two
With nothing to mar our joy

Professional or not, he couldn't help it. He heard his voice catch, felt a tear slip between his closed lids. Damn it to hell, he thought. He paused, lost, forgot what came next, then remembered, because the exact moment came back to him, the one when he'd first told Ilse that he loved her.

I would say such wonderful things to you
There would be such wonderful things to do
If you were the only girl in the world
And I were the only boy

He faltered on the high note, the words, the tune, drying on his lips. He felt a hand on his arm, squeezing him, heard Molly start to sing, her and then the rest of the pub, continuing what he could not.

He opened his eyes, to thank Molly for rescuing him. But it wasn't the Globe's landlady standing there, holding him. It was . . . her. And he was grateful for that too, grateful that he'd finally drunk himself to the place where he could see her again. Where he could say goodbye to her.

"Goodbye, Ilse," he said.

Her eyebrows rose. That look came into her eyes, the one he most remembered, the one that was always followed by her laugh. He'd seen the one, heard the other . . . on a beach in Suffolk. Outside a house in Hampstead. In a hallway in Oslo. In so many dreams between and since.

Both came now. "Goodbye?" she said, turning to smile at Molly, who was standing beside her, before turning back. "But Billy... I've only just got here."

And then she laughed.

AFTERWORD

Salt Spring Island. August 2023

Someday I'll Find You was the novel I *had* to write. Yet for so many reasons it has taken me this long to get to it. Novel number twenty-two in fact (a total I cannot quite believe).

Why did I have to write it? Why the delay? I'll try to explain.

The glimmerings of this story began, literally I suppose, at my father's knee. Even though he and my protagonist, Billy Coke, differ in so many ways, my dad *was* Flight Lieutenant Peter Humphreys, RAFVR (the VR stands for "Volunteer Reserve," because he volunteered six months before the war broke out). He was also an actor and a storyteller (apples and their distance from trees come to mind here). Unlike many who came through it, he was happy to talk about his war. Mostly. The glorious side, anyway. "So there I was in a dogfight over Tobruk, cannonball in the glycol, chased back to base by Messerschmitts . . ."

The less glorious side, the damage within, he didn't discuss. That, my brother and I had to observe, learn to deal with more—and less—successfully.

You'll notice I didn't say that the story began at my *parents'* knees. My mother, Ingegerd Holter, also had extraordinary tales to tell—but she almost never did. Partly that was her nature, her reserve. Partly because her life and work in occupied Norway was rarely "glorious." It was alternately dull and terrifying. She lost people too, sometimes in horrible ways, and only just escaped with her life. Finally, I think she didn't speak too much because of things my research into her, and the world of World War Two espionage, uncovered—if she was, as we now suspect, a spy for the British SOE rather than one of the Norwegian resistance groups, she would have signed Britain's Official Secrets Act which forbade her from disclosing almost anything at all, ever. And my mother took every promise she made most seriously.

Still, the fighter pilot and the spy . . . How could I not write that?

I delayed for several reasons. Some professional—publishers' plans, agents' ideas, editors' comings and goings. Most personal, and these were . . . layered.

My dad died in 1986. My mum lived till she was 98, and only died in 2013 with, as we say in England, "all her dogs barking"—still engaged, still vibrant in mind if not so much in body. But her younger sister, my aunt (*tante* in Norwegian) Jorunn, who served in the Norwegian navy during the war, died aged 104 in 2020—and it was partly for her that I couldn't yet tackle the subjects I knew I must. One especially. Because, to the sisters' shame, their father, my grandfather Karl Holter, was a Nazi. In 1936, like my fictional Wilhelm, Karl won a writing prize (though in his case, for a play). In Berlin to receive the award, he shook Göring's hand.

What the Nazis perpetrated on the world, upon their enemies and their own people, added new depths to the word *atrocity*. It is hard to read about, let alone write. But like the actor I am, I still needed to find my Nazi characters' "motivations." I do not believe that many people wake up each morning and say, "I am a monster. How can I be monstrous today?" In the end, I let much of their philosophy be spoken by a loving, devoted grandmother. Because so many people, from the very young to the very old, across Europe of the time—but most especially in Germany—did believe in the philosophy. Did see Hitler as a saviour from the awful times they'd endured after the First World War. Did, in the 1930s at least, see the horror in Stalin's Russia, where millions were known to have been slaughtered and starved to death years before the Nazis fully geared up their killing machines.

Am I excusing my grandfather? No. I still believe, as my mother and aunt believed, that however much he was anti-Bolshevik and anti-British (known to many as the "Evil Empire" of its day), pro-German (and he was half German), he should still have recognized true evil and stopped aiding it. He didn't—he continued as a journalist and propagandist for "the cause" until the war's end, and spent several years in prison because of it. I cannot excuse him. But I did strive to understand him in order to write the book—just not until now. Because this is my family's dirty linen, and my aunt, a proud and private woman who was alert right to the end, would not have wanted that washed in public.

However—and of course—my family's story is not my characters' story. I have fictionalized, dramatized. The fiction differs from the reality in fundamental ways.

My father, Peter Humphreys was an actor, but not a singer—though he had a whisky-and-cigarette voice and could charm the birds from the trees when he chose to. He was certainly not an anarchist—rather the opposite. He *was* a fighter pilot—though if he had a grave (another long story) he'd be rolling over in it now since I have Billy fly the more glamorous Spitfire rather than the workhorse Hurricane, as Dad did.

My mother, Ingegerd Holter, was not a classical flautist, but she *was* a spy and a true Norse beauty—Oslo Princess 1936, essentially Miss Oslo. She didn't go back and forth to Norway, however; she was there from the invasion on, worked undercover for a year and only narrowly escaped with her life across the border to Sweden when her network was busted. Also, my parents didn't meet as the bombs fell on London in 1940 but in Scotland in 1944, both on leave. It was certainly *un coup de foudre*—that lightning bolt of sudden intense love that Billy is struck by on seeing Ilse. Dad proposed after three days, Mum held him off for five weeks, and they married in London.

So far, so different. And yet, and yet? A novel with such a personal origin can't help but be personal. The storyline may differ but the little details that hold it together, its glue perhaps, are made up of those wonderful oscillations (a favourite writing word of mine) between what my research into those times has given me and my protagonists' imagined reactions to circumstance. Between plot and character. Between structure—much dictated by the war's actual events—and, again, character. Together with those mysterious collisions in a writer's mind between his own history, his experiences, and the people and places he has observed.

There are too many examples of these in the novel to fully list. We'd be here all night! Here, though, are a selected few:

St. Giles' Cripplegate. The church where Ilse plays her flute at the beginning of the novel and rushes from to her fate, running into Billy—this church was behind my drama college, the Guildhall School, in London's Barbican. But the priest in the novel was wrong when he urged the musicians to shelter there, saying that Hitler wouldn't destroy what the Great Fire of London had failed to . . . because the church was burned to the ground later that same terrible night, and anyone sheltering in it died. The building I often visited was a beautiful reconstruction. (It also features in my novel *Fire*, about that first Great Fire of London).

"Do you think we will win this war?" It is the question the Irish lieutenant asks Ilse in her interview at SOE. Her response is that she never doubts that Nazism will be defeated. Which is what my mother told me when I asked her once: "I never, for a moment, believed that they would win in the end." Quite the belief to hold when you've watched the Germans march up your high street on April 9, 1940.

Theatre Royal, Bath. Like Billy, my father was in repertory theatre there before the war. Unlike Billy, he volunteered for the RAF six months before the war came ("I knew it was coming and I was damned if I was going to be shot in a trench," he told me) and was accepted. One of the great resources for this novel was my father's "Pilot's Logbook." It lists, in his beautiful copperplate handwriting, every flight he took—from his first lesson as a pupil in a Tiger Moth on April 8, 1939 to his very last flight, flying an Anson solo on October 8, 1945. It includes, on April 24, 1941, the time he "scrambled" over Tobruk and was shot down. He wrote: "Missed a 109. Hit in glycol by a 109. Chased home by four and a 110." Similar to what happens to Billy over Sicily.

That was one of my father's grandstand stories. His recounting completely left out the sheer terror he must have felt. Reading as I have done some wonderful accounts of pilots in World War Two (see the Bibliography) and reading also about PTSD, there is little doubt in my mind that my father suffered from it. So many who survived the war were undiagnosed, received no counselling or care. They dealt with it in their own ways. Or not.

North Africa Squadron 73. I made Billy's North Africa squadron No. 73, same as my dad's. (I like the idea of them flying together!) I did however change Billy's RCAF squadron in Sicily from 91 to 92, in case there are Canadian Spitfire pilots alive who might object. Also, like Billy, in 1944 Dad did end up at RAF Hendon in a communications squadron. And like Billy, Dad always wore his "blue polka-dotted silk scarf," which I still have.

The Razor's Edge. This wonderful book by W. Somerset Maugham is kind of the previous generation's *On the Road*—a young man travels the world in search of meaning. I wanted Billy to read a novel and was delighted when Google offered this one as a bestseller of 1944— especially as my grandfather, Cecil Humphreys, was in the 1946 film based on the book, playing the guru atop the Himalaya that Larry Darrell (Tyrone Power in the movie) seeks meaning from!

Noël Coward. He was a playwright, composer and consummate entertainer. He wrote the play *Private Lives* and a song for it that I have taken as the title of my novel: "Someday I'll Find You." My father was briefly his pilot during the war, when Noël was in the Middle East "entertaining the troops." Noël was delighted to meet Cecil Humphreys' son (writing in his *Middle East Diaries* that "the blood of Wardour Street flows in these desert sands!") They took to each other, kept in touch. In 1944, my father sent Noël an early play he'd written and Noël returned a critique which begins with the immortal sentence: "Be prepared—I am going to be rather beastly to you." Despite the literary savaging, they stayed friends, and the playwright showed up to my parents' wedding reception at the Savoy

Hotel, fashionably late, with two bottles of champagne (in London in 1944!).

Harald Hårfagres gate. Ilse's address in Oslo is based on my wonderful cousin Line Beck's apartment. A beautiful 1920s four-storey building, four-sided around a communal garden, the apartment had everything I needed within and without, with its attic running around the four buildings that make up the square. The Germans did raid it, once seeking one of the commandos from the famous attack on the heavy water factory in Telemark (Kirk Douglas starred in the great film *The Heroes of Telemark*). The commando was hiding out at his parents' but managed to escape over the roof.

Codes. My elder brother, Alan Humphreys, has been a great support throughout my writing career and particularly with this book, sharing reminiscences of our parents and filling the gaps, especially in our mother's story. Also, being a former Morse code radio operator in the Merchant Navy and subsequently in communications in Canada's Foreign Affairs department serving at embassies across the world, he was invaluable in the code sections of this book, making them authentic and plausible.

The Cokes. Some readers who have read me before will recognize the name. Captain William Coke is the seventeenth-century highwayman and protagonist of my novels *Plague* and *Fire*. Billy is his namesake and descendent. Several of my novels have some such familial connections. I hope it amuses a few people other than myself. (Now I simply must go back and write the novel about how Captain Coke becomes a knight and founds a regiment. One day!)

Salt Spring Island. I wrote most of this novel where I reside: beautiful Salt Spring Island, in British Columbia, on Canada's western coast. This is where I met "the widow-maker" that killed Billy's father, when an arborist taking down some trees on my land was struck by one, though fortunately escaped with only bruises. It seemed appropriate to have Billy hail from here. And though the circumstances are very different, I too was plucked at the same age from the west coast (further down, Southern California), separated from my father and sent to an English private school. If I did not become an anarchist—though I was once arrested in Parliament Square, London, for protesting the first Gulf War—at least I do know something about being a "fish out of water."

There are so many other tales I could still discuss. Far too many to recount here, though I do intend to write more at publication time. Should anyone reading this now be interested, please check out my blog at my website.

I have listed most of my sources in the Bibliography if anyone wants to further understand that world, at that time. Acknowledgements also follow, for all the people who have made this novel possible. Writing a novel truly is a team game and *Someday I'll Find You* would have been impossible to pull off without their support and insights.

I am a lucky man indeed. And so happy that this book is finally off my chest and off my desk. I hope you've found it both the adventure and the love story I set out to write, as well as an examination of men and women at war. I have learned so much writing it. Exploring the world in which my parents came of age—those terrible, terrifying yet sometimes thrilling times and places—I did what a writer does: tried to imagine how a person might react to stress and circumstance. That these characters are at least partially based on my mother and father has helped me know them so much better—while making me miss them so much more. If only I could talk to them now!

Perhaps, in a way, I have.

ACKNOWLEDGMENTS

Contrary to popular belief, writing a novel is a *team* game. I have been especially blessed by the team I have played with on *Someday I'll Find You*. I know I will miss someone out so apologies in advance. Here, in no particular order, I deeply thank:

My parents, Peter and Ingegerd Humphreys. My partner, Cat Cooper.

Colonel Joshua Kutryk, astronaut, RCAF fighter and test pilot, who knows more about dogfights, aerobatics, stalling speeds and strafing than any man alive. (He's also married to my niece!)

Alan Humphreys, brother, Morse operator, codes expert.

Karim Jadwat and Amanda Knight, for their deep friendship and for hosting me each time I researched in London.

Jon Wood, formerly my editor at Hachette, now my agent at Rogers, Coleridge and White, London. Always my supporter and my friend.

George Crotty, cello virtuoso and adviser on all things musical.

This novel was originally published by Doubleday Canada and only in that country. Their support was huge and I'd like to thank everyone there. As well as all those on the front line: every amazing bookseller!

Line Beck, cousin, owner of "Ilse's apartment" in Oslo and guru on all things Norwegian—especially the lamb stew!

Janet (J. L.) Oakley for pulling me deep into the Norwegian resistance by letting me be her audiobook narrator for her wonderful books *The Jøssing Affair* and *The Quisling Factor*.

Nuria Belastegui and her friends for all things Basque.

Mark Leslie Lefebvre for his friendship and self-publishing smarts. This edition would not be in your hands without him.

Finally, my wonderful editor, Melanie Tutino, whose endless support, gentle criticism and subtle urging to always strive for clarity had such a profound effect on making this novel as strong and as powerful as it can be. Grazie mille!

BIBLIOGRAPHY

My background reading on World War Two has been going on for a lifetime. Here are many of the essential reads. Also, I can't list the innumerable websites I visited but the internet is an extraordinary resource for everything from tram stations in wartime Oslo to the price of a gin in a London pub, and everything in between. I love history and have tried to get all the details right. I know, however, that I am not a fighter pilot, a code breaker, a member of the Nazi Party nor all the other things I needed to imagine I was to create this novel. So apologies to all the readers who know more than me about some things. I look forward to your letters.

General History
Boyd, Julia. *Travelers in the Third Reich: The Rise of Fascism 1919–1945*. New York: Pegasus Books, 2019.

Boyes, Roger, and Adam Lebor. *Surviving Hitler: Choices, Corruption and Compromise in the Third Reich*. London: Simon & Schuster, 2000.

Brendon, Piers. *The Dark Valley: A Panorama of the 1930s*. New York: Vintage, 2002.

Farson, Negley. *Bomber's Moon*. London: Victor Gollancz Ltd., 1941.

Johnson, David. *The London Blitz: The City Ablaze*. New York: Stein & Day, 1982.

Rankin, Nicholas. *Telegram from Guernica*. London: Faber & Faber, 2012.

Remak, Joachim, ed. *The Nazi Years: A Documentary History*. Long Grove: Waveland Press, 1990.

Shirer, William L. *The Nightmare Years 1930–1940*. Boston: Little, Brown & Co., 1984.

Thomas, Hugh. *The Spanish Civil War*. New York: Modern Library, 2001.

Ziegler, Philip. *London at War*. New York: Knopf, 1995.

Spies
Adamson, Hans Christian, and Per Kelm. *Blood on the Midnight Sun*. New York: W. W. Norton & Co., 1964.

Bull, Stephen, ed. *The Secret Agent's Handbook Pocket Manual*. London: Conway, 2009.

Cookridge, E. H. *Inside SOE: The First Full Story of Special Operations Executive in Western Europe, 1950–1945*. London: Arthur Barker Ltd., 1966.

Gjelsvik, Tore. *Norwegian Resistance: 1940–1945*. Toronto: University of Toronto Press, 1979.

Olsen, Oluf Reed. *Two Eggs on My Plate*. London: George Allen & Unwin Ltd., 1952.

The German Secret Service (Abwehr), declassified secret report. London: War Office, 1942.

Flying

Peter Humphreys' Pilot's Flying Log Book, Royal Air Force. London: 1939–1945.

Bashow, David L. *All the Fine Young Eagles: In the Cockpit with Canada's Second World War Fighter Pilots.* Vancouver: Douglas & McIntyre, 2016.

Dempster, Derek, and Derek Wood. *The Narrow Margin: The Battle of Britain and the Rise of Air Power 1930–1949.* Barnsley: Pen & Sword, 2003.

Overy, Richard J. *Battle of Britain.* New York: W. W. Norton & Co., 2002.

Partridge, Eric. *A Dictionary of RAF Slang.* London: Michael Joseph, 2017.

Robson, Martin. *The Hurricane Pocket Manual: All Marks in Service 1939–1945.* Oxford: Osprey Publishing, 2019.

Novels

Bates, H. E. *Fair Stood the Wind for France.* Whitefish: Kessinger Publishing, 2010.

Maugham, W. Somerset. *The Razor's Edge.* New York: Vintage, 2003.

ABOUT THE AUTHOR

An award-winning novelist, playwright, actor and teacher, C.C. (Chris) Humphreys has written 22 novels including *Vlad, The Last Confession* and *Plague* which won the 2015 CWA Best Crime Novel Award. He has a MFA in Creative Writing and has been translated into 13 languages. Find him at:

https://www.authorchrishumphreys.com/

ALSO BY C. C. HUMPHREYS

The French Executioner

Blood Ties

Jack Absolute

The Blooding of Jack Absolute

Absolute Honour

Vlad, The Last Confession

A Place Called Armageddon

Shakespeare's Rebel

Plague

Fire

Chasing the Wind

One London Day

Someday I'll Find You

(as Chris Humphreys)

The Runestone Saga:

- The Fetch

- Vendetta

- Possession

The Tapestry Trilogy:

- The Hunt of the Unicorn

- The Hunt of the Dragon

- The Hunt of the Shapeshifters

The Immortals' Blood Trilogy:

- Smoke in the Glass
- The Coming of the Dark
- The Wars of Gods and Men